My LITTLE PONY

THE MANGA

A Day in the Life of Equestria

Vol. 2

story by
David Lumsdon

art by
Shiei

toning by
Ludwig Sacramento

lettering by
Nicky Lim

Licensed by:

Seven Seas

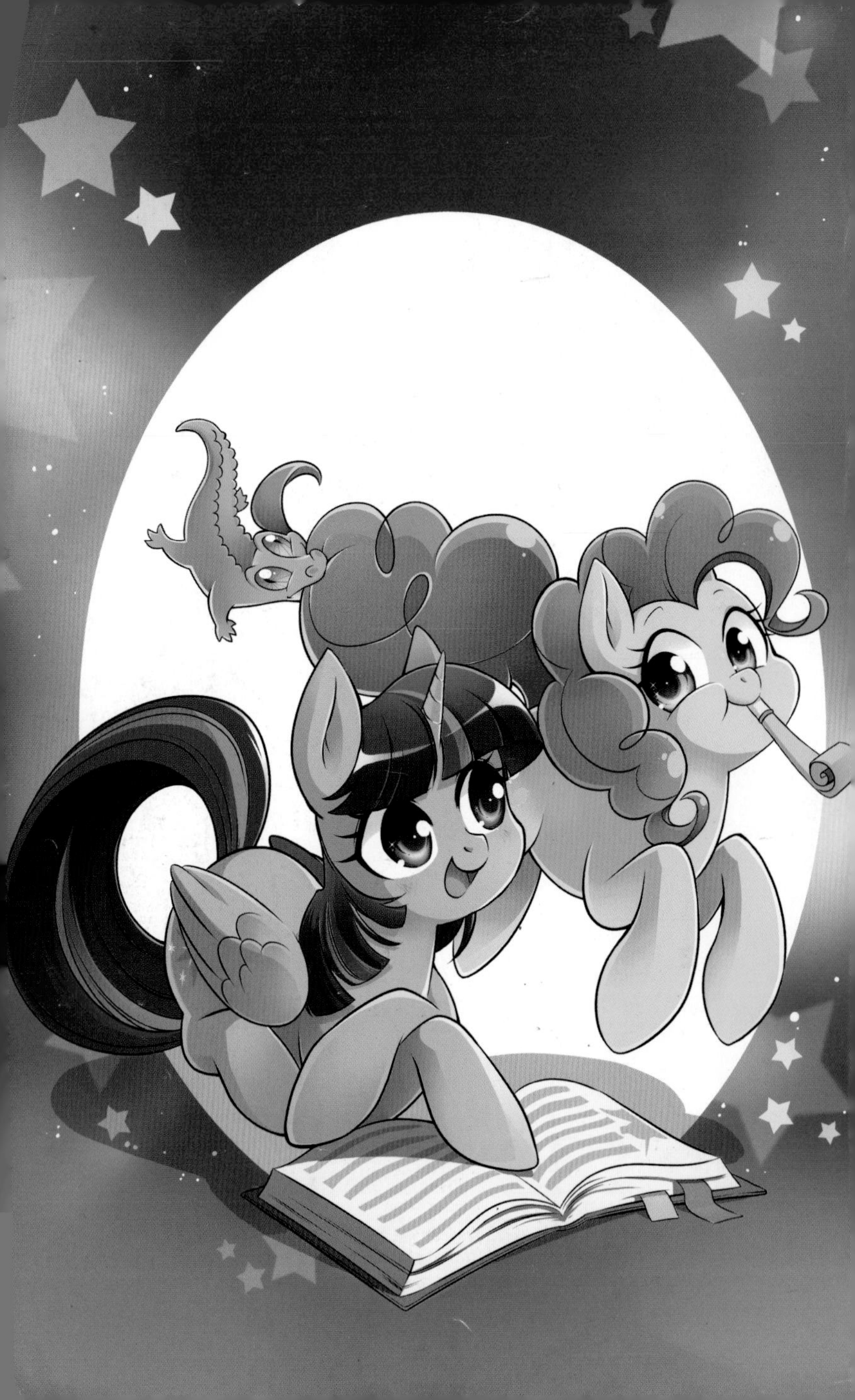

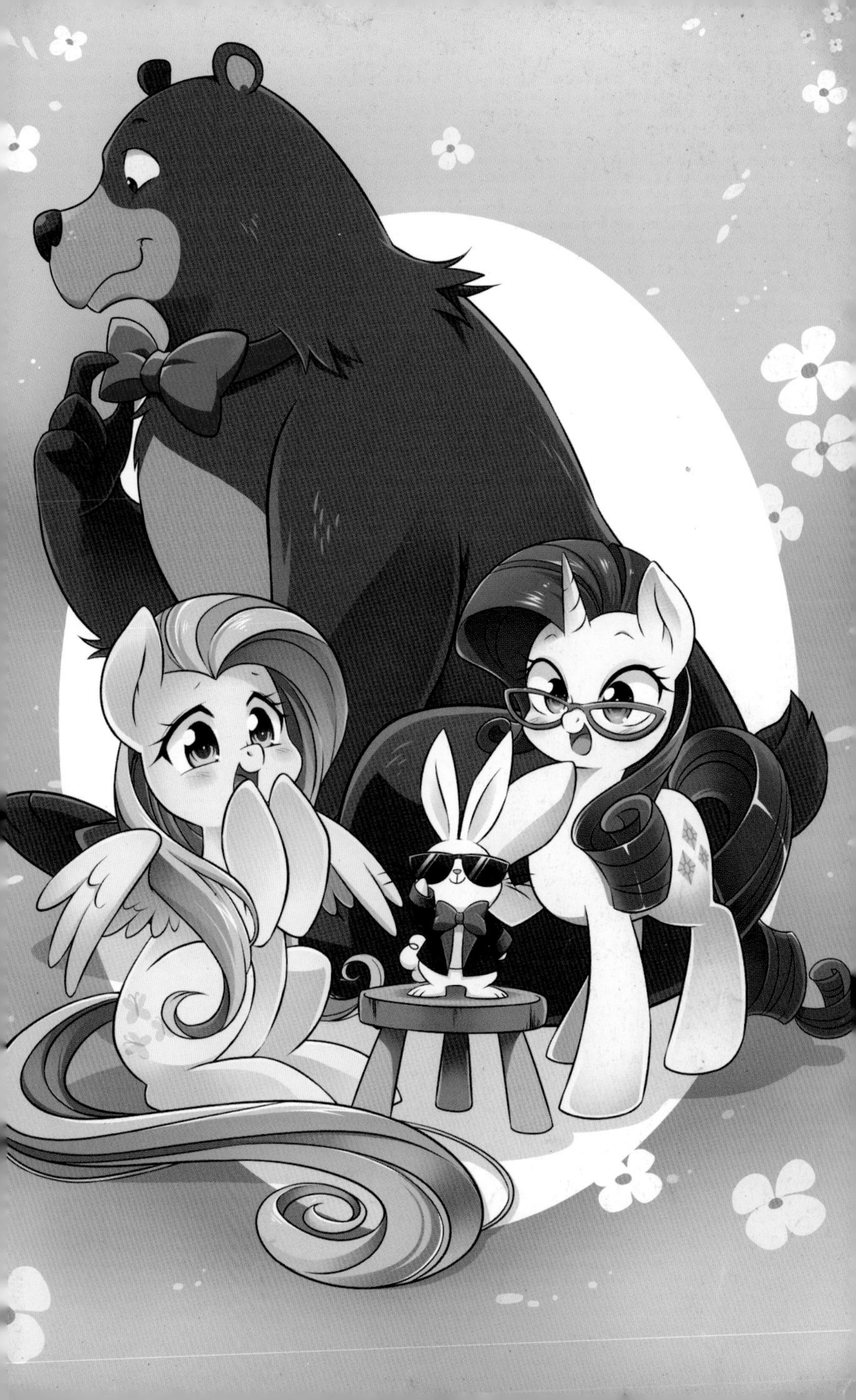

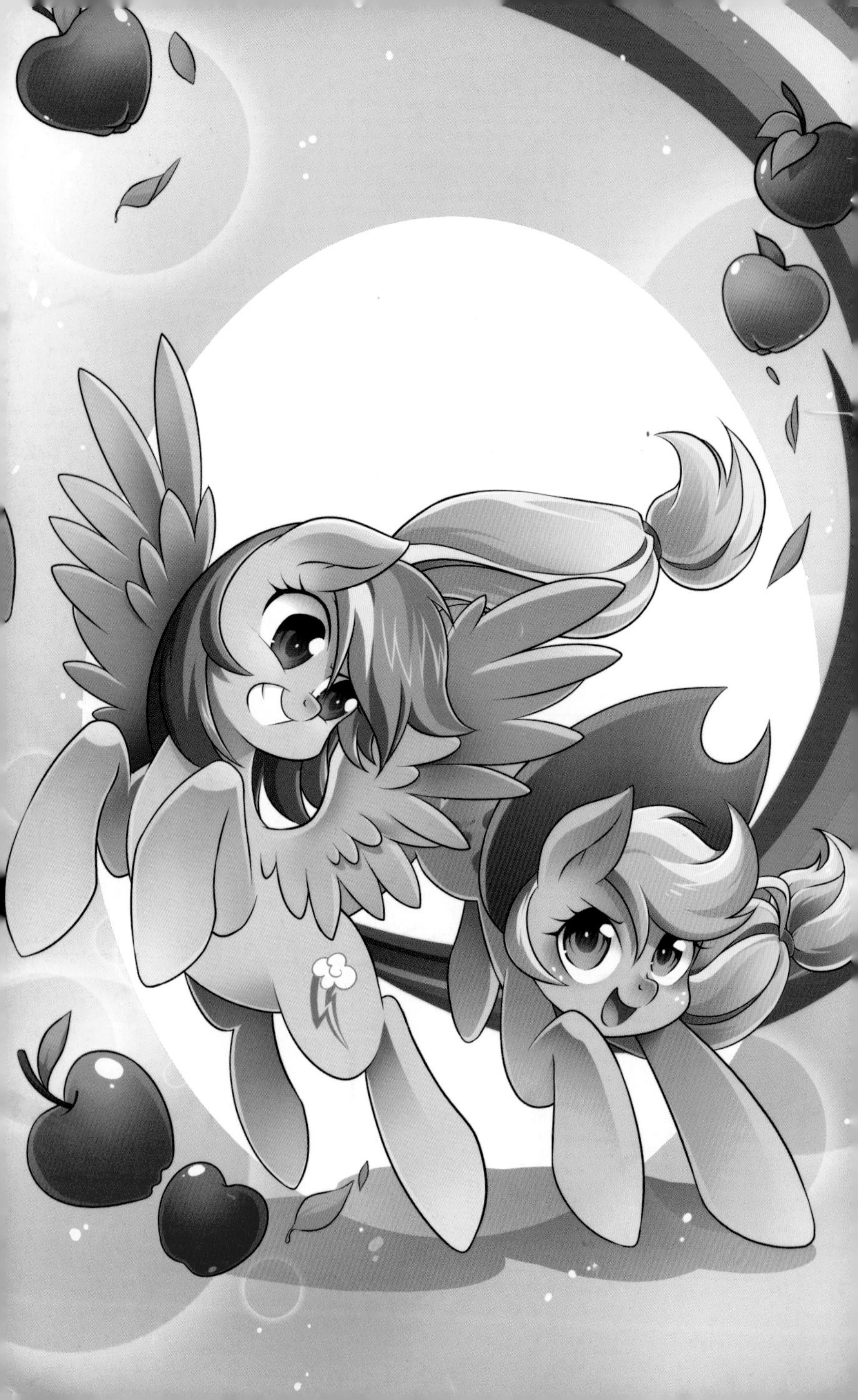

TABLE OF CONTENTS

CHAPTER 1

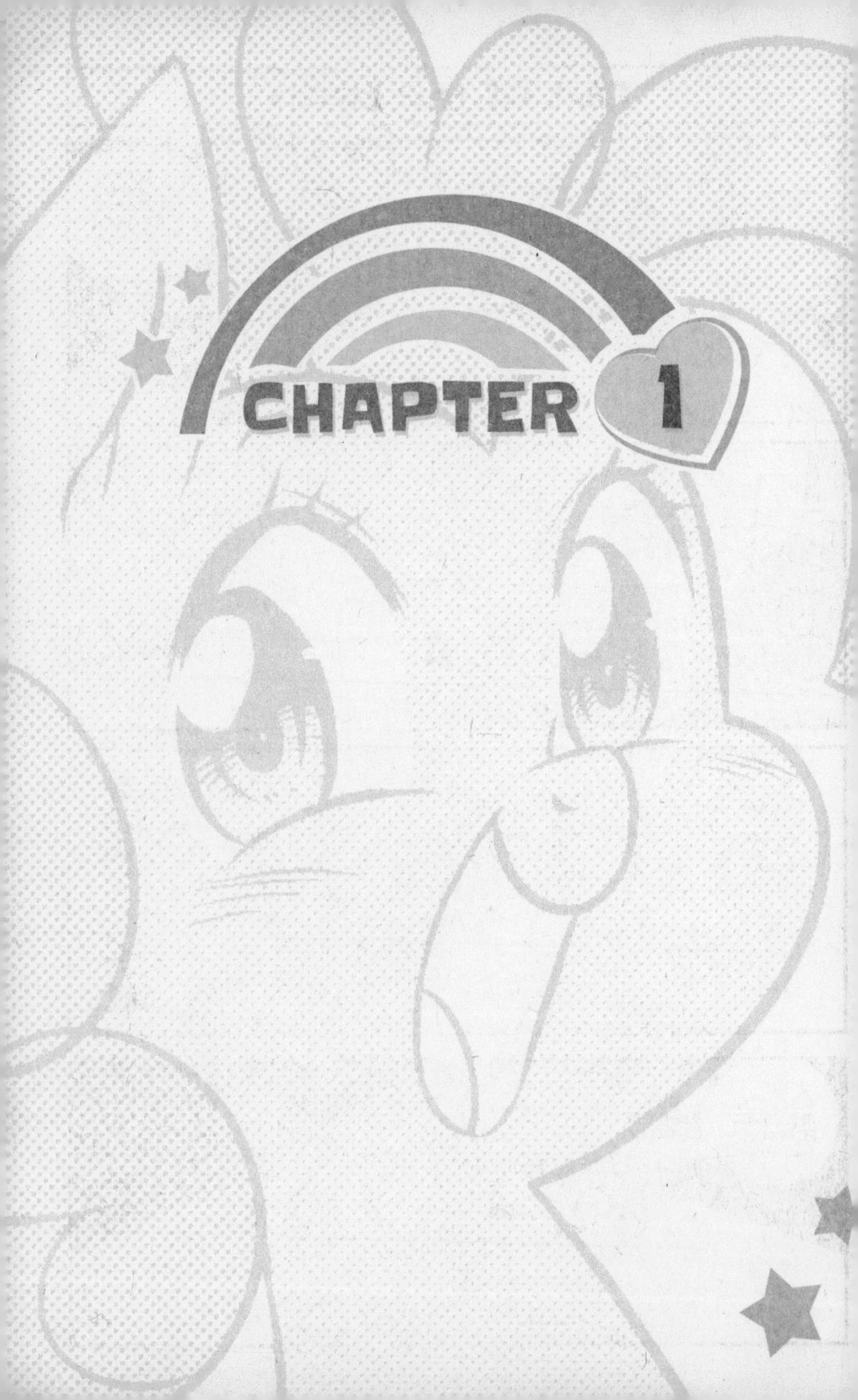

Out of the Loop

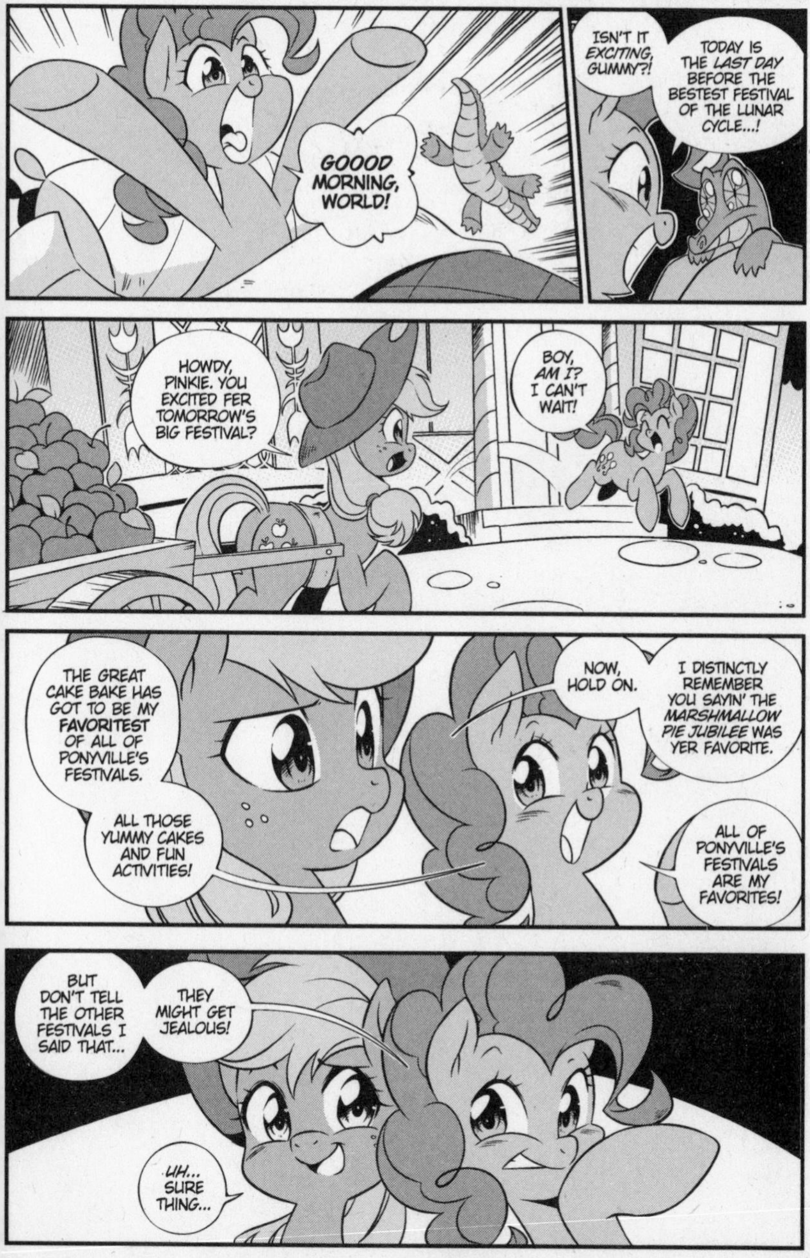
GOOOD MORNING, WORLD!
ISN'T IT *EXCITING,* GUMMY?!
TODAY IS THE *LAST DAY* BEFORE THE BESTEST FESTIVAL OF THE LUNAR CYCLE...!
HOWDY, PINKIE. YOU EXCITED FER TOMORROW'S BIG FESTIVAL?
BOY, *AM I?* I CAN'T WAIT!
THE GREAT CAKE BAKE HAS GOT TO BE MY **FAVORITEST** OF ALL OF PONYVILLE'S FESTIVALS.
ALL THOSE YUMMY CAKES AND FUN ACTIVITIES!
NOW, HOLD ON.
I DISTINCTLY REMEMBER YOU SAYIN' THE *MARSHMALLOW PIE JUBILEE* WAS YER FAVORITE.
ALL OF PONYVILLE'S FESTIVALS ARE MY FAVORITES!
BUT DON'T TELL THE OTHER FESTIVALS I SAID THAT...
THEY MIGHT GET JEALOUS!
UH... SURE THING...

Bobbing for Trouble

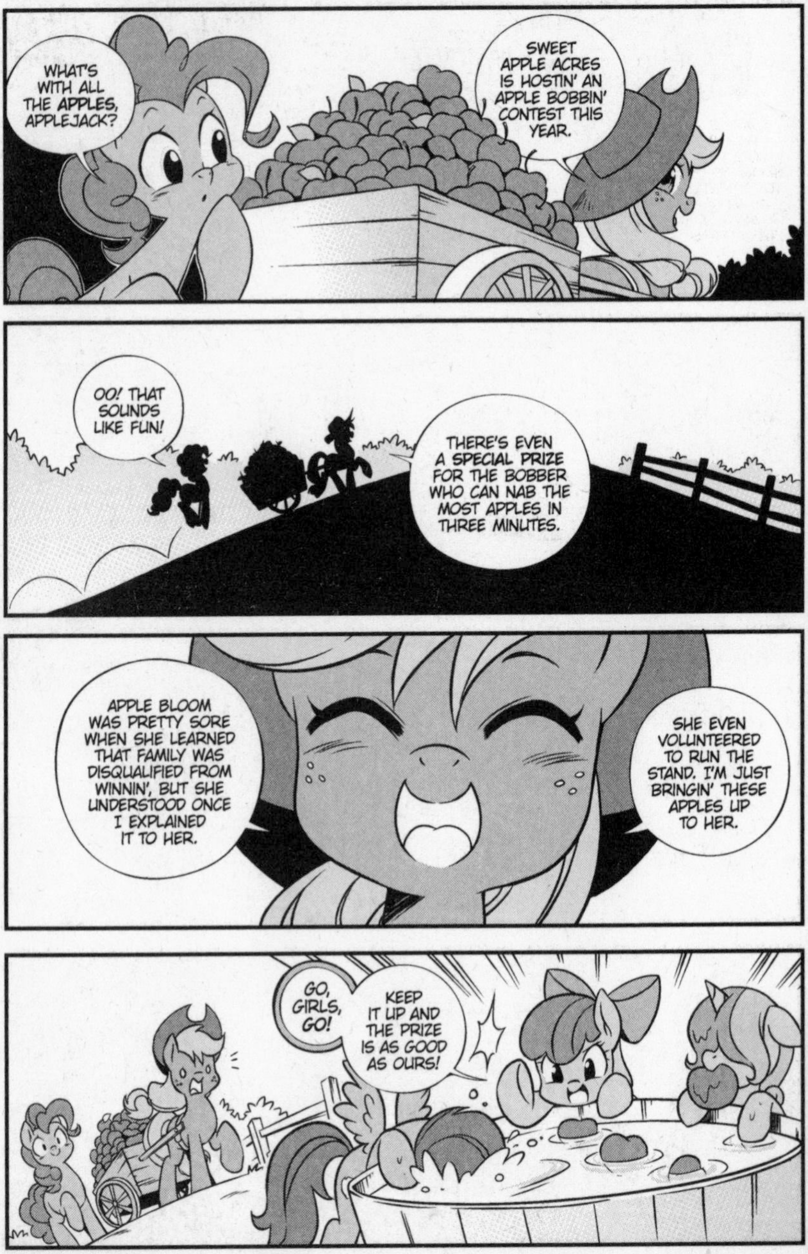
WHAT'S WITH ALL THE APPLES, APPLEJACK?
SWEET APPLE ACRES IS HOSTIN' AN APPLE BOBBIN' CONTEST THIS YEAR.
OO! THAT SOUNDS LIKE FUN!
THERE'S EVEN A SPECIAL PRIZE FOR THE BOBBER WHO CAN NAB THE MOST APPLES IN THREE MINUTES.
APPLE BLOOM WAS PRETTY SORE WHEN SHE LEARNED THAT FAMILY WAS DISQUALIFIED FROM WINNIN', BUT SHE UNDERSTOOD ONCE I EXPLAINED IT TO HER.
SHE EVEN VOLUNTEERED TO RUN THE STAND. I'M JUST BRINGIN' THESE APPLES UP TO HER.
GO, GIRLS, GO!
KEEP IT UP AND THE PRIZE IS AS GOOD AS OURS!

Go, Cart, Go!

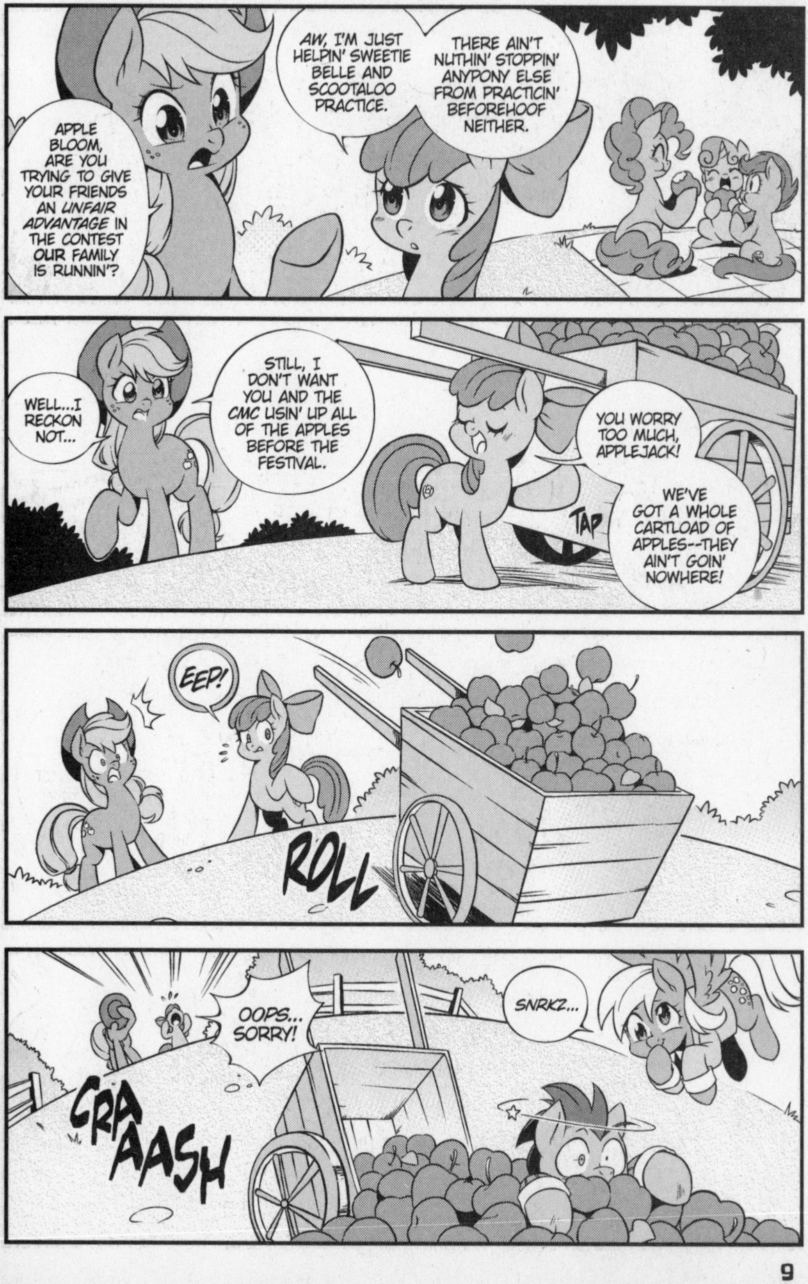
APPLE BLOOM, ARE YOU TRYING TO GIVE YOUR FRIENDS AN *UNFAIR ADVANTAGE* IN THE CONTEST OUR FAMILY IS RUNNIN'?
AW, I'M JUST HELPIN' SWEETIE BELLE AND SCOOTALOO PRACTICE.
THERE AIN'T NUTHIN' STOPPIN' ANYPONY ELSE FROM PRACTICIN' BEFOREHOOF NEITHER.
WELL...I RECKON NOT...
STILL, I DON'T WANT YOU AND THE *CMC* USIN' UP ALL OF THE APPLES BEFORE THE FESTIVAL.
YOU WORRY TOO MUCH, APPLEJACK!
TAP
WE'VE GOT A WHOLE CARTLOAD OF APPLES--THEY AIN'T GOIN' NOWHERE!
EEP!
ROLL
CRAAASH
OOPS... SORRY!
SNRKZ...

A Taste for Fashion

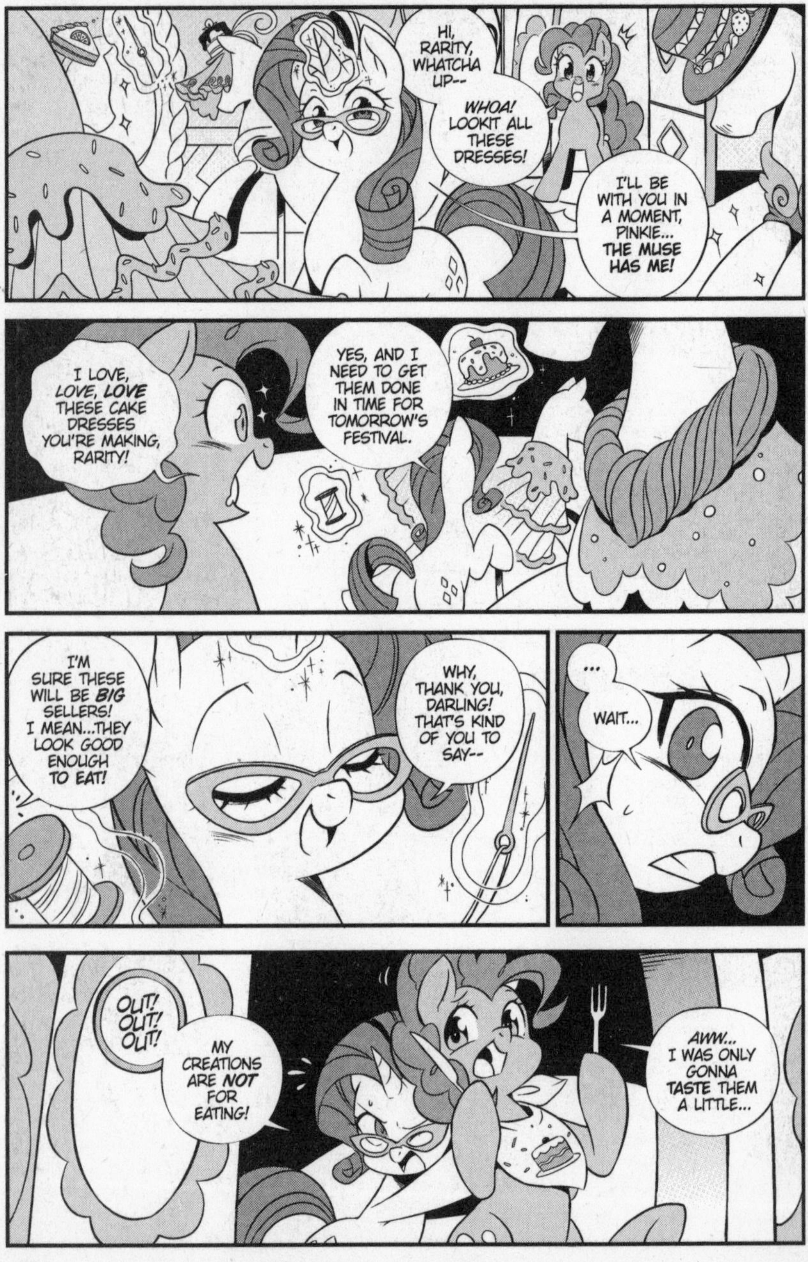
HI, RARITY, WHATCHA UP--
WHOA! LOOKIT ALL THESE DRESSES!
I'LL BE WITH YOU IN A MOMENT, PINKIE... **THE MUSE HAS ME!**
I LOVE, *LOVE*, ***LOVE*** THESE CAKE DRESSES YOU'RE MAKING, RARITY!
YES, AND I NEED TO GET THEM DONE IN TIME FOR TOMORROW'S FESTIVAL.
I'M SURE THESE WILL BE ***BIG*** SELLERS! I MEAN...THEY LOOK GOOD ENOUGH TO EAT!
WHY, THANK YOU, DARLING! THAT'S KIND OF YOU TO SAY--
...
WAIT...
OUT! OUT! OUT!
MY CREATIONS ARE ***NOT*** FOR EATING!
AWW... I WAS ONLY GONNA TASTE THEM A LITTLE...

Sphere of Study

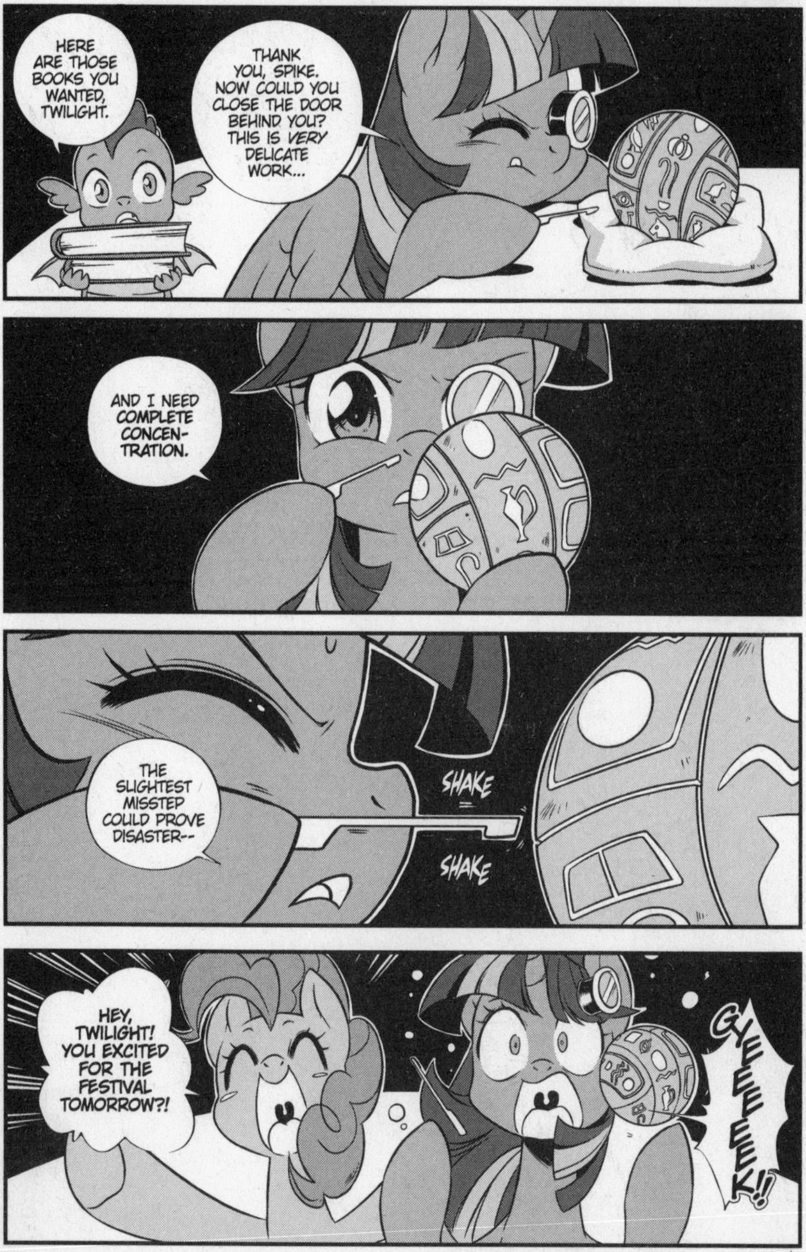
HERE ARE THOSE BOOKS YOU WANTED, TWILIGHT.
THANK YOU, SPIKE. NOW COULD YOU CLOSE THE DOOR BEHIND YOU? THIS IS *VERY* DELICATE WORK...
AND I NEED COMPLETE CONCEN-TRATION.
THE SLIGHTEST MISSTEP COULD PROVE DISASTER--
SHAKE
SHAKE
HEY, TWILIGHT! YOU EXCITED FOR THE FESTIVAL TOMORROW?!
GYEEEEEK!!

Balance of Terror

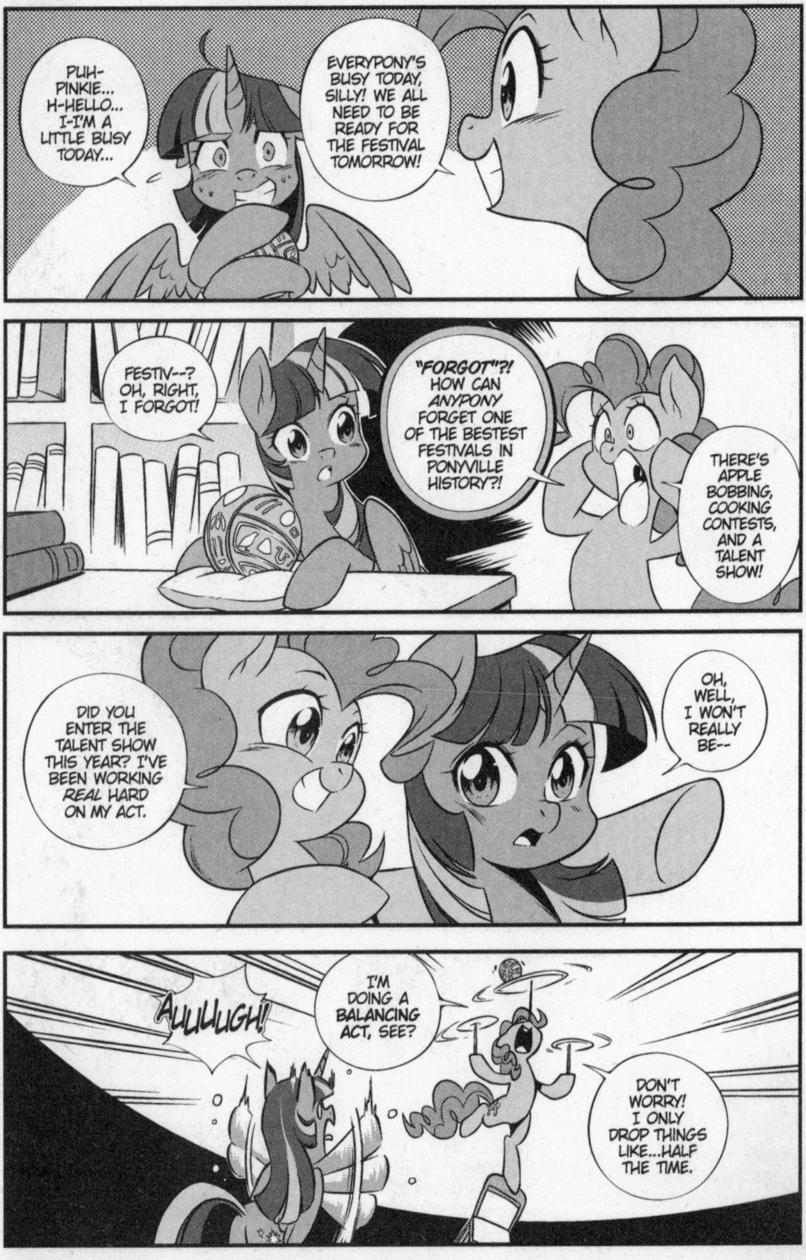

PUH-PINKIE... H-HELLO... I-I'M A LITTLE BUSY TODAY...
EVERYPONY'S BUSY TODAY, SILLY! WE ALL NEED TO BE READY FOR THE FESTIVAL TOMORROW!
FESTIV--? OH, RIGHT, I FORGOT!
"FORGOT"?! HOW CAN *ANYPONY* FORGET ONE OF THE BESTEST FESTIVALS IN PONYVILLE HISTORY?!
THERE'S APPLE BOBBING, COOKING CONTESTS, AND A TALENT SHOW!
DID YOU ENTER THE TALENT SHOW THIS YEAR? I'VE BEEN WORKING *REAL* HARD ON MY ACT.
OH, WELL, I WON'T REALLY BE--
I'M DOING A BALANCING ACT, SEE?
AUUUUGH!
DON'T WORRY! I ONLY DROP THINGS LIKE...HALF THE TIME.

Shattering Expectations

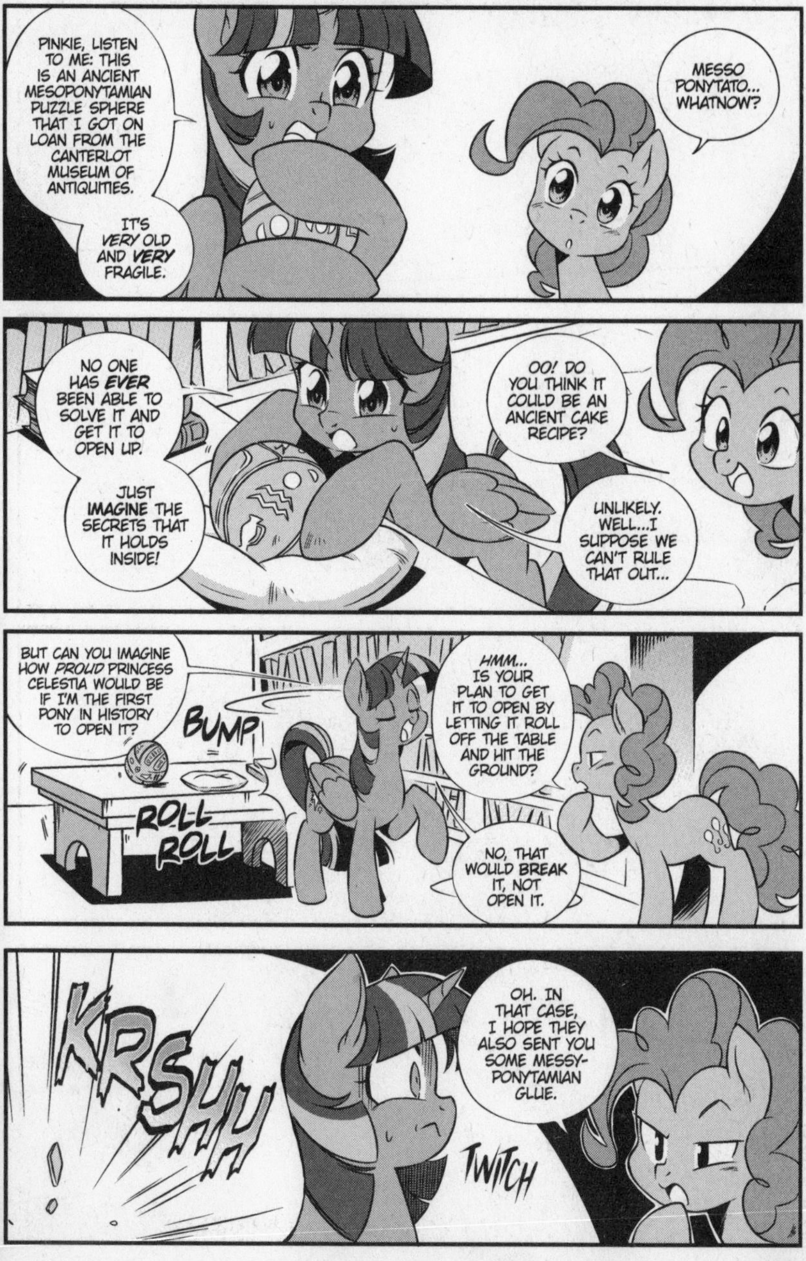
PINKIE, LISTEN TO ME: THIS IS AN ANCIENT MESOPONYTAMIAN PUZZLE SPHERE THAT I GOT ON LOAN FROM THE CANTERLOT MUSEUM OF ANTIQUITIES.
IT'S *VERY* OLD AND ***VERY*** FRAGILE.
MESSO PONYTATO... WHATNOW?
NO ONE HAS ***EVER*** BEEN ABLE TO SOLVE IT AND GET IT TO OPEN UP.
JUST **IMAGINE** THE SECRETS THAT IT HOLDS INSIDE!
OO! DO YOU THINK IT COULD BE AN ANCIENT CAKE RECIPE?
UNLIKELY. WELL...I SUPPOSE WE CAN'T RULE THAT OUT...
BUT CAN YOU IMAGINE HOW *PROUD* PRINCESS CELESTIA WOULD BE IF I'M THE FIRST PONY IN HISTORY TO OPEN IT?
BUMP
ROLL ROLL
HMM... IS YOUR PLAN TO GET IT TO OPEN BY LETTING IT ROLL OFF THE TABLE AND HIT THE GROUND?
NO, THAT WOULD **BREAK** IT, NOT OPEN IT.
KRSHH
OH. IN THAT CASE, I HOPE THEY ALSO SENT YOU SOME MESSY-PONYTAMIAN GLUE.
TWITCH

Just Wingin' It

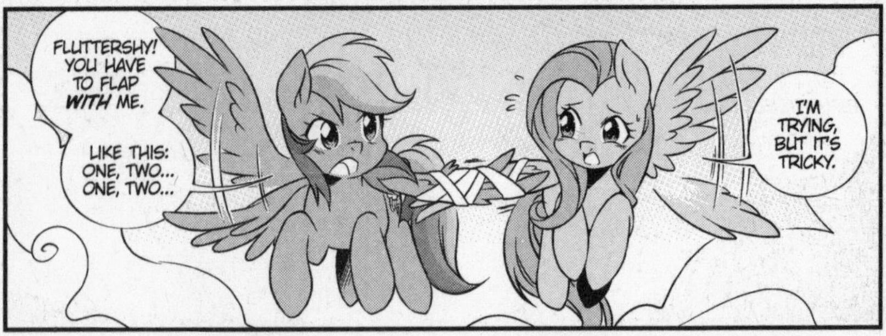
FLUTTERSHY! YOU HAVE TO FLAP *WITH* ME.
LIKE THIS: ONE, TWO... ONE, TWO...
I'M TRYING, BUT IT'S TRICKY.

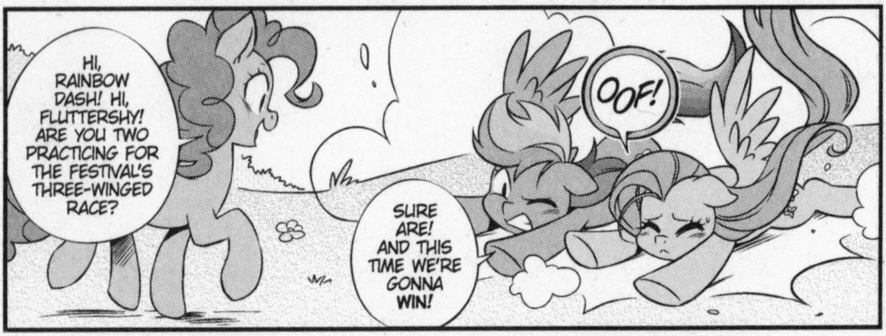
HI, RAINBOW DASH! HI, FLUTTERSHY! ARE YOU TWO PRACTICING FOR THE FESTIVAL'S THREE-WINGED RACE?
OOF!
SURE ARE! AND THIS TIME WE'RE GONNA **WIN!**

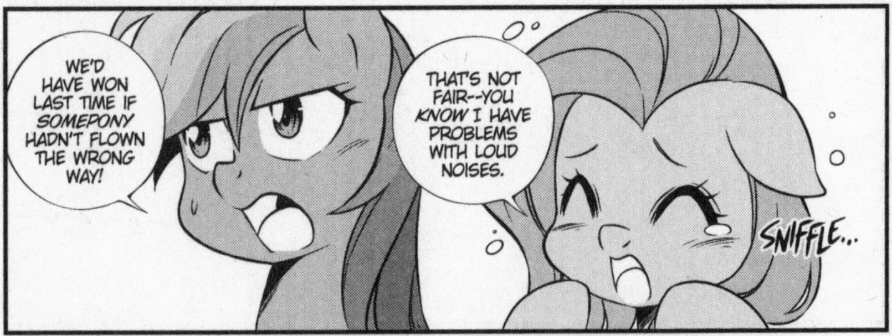
WE'D HAVE WON LAST TIME IF *SOMEPONY* HADN'T FLOWN THE WRONG WAY!
THAT'S NOT FAIR--YOU *KNOW* I HAVE PROBLEMS WITH LOUD NOISES.
SNIFFLE...

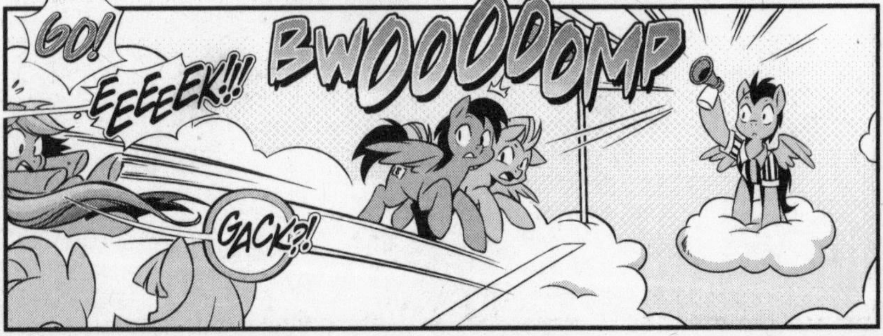
GO!
BWOOOOOOMP
EEEEEEK!!!
GACK?!

Race to the Top

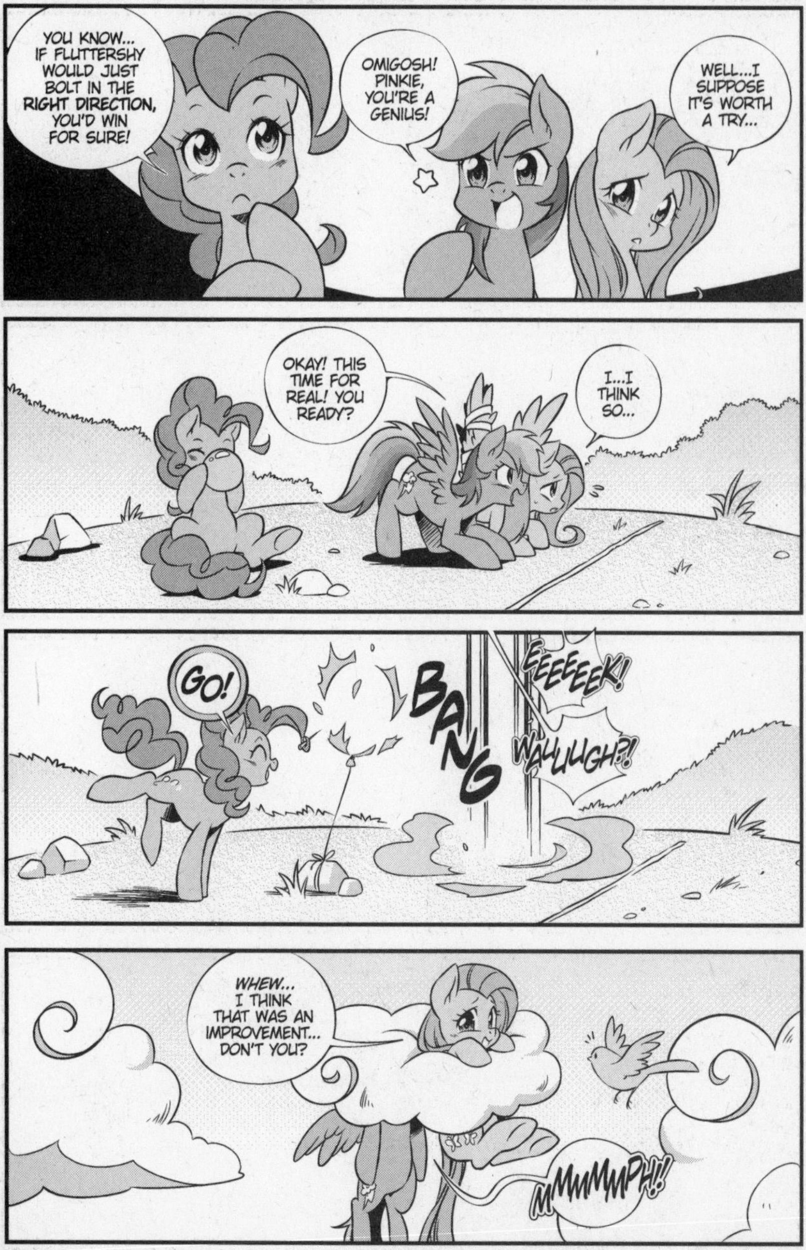

YOU KNOW... IF FLUTTERSHY WOULD JUST BOLT IN THE RIGHT DIRECTION, YOU'D WIN FOR SURE!
OMIGOSH! PINKIE, YOU'RE A GENIUS!
WELL...I SUPPOSE IT'S WORTH A TRY...
OKAY! THIS TIME FOR REAL! YOU READY?
I...I THINK SO...
GO!
BANG
EEEEEEK!
WAUUUGH?!
WHEW... I THINK THAT WAS AN IMPROVEMENT... DON'T YOU?
MMMMMPH!!

Going Nowhere Fast

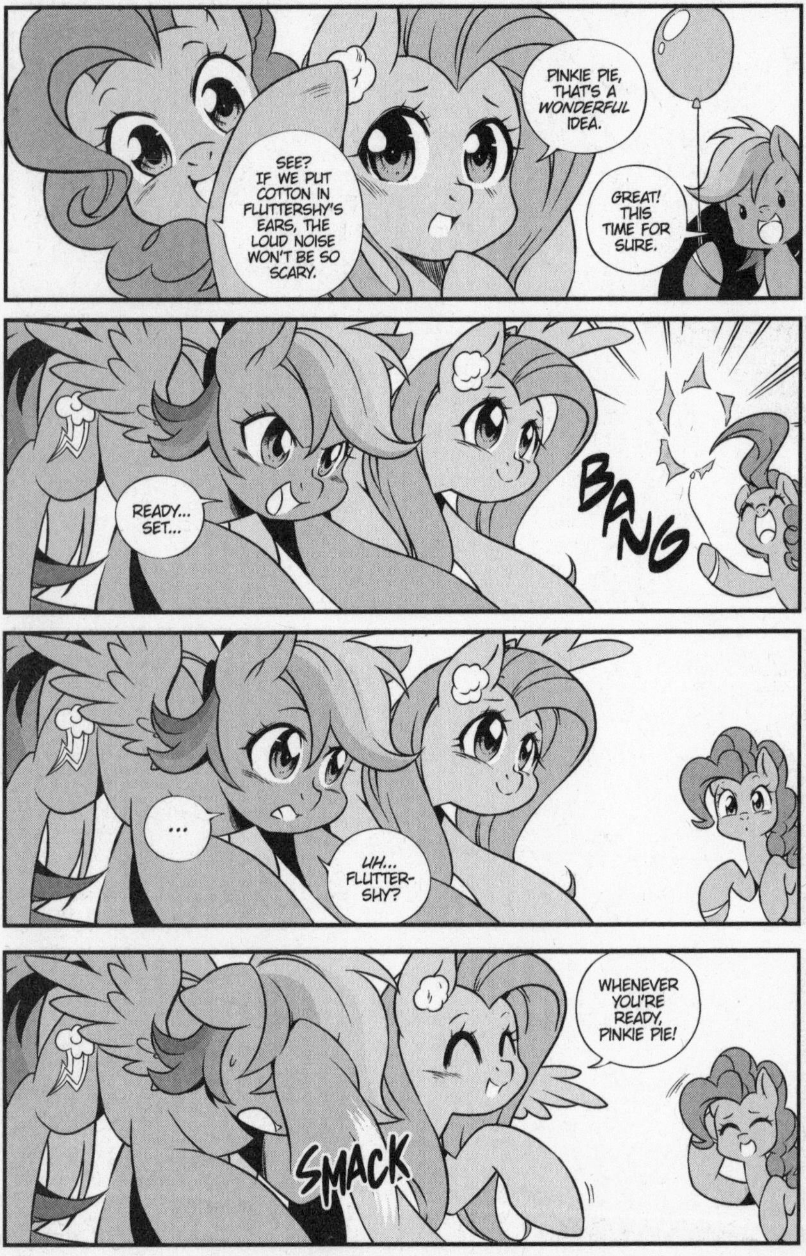
SEE? IF WE PUT COTTON IN FLUTTERSHY'S EARS, THE LOUD NOISE WON'T BE SO SCARY.
PINKIE PIE, THAT'S A *WONDERFUL* IDEA.
GREAT! THIS TIME FOR SURE.
READY... SET...
BANG
...
UH... FLUTTER-SHY?
WHENEVER YOU'RE READY, PINKIE PIE!
SMACK

Sofa so Good

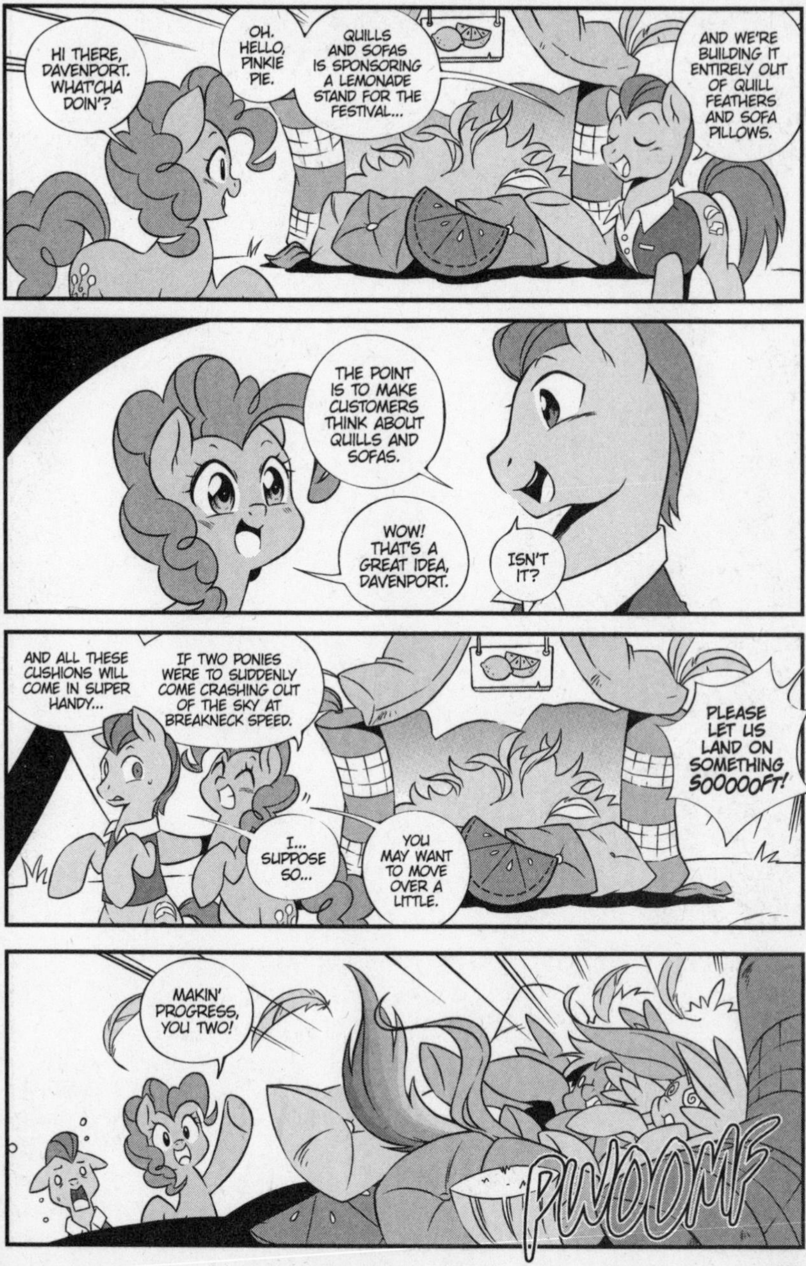
HI THERE, DAVENPORT. WHAT'CHA DOIN'?
OH. HELLO, PINKIE PIE.
QUILLS AND SOFAS IS SPONSORING A LEMONADE STAND FOR THE FESTIVAL...
AND WE'RE BUILDING IT ENTIRELY OUT OF QUILL FEATHERS AND SOFA PILLOWS.
THE POINT IS TO MAKE CUSTOMERS THINK ABOUT QUILLS AND SOFAS.
WOW! THAT'S A GREAT IDEA, DAVENPORT.
ISN'T IT?
AND ALL THESE CUSHIONS WILL COME IN SUPER HANDY...
IF TWO PONIES WERE TO SUDDENLY COME CRASHING OUT OF THE SKY AT BREAKNECK SPEED.
I... SUPPOSE SO...
YOU MAY WANT TO MOVE OVER A LITTLE.
PLEASE LET US LAND ON SOMETHING SOOOOOFT!
MAKIN' PROGRESS, YOU TWO!
PWOOMF

Did You Remember to Brush Your Gums?

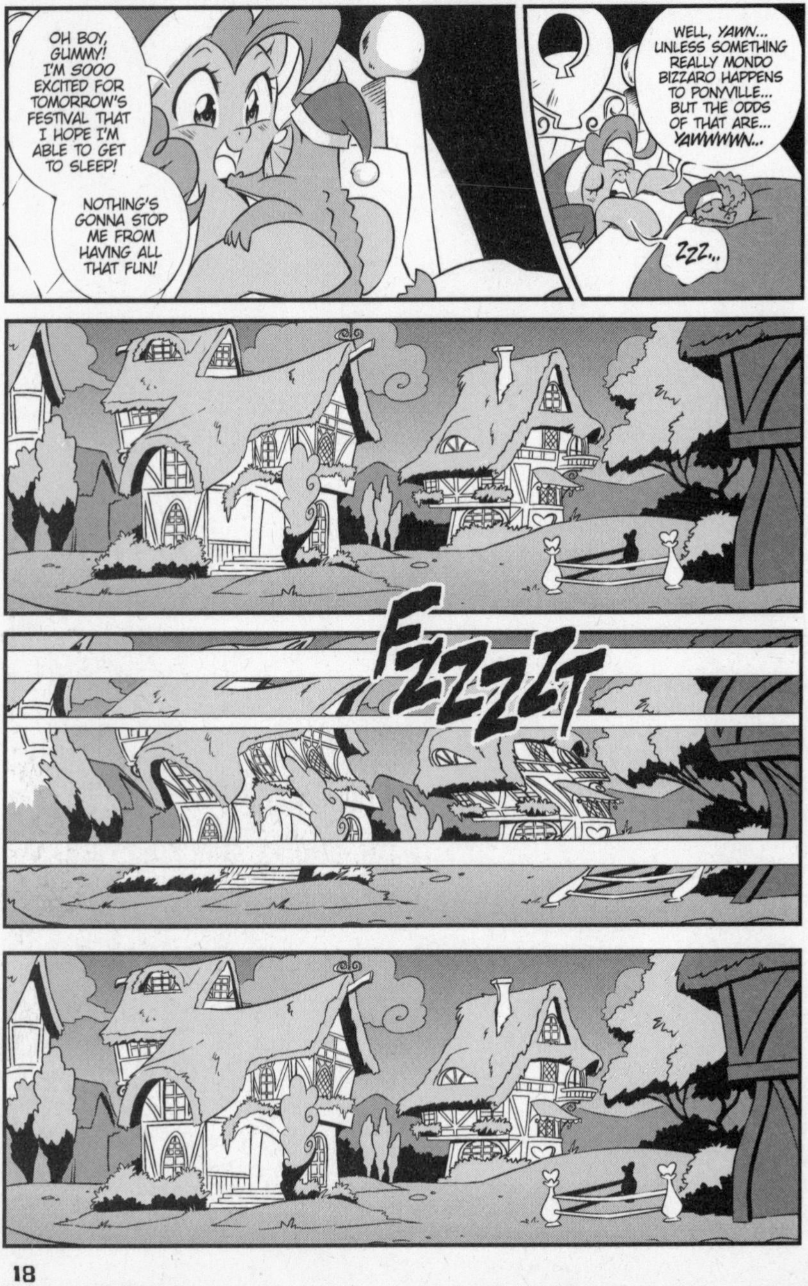

OH BOY, GUMMY! I'M SOOO EXCITED FOR TOMORROW'S FESTIVAL THAT I HOPE I'M ABLE TO GET TO SLEEP!
NOTHING'S GONNA STOP ME FROM HAVING ALL THAT FUN!
WELL, YAWN... UNLESS SOMETHING REALLY MONDO BIZZARO HAPPENS TO PONYVILLE... BUT THE ODDS OF THAT ARE... YAWWWWN...
ZZZ...
FZZZZT

CHAPTER 2

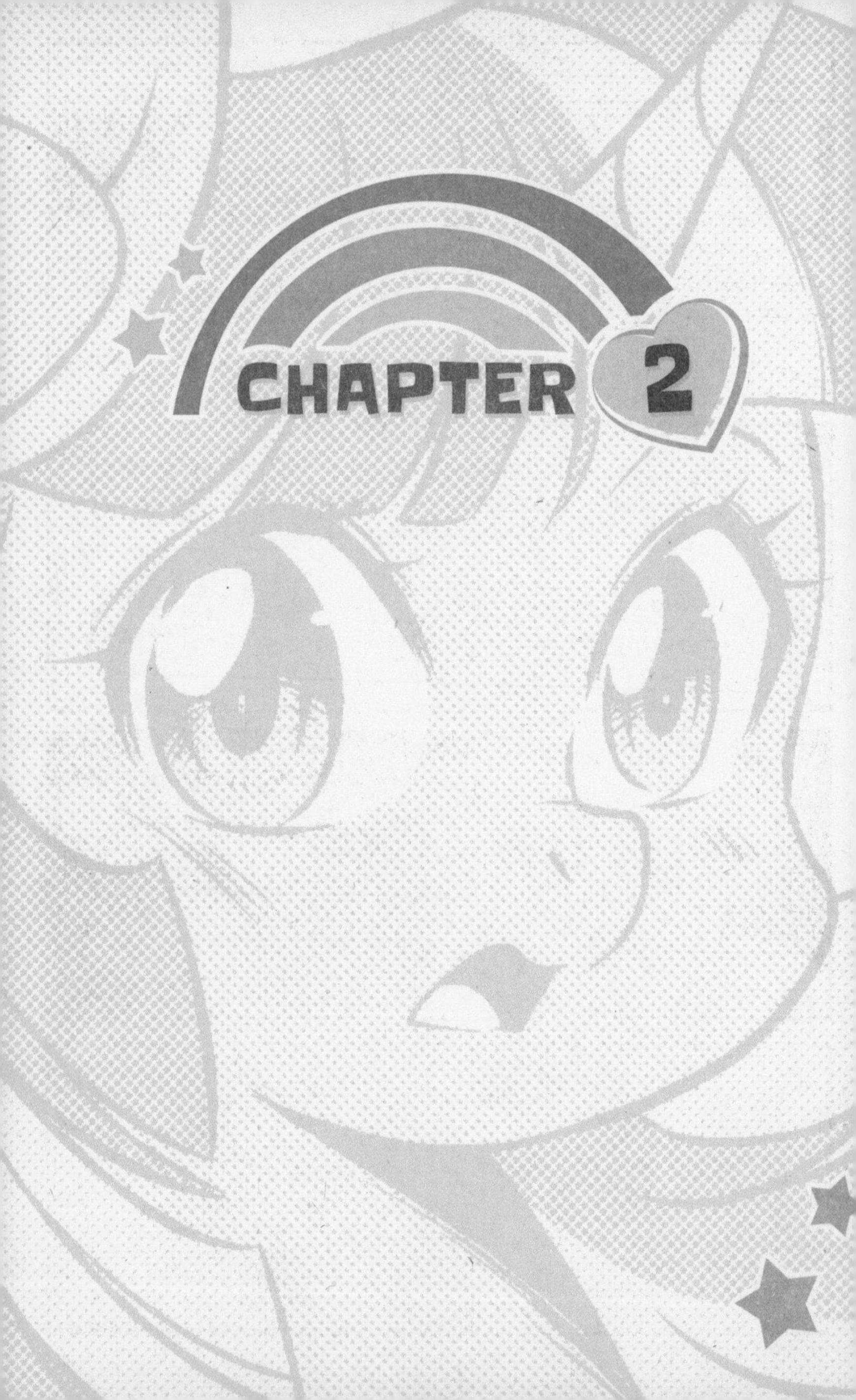

Blabblejack

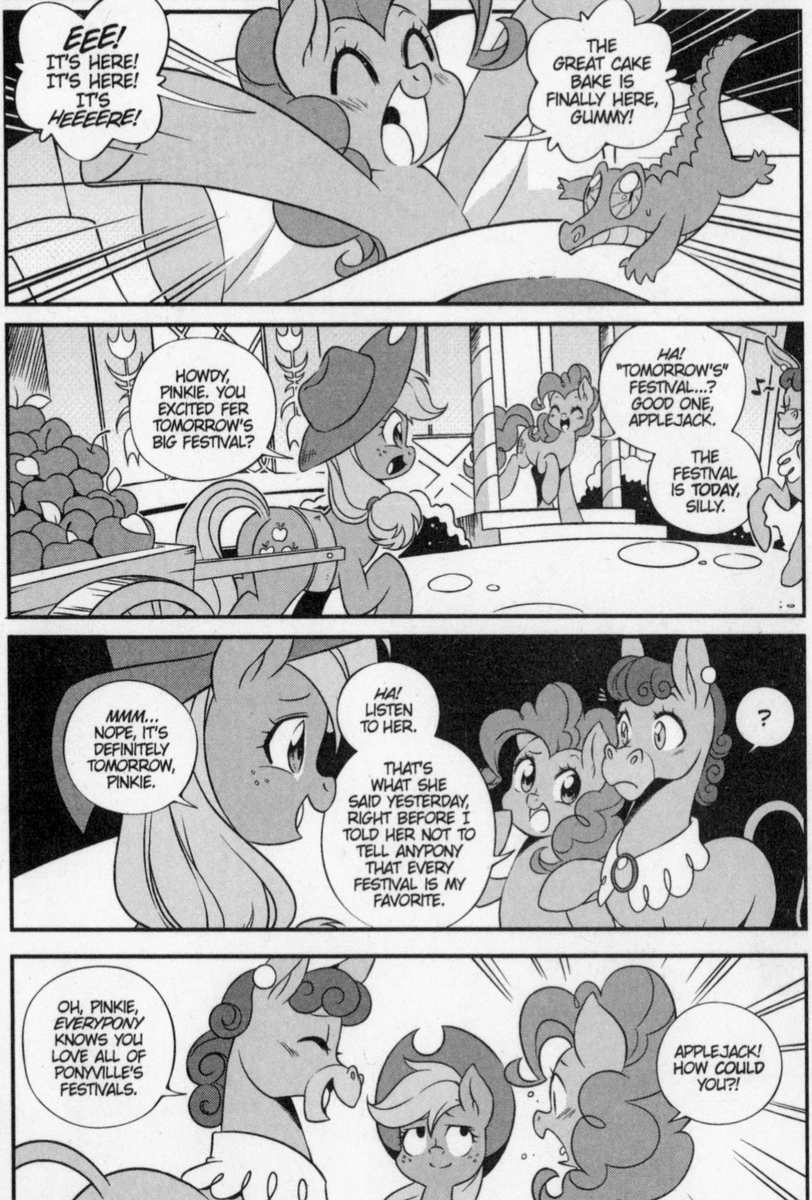

EEE! IT'S HERE! IT'S HERE! IT'S HEEEERE!
THE GREAT CAKE BAKE IS FINALLY HERE, GUMMY!
HOWDY, PINKIE. YOU EXCITED FER TOMORROW'S BIG FESTIVAL?
HA! "TOMORROW'S" FESTIVAL...? GOOD ONE, APPLEJACK.
THE FESTIVAL IS TODAY, SILLY.
MMM... NOPE, IT'S DEFINITELY TOMORROW, PINKIE.
HA! LISTEN TO HER.
THAT'S WHAT SHE SAID YESTERDAY, RIGHT BEFORE I TOLD HER NOT TO TELL ANYPONY THAT EVERY FESTIVAL IS MY FAVORITE.
?
OH, PINKIE, EVERYPONY KNOWS YOU LOVE ALL OF PONYVILLE'S FESTIVALS.
APPLEJACK! HOW COULD YOU?!

Carting Trouble

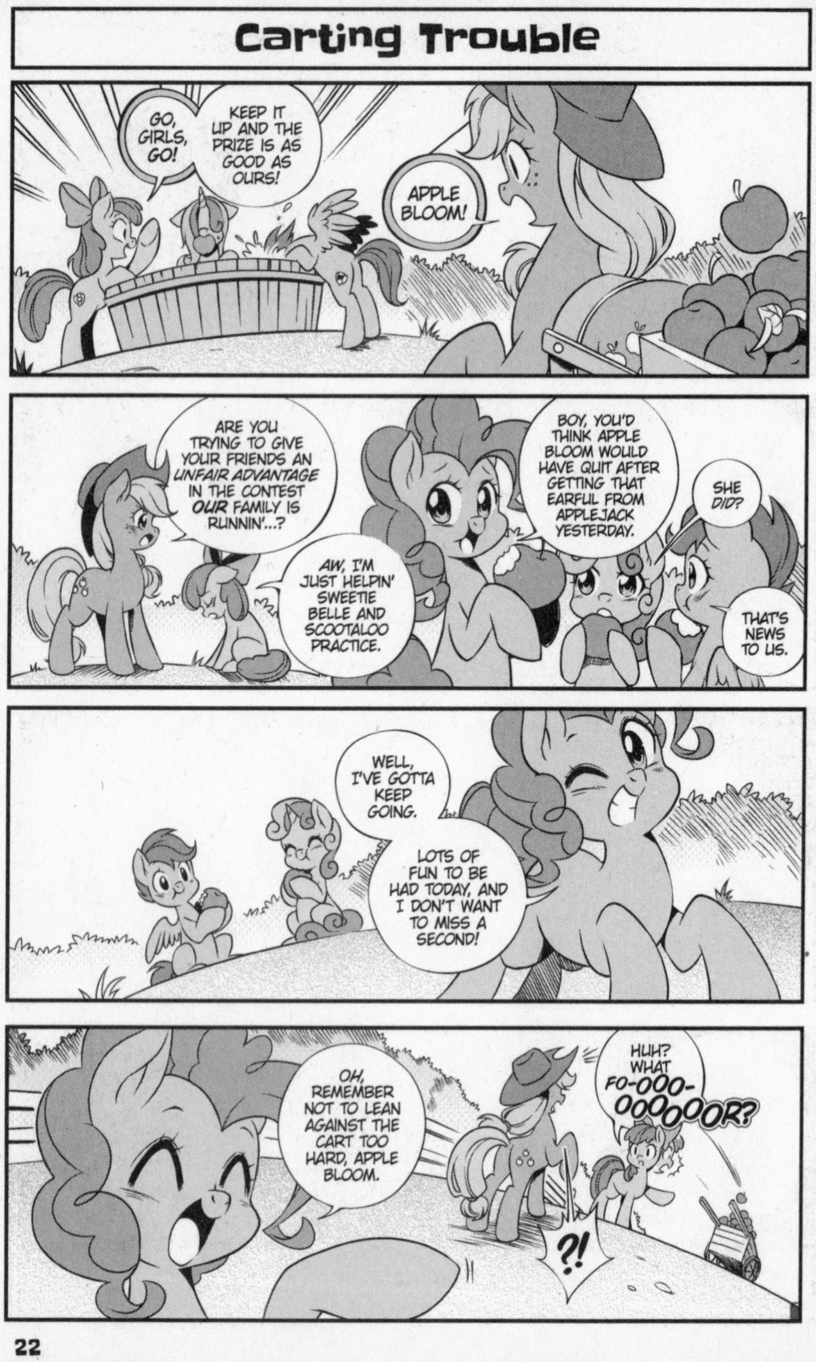

GO, GIRLS, GO!
KEEP IT UP AND THE PRIZE IS AS GOOD AS OURS!
APPLE BLOOM!
ARE YOU TRYING TO GIVE YOUR FRIENDS AN UNFAIR ADVANTAGE IN THE CONTEST OUR FAMILY IS RUNNIN'...?
AW, I'M JUST HELPIN' SWEETIE BELLE AND SCOOTALOO PRACTICE.
BOY, YOU'D THINK APPLE BLOOM WOULD HAVE QUIT AFTER GETTING THAT EARFUL FROM APPLEJACK YESTERDAY.
SHE DID?
THAT'S NEWS TO US.
WELL, I'VE GOTTA KEEP GOING.
LOTS OF FUN TO BE HAD TODAY, AND I DON'T WANT TO MISS A SECOND!
OH, REMEMBER NOT TO LEAN AGAINST THE CART TOO HARD, APPLE BLOOM.
HUH? WHAT FO-OOO-OOOOOOR?
?!

Skirting Good Taste

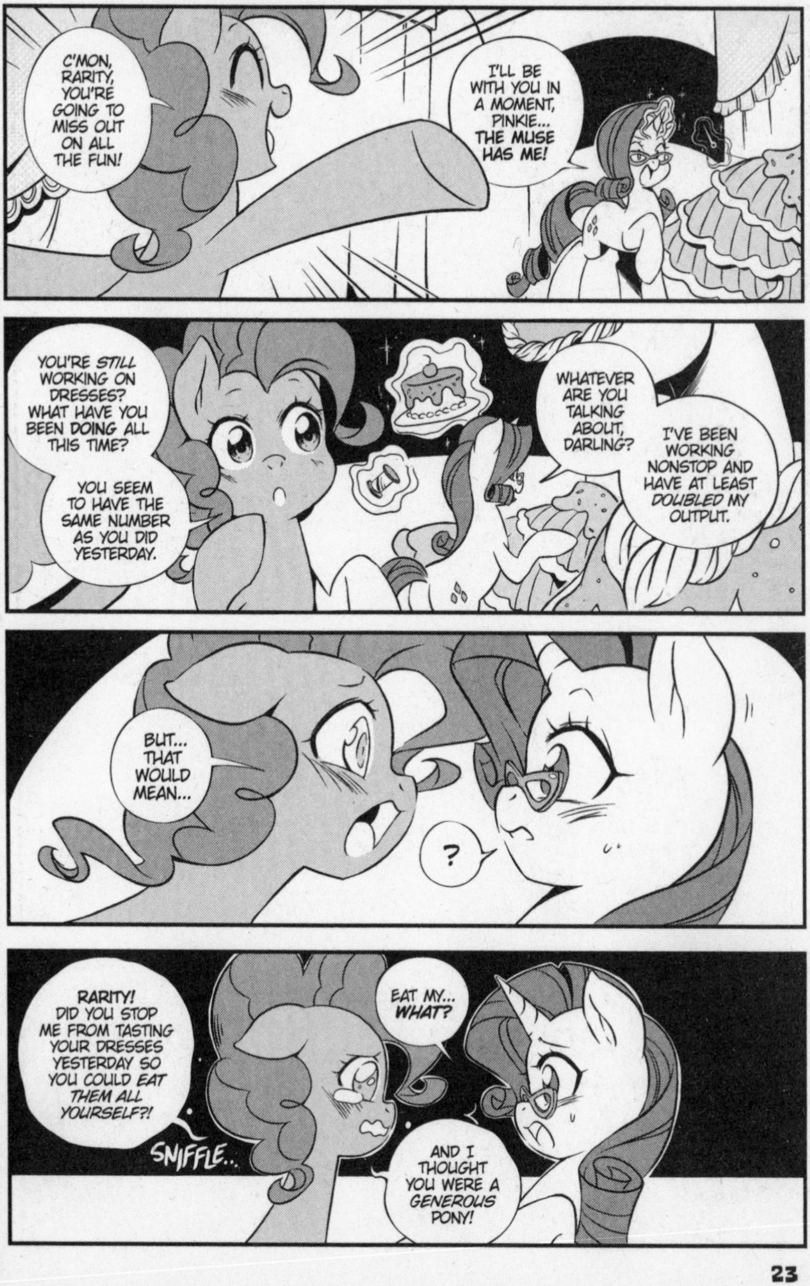
C'MON, RARITY, YOU'RE GOING TO MISS OUT ON ALL THE FUN!
I'LL BE WITH YOU IN A MOMENT, PINKIE... THE MUSE HAS ME!
YOU'RE *STILL* WORKING ON DRESSES? WHAT HAVE YOU BEEN DOING ALL THIS TIME?
YOU SEEM TO HAVE THE SAME NUMBER AS YOU DID YESTERDAY.
WHATEVER ARE YOU TALKING ABOUT, DARLING?
I'VE BEEN WORKING NONSTOP AND HAVE AT LEAST *DOUBLED* MY OUTPUT.
BUT... THAT WOULD MEAN...
?
RARITY! DID YOU STOP ME FROM TASTING YOUR DRESSES YESTERDAY SO YOU COULD *EAT THEM ALL* YOURSELF?!
EAT MY... ***WHAT?***
SNIFFLE...
AND I THOUGHT YOU WERE A *GENEROUS* PONY!

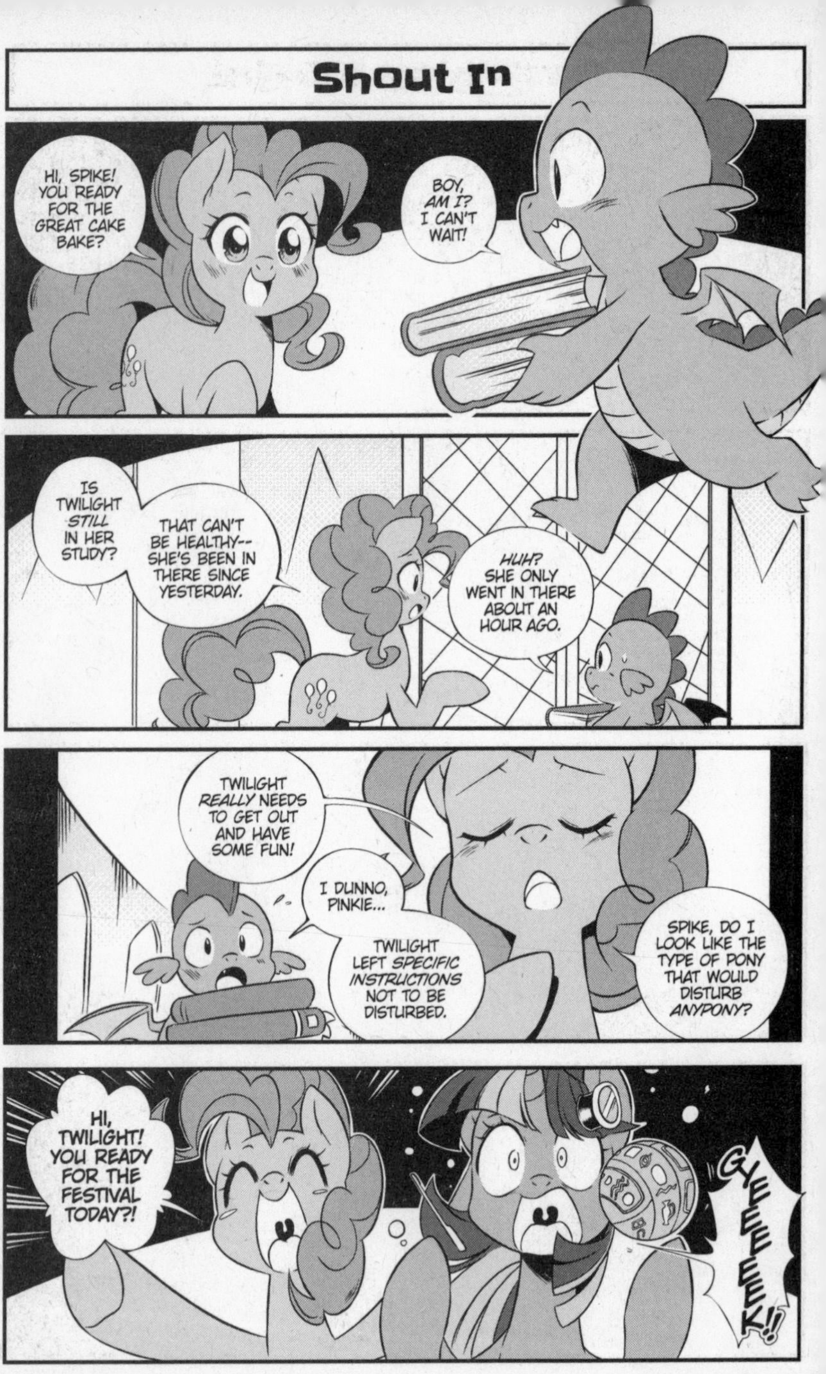
Shout In
HI, SPIKE! YOU READY FOR THE GREAT CAKE BAKE?
BOY, *AM I?* I CAN'T WAIT!
IS TWILIGHT *STILL* IN HER STUDY?
THAT CAN'T BE HEALTHY-- SHE'S BEEN IN THERE SINCE YESTERDAY.
HUH? SHE ONLY WENT IN THERE ABOUT AN HOUR AGO.
TWILIGHT *REALLY* NEEDS TO GET OUT AND HAVE SOME FUN!
I DUNNO, PINKIE...
TWILIGHT LEFT *SPECIFIC INSTRUCTIONS* NOT TO BE DISTURBED.
SPIKE, DO I LOOK LIKE THE TYPE OF PONY THAT WOULD DISTURB *ANYPONY?*
HI, TWILIGHT! YOU READY FOR THE FESTIVAL TODAY?!
GYEEEEEK!!

Smashing Insight

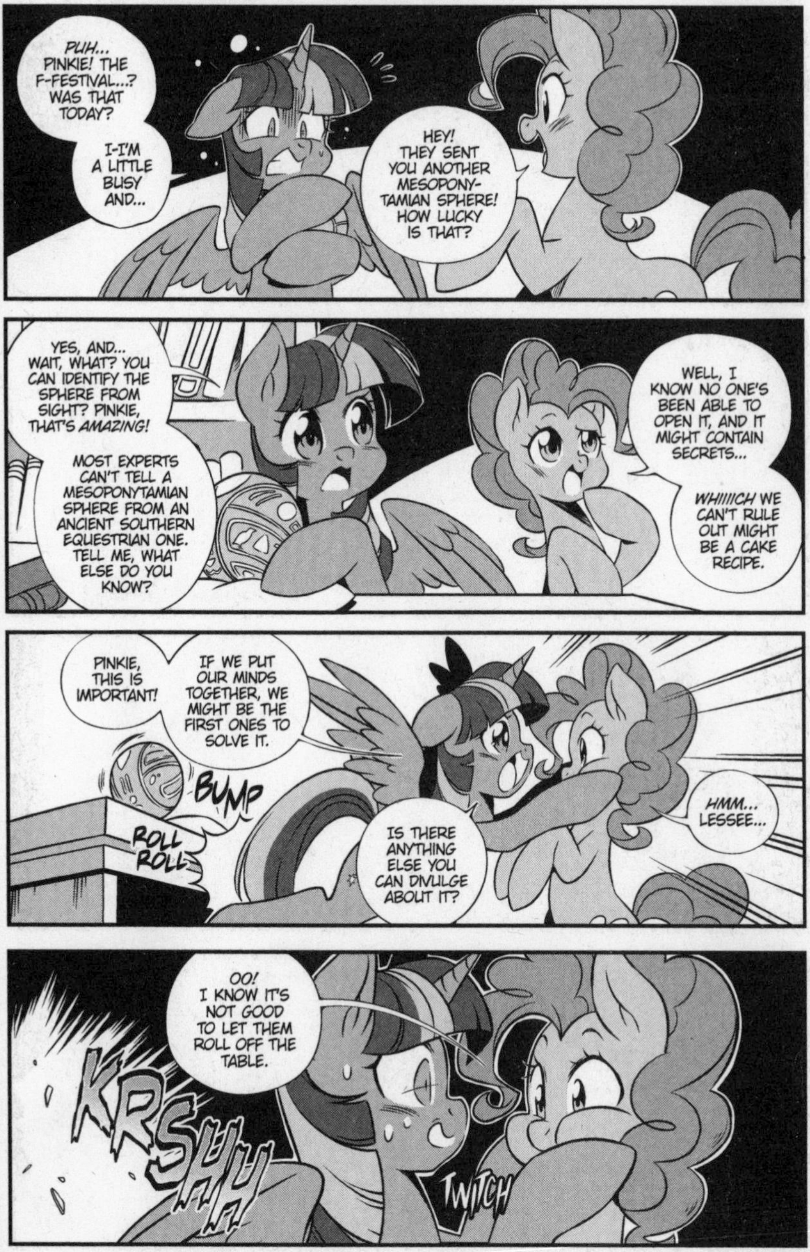
PUH... PINKIE! THE F-FESTIVAL...? WAS THAT TODAY?
I-I'M A LITTLE BUSY AND...
HEY! THEY SENT YOU ANOTHER MESOPONY-TAMIAN SPHERE! HOW LUCKY IS THAT?
YES, AND... WAIT, WHAT? YOU CAN IDENTIFY THE SPHERE FROM SIGHT? PINKIE, THAT'S *AMAZING!*
MOST EXPERTS CAN'T TELL A MESOPONYTAMIAN SPHERE FROM AN ANCIENT SOUTHERN EQUESTRIAN ONE. TELL ME, WHAT ELSE DO YOU KNOW?
WELL, I KNOW NO ONE'S BEEN ABLE TO OPEN IT, AND IT MIGHT CONTAIN SECRETS...
WHIIIICH WE CAN'T RULE OUT MIGHT BE A CAKE RECIPE.
PINKIE, THIS IS IMPORTANT!
IF WE PUT OUR MINDS TOGETHER, WE MIGHT BE THE FIRST ONES TO SOLVE IT.
BUMP
ROLL ROLL
IS THERE ANYTHING ELSE YOU CAN DIVULGE ABOUT IT?
HMM... LESSEE...
OO! I KNOW IT'S NOT GOOD TO LET THEM ROLL OFF THE TABLE.
KRSHH
TWITCH

Forget-foals

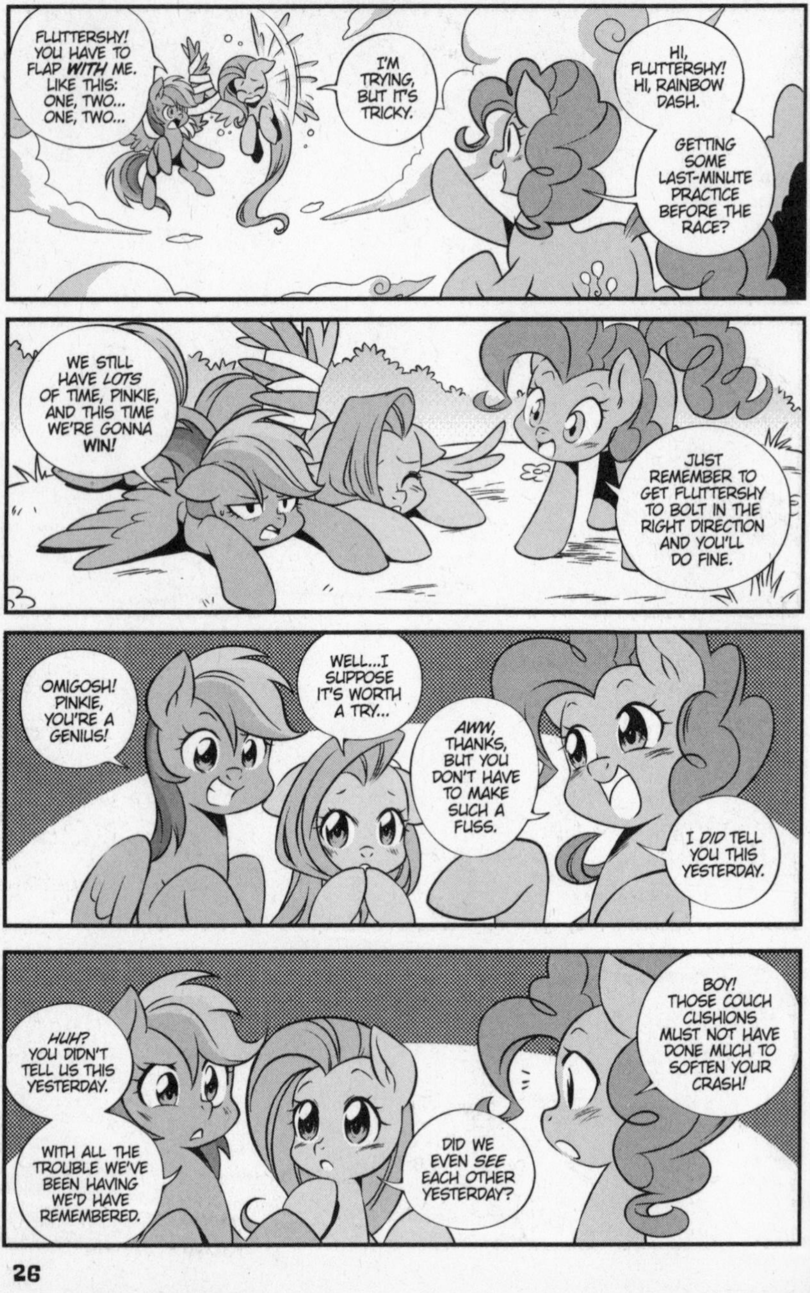
FLUTTERSHY! YOU HAVE TO FLAP ***WITH*** ME. LIKE THIS: ONE, TWO... ONE, TWO...
I'M TRYING, BUT IT'S TRICKY.
HI, FLUTTERSHY! HI, RAINBOW DASH.
GETTING SOME LAST-MINUTE PRACTICE BEFORE THE RACE?
WE STILL HAVE *LOTS* OF TIME, PINKIE, AND THIS TIME WE'RE GONNA **WIN!**
JUST REMEMBER TO GET FLUTTERSHY TO BOLT IN THE RIGHT DIRECTION AND YOU'LL DO FINE.
OMIGOSH! PINKIE, YOU'RE A GENIUS!
WELL...I SUPPOSE IT'S WORTH A TRY...
AWW, THANKS, BUT YOU DON'T HAVE TO MAKE SUCH A FUSS.
I *DID* TELL YOU THIS YESTERDAY.
HUH? YOU DIDN'T TELL US THIS YESTERDAY.
WITH ALL THE TROUBLE WE'VE BEEN HAVING WE'D HAVE REMEMBERED.
DID WE EVEN *SEE* EACH OTHER YESTERDAY?
BOY! THOSE COUCH CUSHIONS MUST NOT HAVE DONE MUCH TO SOFTEN YOUR CRASH!

See You Next Fall

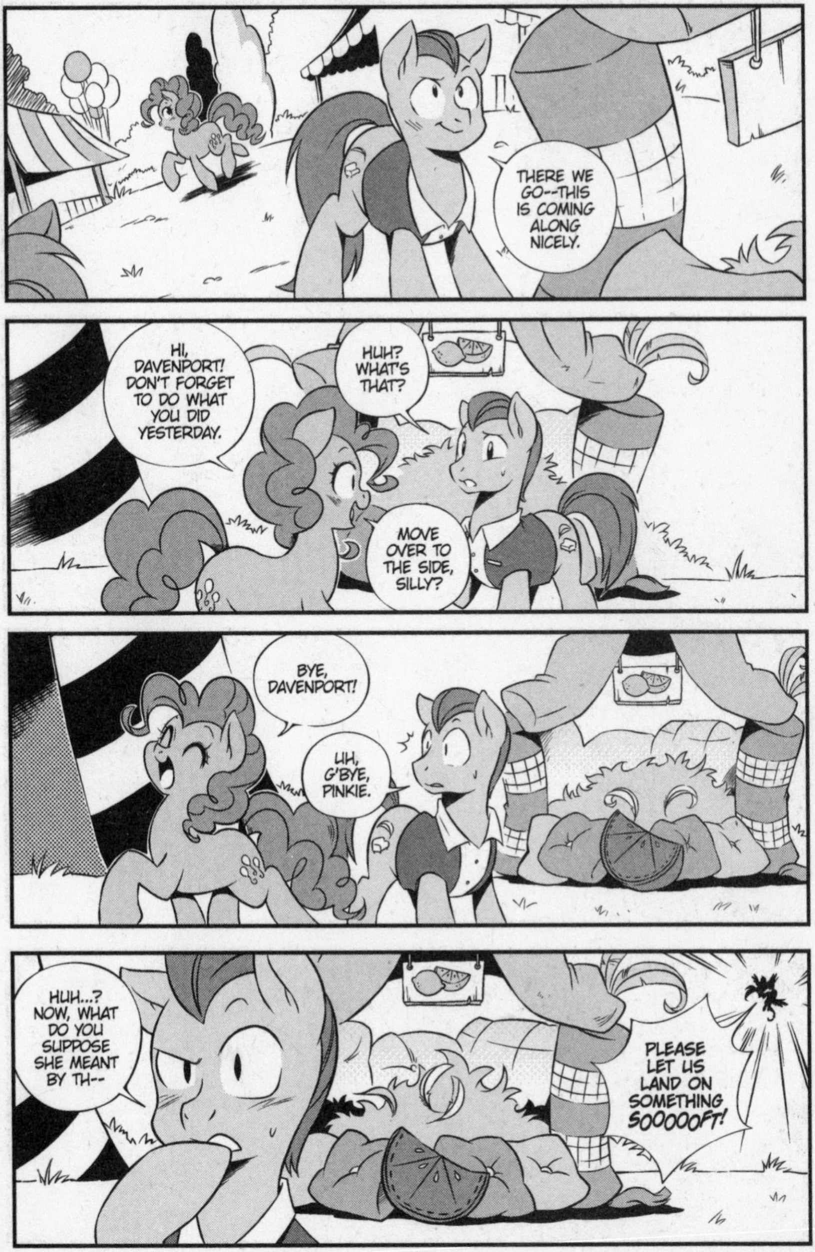

THERE WE GO--THIS IS COMING ALONG NICELY.
HI, DAVENPORT! DON'T FORGET TO DO WHAT YOU DID YESTERDAY.
HUH? WHAT'S THAT?
MOVE OVER TO THE SIDE, SILLY?
BYE, DAVENPORT!
UH, G'BYE, PINKIE.
HUH...? NOW, WHAT DO YOU SUPPOSE SHE MEANT BY TH--
PLEASE LET US LAND ON SOMETHING SOOOOOFT!

Are you Ready to Rock?

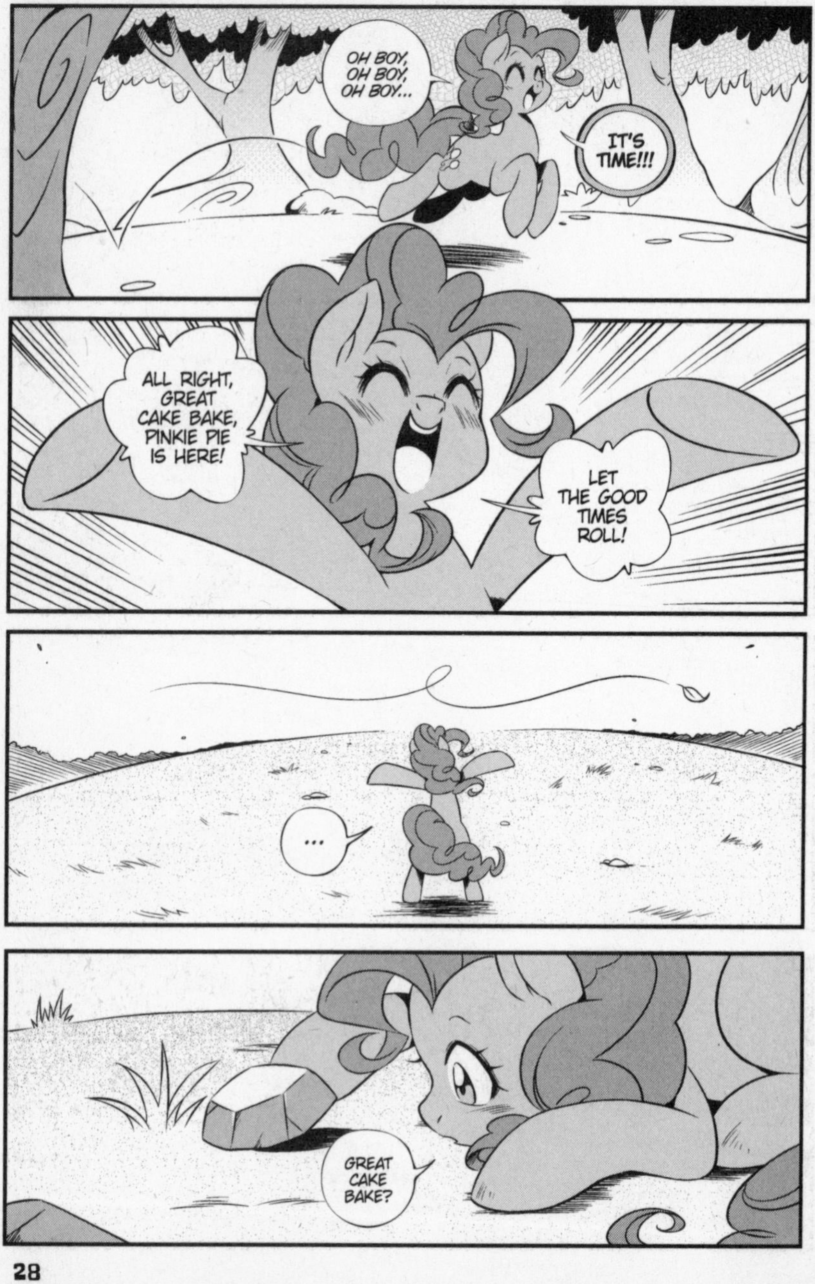
OH BOY, OH BOY, OH BOY...
IT'S TIME!!!
ALL RIGHT, GREAT CAKE BAKE, PINKIE PIE IS HERE!
LET THE GOOD TIMES ROLL!
...
GREAT CAKE BAKE?

Pink-A-Boo!

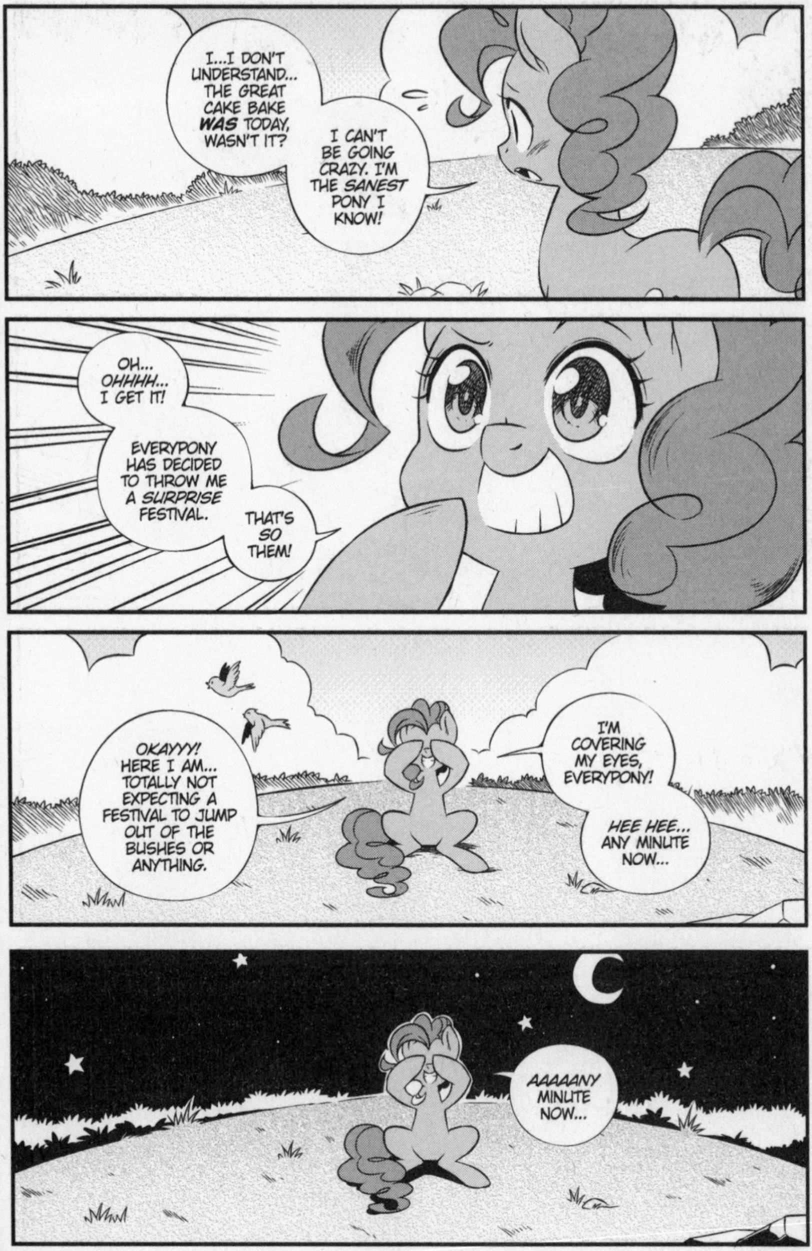
I...I DON'T UNDERSTAND... THE GREAT CAKE BAKE **WAS** TODAY, WASN'T IT?
I CAN'T BE GOING CRAZY. I'M THE *SANEST* PONY I KNOW!
OH... *OHHHH...* I GET IT!
EVERYPONY HAS DECIDED TO THROW ME A *SURPRISE* FESTIVAL.
THAT'S *SO* THEM!
OKAYYY! HERE I AM... TOTALLY NOT EXPECTING A FESTIVAL TO JUMP OUT OF THE BUSHES OR ANYTHING.
I'M COVERING MY EYES, EVERYPONY!
HEE HEE... ANY MINUTE NOW...
AAAAANY MINUTE NOW...

What a Roomy Meadow

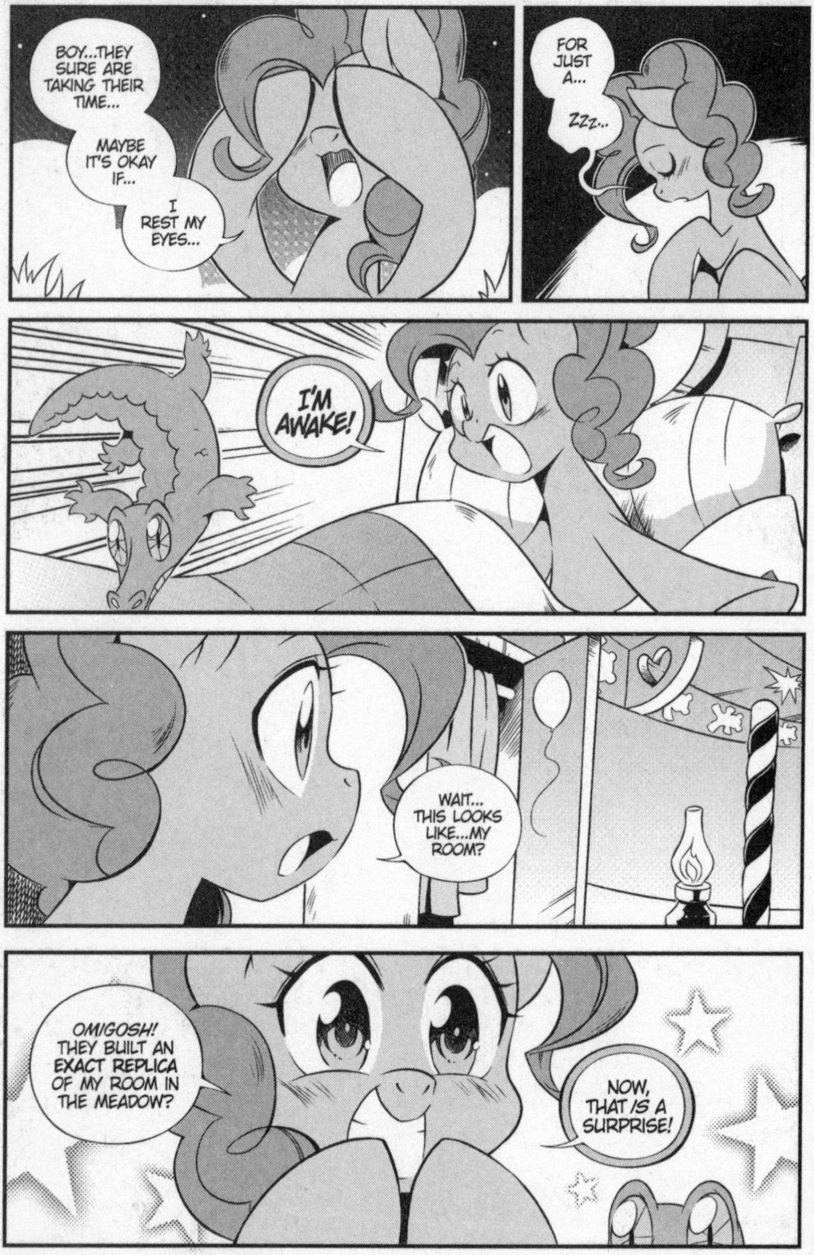
BOY...THEY SURE ARE TAKING THEIR TIME...
MAYBE IT'S OKAY IF...
I REST MY EYES...
FOR JUST A...
ZZZ...
I'M AWAKE!
WAIT... THIS LOOKS LIKE...MY ROOM?
OMIGOSH! THEY BUILT AN EXACT REPLICA OF MY ROOM IN THE MEADOW?
NOW, THAT IS A SURPRISE!

Funfair? More Like "Unfair"!

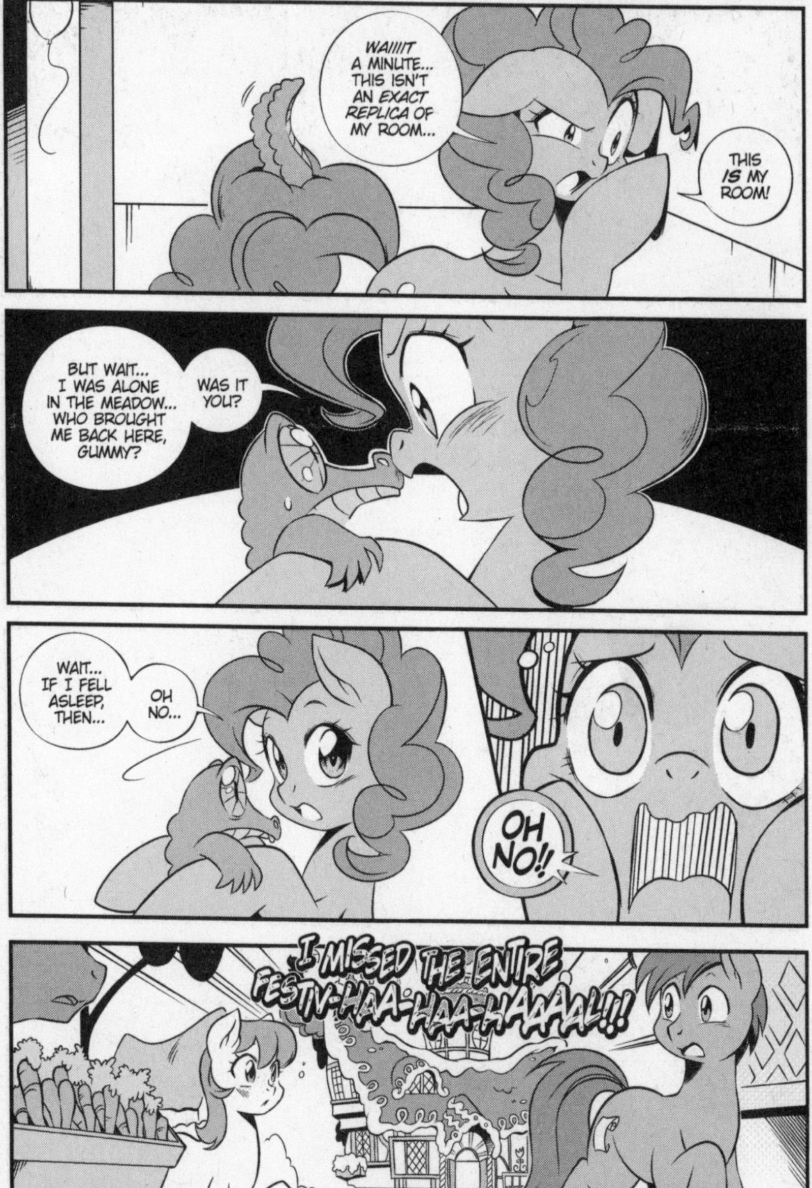
WAIIIIT A MINUTE... THIS ISN'T AN *EXACT REPLICA* OF MY ROOM...
THIS *IS* MY ROOM!
BUT WAIT... I WAS ALONE IN THE MEADOW... WHO BROUGHT ME BACK HERE, GUMMY?
WAS IT YOU?
WAIT... IF I FELL ASLEEP, THEN...
OH NO...
OH NO!!
I MISSED THE ENTIRE FESTIV-HAA-HAA-HAAAAL!!!

Pink'd

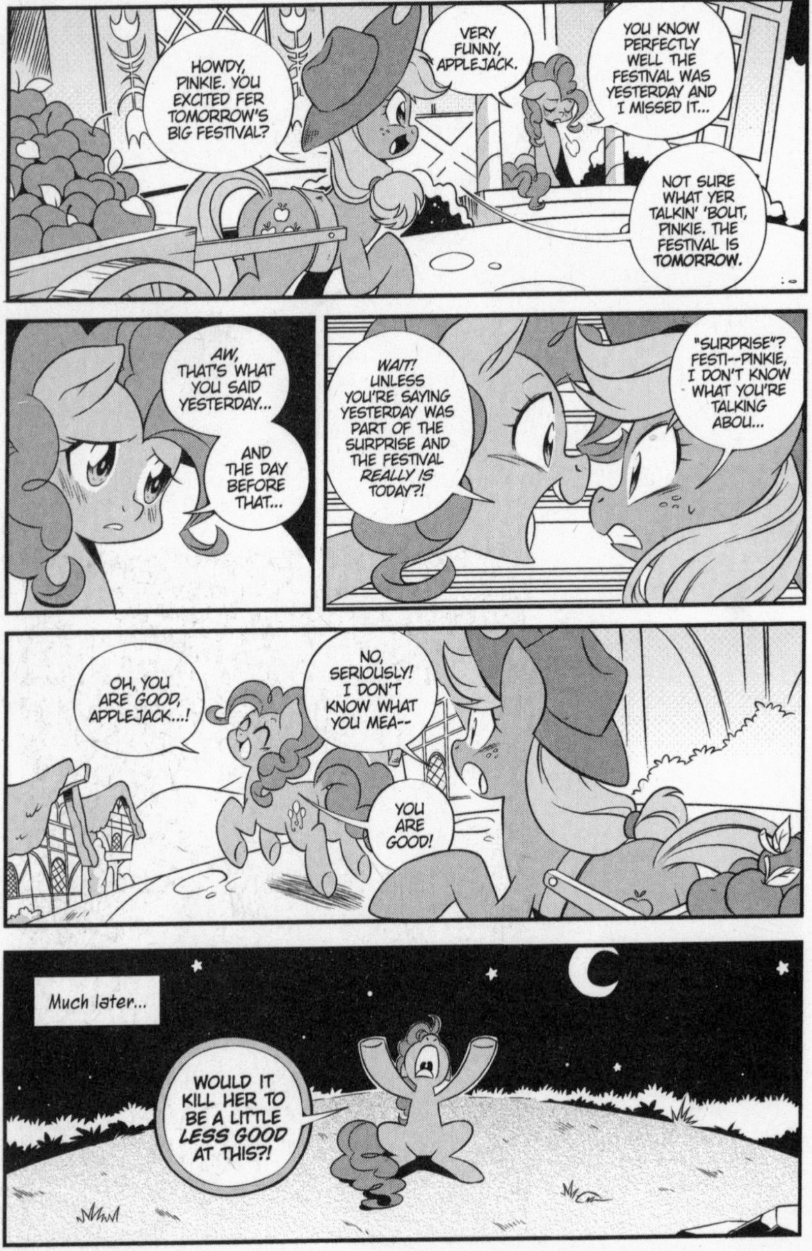

HOWDY, PINKIE. YOU EXCITED FER TOMORROW'S BIG FESTIVAL?
VERY FUNNY, APPLEJACK.
YOU KNOW PERFECTLY WELL THE FESTIVAL WAS YESTERDAY AND I MISSED IT...
NOT SURE WHAT YER TALKIN' 'BOUT, PINKIE. THE FESTIVAL IS TOMORROW.
AW, THAT'S WHAT YOU SAID YESTERDAY...
AND THE DAY BEFORE THAT...
WAIT! UNLESS YOU'RE SAYING YESTERDAY WAS PART OF THE SURPRISE AND THE FESTIVAL *REALLY IS* TODAY?!
"SURPRISE"? FESTI--PINKIE, I DON'T KNOW WHAT YOU'RE TALKING ABOU...
OH, YOU ARE GOOD, APPLEJACK...!
NO, SERIOUSLY! I DON'T KNOW WHAT YOU MEA--
YOU ARE GOOD!
Much later...
WOULD IT KILL HER TO BE A LITTLE ***LESS GOOD*** AT THIS?!

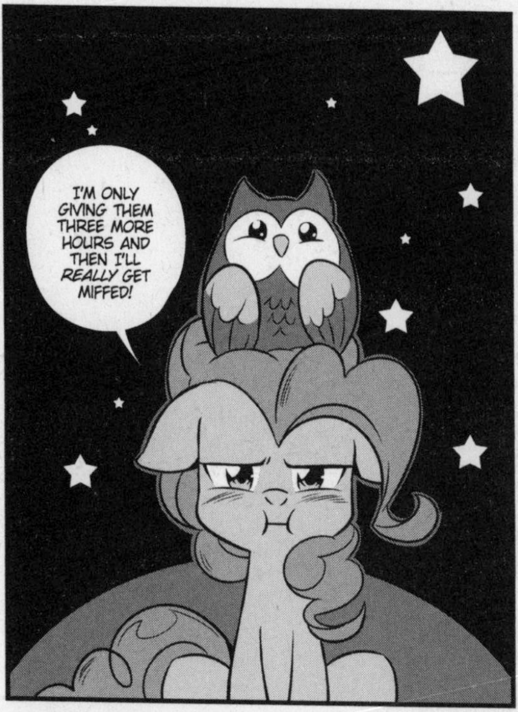
I'M ONLY GIVING THEM THREE MORE HOURS AND THEN I'LL *REALLY* GET MIFFED!

CHAPTER 3

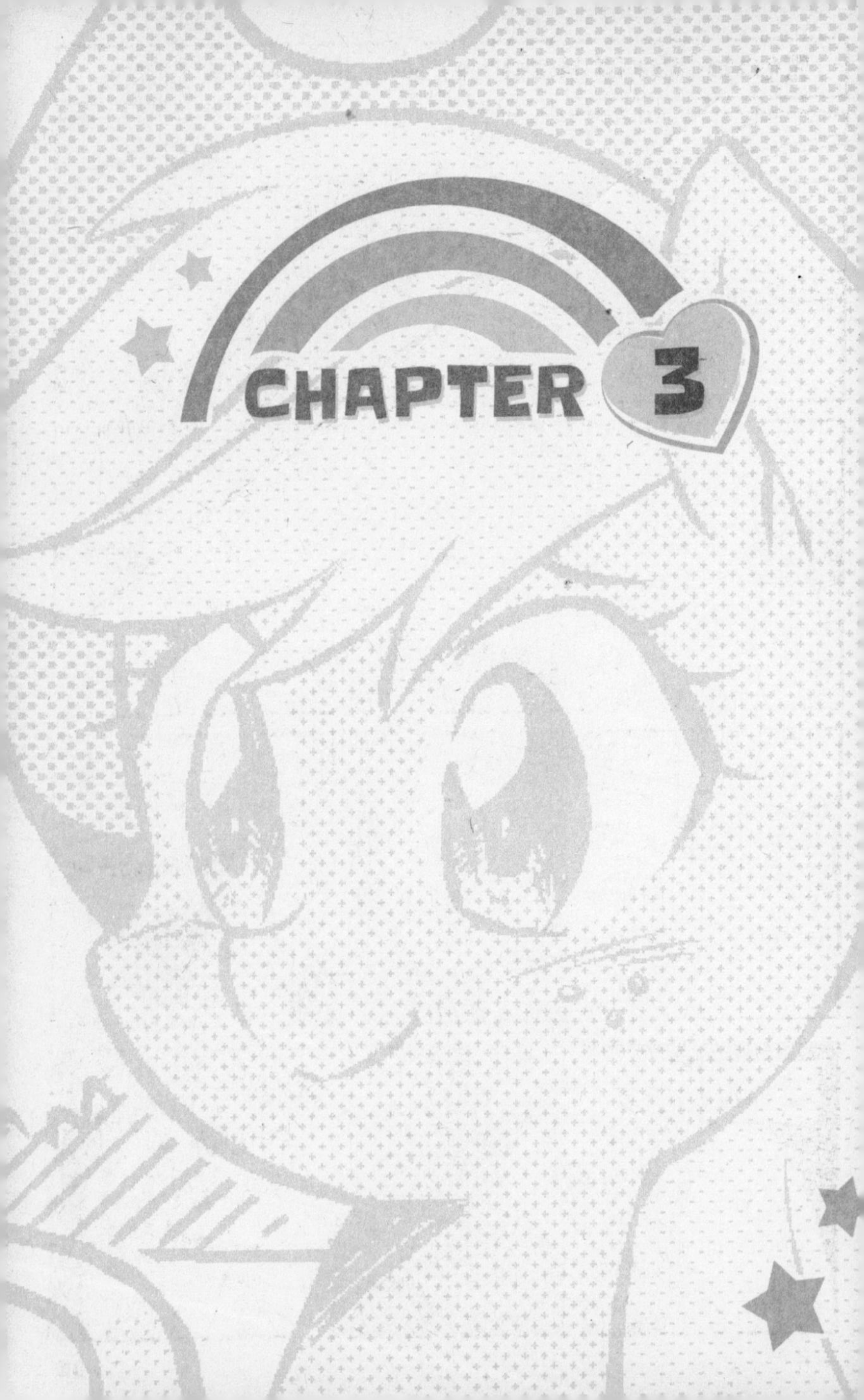

Stop Me if You've Heard this One...

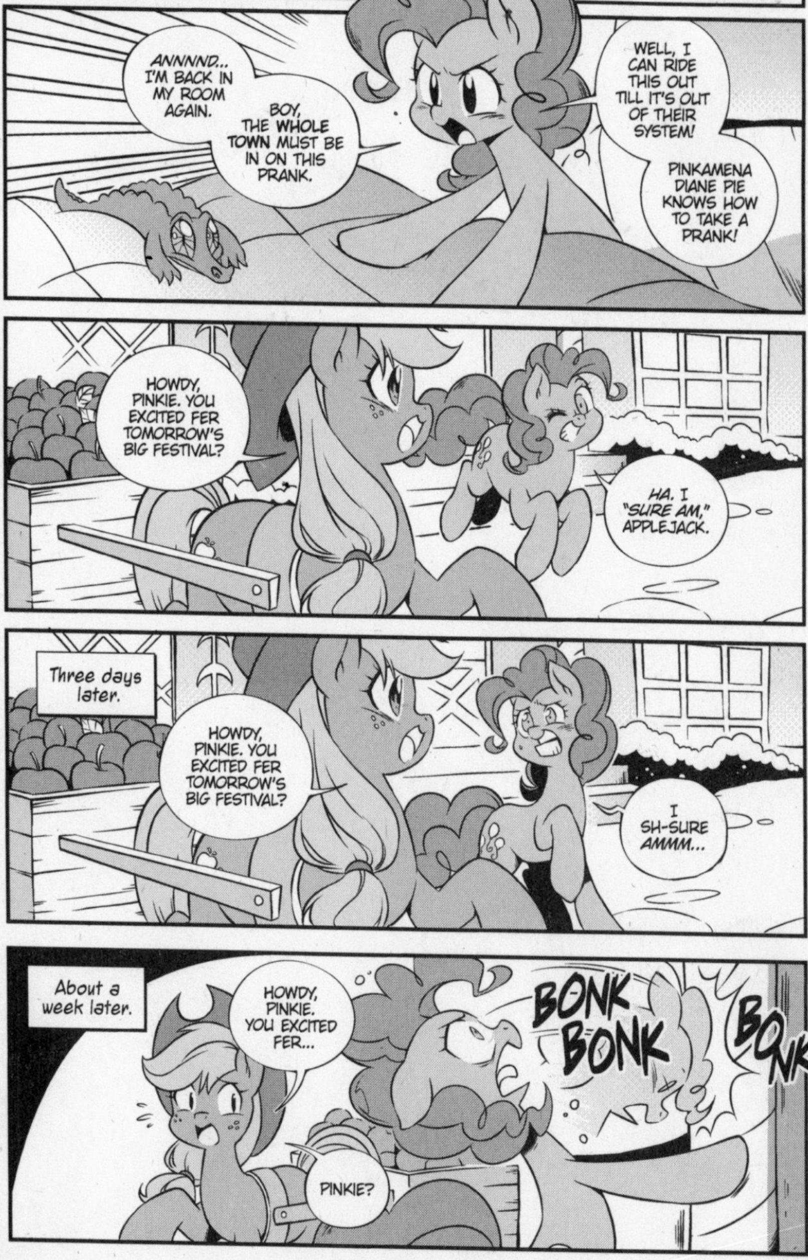

ANNNND... I'M BACK IN MY ROOM AGAIN.
BOY, THE WHOLE TOWN MUST BE IN ON THIS PRANK.
WELL, I CAN RIDE THIS OUT TILL IT'S OUT OF THEIR SYSTEM!
PINKAMENA DIANE PIE KNOWS HOW TO TAKE A PRANK!
HOWDY, PINKIE. YOU EXCITED FER TOMORROW'S BIG FESTIVAL?
HA. I "SURE AM," APPLEJACK.
Three days later.
HOWDY, PINKIE. YOU EXCITED FER TOMORROW'S BIG FESTIVAL?
I SH-SURE AMMM...
About a week later.
HOWDY, PINKIE. YOU EXCITED FER...
BONK
BONK
BONK
PINKIE?

Pie Give Up!

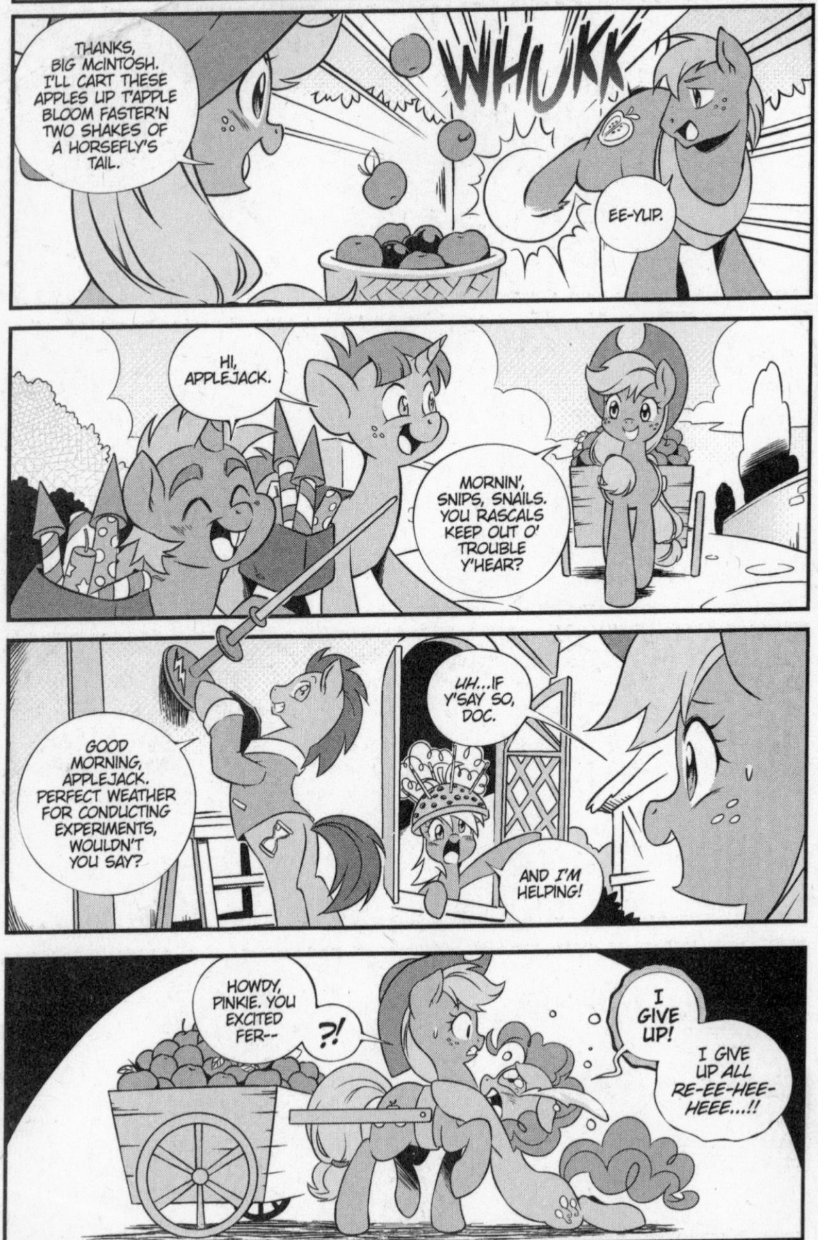
THANKS, BIG McINTOSH. I'LL CART THESE APPLES UP T'APPLE BLOOM FASTER'N TWO SHAKES OF A HORSEFLY'S TAIL.
WHUKK
EE-YUP.
HI, APPLEJACK.
MORNIN', SNIPS, SNAILS. YOU RASCALS KEEP OUT O' TROUBLE Y'HEAR?
GOOD MORNING, APPLEJACK. PERFECT WEATHER FOR CONDUCTING EXPERIMENTS, WOULDN'T YOU SAY?
AND I'M HELPING!
UH...IF Y'SAY SO, DOC.
HOWDY, PINKIE. YOU EXCITED FER--
?!
I GIVE UP!
I GIVE UP ALL RE-EE-HEE-HEEE...!!

Pie in the Sky

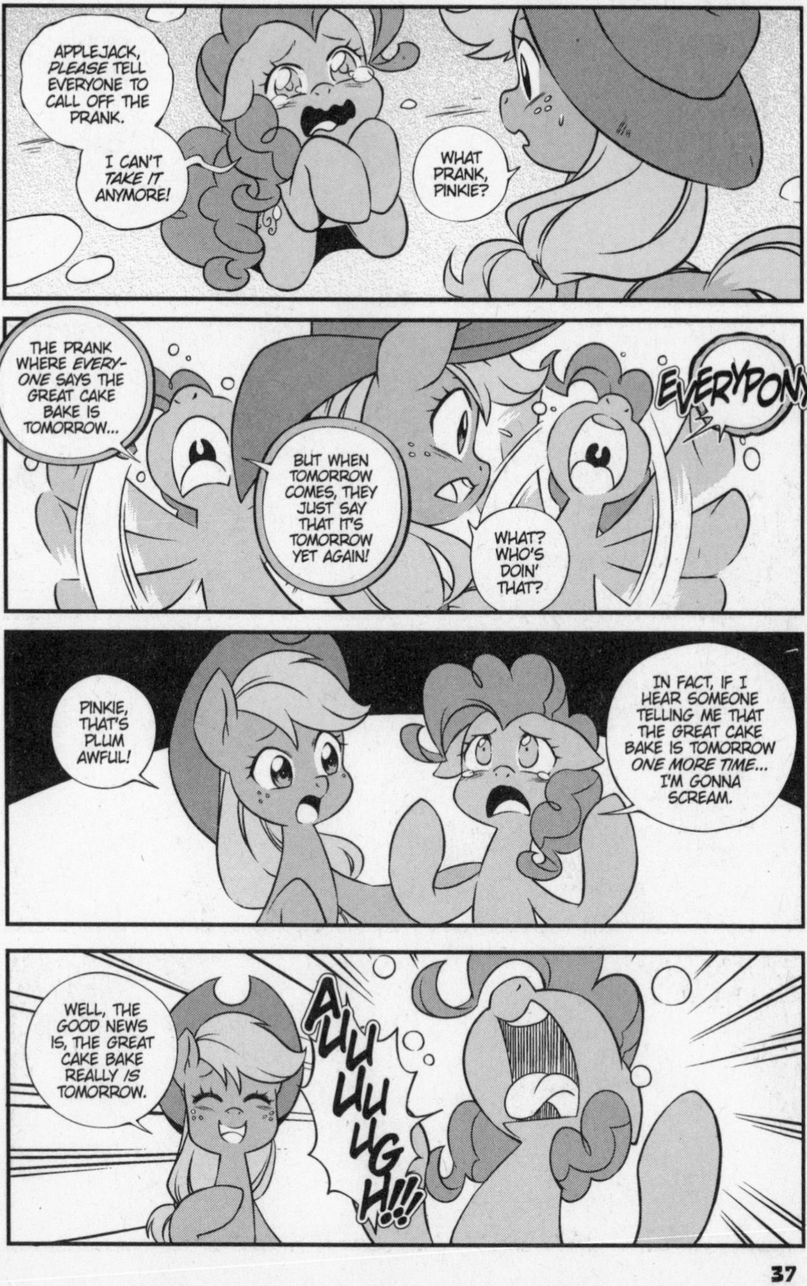
APPLEJACK, *PLEASE* TELL EVERYONE TO CALL OFF THE PRANK.
I CAN'T *TAKE IT* ANYMORE!
WHAT PRANK, PINKIE?
THE PRANK WHERE *EVERY-ONE* SAYS THE GREAT CAKE BAKE IS TOMORROW...
BUT WHEN TOMORROW COMES, THEY JUST SAY THAT IT'S TOMORROW YET AGAIN!
EVERYPONY!
WHAT? WHO'S DOIN' THAT?
PINKIE, THAT'S PLUM AWFUL!
IN FACT, IF I HEAR SOMEONE TELLING ME THAT THE GREAT CAKE BAKE IS TOMORROW *ONE MORE TIME*... I'M GONNA SCREAM.
WELL, THE GOOD NEWS IS, THE GREAT CAKE BAKE REALLY *IS* TOMORROW.
AUUUUUUGH!!!

Turnabout is Mare Play

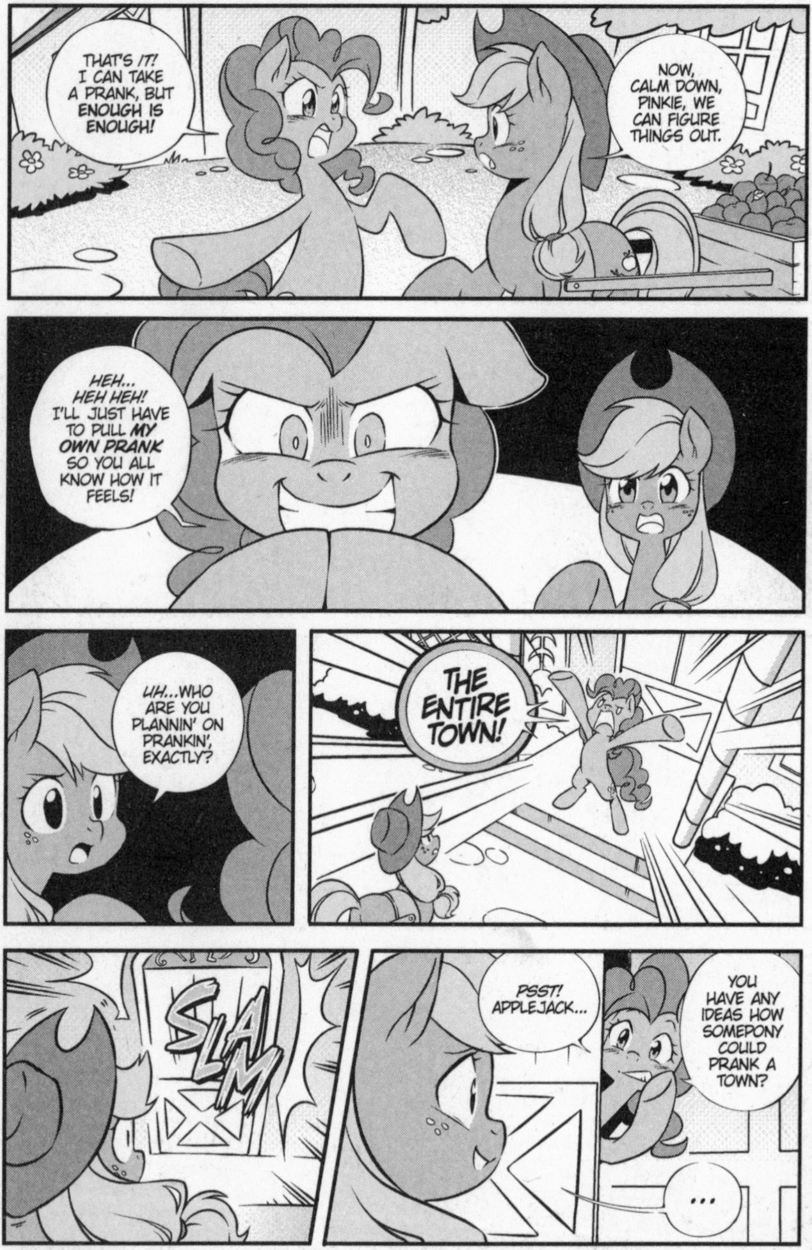

THAT'S IT! I CAN TAKE A PRANK, BUT ENOUGH IS ENOUGH!
NOW, CALM DOWN, PINKIE, WE CAN FIGURE THINGS OUT.
HEH... HEH HEH! I'LL JUST HAVE TO PULL MY OWN PRANK SO YOU ALL KNOW HOW IT FEELS!
UH...WHO ARE YOU PLANNIN' ON PRANKIN', EXACTLY?
THE ENTIRE TOWN!
SLAM
PSST! APPLEJACK...
YOU HAVE ANY IDEAS HOW SOMEPONY COULD PRANK A TOWN?
...

A Plot is 'Stached

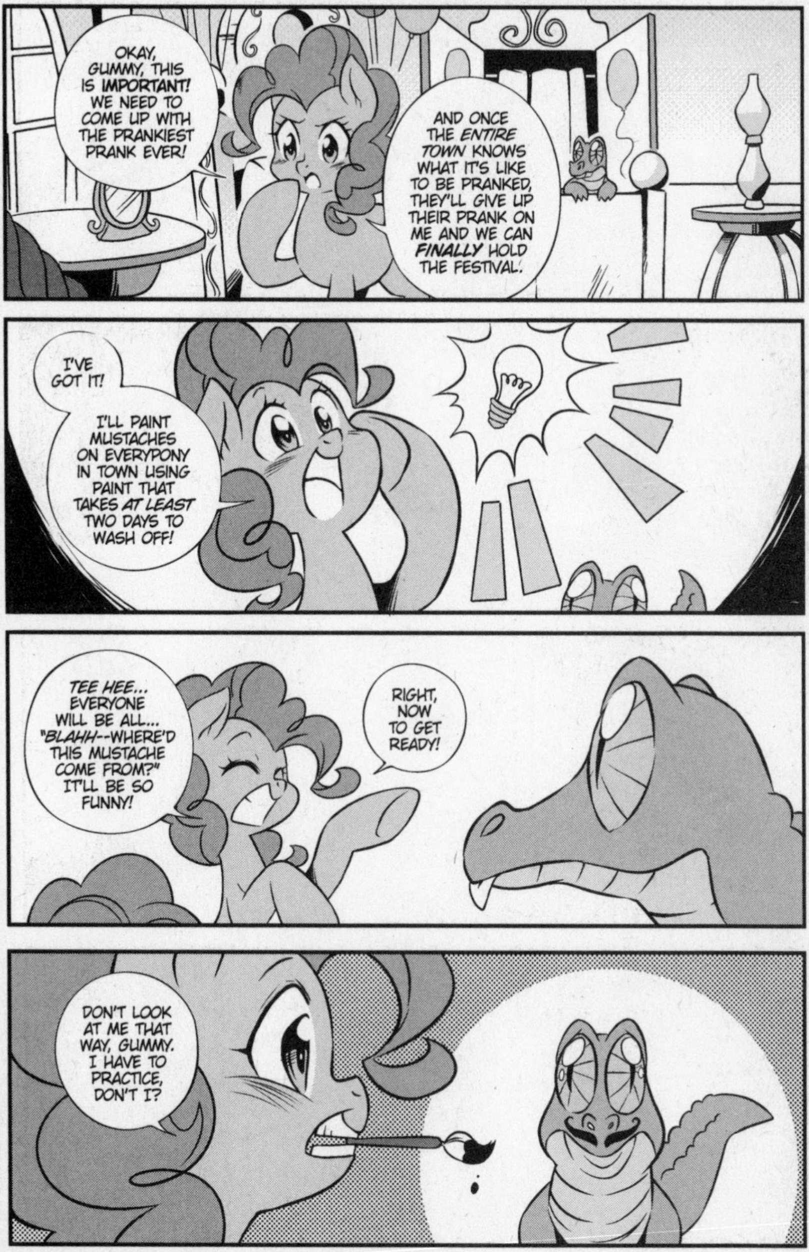

OKAY, GUMMY, THIS IS **IMPORTANT!** WE NEED TO COME UP WITH THE PRANKIEST PRANK EVER!
AND ONCE THE *ENTIRE TOWN* KNOWS WHAT IT'S LIKE TO BE PRANKED, THEY'LL GIVE UP THEIR PRANK ON ME AND WE CAN ***FINALLY*** HOLD THE FESTIVAL.
I'VE GOT IT!
I'LL PAINT MUSTACHES ON EVERYPONY IN TOWN USING PAINT THAT TAKES *AT LEAST* TWO DAYS TO WASH OFF!
TEE HEE... EVERYONE WILL BE ALL... "*BLAHH*--WHERE'D THIS MUSTACHE COME FROM?" IT'LL BE SO FUNNY!
RIGHT, NOW TO GET READY!
DON'T LOOK AT ME THAT WAY, GUMMY. I HAVE TO PRACTICE, DON'T I?

Pie on the Sly

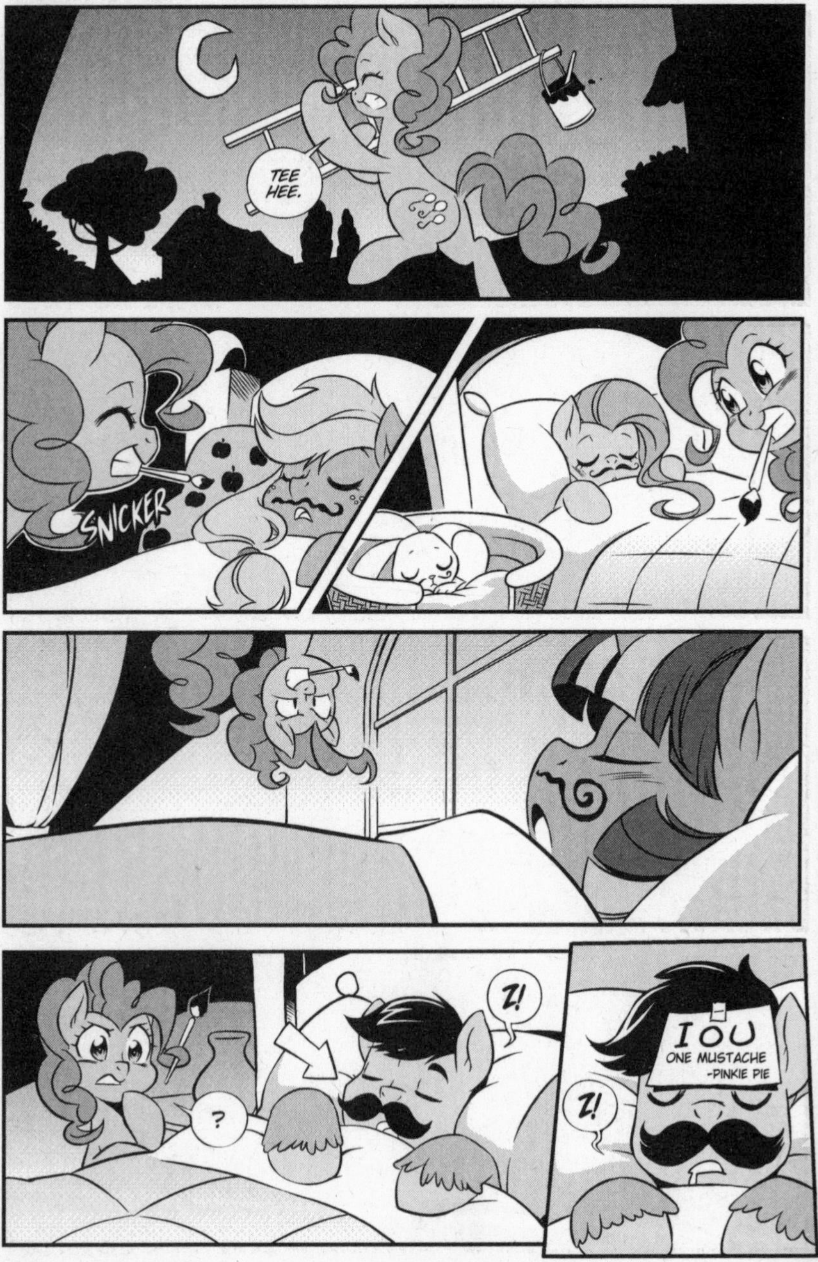
TEE HEE.
SNICKER
Z!
?
IOU
ONE MUSTACHE
-PINKIE PIE
Z!

Where'd You Stash the 'Stache?

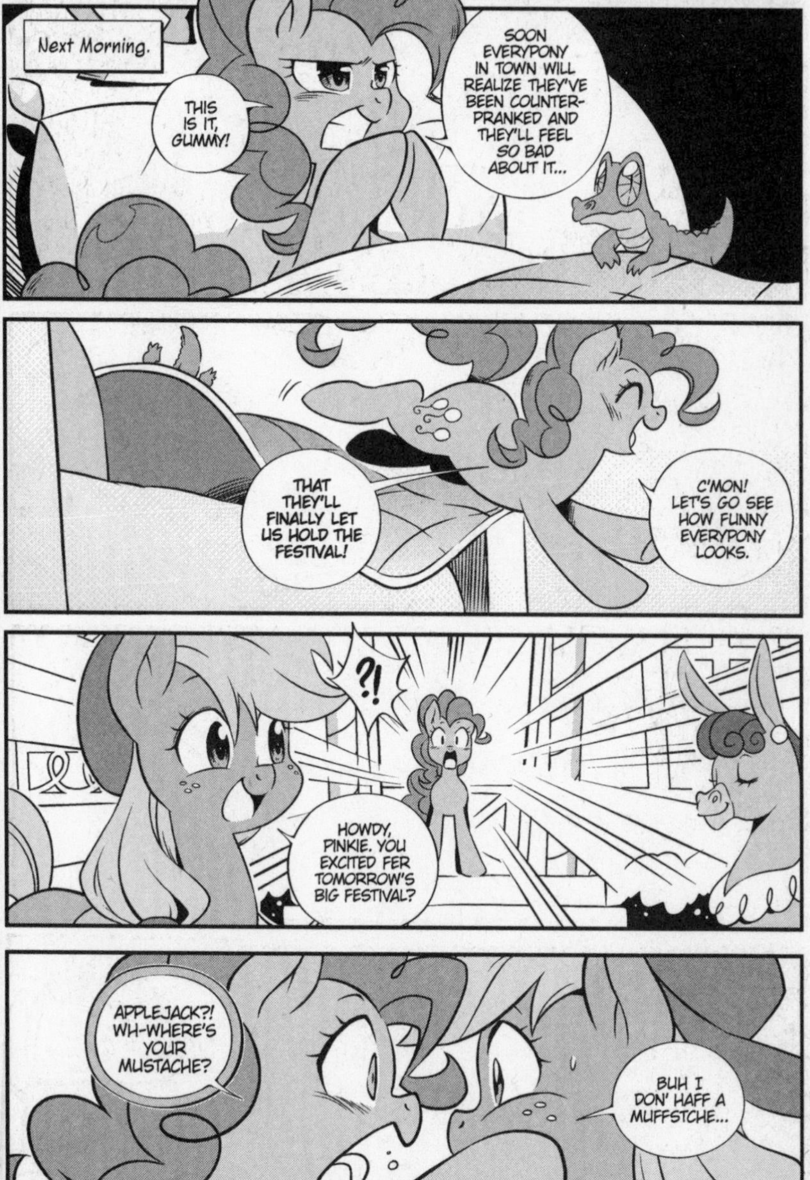
Next Morning.
THIS IS IT, GUMMY!
SOON EVERYPONY IN TOWN WILL REALIZE THEY'VE BEEN COUNTER-PRANKED AND THEY'LL FEEL SO BAD ABOUT IT...
THAT THEY'LL FINALLY LET US HOLD THE FESTIVAL!
C'MON! LET'S GO SEE HOW FUNNY EVERYPONY LOOKS.
?!
HOWDY, PINKIE. YOU EXCITED FER TOMORROW'S BIG FESTIVAL?
APPLEJACK?! WH-WHERE'S YOUR MUSTACHE?
BUH I DON' HAFF A MUFFSTCHE...

Scoop the Loop

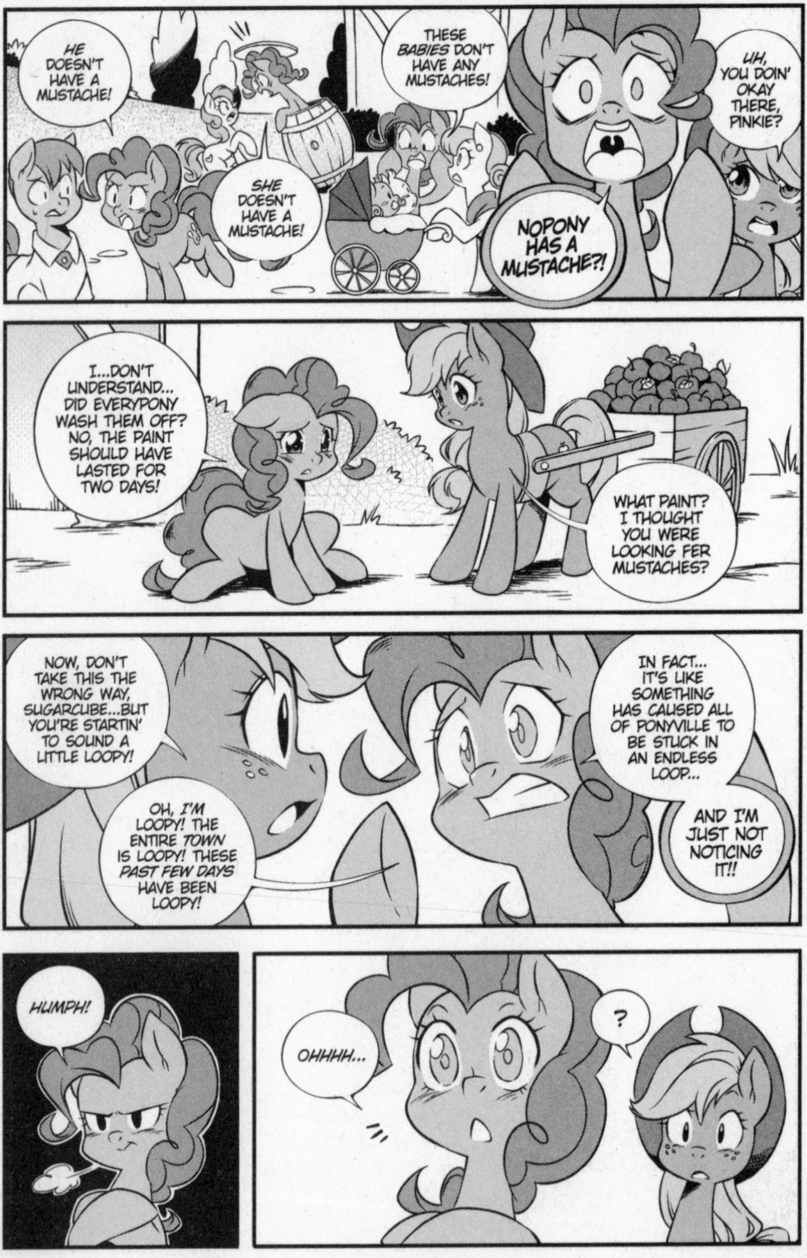

HE DOESN'T HAVE A MUSTACHE!
SHE DOESN'T HAVE A MUSTACHE!
THESE BABIES DON'T HAVE ANY MUSTACHES!
NOPONY HAS A MUSTACHE?!
UH, YOU DOIN' OKAY THERE, PINKIE?
I...DON'T UNDERSTAND... DID EVERYPONY WASH THEM OFF? NO, THE PAINT SHOULD HAVE LASTED FOR TWO DAYS!
WHAT PAINT? I THOUGHT YOU WERE LOOKING FER MUSTACHES?
NOW, DON'T TAKE THIS THE WRONG WAY, SUGARCUBE...BUT YOU'RE STARTIN' TO SOUND A LITTLE LOOPY!
OH, I'M LOOPY! THE ENTIRE TOWN IS LOOPY! THESE PAST FEW DAYS HAVE BEEN LOOPY!
IN FACT... IT'S LIKE SOMETHING HAS CAUSED ALL OF PONYVILLE TO BE STUCK IN AN ENDLESS LOOP...
AND I'M JUST NOT NOTICING IT!!
HUMPH!
OHHHH...
?

Some O'Her Repeats

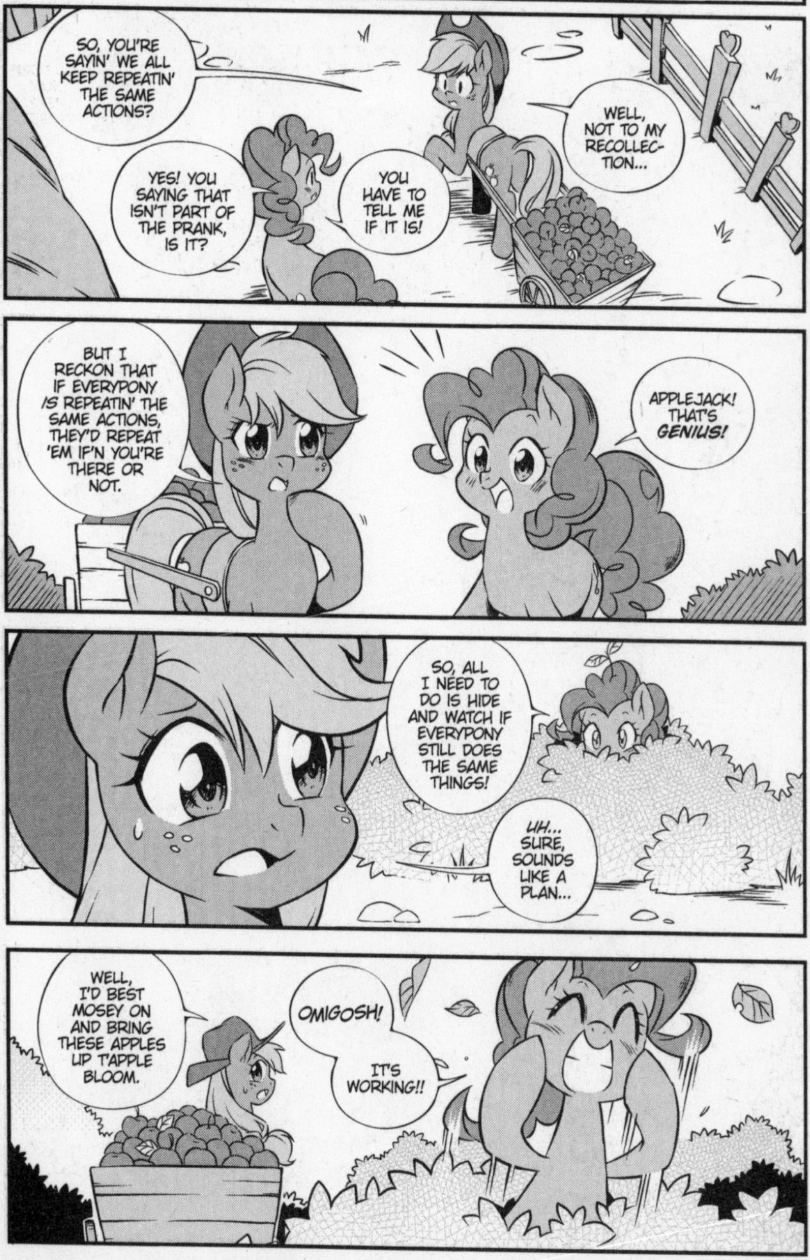
SO, YOU'RE SAYIN' WE ALL KEEP REPEATIN' THE SAME ACTIONS?
YES! YOU SAYING THAT ISN'T PART OF THE PRANK, IS IT?
YOU HAVE TO TELL ME IF IT IS!
WELL, NOT TO MY RECOLLEC-TION...
BUT I RECKON THAT IF EVERYPONY IS REPEATIN' THE SAME ACTIONS, THEY'D REPEAT 'EM IF'N YOU'RE THERE OR NOT.
APPLEJACK! THAT'S GENIUS!
SO, ALL I NEED TO DO IS HIDE AND WATCH IF EVERYPONY STILL DOES THE SAME THINGS!
UH... SURE, SOUNDS LIKE A PLAN...
WELL, I'D BEST MOSEY ON AND BRING THESE APPLES UP T'APPLE BLOOM.
OMIGOSH!
IT'S WORKING!!

Pinkie Pie Private Eye

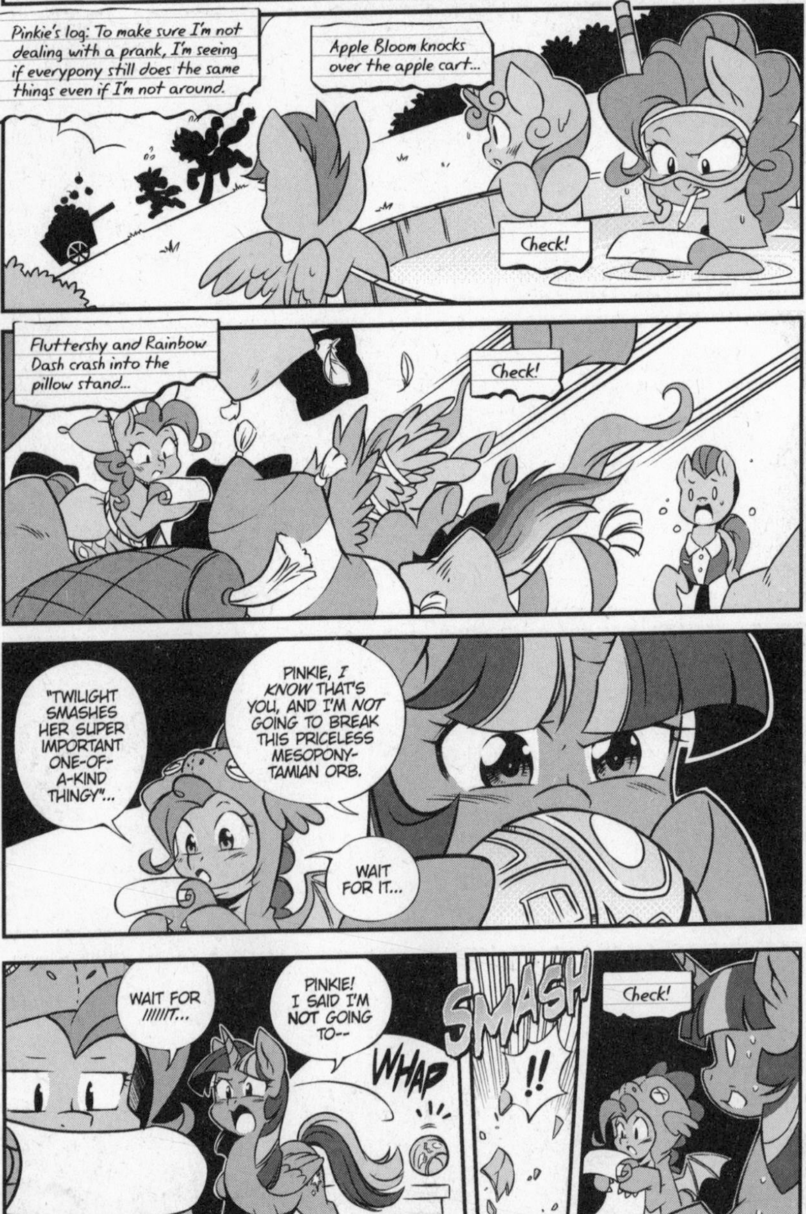
Pinkie's log: To make sure I'm not dealing with a prank, I'm seeing if everypony still does the same things even if I'm not around.
Apple Bloom knocks over the apple cart...
Check!
Fluttershy and Rainbow Dash crash into the pillow stand...
Check!
"TWILIGHT SMASHES HER SUPER IMPORTANT ONE-OF-A-KIND THINGY"...
PINKIE, I KNOW THAT'S YOU, AND I'M NOT GOING TO BREAK THIS PRICELESS MESOPONY-TAMIAN ORB.
WAIT FOR IT...
WAIT FOR //////IT...
PINKIE! I SAID I'M NOT GOING TO--
WHAP
SMASH
!!
Check!

Getting to the Core of the Matter

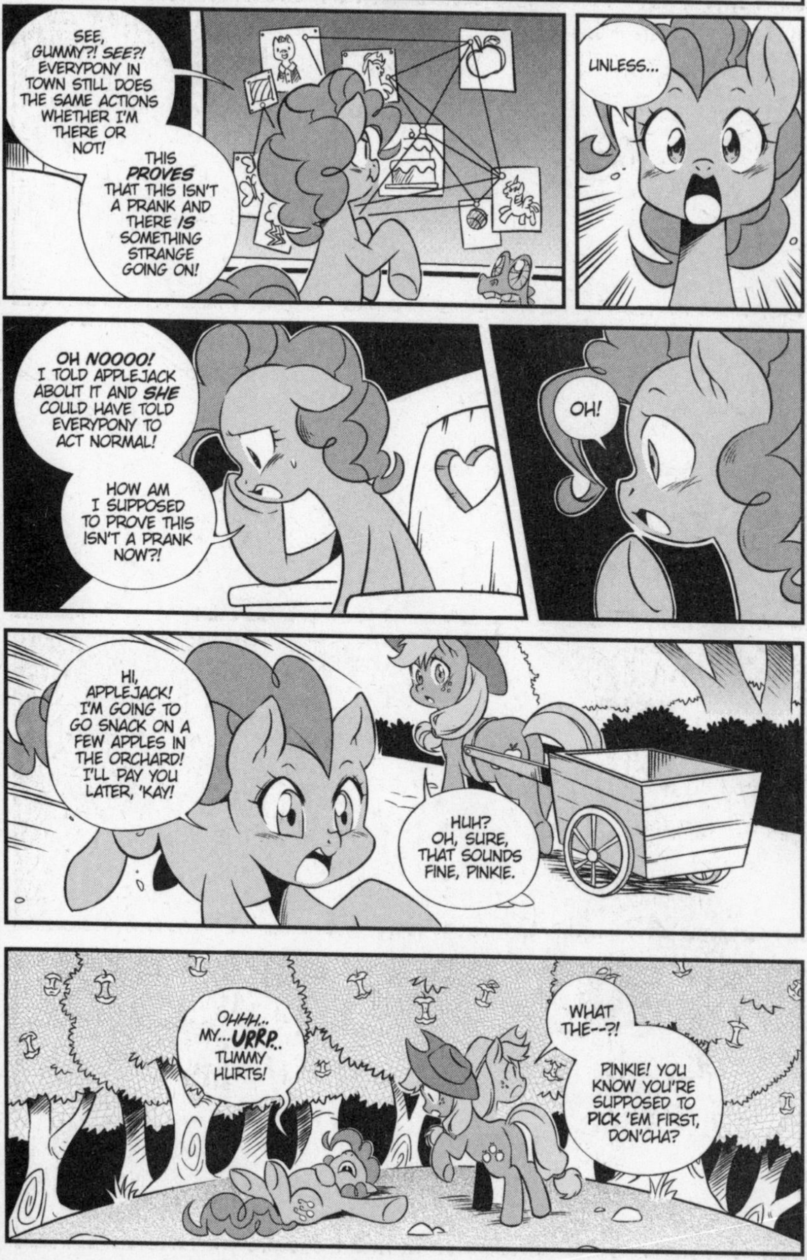

SEE, GUMMY?! SEE?! EVERYPONY IN TOWN STILL DOES THE SAME ACTIONS WHETHER I'M THERE OR NOT!
THIS **PROVES** THAT THIS ISN'T A PRANK AND THERE *IS* SOMETHING STRANGE GOING ON!
UNLESS...
OH *NOOOO!* I TOLD APPLEJACK ABOUT IT AND *SHE* COULD HAVE TOLD EVERYPONY TO ACT NORMAL!
HOW AM I SUPPOSED TO PROVE THIS ISN'T A PRANK NOW?!
OH!
HI, APPLEJACK! I'M GOING TO GO SNACK ON A FEW APPLES IN THE ORCHARD! I'LL PAY YOU LATER, 'KAY!
HUH? OH, SURE, THAT SOUNDS FINE, PINKIE.
OHHH.. MY...**URRP**.. TUMMY HURTS!
WHAT THE--?!
PINKIE! YOU KNOW YOU'RE SUPPOSED TO PICK 'EM FIRST, DON'CHA?

Nooooooo-It-All

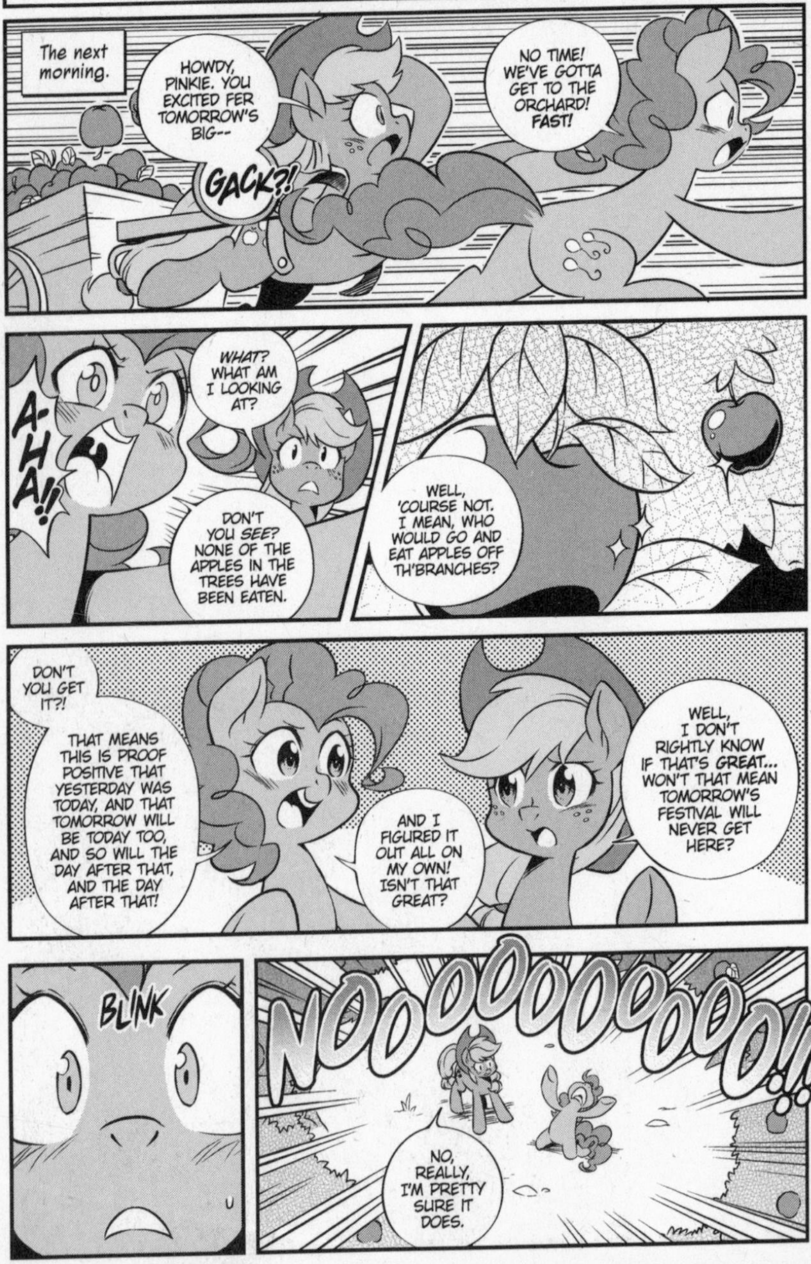
The next morning.
HOWDY, PINKIE. YOU EXCITED FER TOMORROW'S BIG--
GACK?!
NO TIME! WE'VE GOTTA GET TO THE ORCHARD! FAST!
A-HA!!
WHAT? WHAT AM I LOOKING AT?
DON'T YOU SEE? NONE OF THE APPLES IN THE TREES HAVE BEEN EATEN.
WELL, 'COURSE NOT. I MEAN, WHO WOULD GO AND EAT APPLES OFF TH'BRANCHES?
DON'T YOU GET IT?!
THAT MEANS THIS IS PROOF POSITIVE THAT YESTERDAY WAS TODAY, AND THAT TOMORROW WILL BE TODAY TOO, AND SO WILL THE DAY AFTER THAT, AND THE DAY AFTER THAT!
AND I FIGURED IT OUT ALL ON MY OWN! ISN'T THAT GREAT?
WELL, I DON'T RIGHTLY KNOW IF THAT'S GREAT... WON'T THAT MEAN TOMORROW'S FESTIVAL WILL NEVER GET HERE?
BLINK
NOOOOOOOOOOOO!!!
NO, REALLY, I'M PRETTY SURE IT DOES.

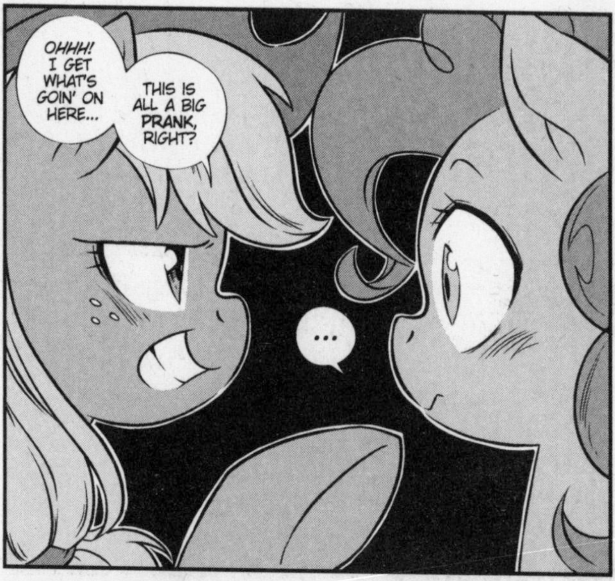
OHHH! I GET WHAT'S GOIN' ON HERE...
THIS IS ALL A BIG PRANK, RIGHT?
...

CHAPTER 4

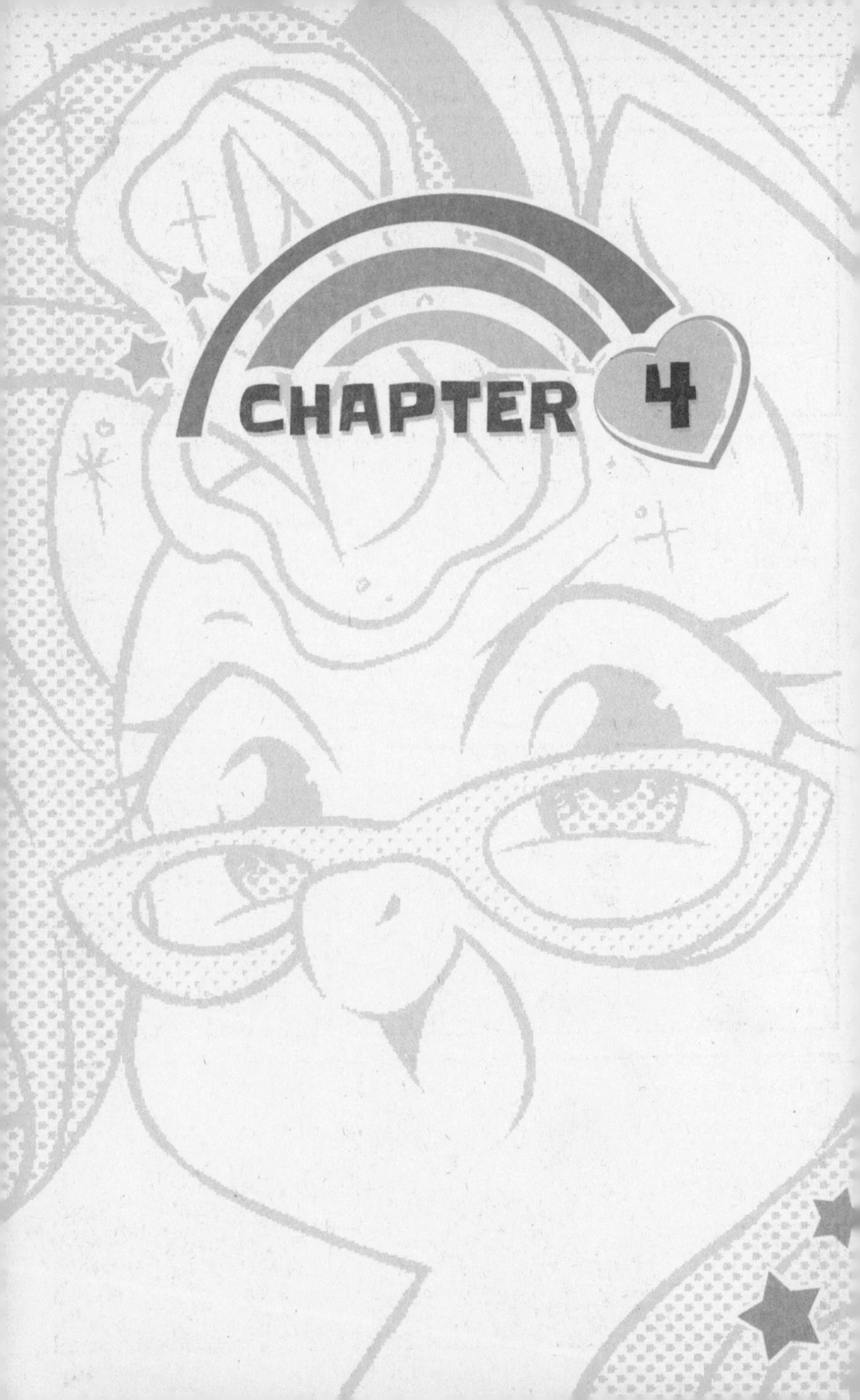

Train of Afterthought

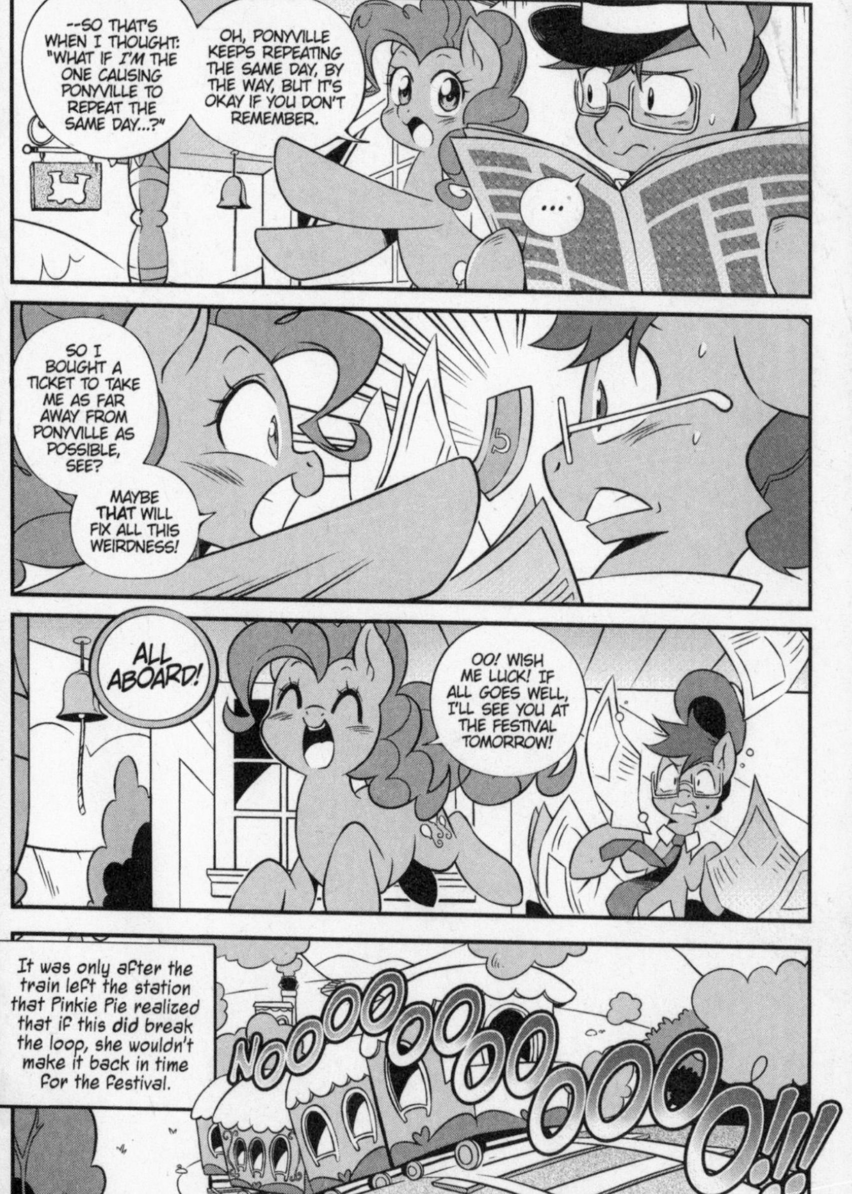

--SO THAT'S WHEN I THOUGHT: "WHAT IF *I'M* THE ONE CAUSING PONYVILLE TO REPEAT THE SAME DAY...?"
OH, PONYVILLE KEEPS REPEATING THE SAME DAY, BY THE WAY, BUT IT'S OKAY IF YOU DON'T REMEMBER.
...
SO I BOUGHT A TICKET TO TAKE ME AS FAR AWAY FROM PONYVILLE AS POSSIBLE, SEE?
MAYBE THAT WILL FIX ALL THIS WEIRDNESS!
ALL ABOARD!
OO! WISH ME LUCK! IF ALL GOES WELL, I'LL SEE YOU AT THE FESTIVAL TOMORROW!
It was only after the train left the station that Pinkie Pie realized that if this did break the loop, she wouldn't make it back in time for the festival.
NOOOOOOOOOOOOOOOO!!!

Quick Trip Home

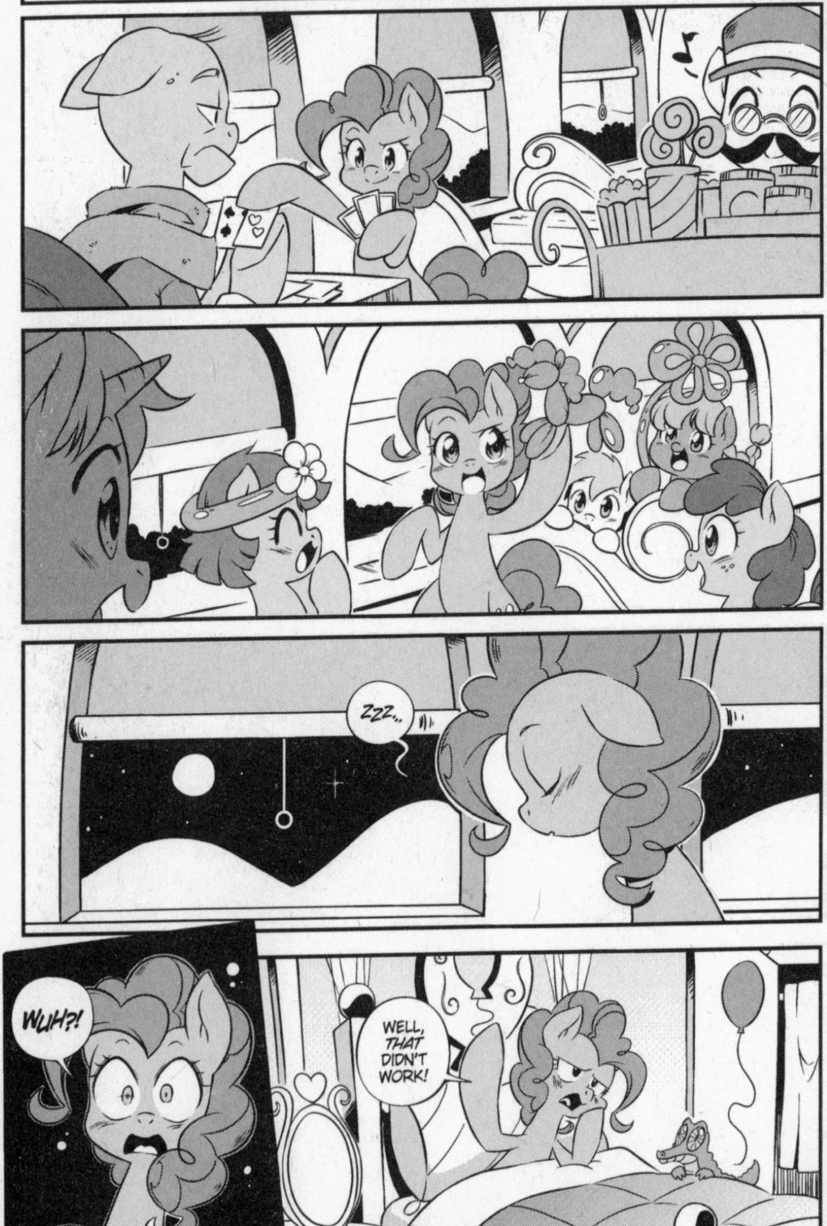
ZZZ..
WUH?!
WELL, *THAT* DIDN'T WORK!

Half-Baked Advice

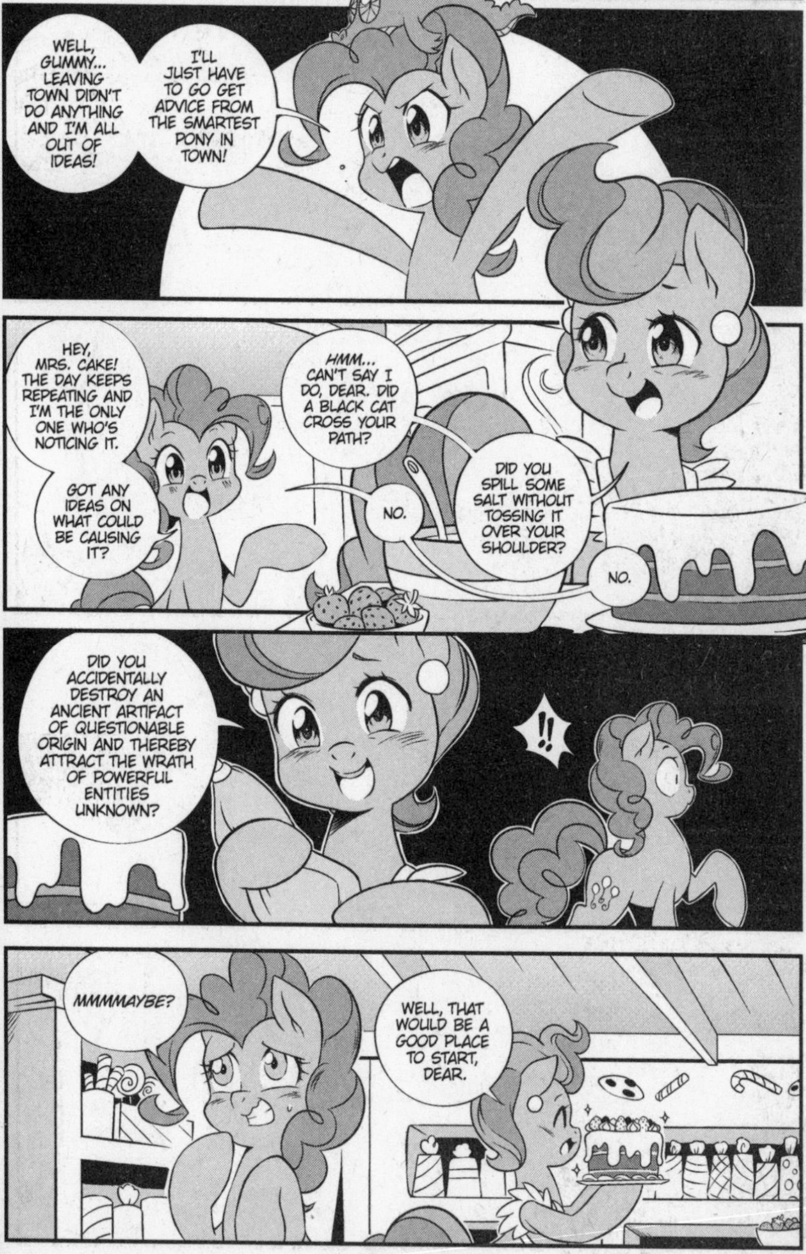
WELL, GUMMY... LEAVING TOWN DIDN'T DO ANYTHING AND I'M ALL OUT OF IDEAS!
I'LL JUST HAVE TO GO GET ADVICE FROM THE SMARTEST PONY IN TOWN!
HEY, MRS. CAKE! THE DAY KEEPS REPEATING AND I'M THE ONLY ONE WHO'S NOTICING IT.
GOT ANY IDEAS ON WHAT COULD BE CAUSING IT?
HMM... CAN'T SAY I DO, DEAR. DID A BLACK CAT CROSS YOUR PATH?
NO.
DID YOU SPILL SOME SALT WITHOUT TOSSING IT OVER YOUR SHOULDER?
NO.
DID YOU ACCIDENTALLY DESTROY AN ANCIENT ARTIFACT OF QUESTIONABLE ORIGIN AND THEREBY ATTRACT THE WRATH OF POWERFUL ENTITIES UNKNOWN?
!!
MMMMAYBE?
WELL, THAT WOULD BE A GOOD PLACE TO START, DEAR.

Let's Get Cracking!

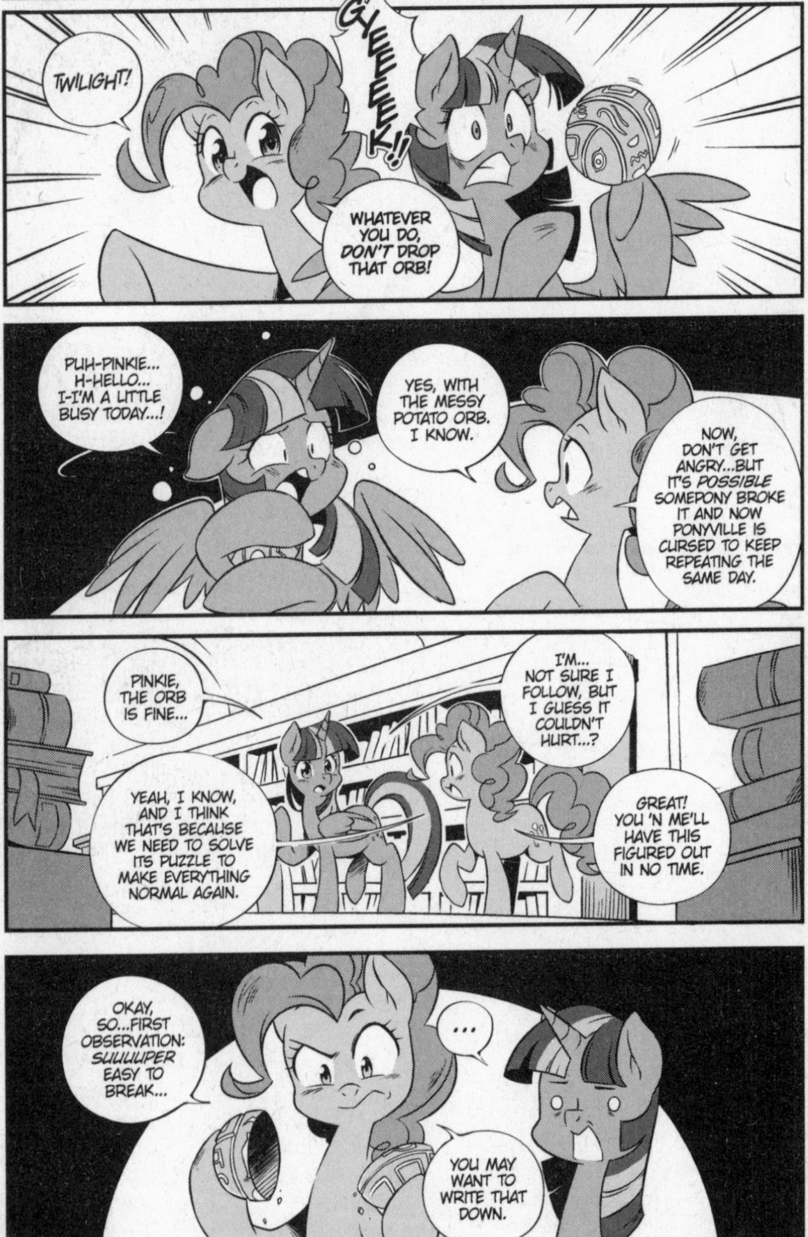

TWILIGHT!
GYEEEEEK!!
WHATEVER YOU DO, DON'T DROP THAT ORB!
PUH-PINKIE... H-HELLO... I-I'M A LITTLE BUSY TODAY...!
YES, WITH THE MESSY POTATO ORB. I KNOW.
NOW, DON'T GET ANGRY...BUT IT'S POSSIBLE SOMEPONY BROKE IT AND NOW PONYVILLE IS CURSED TO KEEP REPEATING THE SAME DAY.
PINKIE, THE ORB IS FINE...
YEAH, I KNOW, AND I THINK THAT'S BECAUSE WE NEED TO SOLVE ITS PUZZLE TO MAKE EVERYTHING NORMAL AGAIN.
I'M... NOT SURE I FOLLOW, BUT I GUESS IT COULDN'T HURT...?
GREAT! YOU 'N ME'LL HAVE THIS FIGURED OUT IN NO TIME.
OKAY, SO...FIRST OBSERVATION: SUUUUPER EASY TO BREAK...
...
YOU MAY WANT TO WRITE THAT DOWN.

Crushing It!

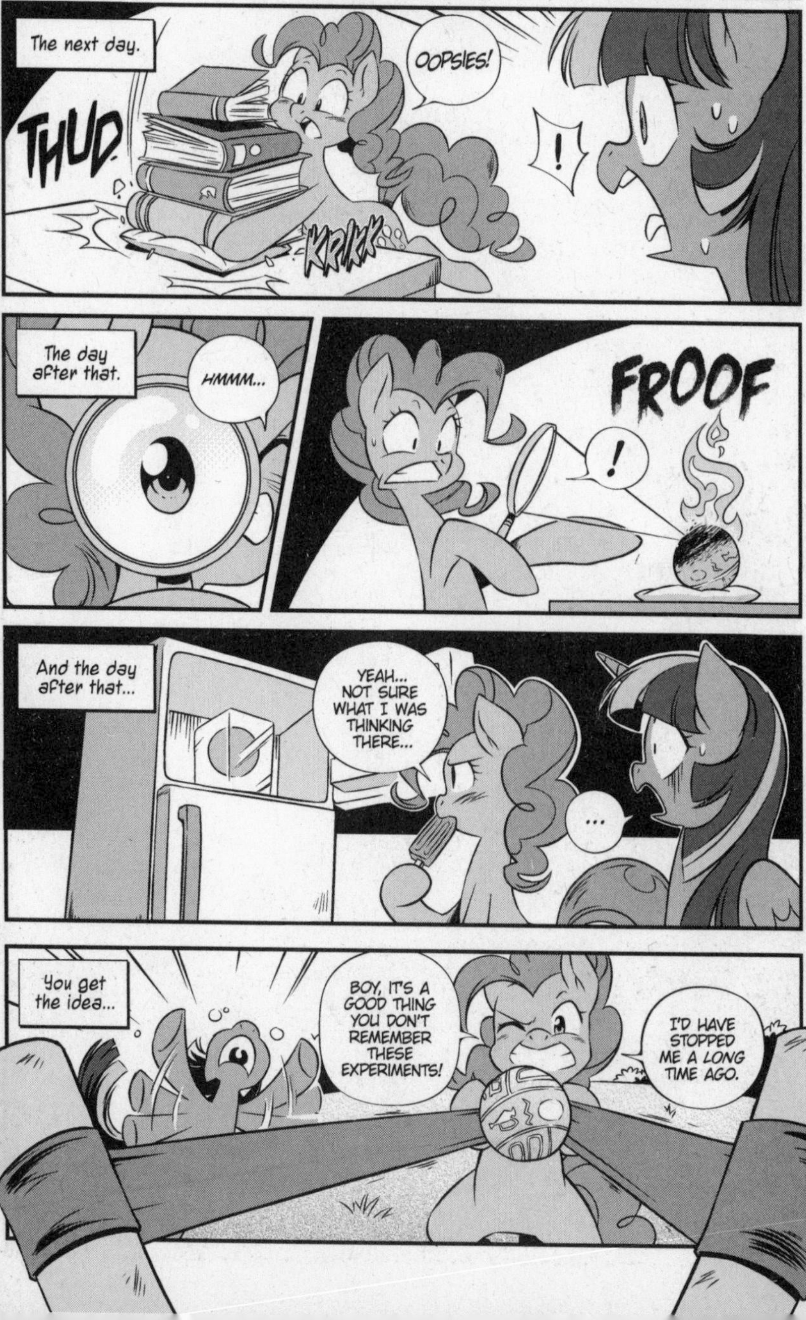

The next day.
THUD
OOPSIES!
KRIKK
!
The day after that.
HMMM...
!
FROOF
And the day after that...
YEAH... NOT SURE WHAT I WAS THINKING THERE...
...
You get the idea...
BOY, IT'S A GOOD THING YOU DON'T REMEMBER THESE EXPERIMENTS!
I'D HAVE STOPPED ME A LONG TIME AGO.

One Good Turn Deserves Another

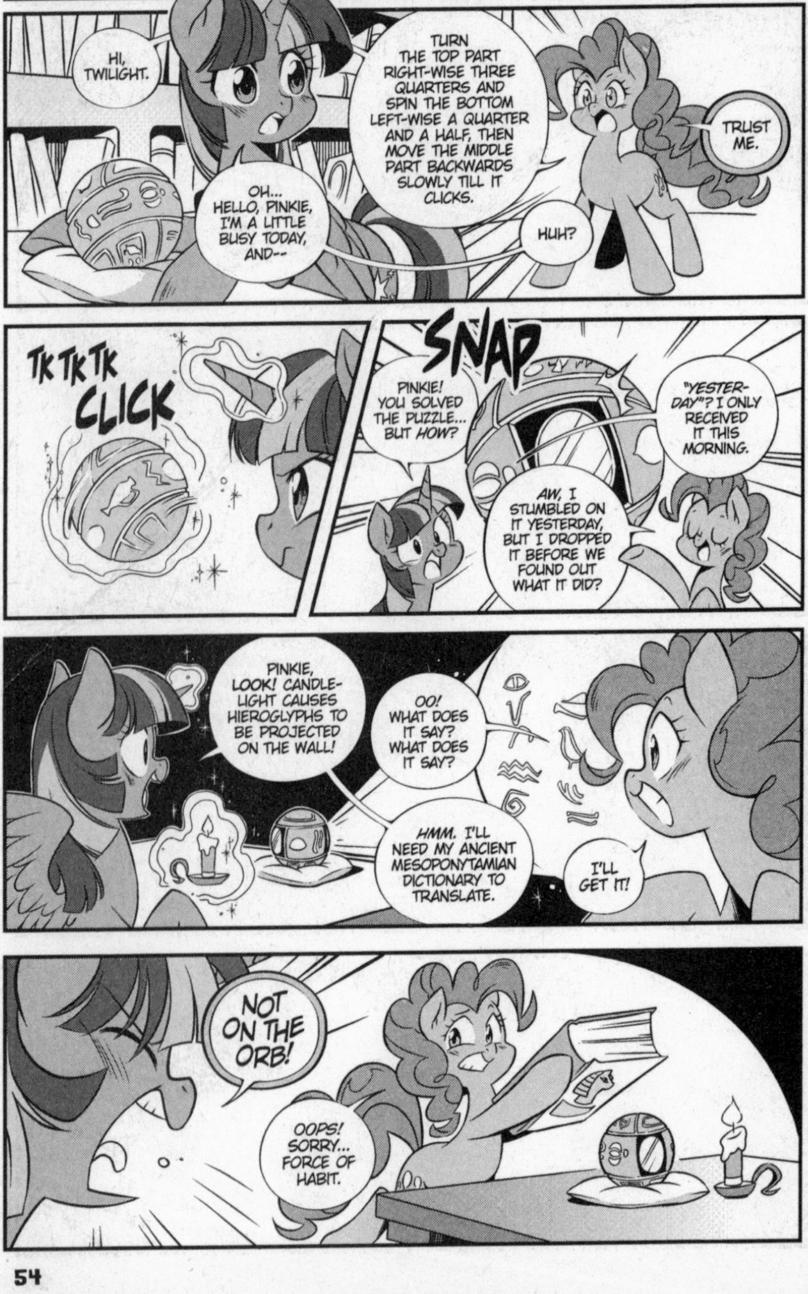
HI, TWILIGHT.
OH... HELLO, PINKIE, I'M A LITTLE BUSY TODAY, AND--
TURN THE TOP PART RIGHT-WISE THREE QUARTERS AND SPIN THE BOTTOM LEFT-WISE A QUARTER AND A HALF, THEN MOVE THE MIDDLE PART BACKWARDS SLOWLY TILL IT CLICKS.
HUH?
TRUST ME.
TK TK TK CLICK
SNAP
PINKIE! YOU SOLVED THE PUZZLE... BUT *HOW*?
AW, I STUMBLED ON IT YESTERDAY, BUT I DROPPED IT BEFORE WE FOUND OUT WHAT IT DID?
"*YESTER-DAY*"? I ONLY RECEIVED IT THIS MORNING.
PINKIE, LOOK! CANDLE-LIGHT CAUSES HIEROGLYPHS TO BE PROJECTED ON THE WALL!
OO! WHAT DOES IT SAY? WHAT DOES IT SAY?
HMM. I'LL NEED MY ANCIENT MESOPONYTAMIAN DICTIONARY TO TRANSLATE.
I'LL GET IT!
NOT ON THE ORB!
OOPS! SORRY... FORCE OF HABIT.

Colt Sweat

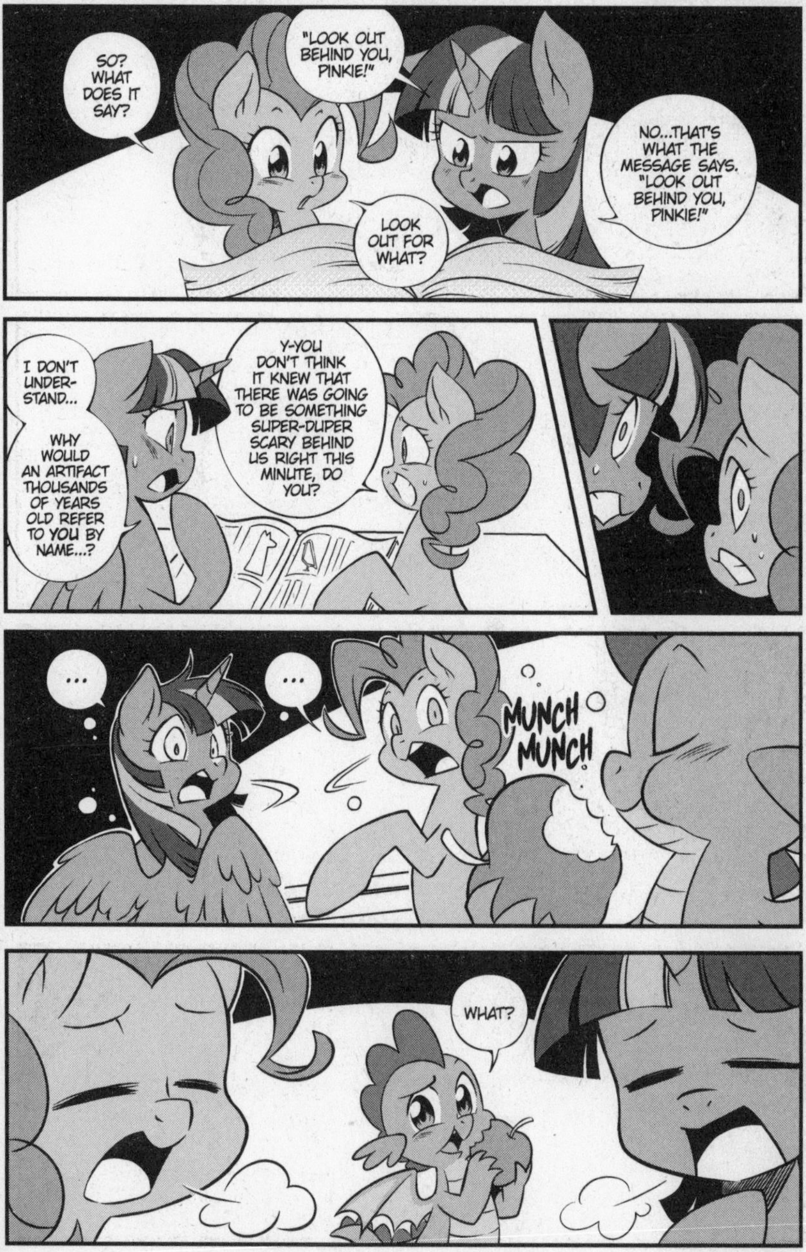
SO? WHAT DOES IT SAY?
"LOOK OUT BEHIND YOU, PINKIE!"
LOOK OUT FOR WHAT?
NO...THAT'S WHAT THE MESSAGE SAYS. "LOOK OUT BEHIND YOU, PINKIE!"
I DON'T UNDER-STAND...
WHY WOULD AN ARTIFACT THOUSANDS OF YEARS OLD REFER TO YOU BY NAME...?
Y-YOU DON'T THINK IT KNEW THAT THERE WAS GOING TO BE SOMETHING SUPER-DUPER SCARY BEHIND US RIGHT THIS MINUTE, DO YOU?
...
...
MUNCH MUNCH
WHAT?

Page Not Found

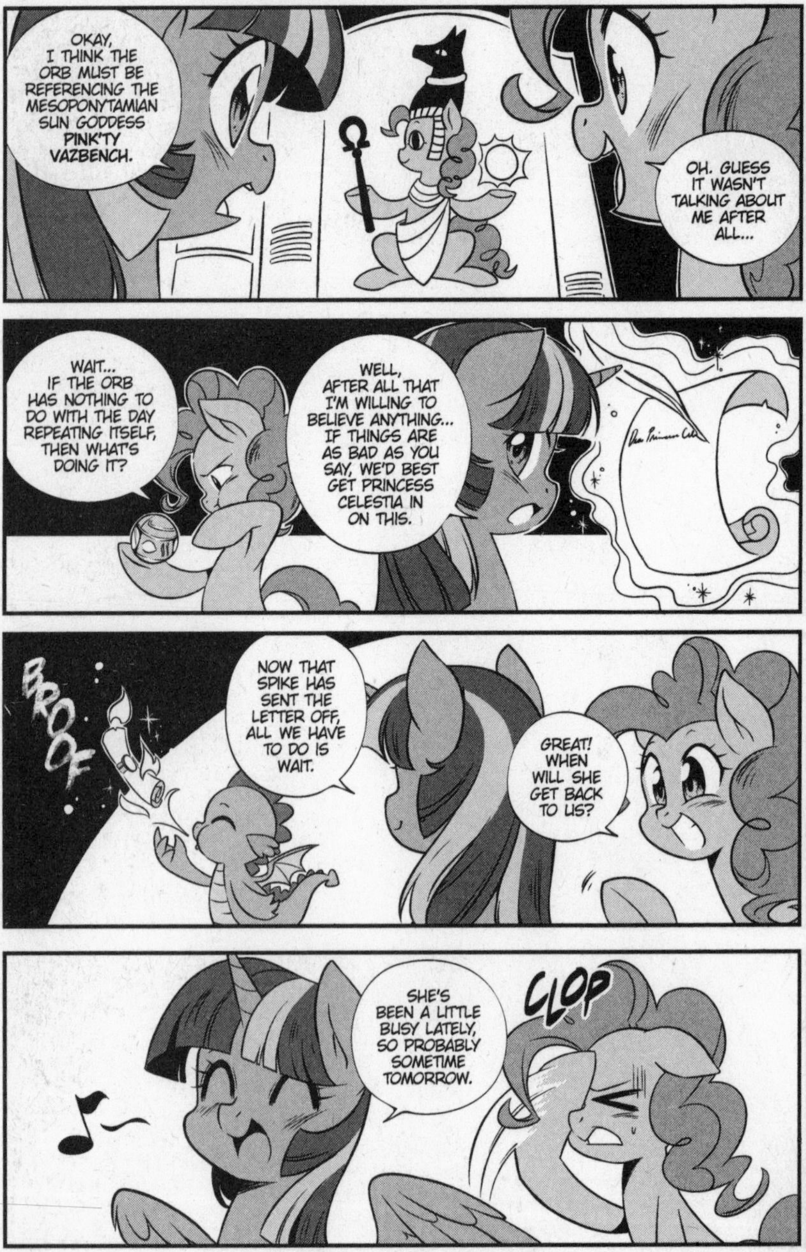
OKAY, I THINK THE ORB MUST BE REFERENCING THE MESOPONYTAMIAN SUN GODDESS PINK'TY VAZBENCH.
OH. GUESS IT WASN'T TALKING ABOUT ME AFTER ALL...
WAIT... IF THE ORB HAS NOTHING TO DO WITH THE DAY REPEATING ITSELF, THEN WHAT'S DOING IT?
WELL, AFTER ALL THAT I'M WILLING TO BELIEVE ANYTHING... IF THINGS ARE AS BAD AS YOU SAY, WE'D BEST GET PRINCESS CELESTIA IN ON THIS.
BROOF
NOW THAT SPIKE HAS SENT THE LETTER OFF, ALL WE HAVE TO DO IS WAIT.
GREAT! WHEN WILL SHE GET BACK TO US?
SHE'S BEEN A LITTLE BUSY LATELY, SO PROBABLY SOMETIME TOMORROW.
CLOP

'Napped Sack

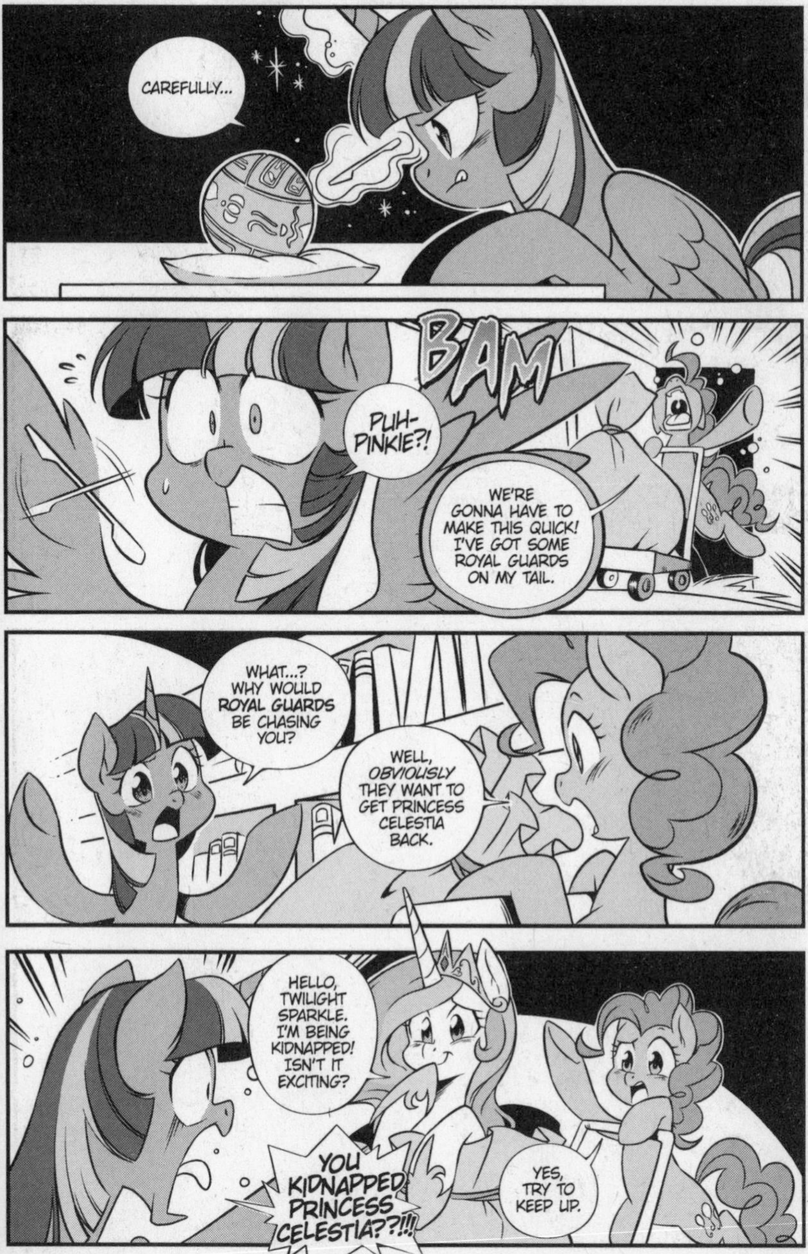
CAREFULLY...
BAM
PUH-PINKIE?!
WE'RE GONNA HAVE TO MAKE THIS QUICK! I'VE GOT SOME ROYAL GUARDS ON MY TAIL.
WHAT...? WHY WOULD ROYAL GUARDS BE CHASING YOU?
WELL, *OBVIOUSLY* THEY WANT TO GET PRINCESS CELESTIA BACK.
HELLO, TWILIGHT SPARKLE. I'M BEING KIDNAPPED! ISN'T IT EXCITING?
YOU KIDNAPPED PRINCESS CELESTIA??!!!
YES, TRY TO KEEP UP.

Party Foal

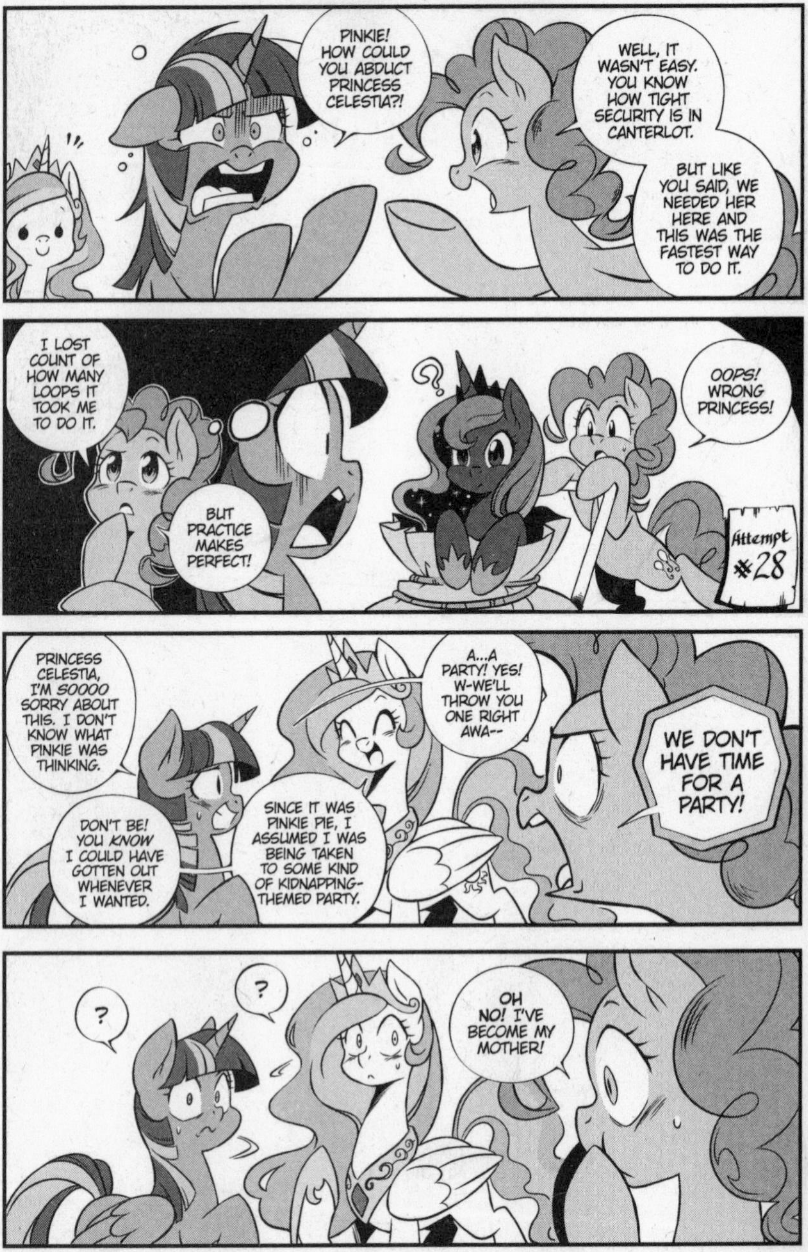
PINKIE! HOW COULD YOU ABDUCT PRINCESS CELESTIA?!
WELL, IT WASN'T EASY. YOU KNOW HOW TIGHT SECURITY IS IN CANTERLOT.
BUT LIKE YOU SAID, WE NEEDED HER HERE AND THIS WAS THE FASTEST WAY TO DO IT.
I LOST COUNT OF HOW MANY LOOPS IT TOOK ME TO DO IT.
BUT PRACTICE MAKES PERFECT!
OOPS! WRONG PRINCESS!
Attempt #28
PRINCESS CELESTIA, I'M SOOOO SORRY ABOUT THIS. I DON'T KNOW WHAT PINKIE WAS THINKING.
DON'T BE! YOU KNOW I COULD HAVE GOTTEN OUT WHENEVER I WANTED.
SINCE IT WAS PINKIE PIE, I ASSUMED I WAS BEING TAKEN TO SOME KIND OF KIDNAPPING-THEMED PARTY.
A...A PARTY! YES! W-WE'LL THROW YOU ONE RIGHT AWA--
WE DON'T HAVE TIME FOR A PARTY!
?
?
OH NO! I'VE BECOME MY MOTHER!

Accom-Pie-Lice

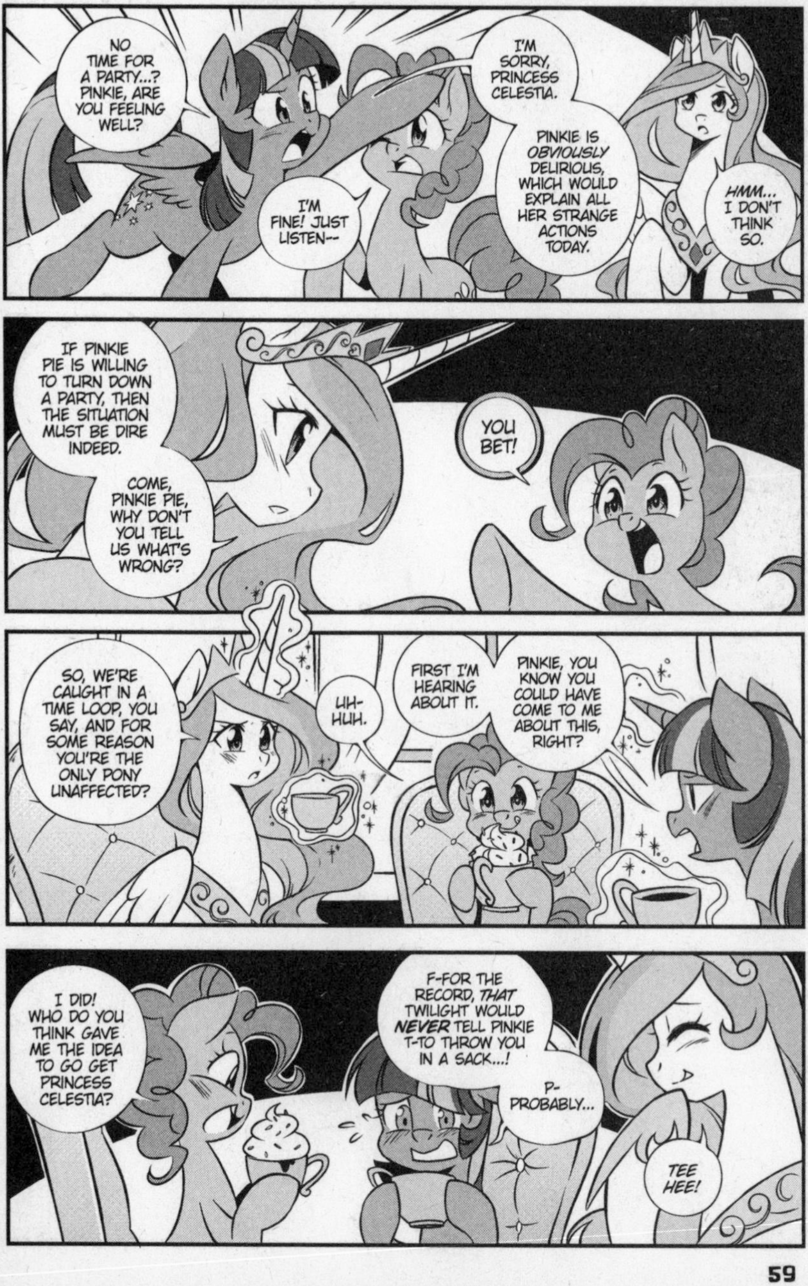

NO TIME FOR A PARTY...? PINKIE, ARE YOU FEELING WELL?
I'M FINE! JUST LISTEN--
I'M SORRY, PRINCESS CELESTIA.
PINKIE IS *OBVIOUSLY* DELIRIOUS, WHICH WOULD EXPLAIN ALL HER STRANGE ACTIONS TODAY.
HMM... I DON'T THINK SO.
IF PINKIE PIE IS WILLING TO TURN DOWN A PARTY, THEN THE SITUATION MUST BE DIRE INDEED.
COME, PINKIE PIE, WHY DON'T YOU TELL US WHAT'S WRONG?
YOU BET!
SO, WE'RE CAUGHT IN A TIME LOOP, YOU SAY, AND FOR SOME REASON YOU'RE THE ONLY PONY UNAFFECTED?
UH-HUH.
FIRST I'M HEARING ABOUT IT.
PINKIE, YOU KNOW YOU COULD HAVE COME TO ME ABOUT THIS, RIGHT?
I DID! WHO DO YOU THINK GAVE ME THE IDEA TO GO GET PRINCESS CELESTIA?
F-FOR THE RECORD, *THAT* TWILIGHT WOULD ***NEVER*** TELL PINKIE T-TO THROW YOU IN A SACK...!
P-PROBABLY...
TEE HEE!

Pie Denied!

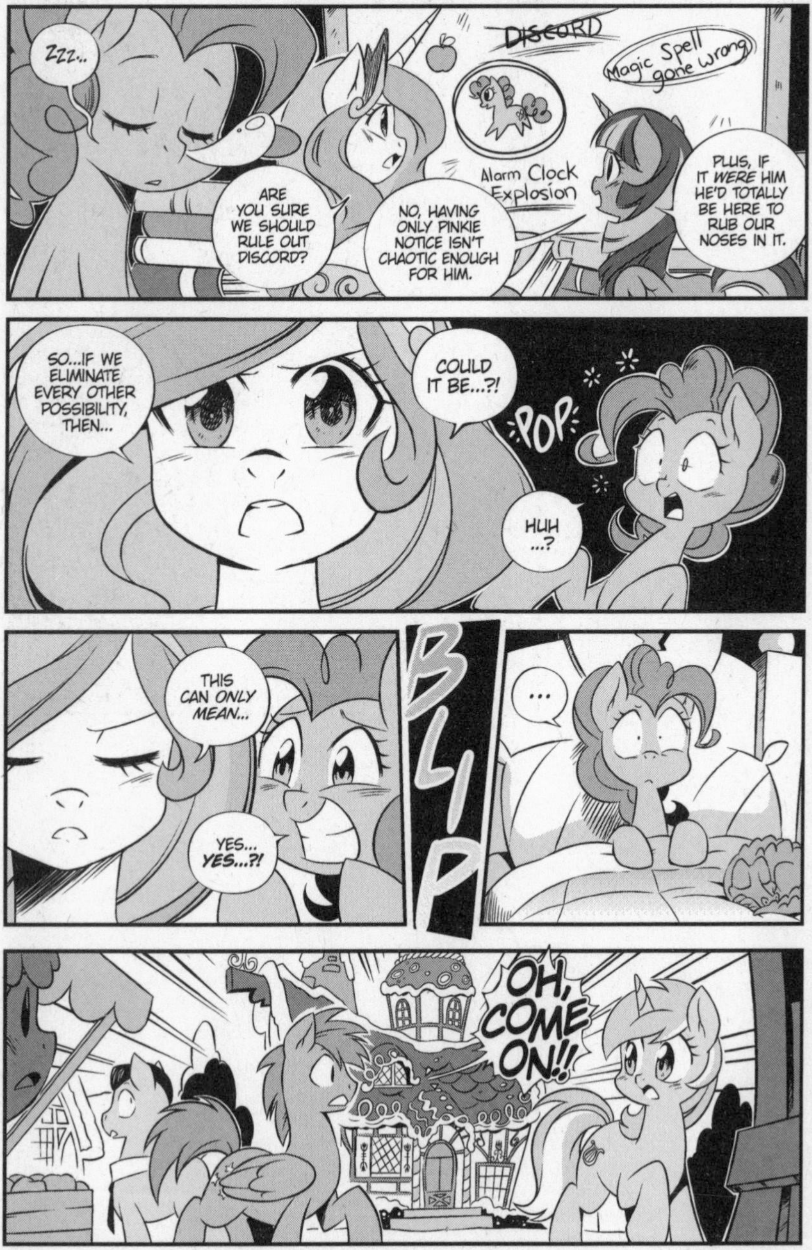

Zzz...
DISCORD
Magic Spell gone wrong
Alarm Clock Explosion
ARE YOU SURE WE SHOULD RULE OUT DISCORD?
NO, HAVING ONLY PINKIE NOTICE ISN'T CHAOTIC ENOUGH FOR HIM.
PLUS, IF IT *WERE* HIM HE'D TOTALLY BE HERE TO RUB OUR NOSES IN IT.
SO...IF WE ELIMINATE EVERY OTHER POSSIBILITY, THEN...
COULD IT BE...?!
POP
HUH ...?
THIS CAN *ONLY* MEAN...
YES... ***YES...?!***
BLIP
...
OH, COME ON!!

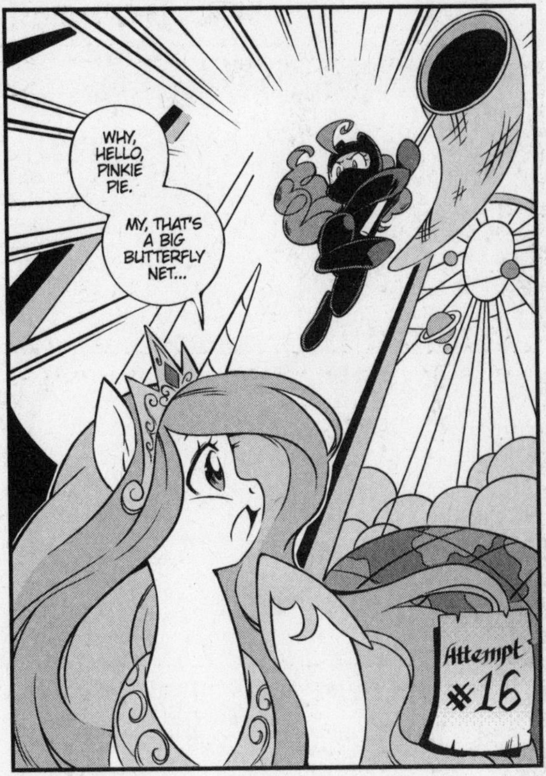
WHY, HELLO, PINKIE PIE.
MY, THAT'S A BIG BUTTERFLY NET...
Attempt #16

CHAPTER 5

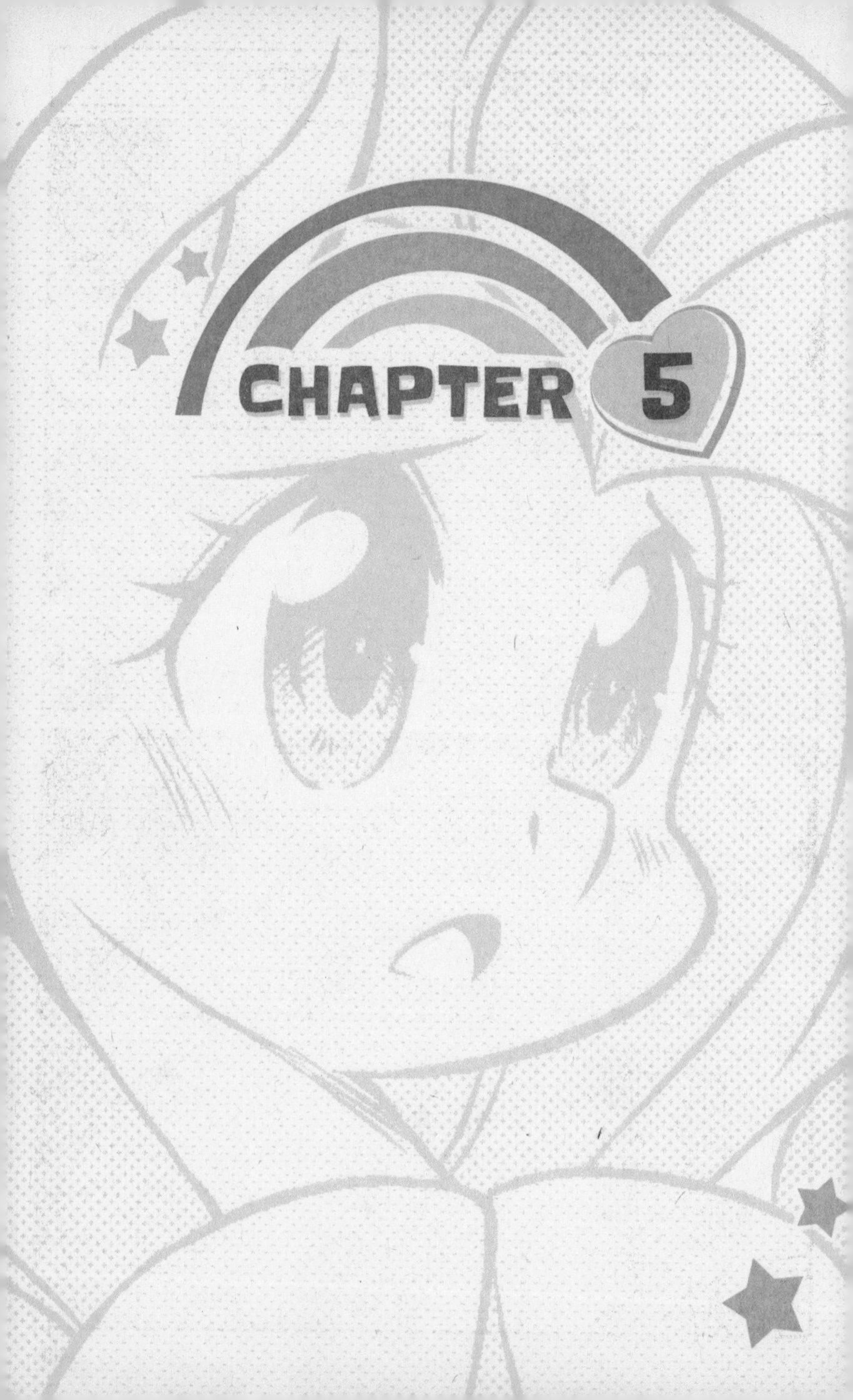

Went Over my Herd

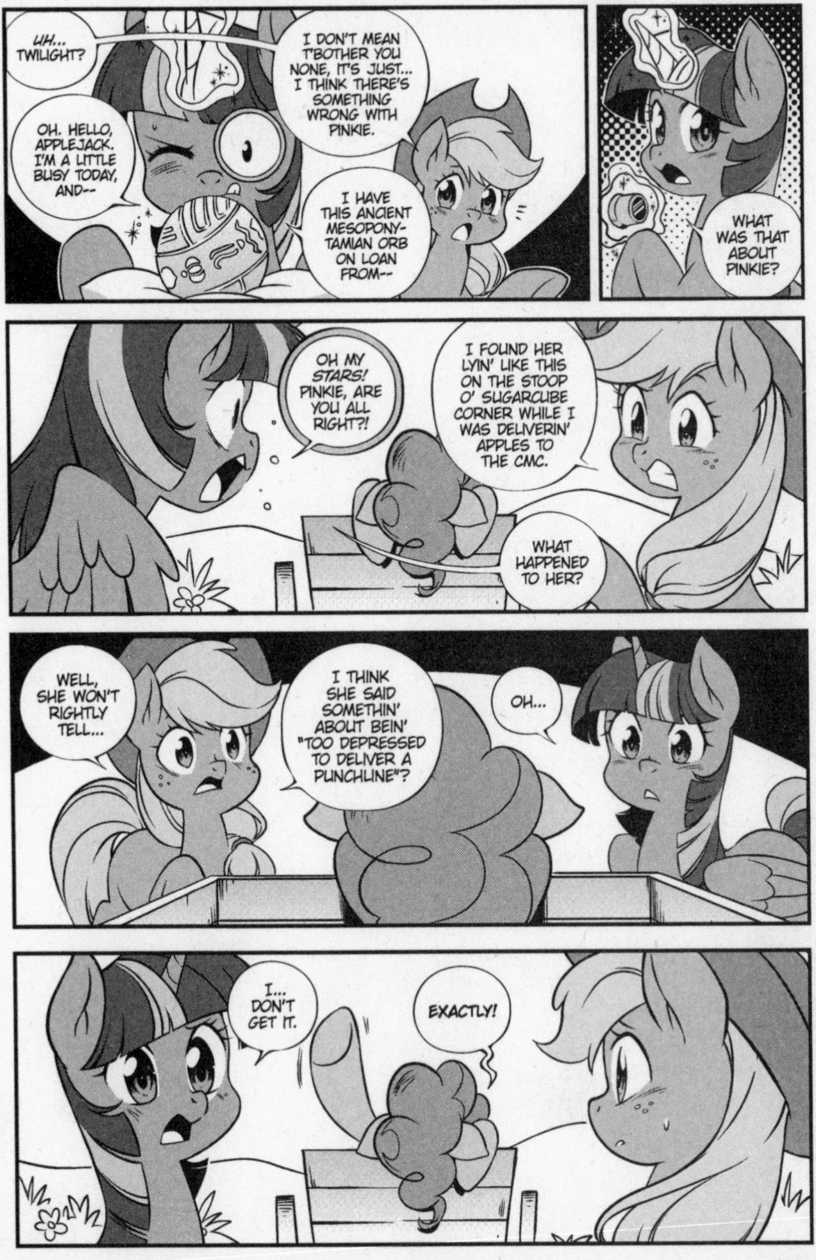

UH... TWILIGHT?
I DON'T MEAN T'BOTHER YOU NONE, IT'S JUST... I THINK THERE'S SOMETHING WRONG WITH PINKIE.
OH. HELLO, APPLEJACK. I'M A LITTLE BUSY TODAY, AND--
I HAVE THIS ANCIENT MESOPONY-TAMIAN ORB ON LOAN FROM--
WHAT WAS THAT ABOUT PINKIE?
OH MY STARS! PINKIE, ARE YOU ALL RIGHT?!
I FOUND HER LYIN' LIKE THIS ON THE STOOP O' SUGARCUBE CORNER WHILE I WAS DELIVERIN' APPLES TO THE CMC.
WHAT HAPPENED TO HER?
WELL, SHE WON'T RIGHTLY TELL...
I THINK SHE SAID SOMETHIN' ABOUT BEIN' "TOO DEPRESSED TO DELIVER A PUNCHLINE"?
OH...
I... DON'T GET IT.
EXACTLY!

Mistaken Piedentity

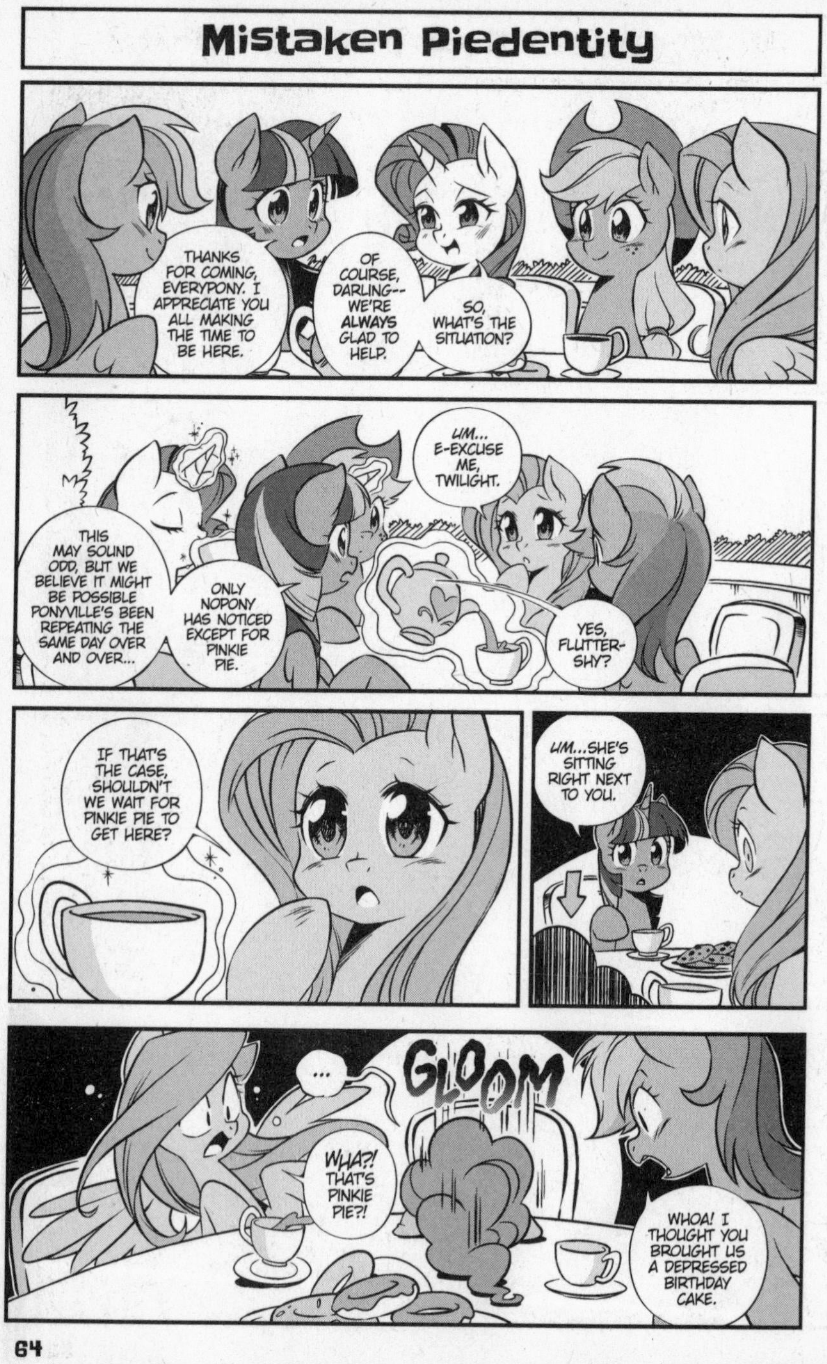
THANKS FOR COMING, EVERYPONY. I APPRECIATE YOU ALL MAKING THE TIME TO BE HERE.
OF COURSE, DARLING-- WE'RE ALWAYS GLAD TO HELP.
SO, WHAT'S THE SITUATION?
THIS MAY SOUND ODD, BUT WE BELIEVE IT MIGHT BE POSSIBLE PONYVILLE'S BEEN REPEATING THE SAME DAY OVER AND OVER...
ONLY NOPONY HAS NOTICED EXCEPT FOR PINKIE PIE.
UM... E-EXCUSE ME, TWILIGHT.
YES, FLUTTER-SHY?
IF THAT'S THE CASE, SHOULDN'T WE WAIT FOR PINKIE PIE TO GET HERE?
UM...SHE'S SITTING RIGHT NEXT TO YOU.
...
GLOOM
WHA?! THAT'S PINKIE PIE?!
WHOA! I THOUGHT YOU BROUGHT US A DEPRESSED BIRTHDAY CAKE.

All Doubts Have Been Dashed

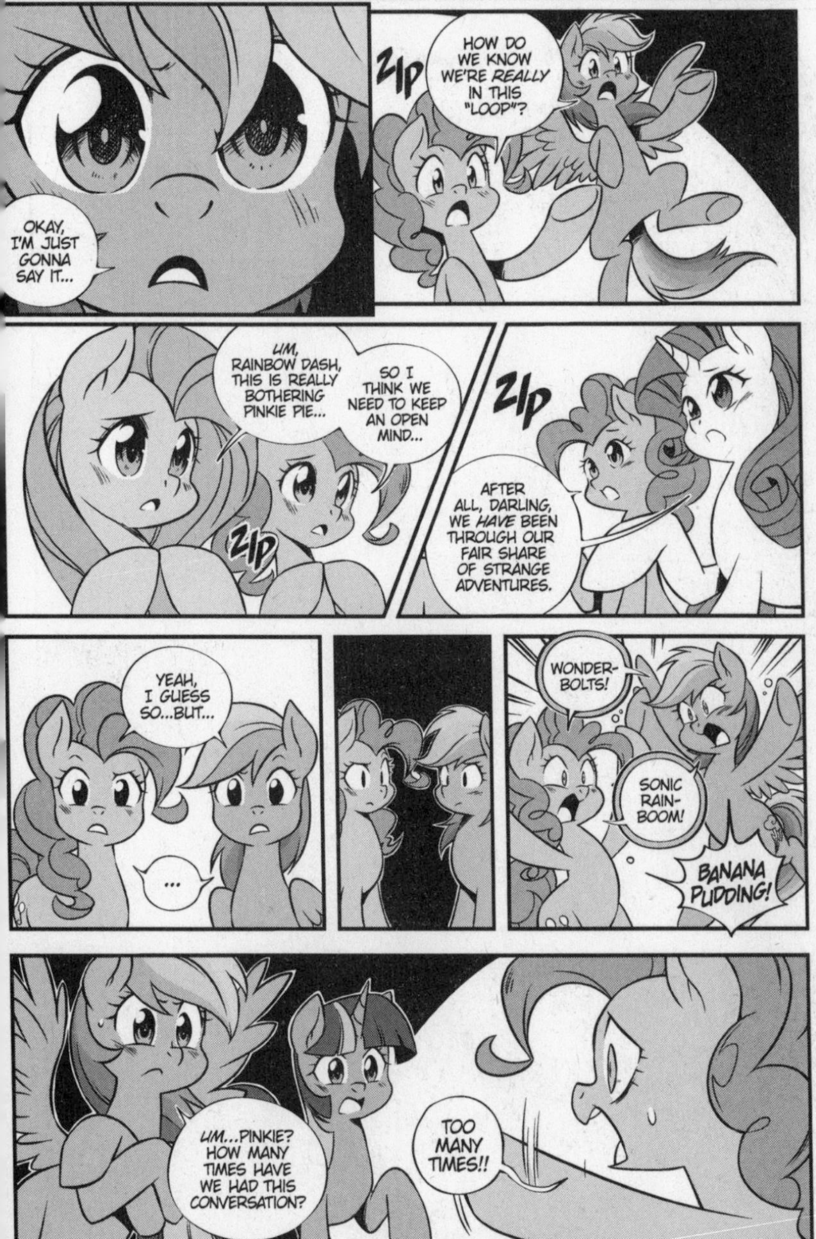

OKAY, I'M JUST GONNA SAY IT...
ZIP
HOW DO WE KNOW WE'RE *REALLY* IN THIS "LOOP"?
UM, RAINBOW DASH, THIS IS REALLY BOTHERING PINKIE PIE...
SO I THINK WE NEED TO KEEP AN OPEN MIND...
ZIP
ZIP
AFTER ALL, DARLING, WE *HAVE* BEEN THROUGH OUR FAIR SHARE OF STRANGE ADVENTURES.
YEAH, I GUESS SO...BUT...
...
WONDER-BOLTS!
SONIC RAIN-BOOM!
BANANA PUDDING!
UM...PINKIE? HOW MANY TIMES HAVE WE HAD THIS CONVERSATION?
TOO MANY TIMES!!

Piecognition

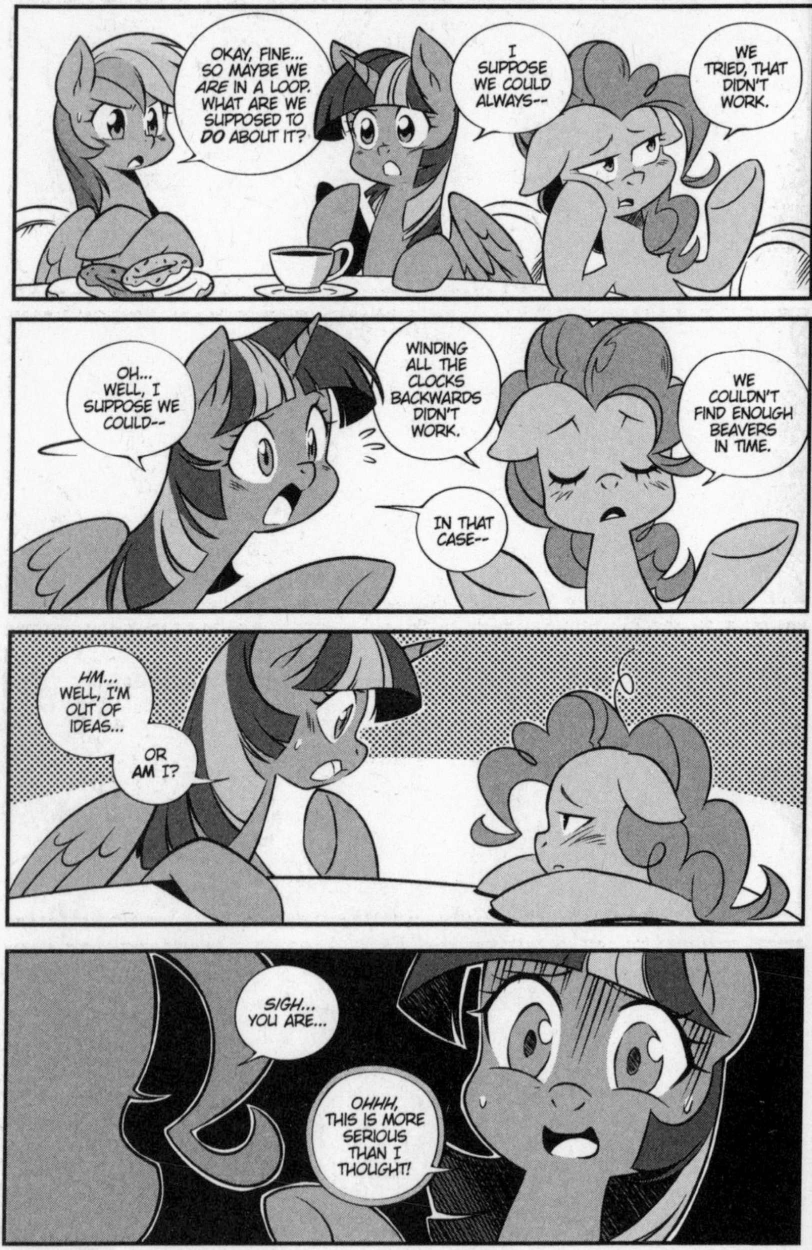
OKAY, FINE... SO MAYBE WE *ARE* IN A LOOP. WHAT ARE WE SUPPOSED TO ***DO*** ABOUT IT?
I SUPPOSE WE COULD ALWAYS--
WE TRIED, THAT DIDN'T WORK.
OH... WELL, I SUPPOSE WE COULD--
WINDING ALL THE CLOCKS BACKWARDS DIDN'T WORK.
WE COULDN'T FIND ENOUGH BEAVERS IN TIME.
IN THAT CASE--
HM... WELL, I'M OUT OF IDEAS...
OR AM I?
SIGH... YOU ARE...
OHHH, THIS IS MORE SERIOUS THAN I THOUGHT!

An Apple Cart a Day Keeps Doc Away

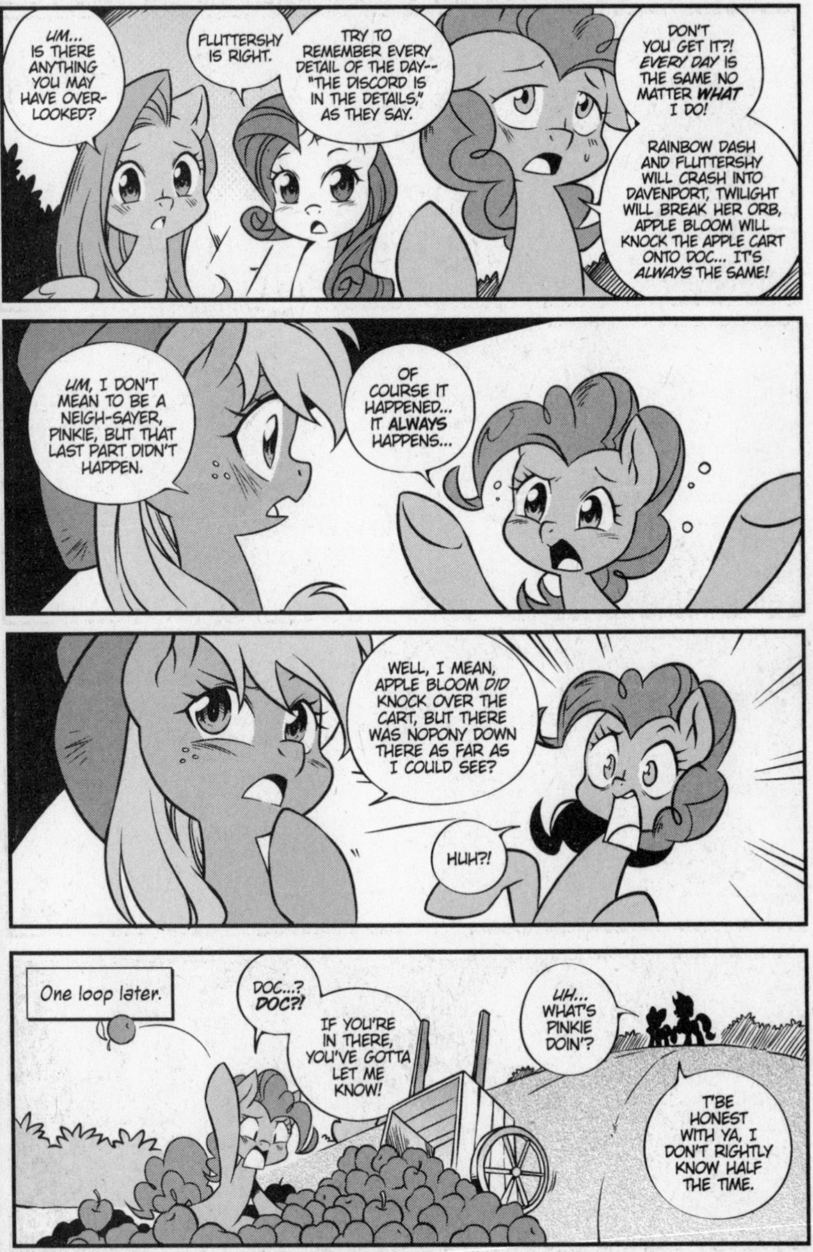

UM... IS THERE ANYTHING YOU MAY HAVE OVER-LOOKED?
FLUTTERSHY IS RIGHT.
TRY TO REMEMBER EVERY DETAIL OF THE DAY-- "THE DISCORD IS IN THE DETAILS," AS THEY SAY.
DON'T YOU GET IT?! EVERY DAY IS THE SAME NO MATTER WHAT I DO!
RAINBOW DASH AND FLUTTERSHY WILL CRASH INTO DAVENPORT, TWILIGHT WILL BREAK HER ORB, APPLE BLOOM WILL KNOCK THE APPLE CART ONTO DOC... IT'S ALWAYS THE SAME!
UM, I DON'T MEAN TO BE A NEIGH-SAYER, PINKIE, BUT THAT LAST PART DIDN'T HAPPEN.
OF COURSE IT HAPPENED... IT ALWAYS HAPPENS...
WELL, I MEAN, APPLE BLOOM DID KNOCK OVER THE CART, BUT THERE WAS NOPONY DOWN THERE AS FAR AS I COULD SEE?
HUH?!
One loop later.
DOC...? DOC?!
IF YOU'RE IN THERE, YOU'VE GOTTA LET ME KNOW!
UH... WHAT'S PINKIE DOIN'?
T'BE HONEST WITH YA, I DON'T RIGHTLY KNOW HALF THE TIME.

Docgone It!

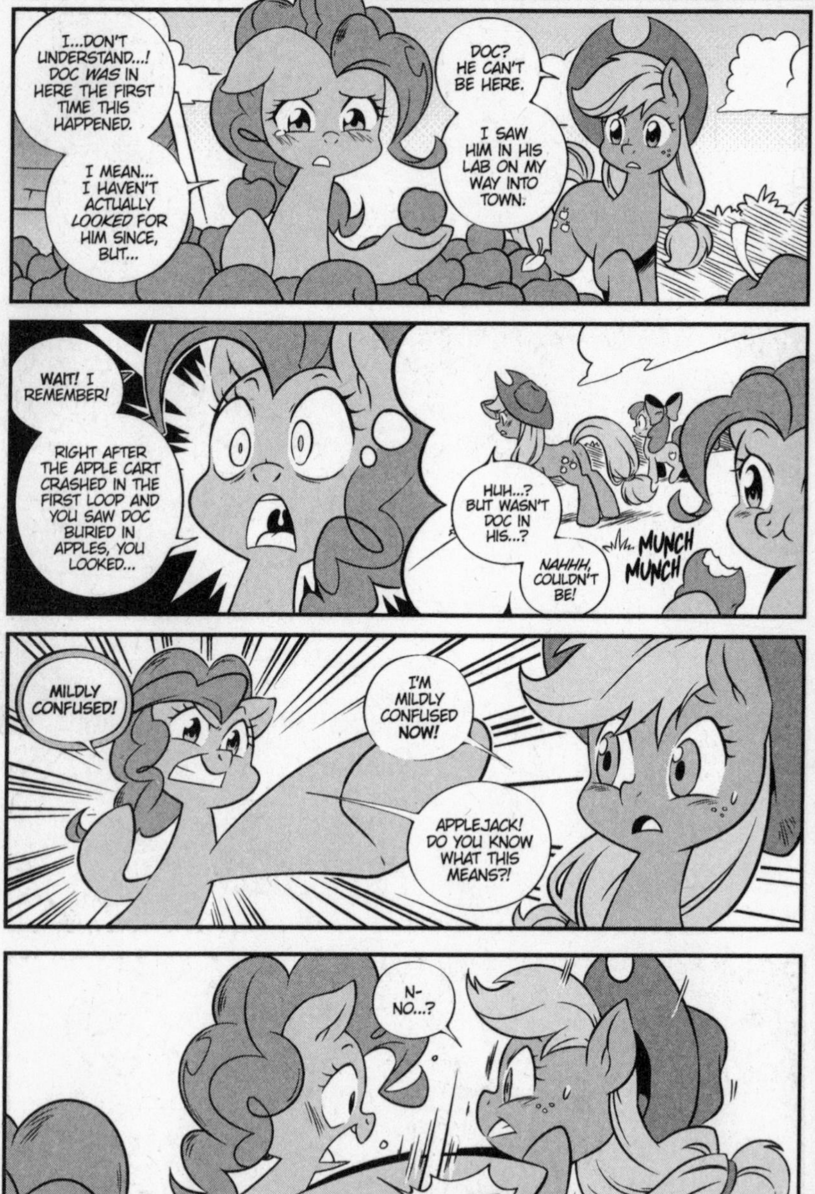
I...DON'T UNDERSTAND...! DOC *WAS* IN HERE THE FIRST TIME THIS HAPPENED.
I MEAN... I HAVEN'T ACTUALLY *LOOKED* FOR HIM SINCE, BUT...
DOC? HE CAN'T BE HERE.
I SAW HIM IN HIS LAB ON MY WAY INTO TOWN.
WAIT! I REMEMBER!
RIGHT AFTER THE APPLE CART CRASHED IN THE FIRST LOOP AND YOU SAW DOC BURIED IN APPLES, YOU LOOKED...
HUH...? BUT WASN'T DOC IN HIS...?
NAHHH, COULDN'T BE!
MUNCH MUNCH
MILDLY CONFUSED!
I'M MILDLY CONFUSED NOW!
APPLEJACK! DO YOU KNOW WHAT THIS MEANS?!
N-NO...?
NEITHER DO I!!

Feeling Loopy

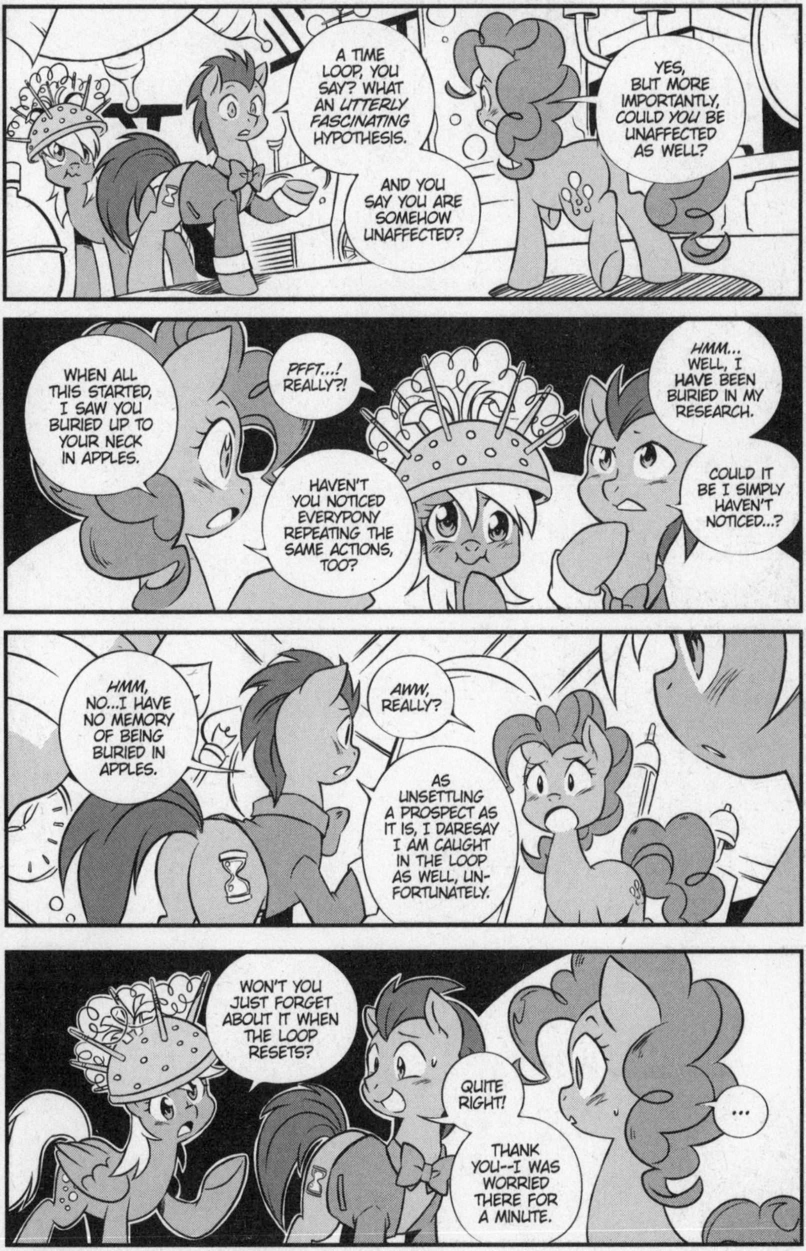
A TIME LOOP, YOU SAY? WHAT AN *UTTERLY FASCINATING* HYPOTHESIS.
AND YOU SAY YOU ARE SOMEHOW UNAFFECTED?
YES, BUT MORE IMPORTANTLY, COULD *YOU* BE UNAFFECTED AS WELL?
WHEN ALL THIS STARTED, I SAW YOU BURIED UP TO YOUR NECK IN APPLES.
PFFT...! REALLY?!
HAVEN'T YOU NOTICED EVERYPONY REPEATING THE SAME ACTIONS, TOO?
HMM... WELL, I HAVE BEEN BURIED IN MY RESEARCH.
COULD IT BE I SIMPLY HAVEN'T NOTICED...?
HMM, NO...I HAVE NO MEMORY OF BEING BURIED IN APPLES.
AWW, REALLY?
AS UNSETTLING A PROSPECT AS IT IS, I DARESAY I AM CAUGHT IN THE LOOP AS WELL, UNFORTUNATELY.
WON'T YOU JUST FORGET ABOUT IT WHEN THE LOOP RESETS?
QUITE RIGHT!
THANK YOU--I WAS WORRIED THERE FOR A MINUTE.
...

Dopplegäng Her

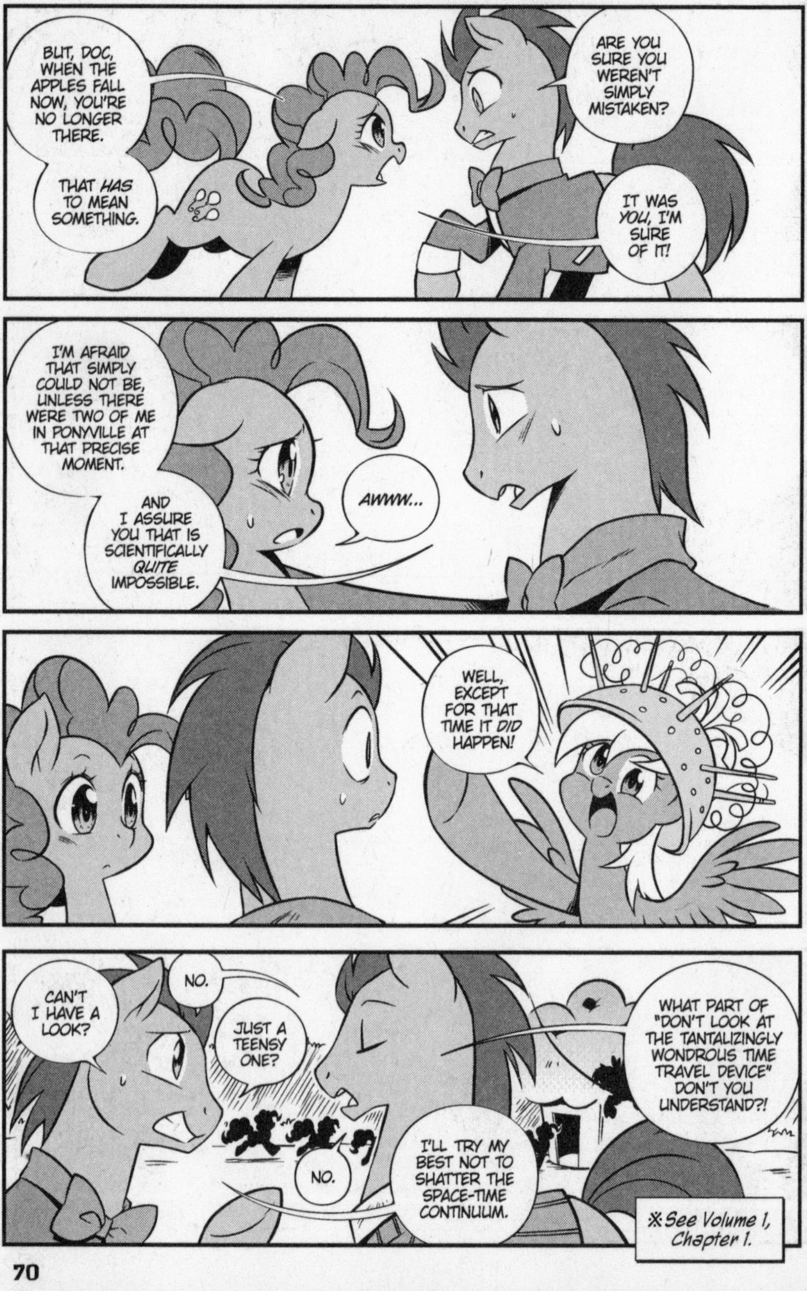
BUT, DOC, WHEN THE APPLES FALL NOW, YOU'RE NO LONGER THERE.
ARE YOU SURE YOU WEREN'T SIMPLY MISTAKEN?
THAT *HAS* TO MEAN SOMETHING.
IT WAS *YOU*, I'M SURE OF IT!
I'M AFRAID THAT SIMPLY COULD NOT BE, UNLESS THERE WERE TWO OF ME IN PONYVILLE AT THAT PRECISE MOMENT.
AWWW...
AND I ASSURE YOU THAT IS SCIENTIFICALLY *QUITE* IMPOSSIBLE.
WELL, EXCEPT FOR THAT TIME IT *DID* HAPPEN!
CAN'T I HAVE A LOOK?
NO.
JUST A TEENSY ONE?
WHAT PART OF "DON'T LOOK AT THE TANTALIZINGLY WONDROUS TIME TRAVEL DEVICE" DON'T YOU UNDERSTAND?!
NO.
I'LL TRY MY BEST NOT TO SHATTER THE SPACE-TIME CONTINUUM.
※*See Volume 1, Chapter 1.*

Muffin to See Here, Folks!

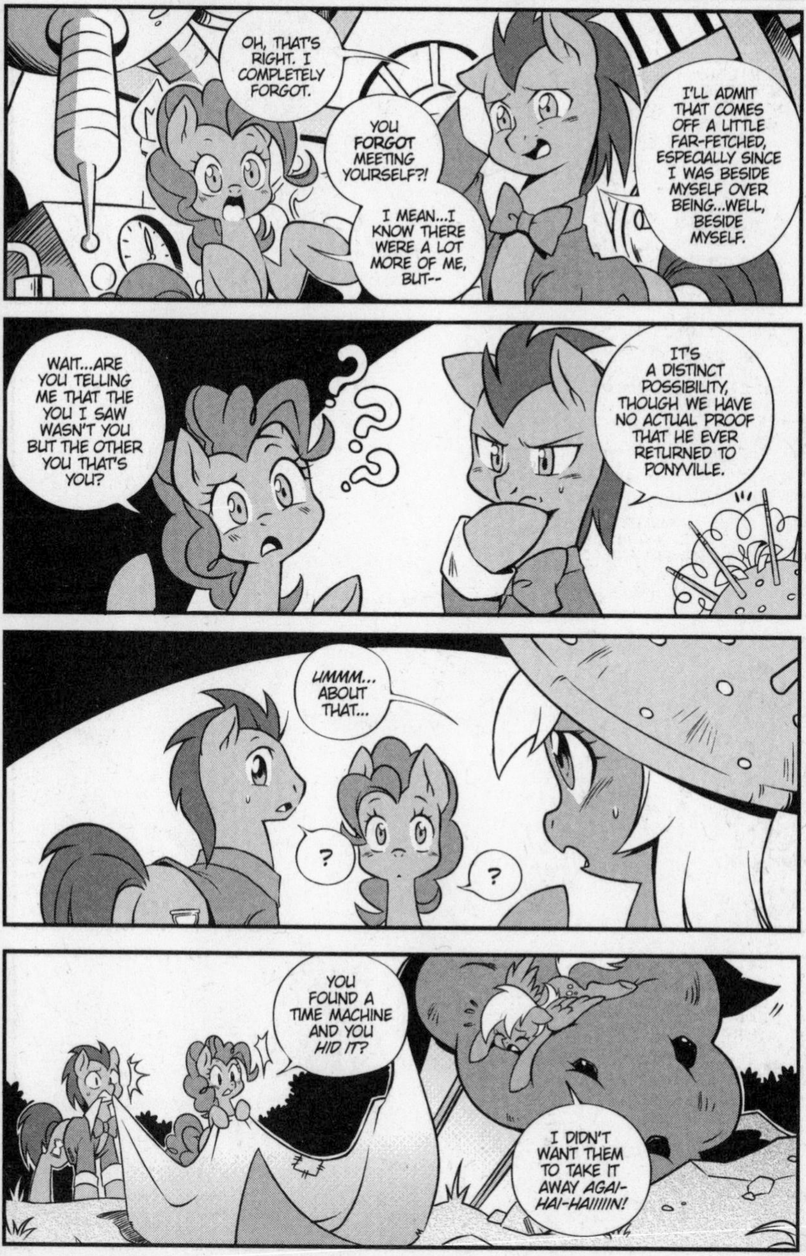

OH, THAT'S RIGHT. I COMPLETELY FORGOT.
YOU FORGOT MEETING YOURSELF?!
I MEAN...I KNOW THERE WERE A LOT MORE OF ME, BUT--
I'LL ADMIT THAT COMES OFF A LITTLE FAR-FETCHED, ESPECIALLY SINCE I WAS BESIDE MYSELF OVER BEING...WELL, BESIDE MYSELF.
WAIT...ARE YOU TELLING ME THAT THE YOU I SAW WASN'T YOU BUT THE OTHER YOU THAT'S YOU?
IT'S A DISTINCT POSSIBILITY, THOUGH WE HAVE NO ACTUAL PROOF THAT HE EVER RETURNED TO PONYVILLE.
UMMM... ABOUT THAT...
?
?
YOU FOUND A TIME MACHINE AND YOU *HID IT*?
I DIDN'T WANT THEM TO TAKE IT AWAY *AGAI-HAI-HAIIIIIN*!

The Proof is in the ~~Pudding~~ Pie

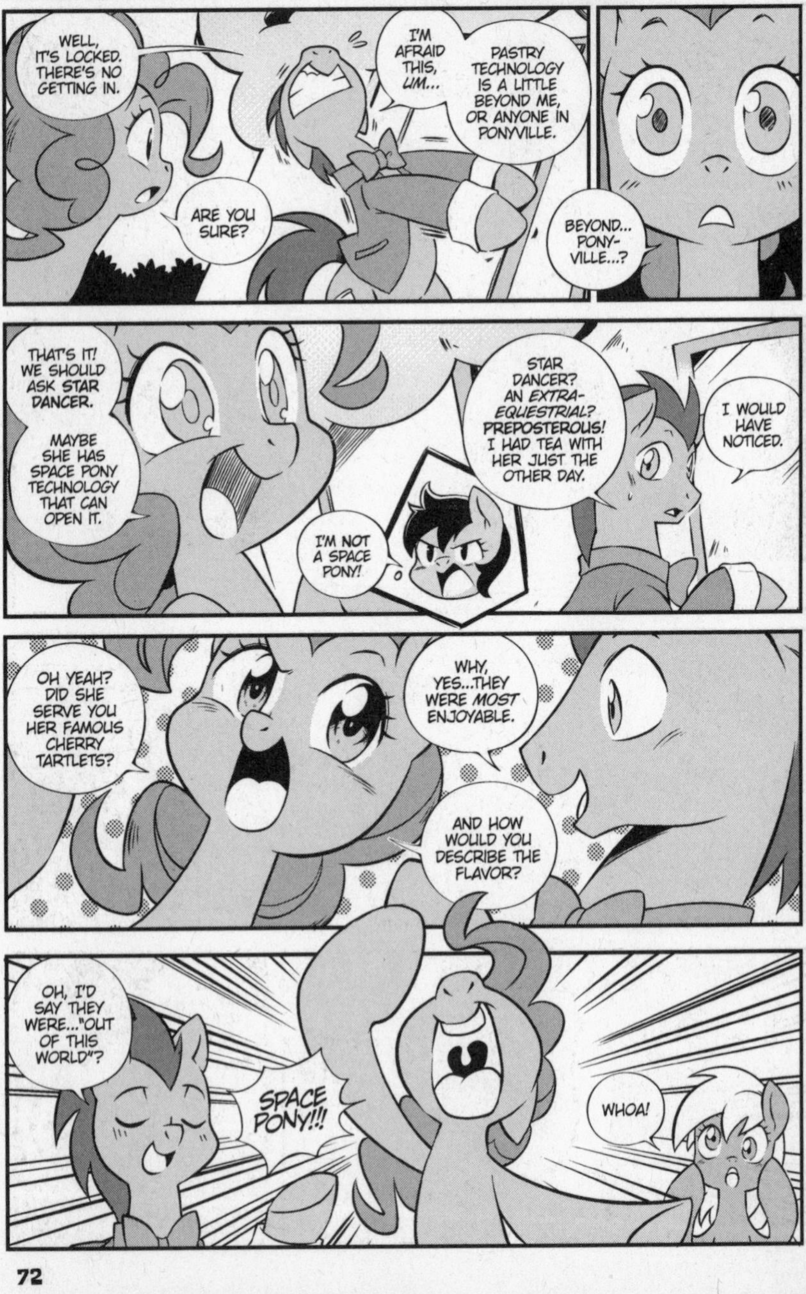

WELL, IT'S LOCKED. THERE'S NO GETTING IN.
I'M AFRAID THIS, *UM*...
PASTRY TECHNOLOGY IS A LITTLE BEYOND ME, OR ANYONE IN PONYVILLE.
ARE YOU SURE?
BEYOND... PONY-VILLE...?
THAT'S IT! WE SHOULD ASK STAR DANCER.
MAYBE SHE HAS SPACE PONY TECHNOLOGY THAT CAN OPEN IT.
I'M NOT A SPACE PONY!
STAR DANCER? AN *EXTRA-EQUESTRIAL?* **PREPOSTEROUS!** I HAD TEA WITH HER JUST THE OTHER DAY.
I WOULD HAVE NOTICED.
OH YEAH? DID SHE SERVE YOU HER FAMOUS CHERRY TARTLETS?
WHY, YES...THEY WERE *MOST* ENJOYABLE.
AND HOW WOULD YOU DESCRIBE THE FLAVOR?
OH, I'D SAY THEY WERE..."OUT OF THIS WORLD"?
SPACE PONY!!!
WHOA!

Pie Dirt

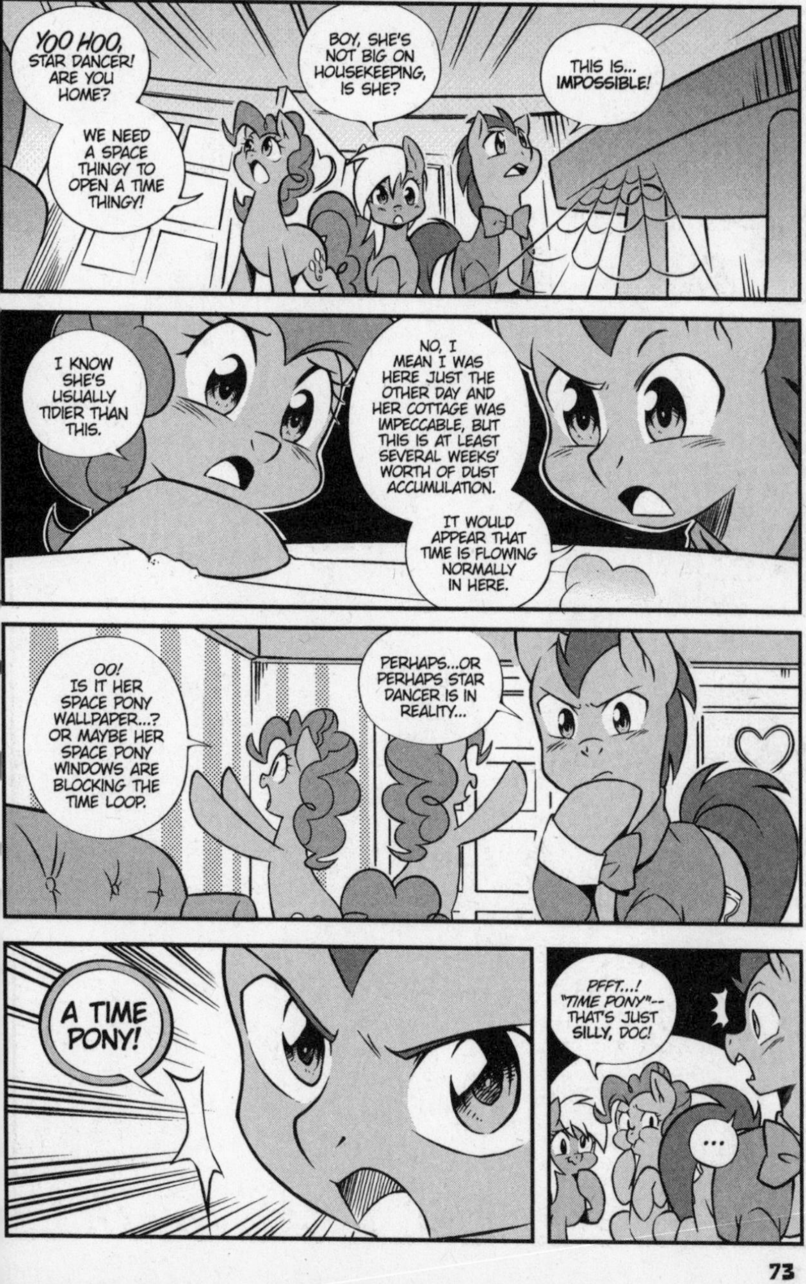
YOO HOO, STAR DANCER! ARE YOU HOME?
WE NEED A SPACE THINGY TO OPEN A TIME THINGY!
BOY, SHE'S NOT BIG ON HOUSEKEEPING, IS SHE?
THIS IS... IMPOSSIBLE!
I KNOW SHE'S USUALLY TIDIER THAN THIS.
NO, I MEAN I WAS HERE JUST THE OTHER DAY AND HER COTTAGE WAS IMPECCABLE, BUT THIS IS AT LEAST SEVERAL WEEKS' WORTH OF DUST ACCUMULATION.
IT WOULD APPEAR THAT TIME IS FLOWING NORMALLY IN HERE.
OO! IS IT HER SPACE PONY WALLPAPER...? OR MAYBE HER SPACE PONY WINDOWS ARE BLOCKING THE TIME LOOP.
PERHAPS...OR PERHAPS STAR DANCER IS IN REALITY...
A TIME PONY!
PFFT...! "TIME PONY"-- THAT'S JUST SILLY, DOC!
...

Vanished Into Pink Hair

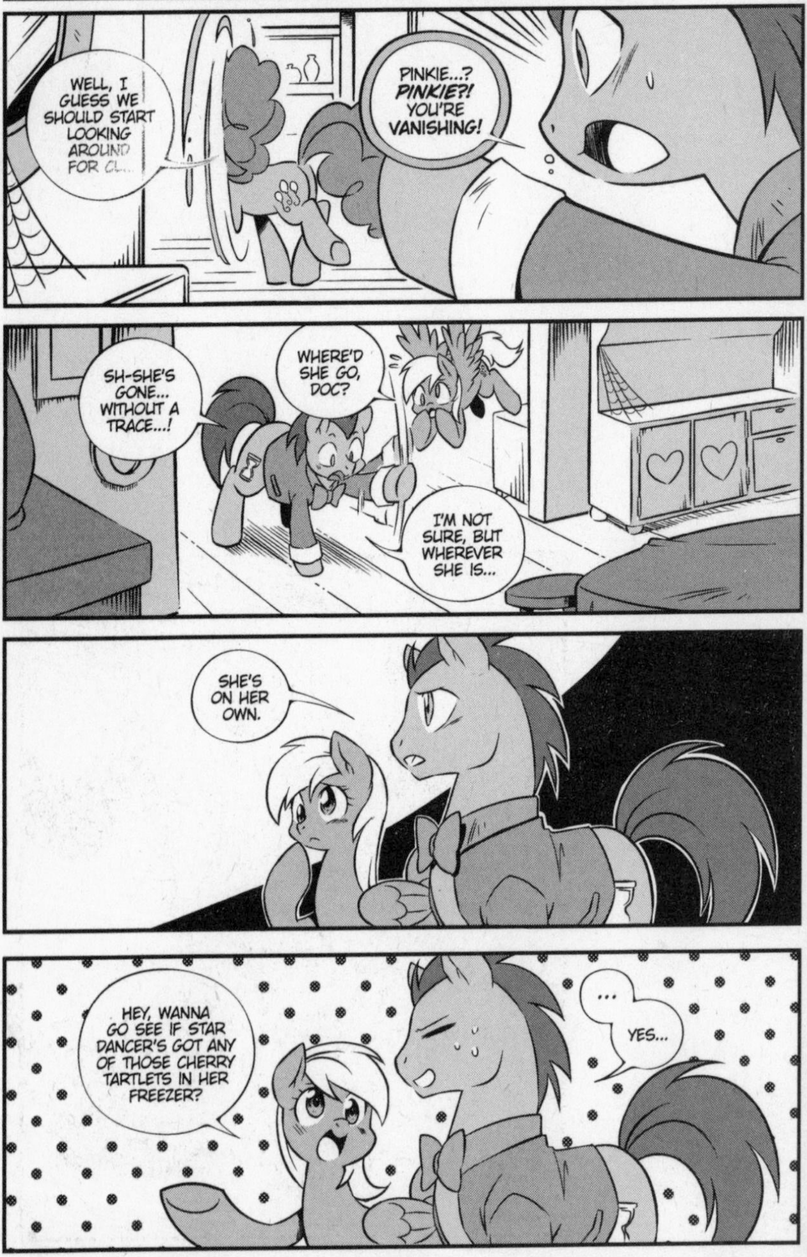
WELL, I GUESS WE SHOULD START LOOKING AROUND FOR CL...
PINKIE...? *PINKIE?!* YOU'RE VANISHING!
SH-SHE'S GONE... WITHOUT A TRACE...!
WHERE'D SHE GO, DOC?
I'M NOT SURE, BUT WHEREVER SHE IS...
SHE'S ON HER OWN.
HEY, WANNA GO SEE IF STAR DANCER'S GOT ANY OF THOSE CHERRY TARTLETS IN HER FREEZER?
...
YES...

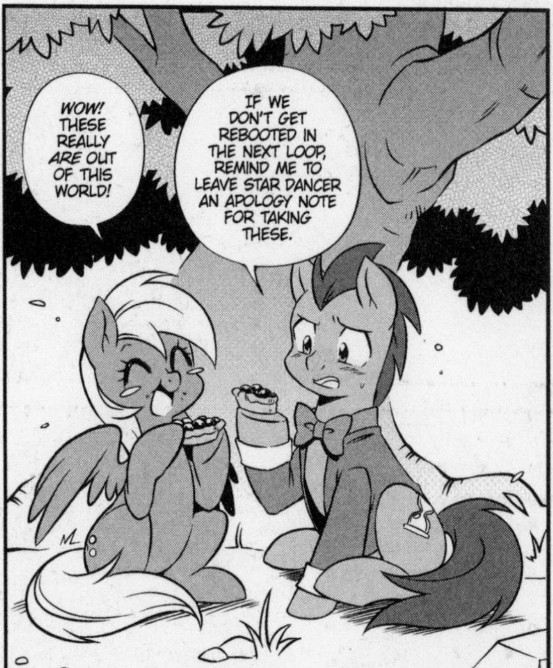
WOW! THESE REALLY ARE OUT OF THIS WORLD!
IF WE DON'T GET REBOOTED IN THE NEXT LOOP, REMIND ME TO LEAVE STAR DANCER AN APOLOGY NOTE FOR TAKING THESE.

CHAPTER 6

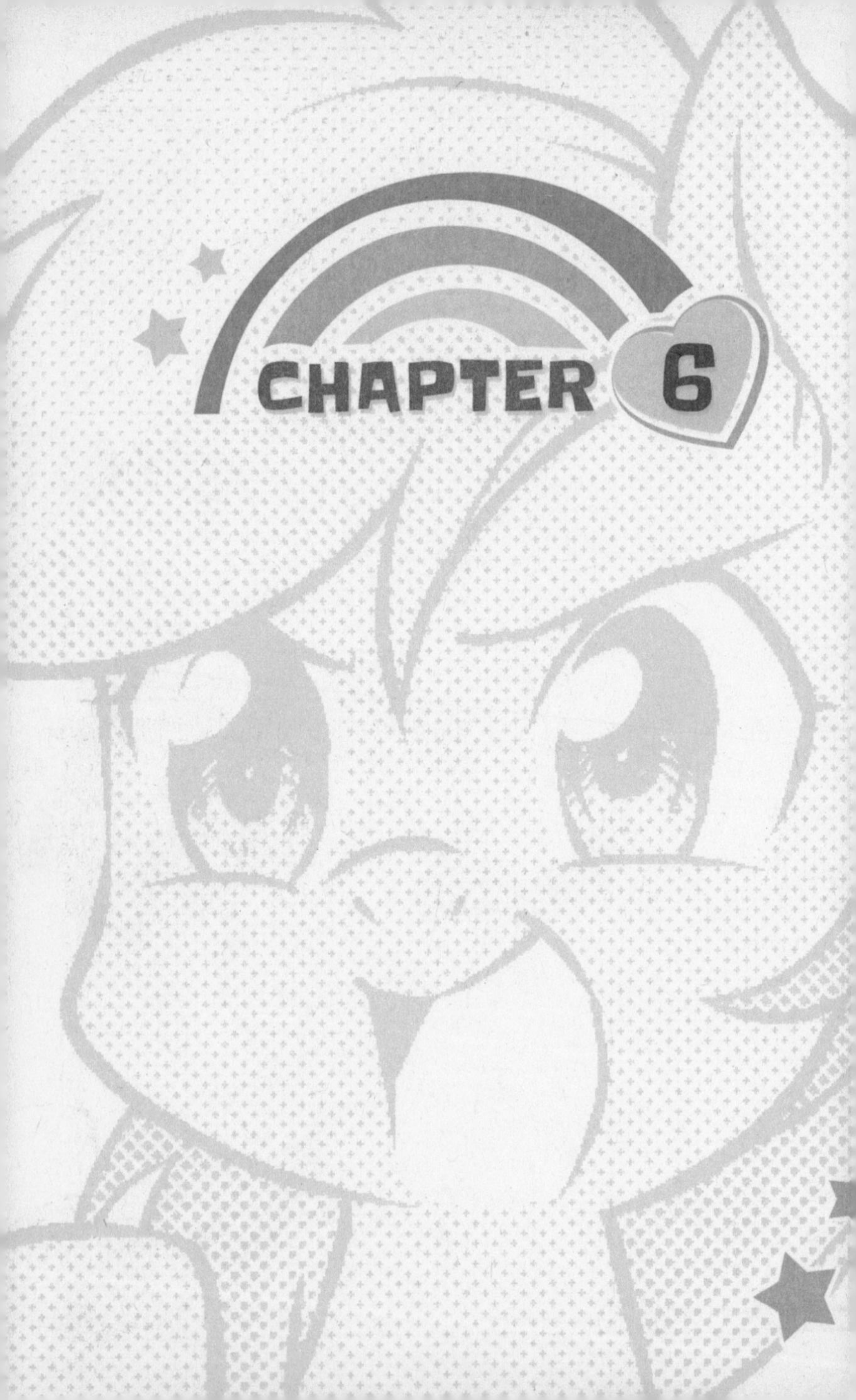

Lost Hallway

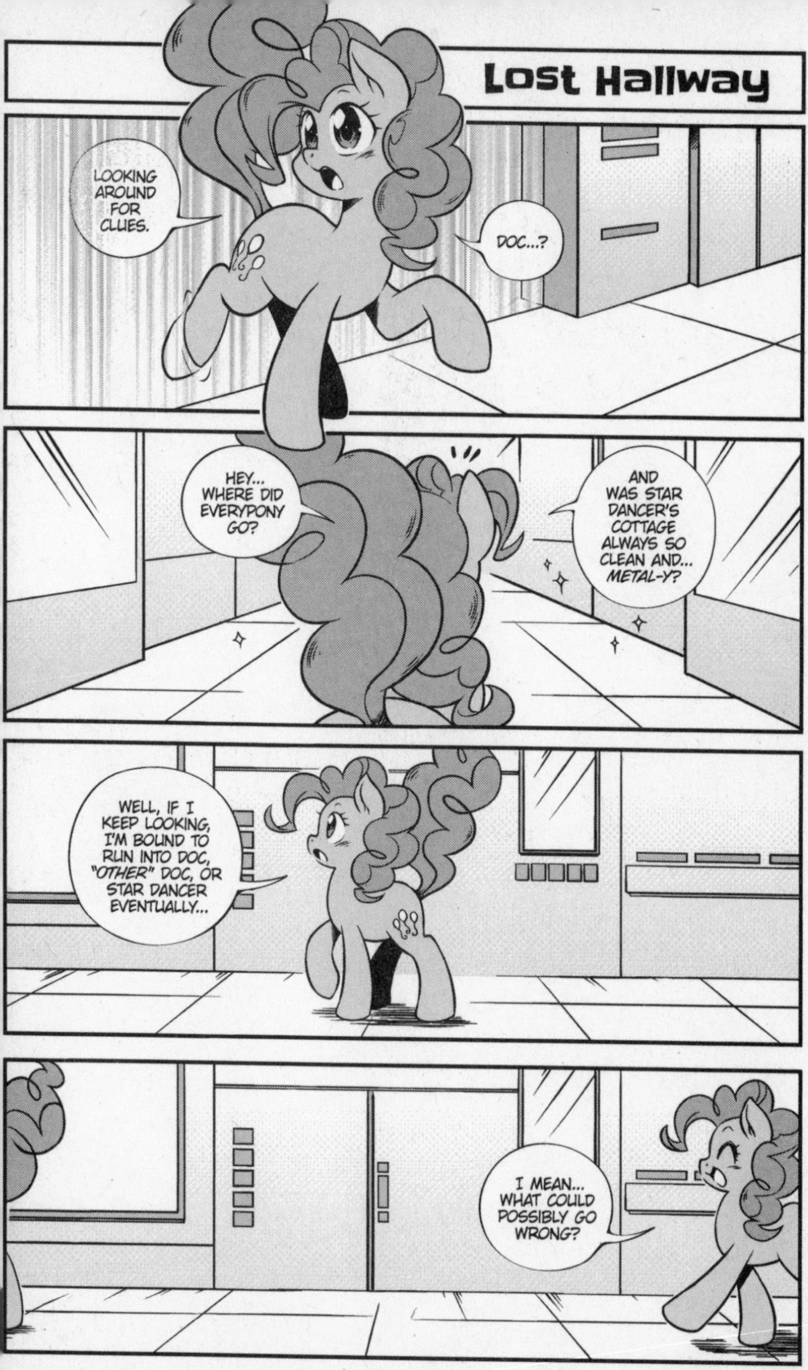

LOOKING AROUND FOR CLUES.
DOC...?
HEY... WHERE DID EVERYPONY GO?
AND WAS STAR DANCER'S COTTAGE ALWAYS SO CLEAN AND... *METAL-Y*?
WELL, IF I KEEP LOOKING, I'M BOUND TO RUN INTO DOC, *"OTHER"* DOC, OR STAR DANCER EVENTUALLY...
I MEAN... WHAT COULD POSSIBLY GO WRONG?

That's Me All Over

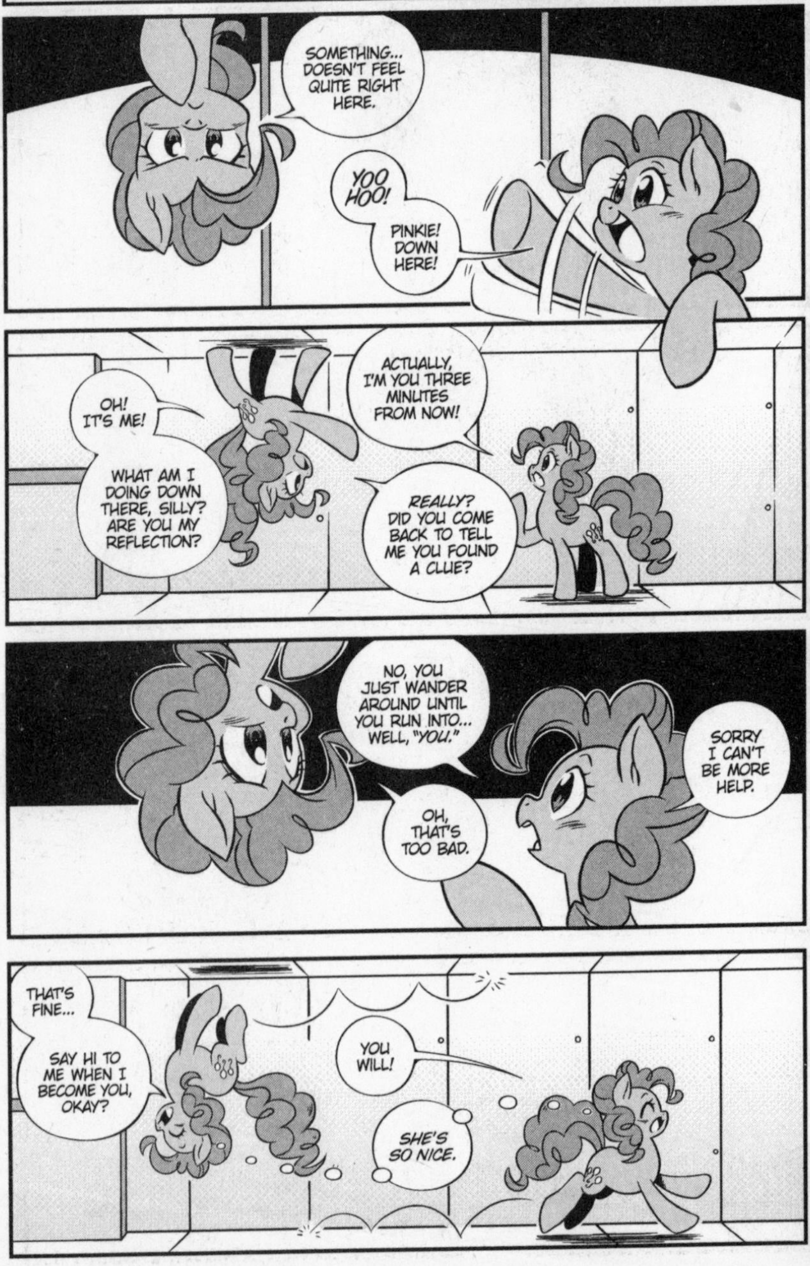

SOMETHING... DOESN'T FEEL QUITE RIGHT HERE.
YOO HOO!
PINKIE! DOWN HERE!
OH! IT'S ME!
WHAT AM I DOING DOWN THERE, SILLY? ARE YOU MY REFLECTION?
ACTUALLY, I'M YOU THREE MINUTES FROM NOW!
REALLY? DID YOU COME BACK TO TELL ME YOU FOUND A CLUE?
NO, YOU JUST WANDER AROUND UNTIL YOU RUN INTO... WELL, "YOU."
OH, THAT'S TOO BAD.
SORRY I CAN'T BE MORE HELP.
THAT'S FINE...
SAY HI TO ME WHEN I BECOME YOU, OKAY?
YOU WILL!
SHE'S SO NICE.

Running Into an Old Friend

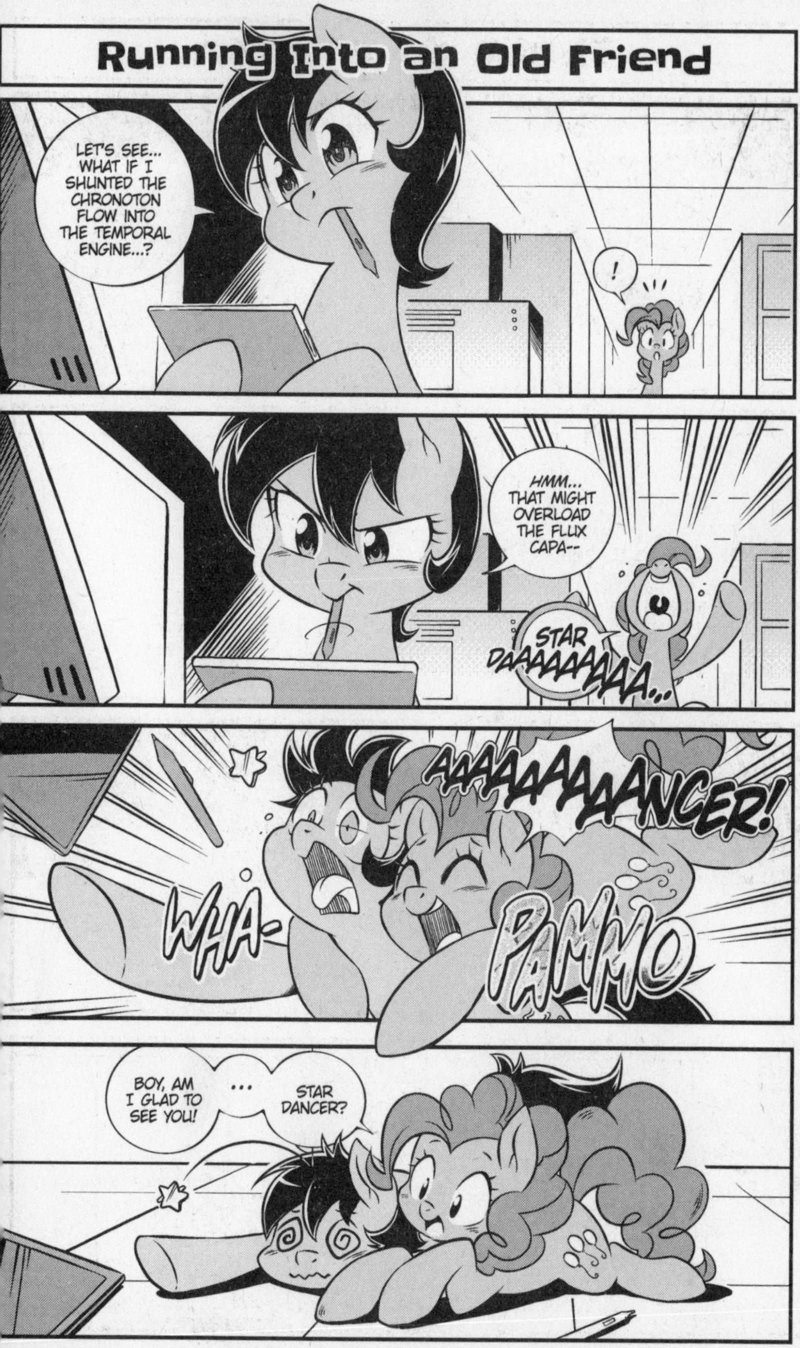

LET'S SEE... WHAT IF I SHUNTED THE CHRONOTON FLOW INTO THE TEMPORAL ENGINE...?
!
HMM... THAT MIGHT OVERLOAD THE FLUX CAPA--
STAR DAAAAAAAAAA...
AAAAAAAAAANCER!
WHA-
PAMMO
BOY, AM I GLAD TO SEE YOU!
...
STAR DANCER?

You Can't Spell "Impossible" Without P.I.E.

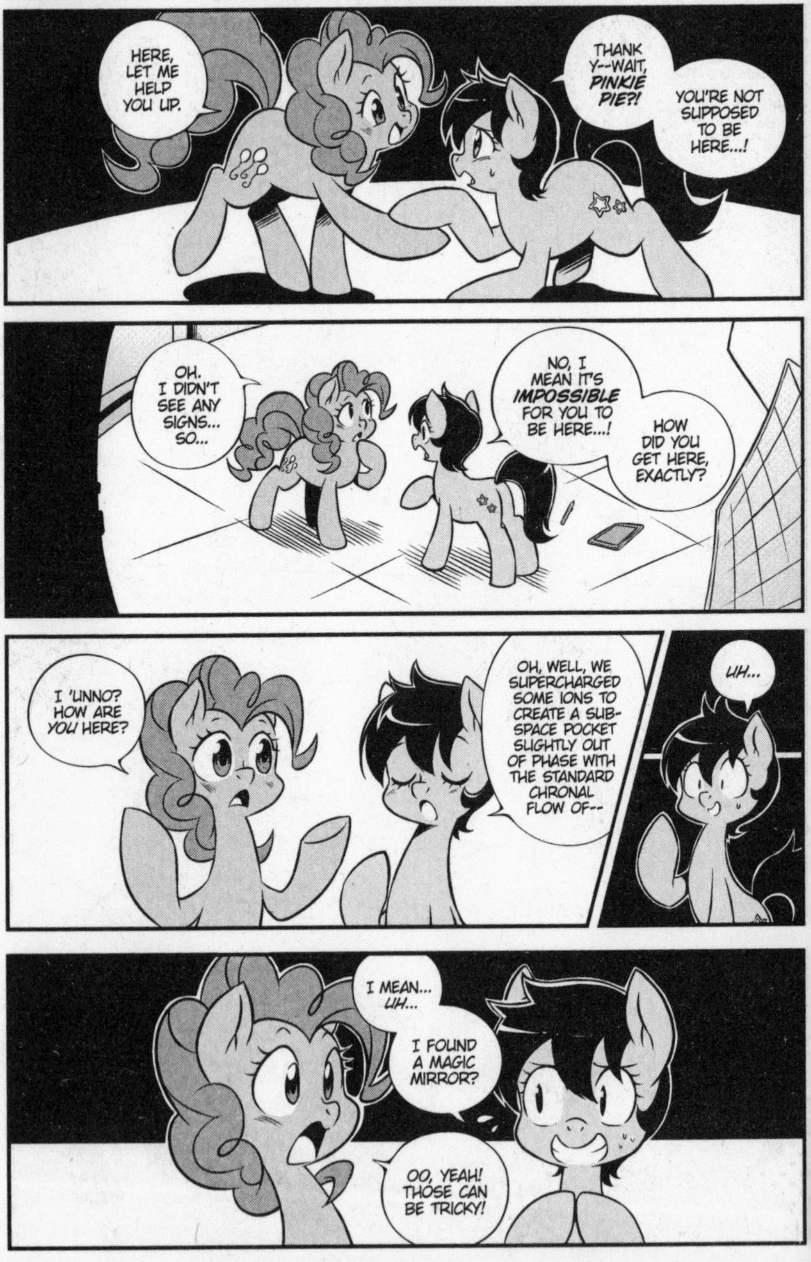
HERE, LET ME HELP YOU UP.
THANK Y--WAIT, *PINKIE PIE?!*
YOU'RE NOT SUPPOSED TO BE HERE...!
OH. I DIDN'T SEE ANY SIGNS... SO...
NO, I MEAN IT'S *IMPOSSIBLE* FOR YOU TO BE HERE...!
HOW DID YOU GET HERE, EXACTLY?
I 'UNNO? HOW ARE *YOU* HERE?
OH, WELL, WE SUPERCHARGED SOME IONS TO CREATE A SUB-SPACE POCKET SLIGHTLY OUT OF PHASE WITH THE STANDARD CHRONAL FLOW OF--
UH...
I MEAN... *UH...*
I FOUND A MAGIC MIRROR?
OO, YEAH! THOSE CAN BE TRICKY!

Pienigma

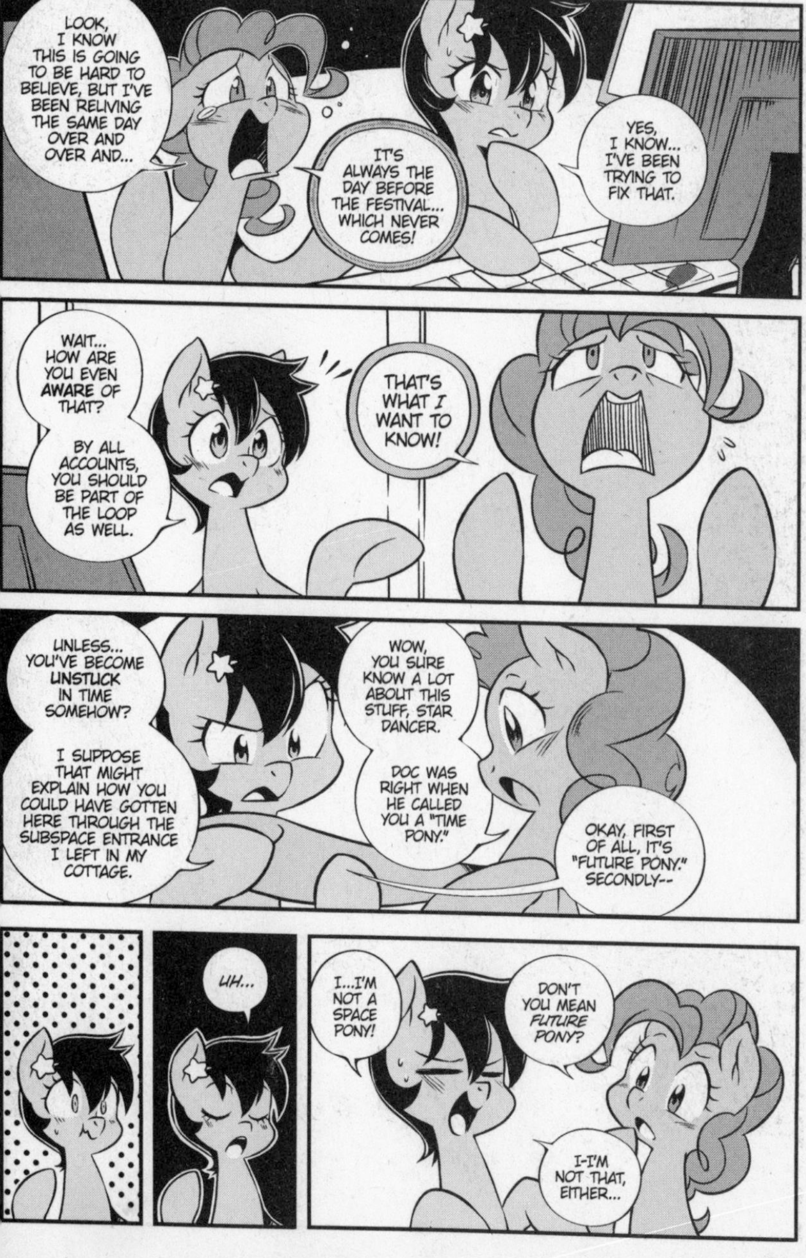

LOOK, I KNOW THIS IS GOING TO BE HARD TO BELIEVE, BUT I'VE BEEN RELIVING THE SAME DAY OVER AND OVER AND...
IT'S ALWAYS THE DAY BEFORE THE FESTIVAL... WHICH NEVER COMES!
YES, I KNOW... I'VE BEEN TRYING TO FIX THAT.
WAIT... HOW ARE YOU EVEN **AWARE** OF THAT?
BY ALL ACCOUNTS, YOU SHOULD BE PART OF THE LOOP AS WELL.
THAT'S WHAT *I* WANT TO KNOW!
UNLESS... YOU'VE BECOME **UNSTUCK** IN TIME SOMEHOW?
I SUPPOSE THAT MIGHT EXPLAIN HOW YOU COULD HAVE GOTTEN HERE THROUGH THE SUBSPACE ENTRANCE I LEFT IN MY COTTAGE.
WOW, YOU SURE KNOW A LOT ABOUT THIS STUFF, STAR DANCER.
DOC WAS RIGHT WHEN HE CALLED YOU A "TIME PONY."
OKAY, FIRST OF ALL, IT'S "FUTURE PONY." SECONDLY--
UH...
I...I'M NOT A SPACE PONY!
DON'T YOU MEAN *FUTURE* PONY?
I-I'M NOT THAT, EITHER...

What's Up, Doc?

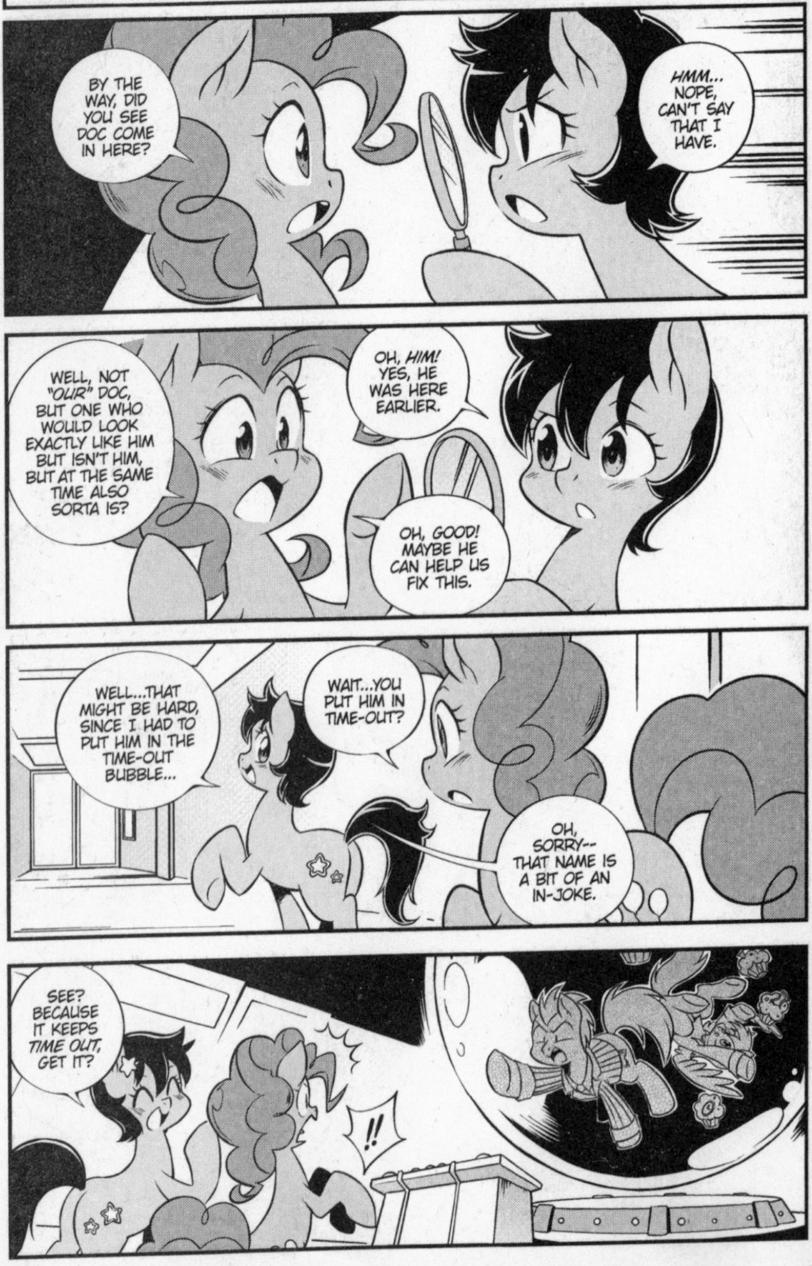
BY THE WAY, DID YOU SEE DOC COME IN HERE?
HMM... NOPE, CAN'T SAY THAT I HAVE.
WELL, NOT *"OUR"* DOC, BUT ONE WHO WOULD LOOK EXACTLY LIKE HIM BUT ISN'T HIM, BUT AT THE SAME TIME ALSO SORTA IS?
OH, *HIM!* YES, HE WAS HERE EARLIER.
OH, GOOD! MAYBE HE CAN HELP US FIX THIS.
WELL...THAT MIGHT BE HARD, SINCE I HAD TO PUT HIM IN THE TIME-OUT BUBBLE...
WAIT...YOU PUT HIM IN TIME-OUT?
OH, SORRY-- THAT NAME IS A BIT OF AN IN-JOKE.
SEE? BECAUSE IT KEEPS *TIME OUT,* GET IT?
!!

A Cause to Un-pause

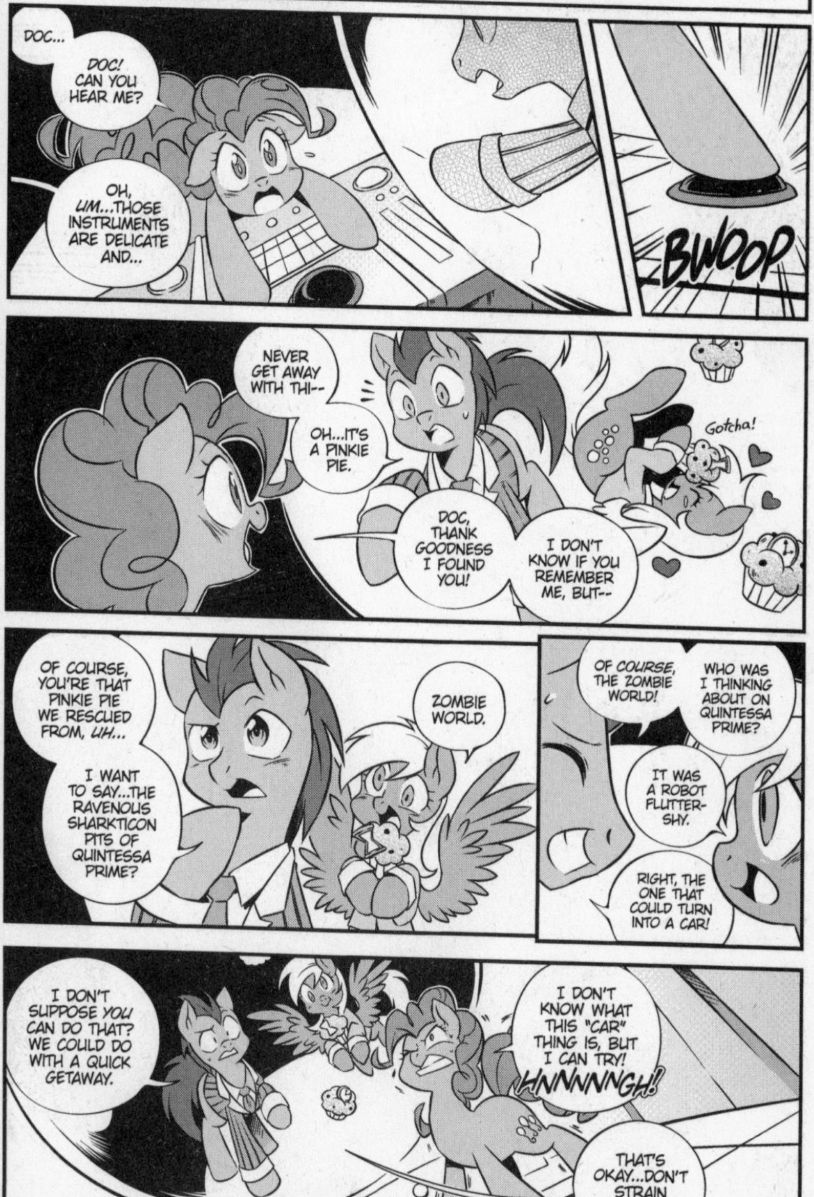
DOC...
DOC! CAN YOU HEAR ME?
OH, UM...THOSE INSTRUMENTS ARE DELICATE AND...
BWOOP
NEVER GET AWAY WITH THI--
OH...IT'S A PINKIE PIE.
Gotcha!
DOC, THANK GOODNESS I FOUND YOU!
I DON'T KNOW IF YOU REMEMBER ME, BUT--
OF COURSE, YOU'RE THAT PINKIE PIE WE RESCUED FROM, UH...
I WANT TO SAY...THE RAVENOUS SHARKTICON PITS OF QUINTESSA PRIME?
ZOMBIE WORLD.
OF COURSE, THE ZOMBIE WORLD!
WHO WAS I THINKING ABOUT ON QUINTESSA PRIME?
IT WAS A ROBOT FLUTTER-SHY.
RIGHT, THE ONE THAT COULD TURN INTO A CAR!
I DON'T SUPPOSE YOU CAN DO THAT? WE COULD DO WITH A QUICK GETAWAY.
I DON'T KNOW WHAT THIS "CAR" THING IS, BUT I CAN TRY!
HNNNNNGH!
THAT'S OKAY...DON'T STRAIN YOURSELF...

Assault of Flattery

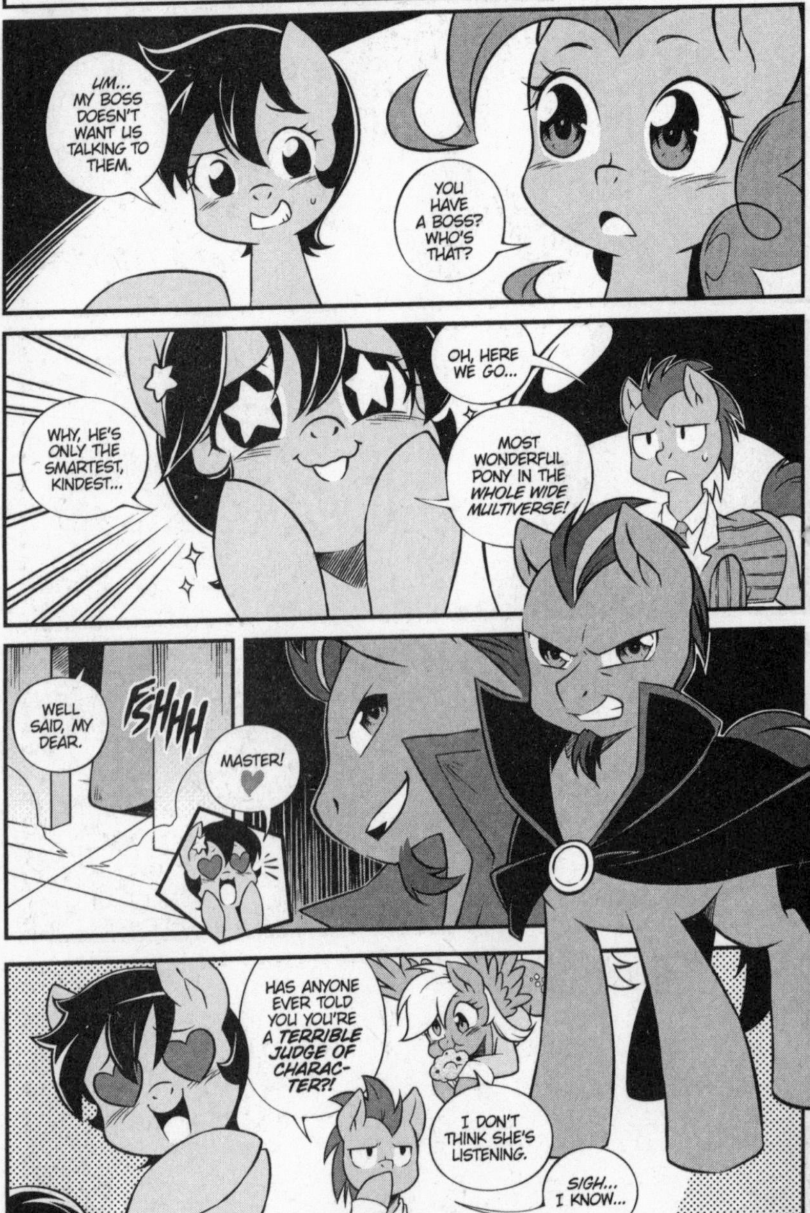
UM... MY BOSS DOESN'T WANT US TALKING TO THEM.
YOU HAVE A BOSS? WHO'S THAT?
WHY, HE'S ONLY THE SMARTEST, KINDEST...
MOST WONDERFUL PONY IN THE *WHOLE WIDE MULTIVERSE!*
OH, HERE WE GO...
WELL SAID, MY DEAR.
FSHHH
MASTER!
HAS ANYONE EVER TOLD YOU YOU'RE A *TERRIBLE JUDGE OF CHARACTER?!*
I DON'T THINK SHE'S LISTENING.
SIGH... I KNOW...

The Long Hello

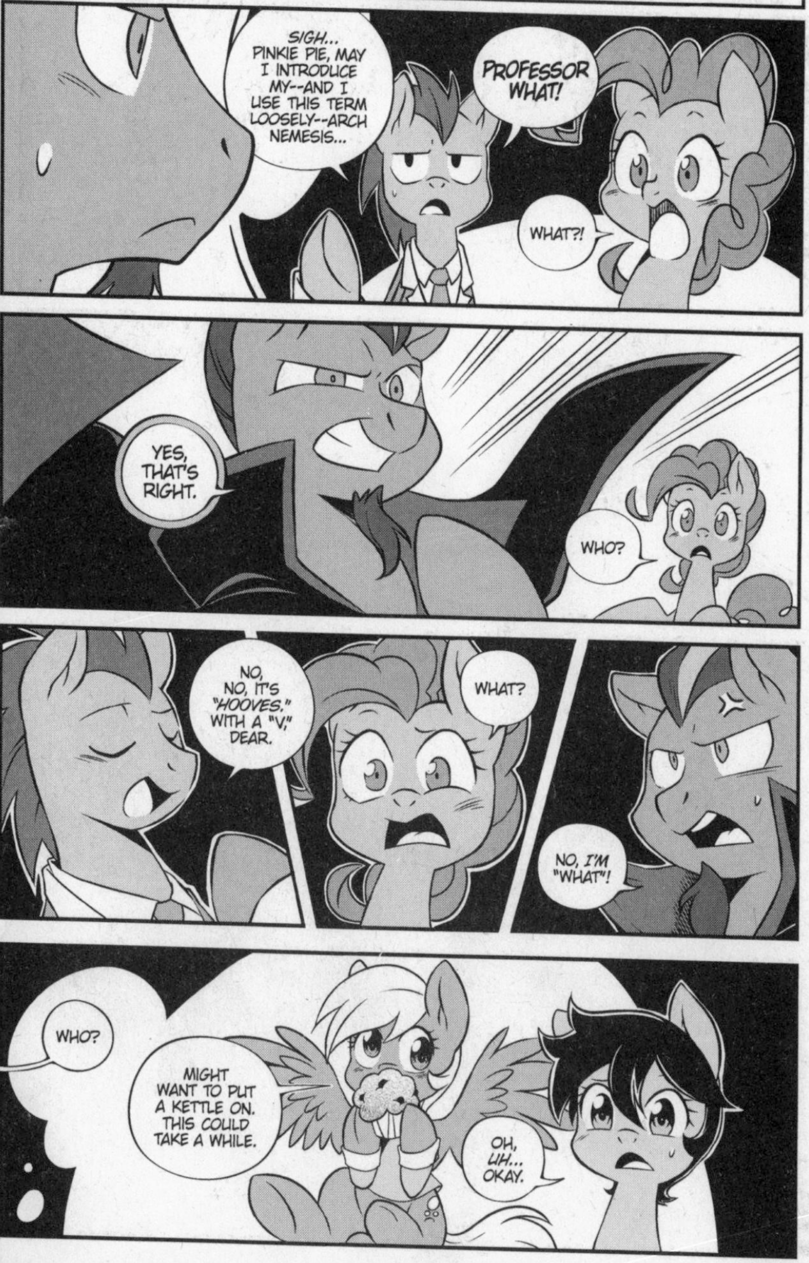

SIGH... PINKIE PIE, MAY I INTRODUCE MY--AND I USE THIS TERM LOOSELY--ARCH NEMESIS...
PROFESSOR WHAT!
WHAT?!
YES, THAT'S RIGHT.
WHO?
NO, NO, IT'S "HOOVES," WITH A "V," DEAR.
WHAT?
NO, I'M "WHAT"!
WHO?
MIGHT WANT TO PUT A KETTLE ON. THIS COULD TAKE A WHILE.
OH, UH... OKAY.

All's Fair in Fairs and War

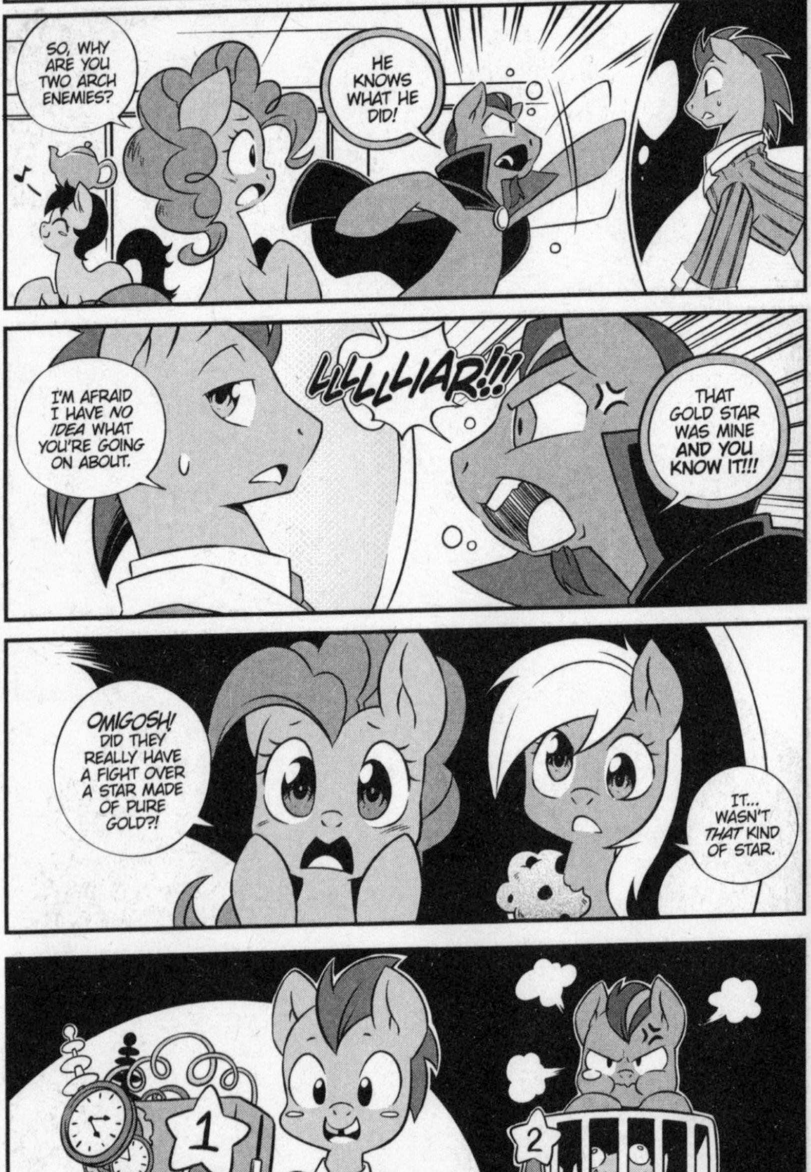
SO, WHY ARE YOU TWO ARCH ENEMIES?
HE KNOWS WHAT HE DID!
I'M AFRAID I HAVE *NO IDEA* WHAT YOU'RE GOING ON ABOUT.
LLLLLLIAR!!!
THAT GOLD STAR WAS MINE AND YOU KNOW IT!!!
OMIGOSH! DID THEY REALLY HAVE A FIGHT OVER A STAR MADE OF PURE GOLD?!
IT... WASN'T *THAT* KIND OF STAR.
1
2

Miffed at Math

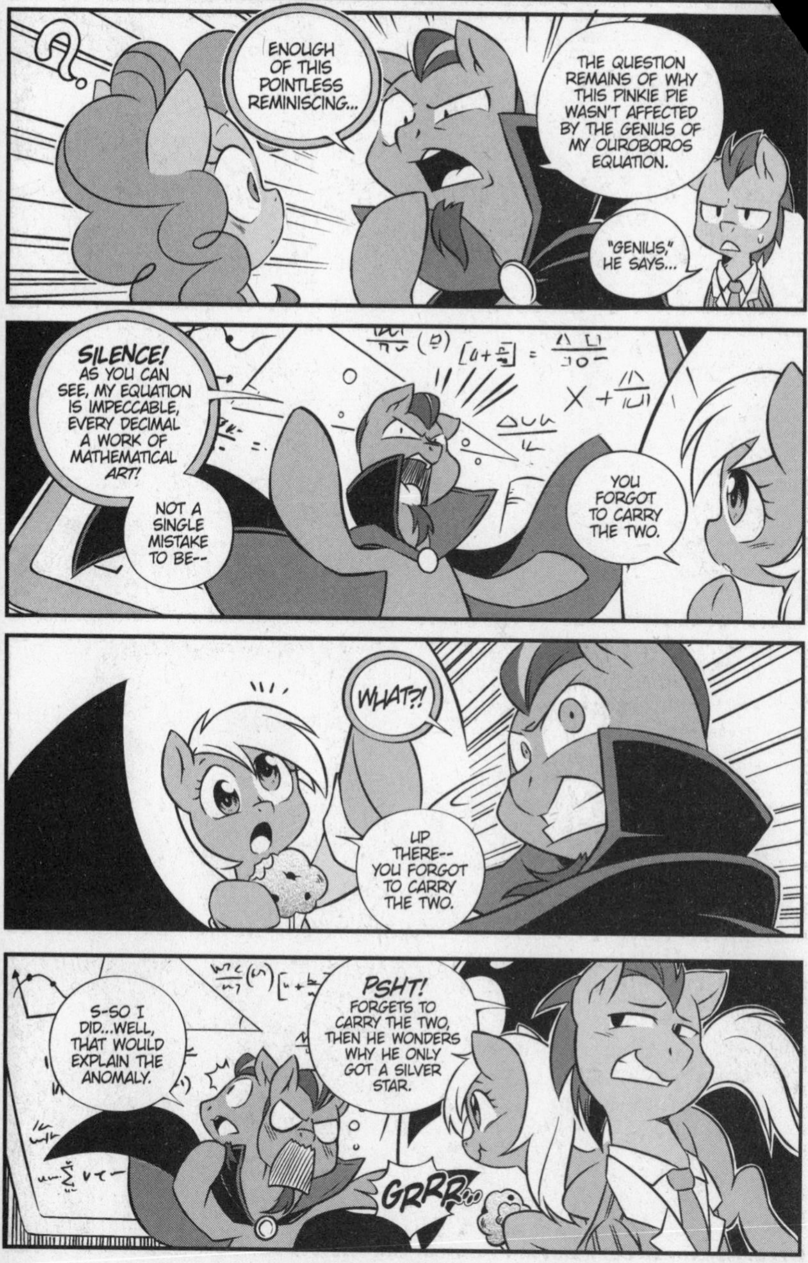

ENOUGH OF THIS POINTLESS REMINISCING...
THE QUESTION REMAINS OF WHY THIS PINKIE PIE WASN'T AFFECTED BY THE GENIUS OF MY OUROBOROS EQUATION.
"GENIUS," HE SAYS...
SILENCE! AS YOU CAN SEE, MY EQUATION IS IMPECCABLE, EVERY DECIMAL A WORK OF MATHEMATICAL ART!
NOT A SINGLE MISTAKE TO BE--
YOU FORGOT TO CARRY THE TWO.
WHAT?!
UP THERE-- YOU FORGOT TO CARRY THE TWO.
S-SO I DID...WELL, THAT WOULD EXPLAIN THE ANOMALY.
PSHT! FORGETS TO CARRY THE TWO, THEN HE WONDERS WHY HE ONLY GOT A SILVER STAR.
GRRR...

Hooves to Blame?!

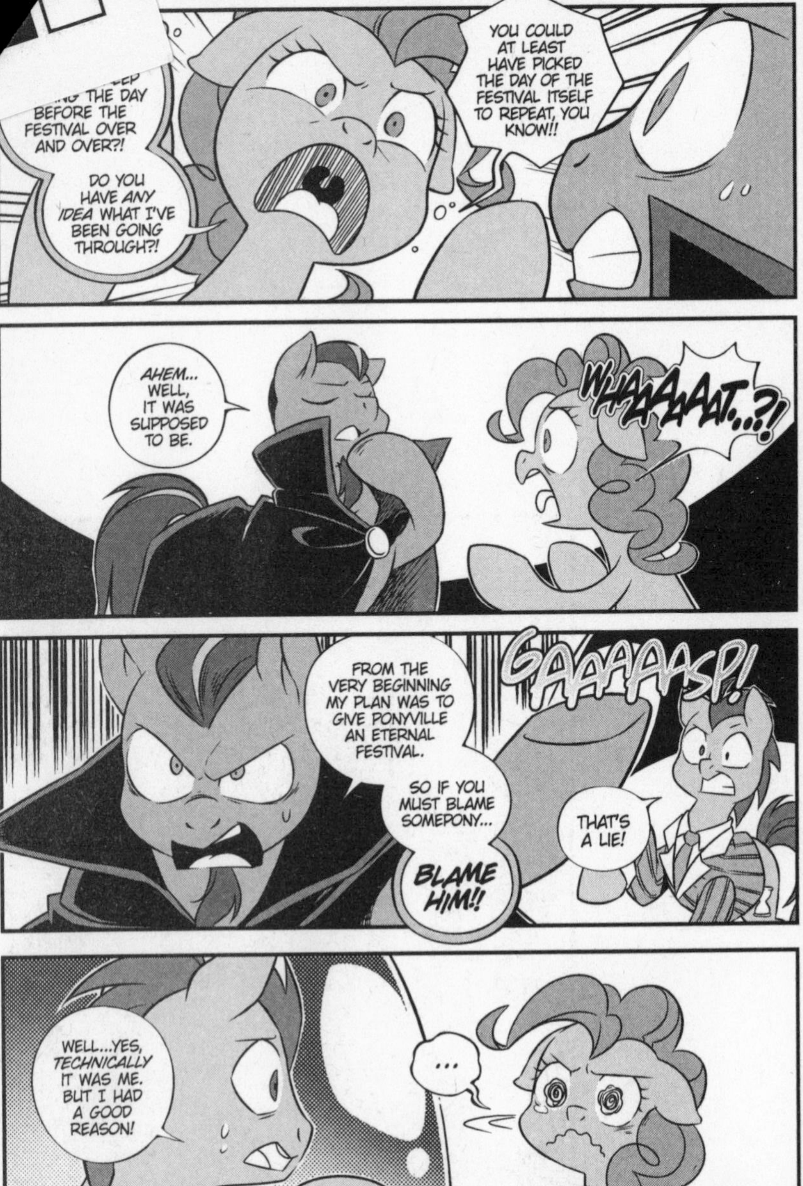
THE DAY BEFORE THE FESTIVAL OVER AND OVER?!
DO YOU HAVE *ANY IDEA* WHAT I'VE BEEN GOING THROUGH?!
YOU COULD AT LEAST HAVE PICKED THE DAY OF THE FESTIVAL ITSELF TO REPEAT, YOU KNOW!!
AHEM... WELL, IT WAS SUPPOSED TO BE.
WHAAAAAAT...?!
FROM THE VERY BEGINNING MY PLAN WAS TO GIVE PONYVILLE AN ETERNAL FESTIVAL.
GAAAAASP!
SO IF YOU MUST BLAME SOMEPONY...
BLAME HIM!!
THAT'S A LIE!
WELL...YES, *TECHNICALLY* IT WAS ME. BUT I HAD A GOOD REASON!
...

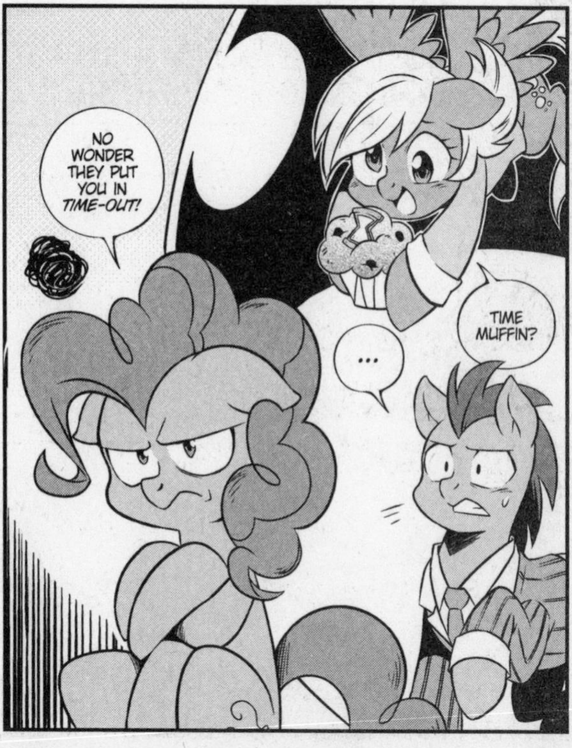
NO WONDER THEY PUT YOU IN *TIME-OUT!*
TIME MUFFIN?
...

CHAPTER 7

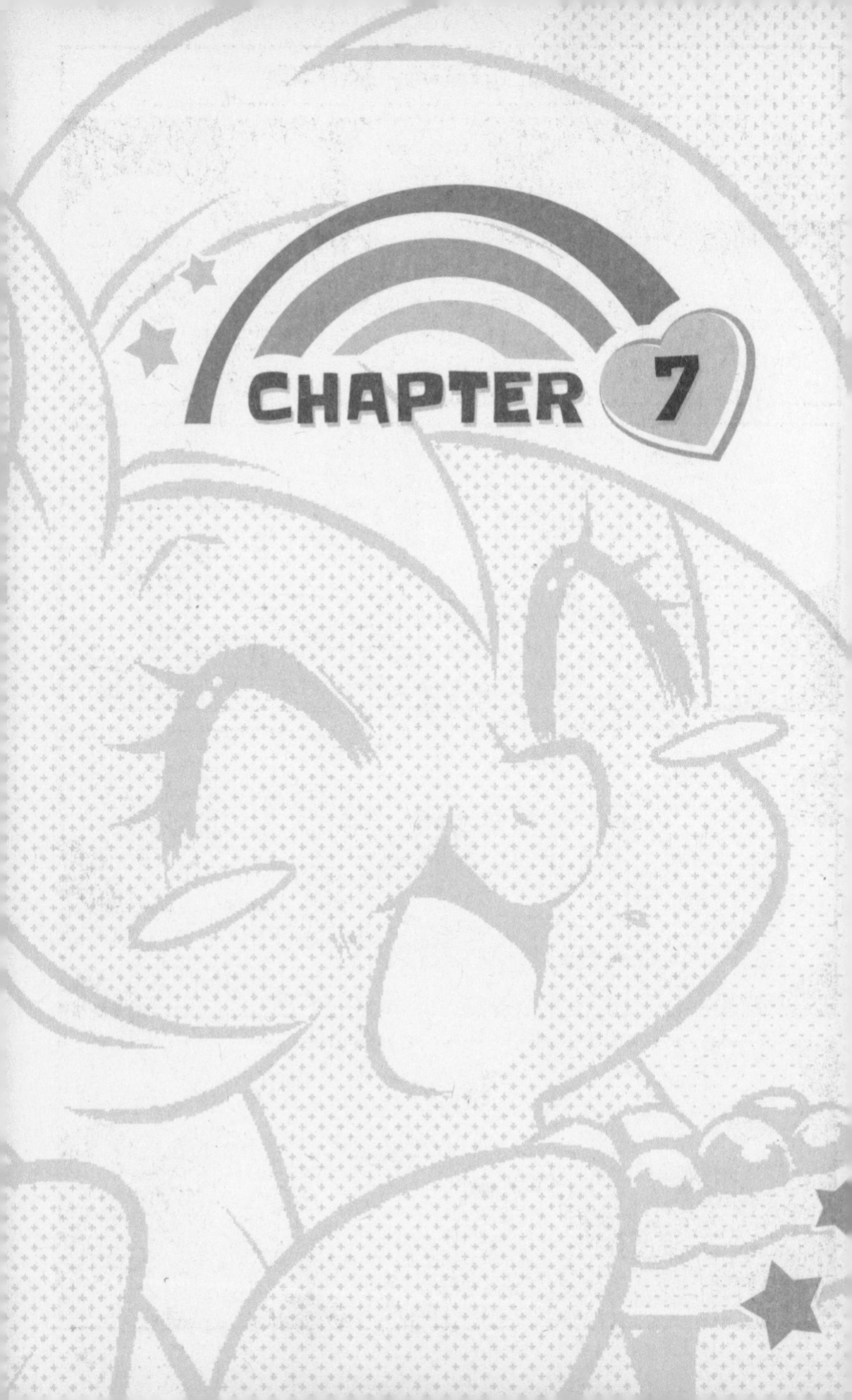

Mine, Mine, Mine!

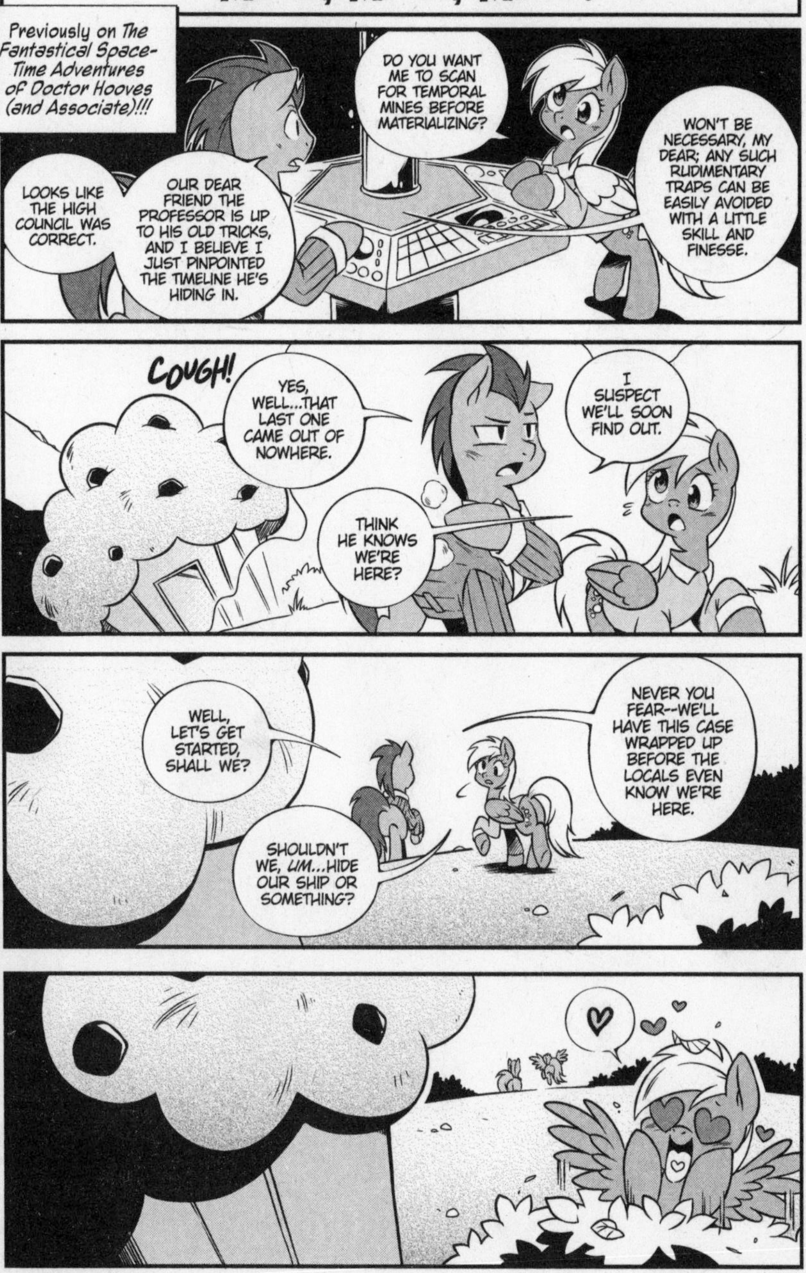
Previously on *The Fantastical Space-Time Adventures of Doctor Hooves (and Associate)*!!!
LOOKS LIKE THE HIGH COUNCIL WAS CORRECT.
OUR DEAR FRIEND THE PROFESSOR IS UP TO HIS OLD TRICKS, AND I BELIEVE I JUST PINPOINTED THE TIMELINE HE'S HIDING IN.
DO YOU WANT ME TO SCAN FOR TEMPORAL MINES BEFORE MATERIALIZING?
WON'T BE NECESSARY, MY DEAR; ANY SUCH RUDIMENTARY TRAPS CAN BE EASILY AVOIDED WITH A LITTLE SKILL AND FINESSE.
COUGH!
YES, WELL...THAT LAST ONE CAME OUT OF NOWHERE.
THINK HE KNOWS WE'RE HERE?
I SUSPECT WE'LL SOON FIND OUT.
WELL, LET'S GET STARTED, SHALL WE?
SHOULDN'T WE, *UM*...HIDE OUR SHIP OR SOMETHING?
NEVER YOU FEAR--WE'LL HAVE THIS CASE WRAPPED UP BEFORE THE LOCALS EVEN KNOW WE'RE HERE.
♥

New Ton o' Trouble

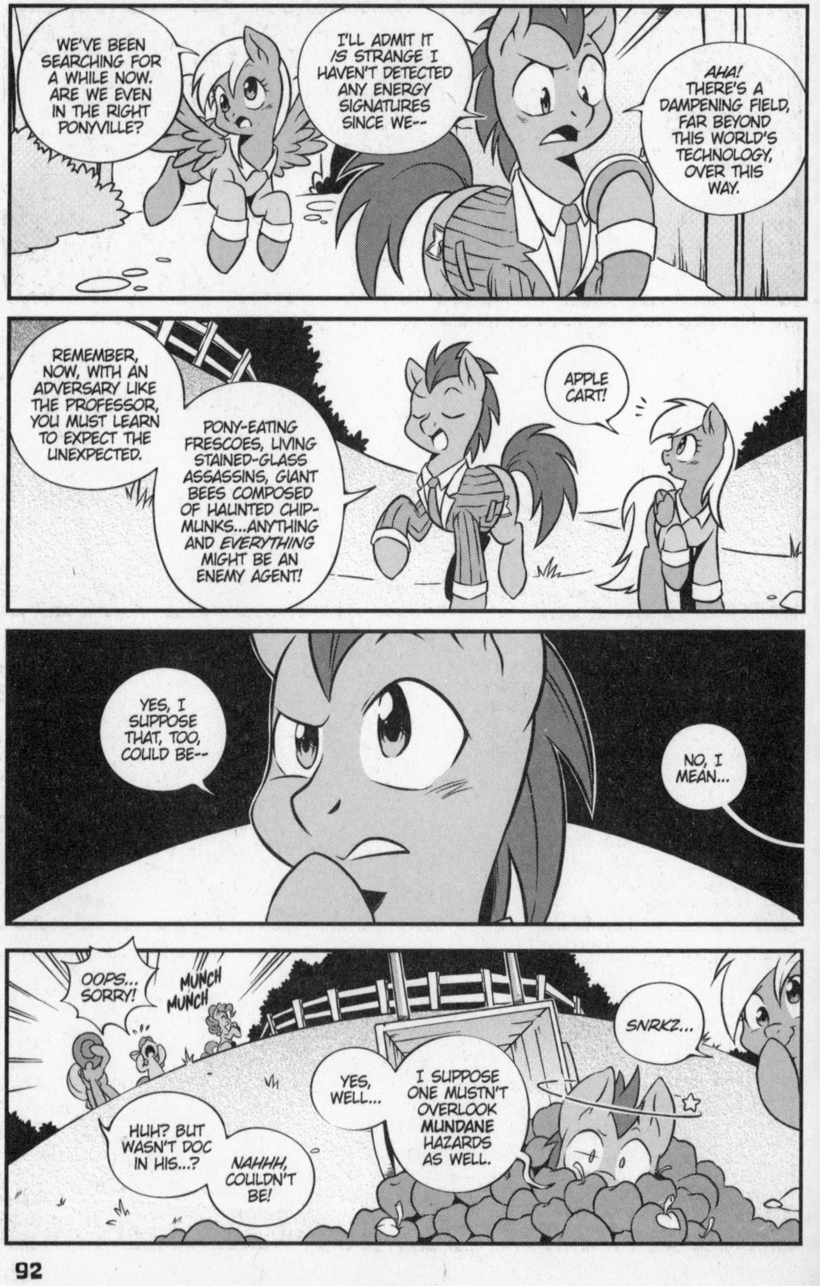
WE'VE BEEN SEARCHING FOR A WHILE NOW. ARE WE EVEN IN THE RIGHT PONYVILLE?
I'LL ADMIT IT *IS* STRANGE I HAVEN'T DETECTED ANY ENERGY SIGNATURES SINCE WE--
AHA! THERE'S A DAMPENING FIELD, FAR BEYOND THIS WORLD'S TECHNOLOGY, OVER THIS WAY.
REMEMBER, NOW, WITH AN ADVERSARY LIKE THE PROFESSOR, YOU MUST LEARN TO EXPECT THE UNEXPECTED.
PONY-EATING FRESCOES, LIVING STAINED-GLASS ASSASSINS, GIANT BEES COMPOSED OF HAUNTED CHIP-MUNKS...ANYTHING AND *EVERYTHING* MIGHT BE AN ENEMY AGENT!
APPLE CART!
YES, I SUPPOSE THAT, TOO, COULD BE--
NO, I MEAN...
OOPS... SORRY!
MUNCH MUNCH
HUH? BUT WASN'T DOC IN HIS...?
NAHHH, COULDN'T BE!
YES, WELL...
I SUPPOSE ONE MUSTN'T OVERLOOK **MUNDANE** HAZARDS AS WELL.
SNRKZ...

Muffinfiltrate

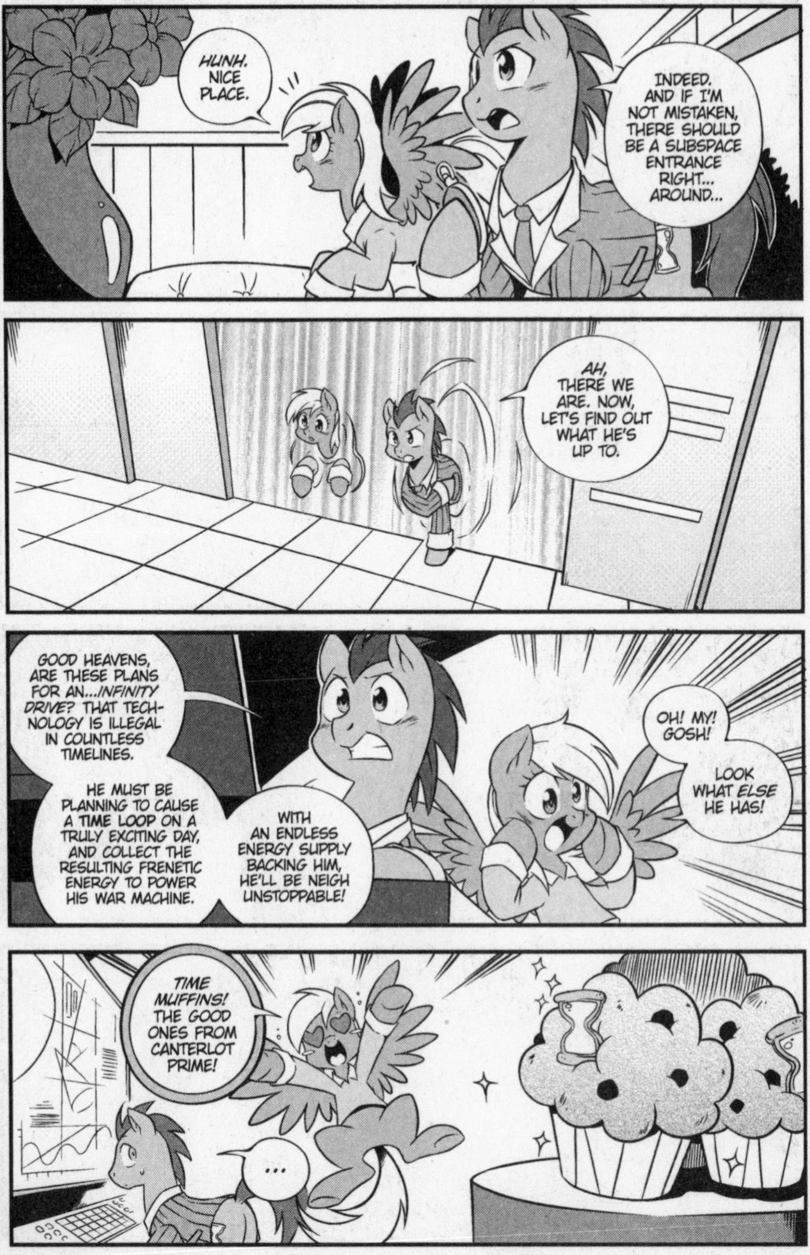
HUNH. NICE PLACE.
INDEED. AND IF I'M NOT MISTAKEN, THERE SHOULD BE A SUBSPACE ENTRANCE RIGHT... AROUND...
AH, THERE WE ARE. NOW, LET'S FIND OUT WHAT HE'S UP TO.
GOOD HEAVENS, ARE THESE PLANS FOR AN...INFINITY DRIVE? THAT TECHNOLOGY IS ILLEGAL IN COUNTLESS TIMELINES.
HE MUST BE PLANNING TO CAUSE A TIME LOOP ON A TRULY EXCITING DAY, AND COLLECT THE RESULTING FRENETIC ENERGY TO POWER HIS WAR MACHINE.
WITH AN ENDLESS ENERGY SUPPLY BACKING HIM, HE'LL BE NEIGH UNSTOPPABLE!
OH! MY! GOSH!
LOOK WHAT ELSE HE HAS!
TIME MUFFINS! THE GOOD ONES FROM CANTERLOT PRIME!
...

Gone Pinkie Gone

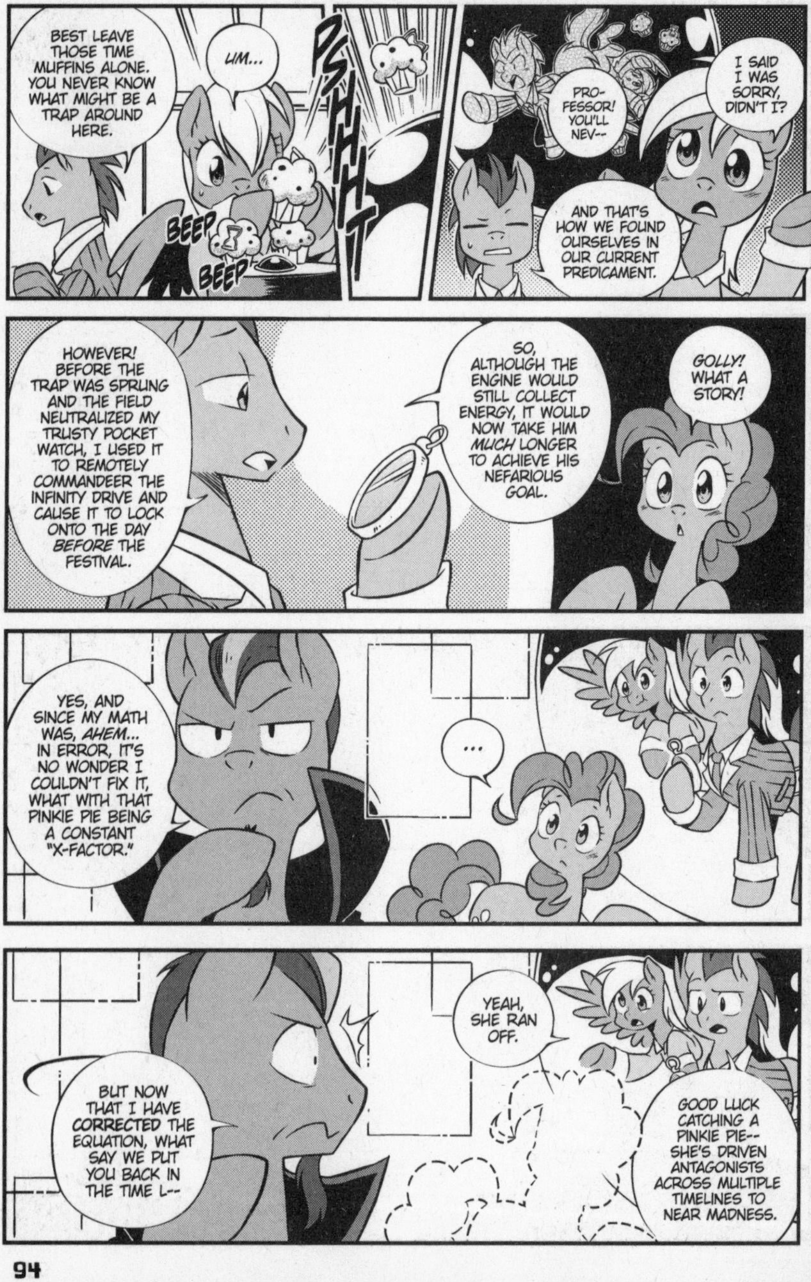

BEST LEAVE THOSE TIME MUFFINS ALONE. YOU NEVER KNOW WHAT MIGHT BE A TRAP AROUND HERE.
UM...
BEEP
BEEP
PSHHHHT
PRO-FESSOR! YOU'LL NEV--
I SAID I WAS SORRY, DIDN'T I?
AND THAT'S HOW WE FOUND OURSELVES IN OUR CURRENT PREDICAMENT.
HOWEVER! BEFORE THE TRAP WAS SPRUNG AND THE FIELD NEUTRALIZED MY TRUSTY POCKET WATCH, I USED IT TO REMOTELY COMMANDEER THE INFINITY DRIVE AND CAUSE IT TO LOCK ONTO THE DAY *BEFORE* THE FESTIVAL.
SO, ALTHOUGH THE ENGINE WOULD STILL COLLECT ENERGY, IT WOULD NOW TAKE HIM *MUCH* LONGER TO ACHIEVE HIS NEFARIOUS GOAL.
GOLLY! WHAT A STORY!
YES, AND SINCE MY MATH WAS, *AHEM*... IN ERROR, IT'S NO WONDER I COULDN'T FIX IT, WHAT WITH THAT PINKIE PIE BEING A CONSTANT "X-FACTOR."
...
BUT NOW THAT I HAVE **CORRECTED** THE EQUATION, WHAT SAY WE PUT YOU BACK IN THE TIME L--
YEAH, SHE RAN OFF.
GOOD LUCK CATCHING A PINKIE PIE-- SHE'S DRIVEN ANTAGONISTS ACROSS MULTIPLE TIMELINES TO NEAR MADNESS.

Timely Warning

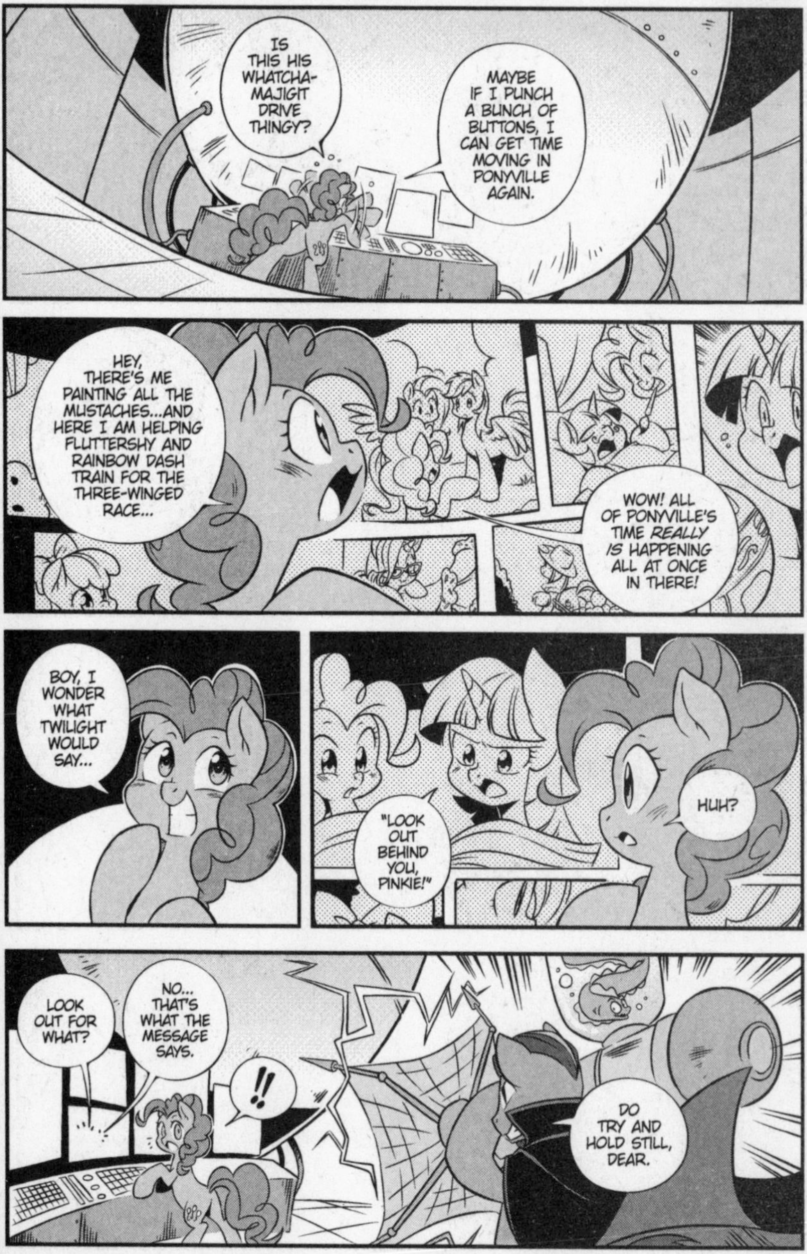

IS THIS HIS WHATCHA-MAJIGIT DRIVE THINGY?
MAYBE IF I PUNCH A BUNCH OF BUTTONS, I CAN GET TIME MOVING IN PONYVILLE AGAIN.
HEY, THERE'S ME PAINTING ALL THE MUSTACHES...AND HERE I AM HELPING FLUTTERSHY AND RAINBOW DASH TRAIN FOR THE THREE-WINGED RACE...
WOW! ALL OF PONYVILLE'S TIME *REALLY* *IS* HAPPENING ALL AT ONCE IN THERE!
BOY, I WONDER WHAT TWILIGHT WOULD SAY...
"LOOK OUT BEHIND YOU, PINKIE!"
HUH?
LOOK OUT FOR WHAT?
NO... THAT'S WHAT THE MESSAGE SAYS.
!!
DO TRY AND HOLD STILL, DEAR.

A Net Loss

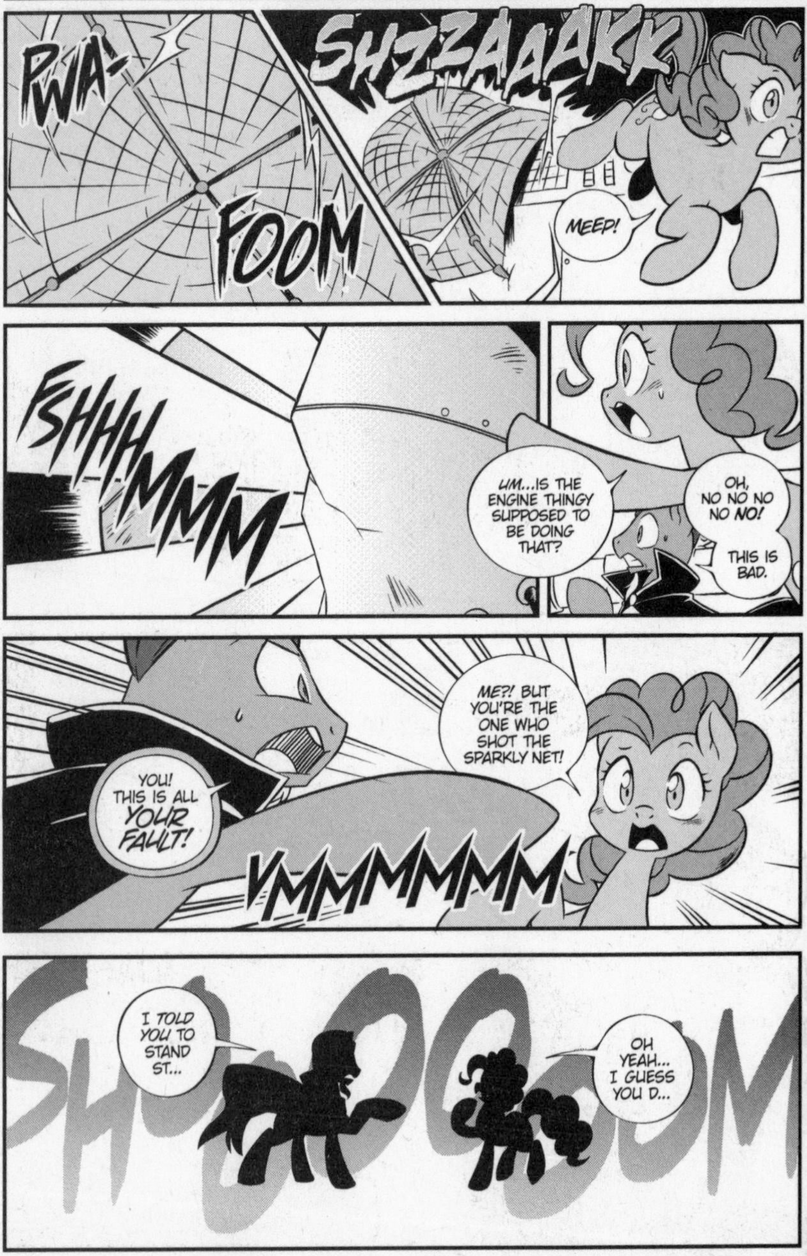
PWA-
FOOM
SHZZAAAKK
MEEP!
FSHHHMMMM
UM...IS THE ENGINE THINGY SUPPOSED TO BE DOING THAT?
OH, NO NO NO NO NO!
THIS IS BAD.
YOU! THIS IS ALL YOUR FAULT!
ME?! BUT YOU'RE THE ONE WHO SHOT THE SPARKLY NET!
VMMMMMMM
I TOLD YOU TO STAND ST...
OH YEAH... I GUESS YOU D...

Tea'd Off

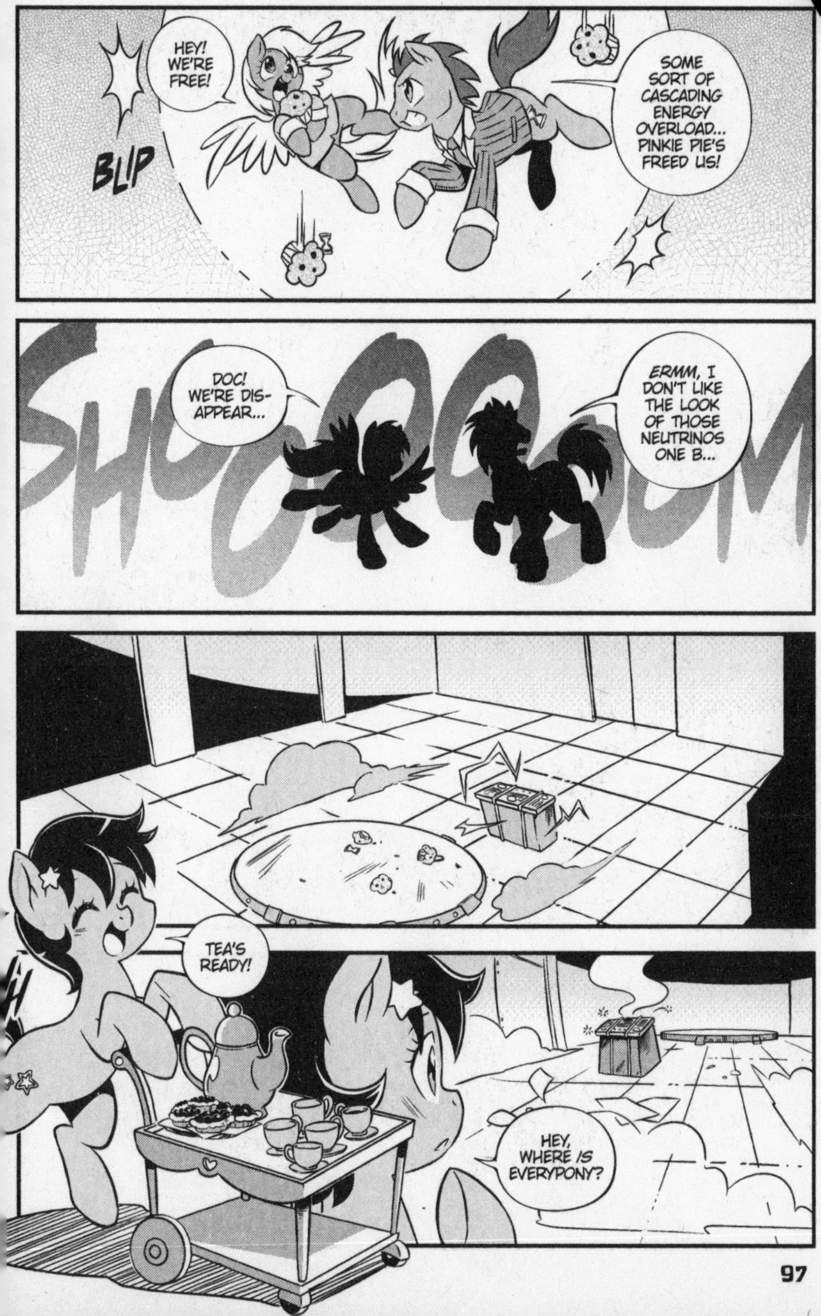
HEY! WE'RE FREE!
BLIP
SOME SORT OF CASCADING ENERGY OVERLOAD... PINKIE PIE'S FREED US!
SHOOOOOM
DOC! WE'RE DIS-APPEAR...
ERMM, I DON'T LIKE THE LOOK OF THOSE NEUTRINOS ONE B...
TEA'S READY!
HEY, WHERE IS EVERYPONY?

Off-the-Cuff Planning

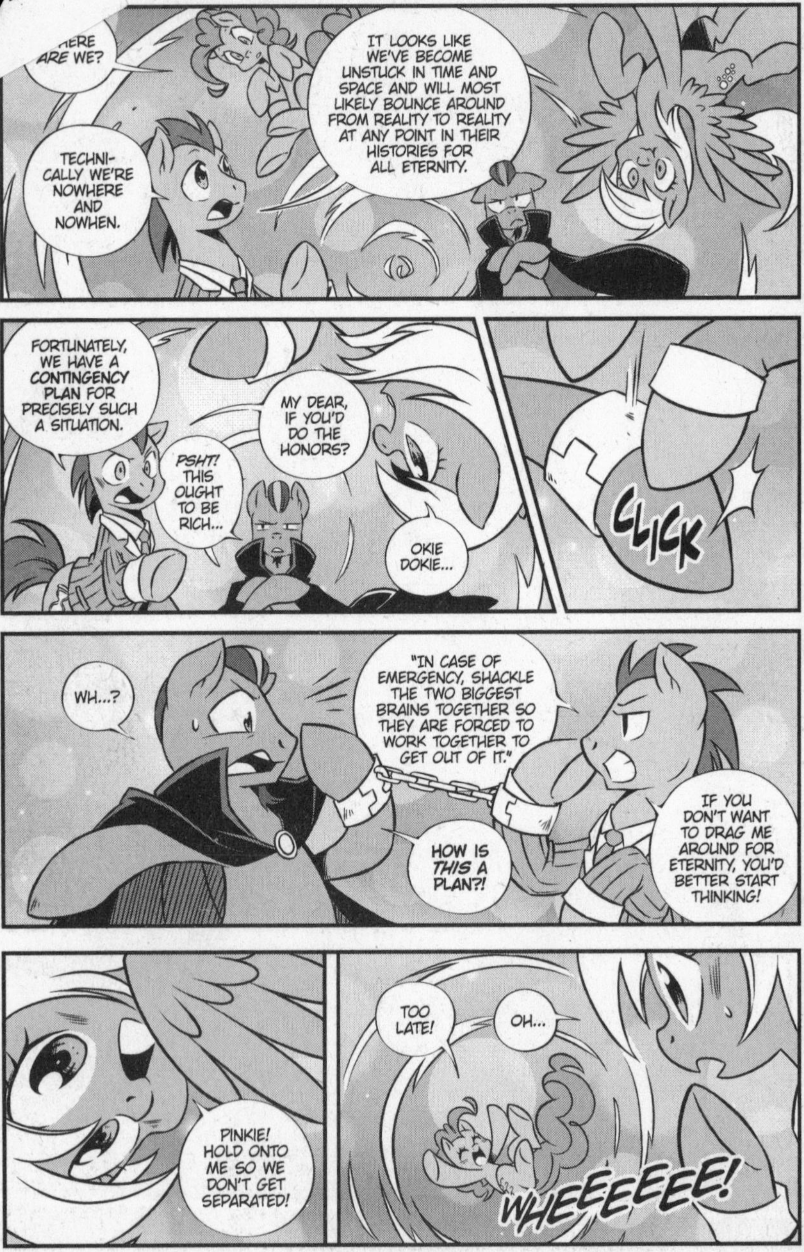

HERE ARE WE?
TECHNICALLY WE'RE NOWHERE AND NOWHEN.
IT LOOKS LIKE WE'VE BECOME UNSTUCK IN TIME AND SPACE AND WILL MOST LIKELY BOUNCE AROUND FROM REALITY TO REALITY AT ANY POINT IN THEIR HISTORIES FOR ALL ETERNITY.
FORTUNATELY, WE HAVE A CONTINGENCY PLAN FOR PRECISELY SUCH A SITUATION.
MY DEAR, IF YOU'D DO THE HONORS?
PSHT! THIS OUGHT TO BE RICH...
OKIE DOKIE...
CLICK
WH...?
"IN CASE OF EMERGENCY, SHACKLE THE TWO BIGGEST BRAINS TOGETHER SO THEY ARE FORCED TO WORK TOGETHER TO GET OUT OF IT."
HOW IS THIS A PLAN?!
IF YOU DON'T WANT TO DRAG ME AROUND FOR ETERNITY, YOU'D BETTER START THINKING!
PINKIE! HOLD ONTO ME SO WE DON'T GET SEPARATED!
TOO LATE!
OH...
WHEEEEEEE!

Cutting Remarks

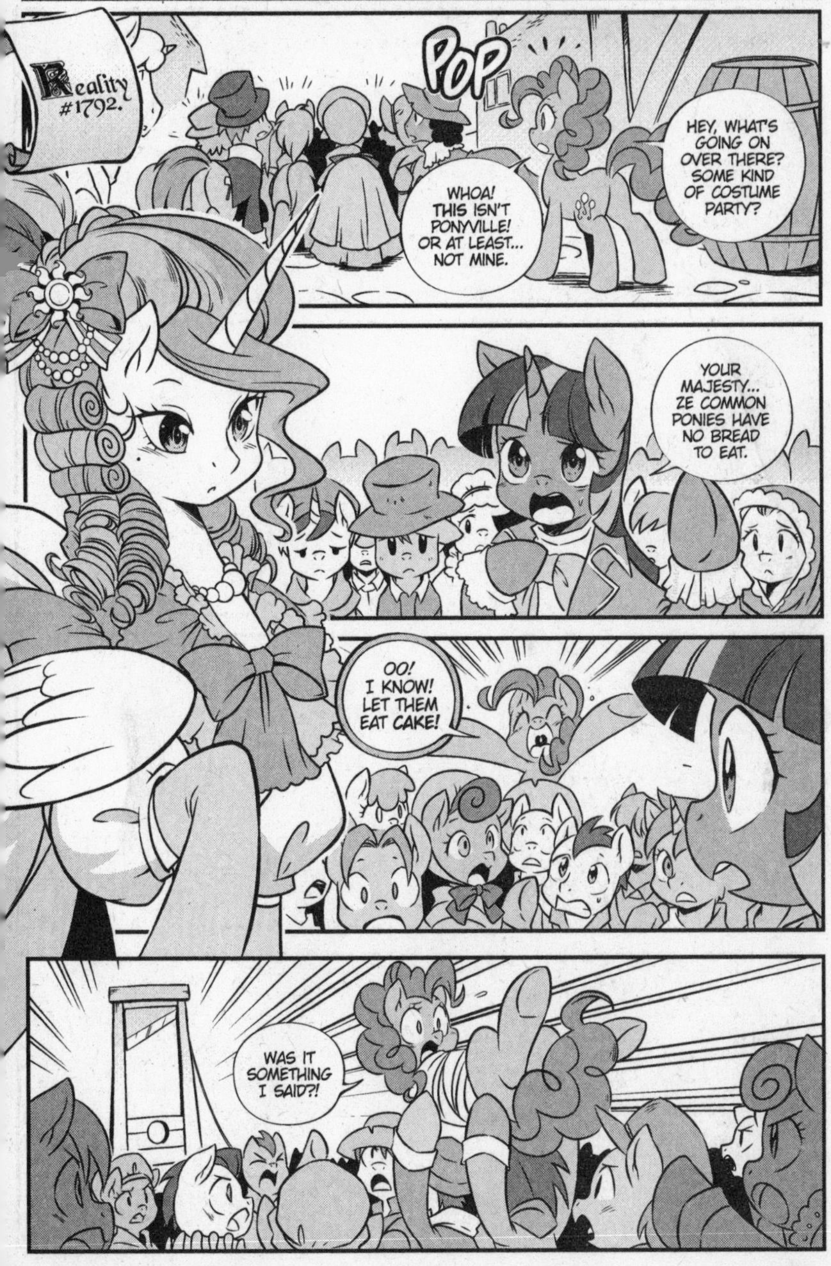
Reality #1792.
POP
WHOA! THIS ISN'T PONYVILLE! OR AT LEAST... NOT MINE.
HEY, WHAT'S GOING ON OVER THERE? SOME KIND OF COSTUME PARTY?
YOUR MAJESTY... ZE COMMON PONIES HAVE NO BREAD TO EAT.
OO! I KNOW! LET THEM EAT CAKE!
WAS IT SOMETHING I SAID?!

A Tiny Problem

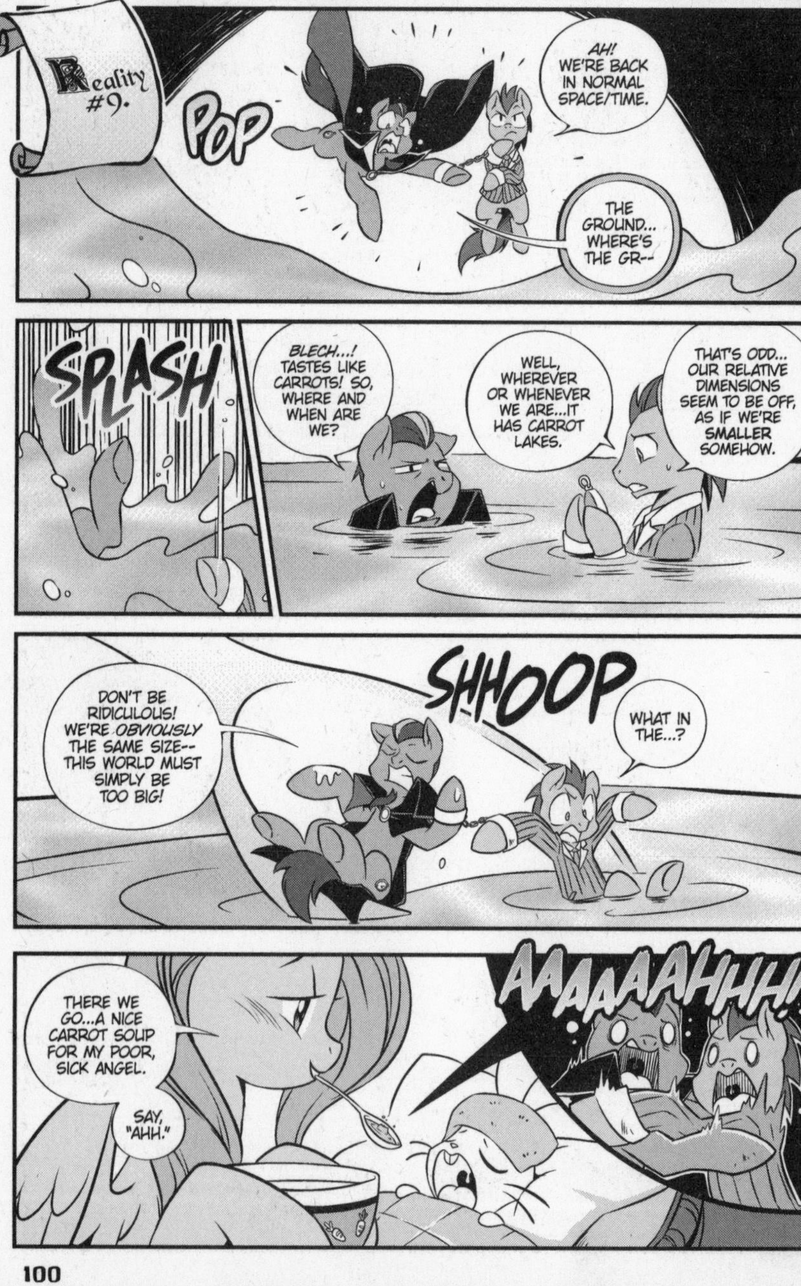

Reality #9.
POP
AH! WE'RE BACK IN NORMAL SPACE/TIME.
THE GROUND... WHERE'S THE GR--
SPLASH
BLECH...! TASTES LIKE CARROTS! SO, WHERE AND WHEN ARE WE?
WELL, WHEREVER OR WHENEVER WE ARE...IT HAS CARROT LAKES.
THAT'S ODD... OUR RELATIVE DIMENSIONS SEEM TO BE OFF, AS IF WE'RE SMALLER SOMEHOW.
DON'T BE RIDICULOUS! WE'RE OBVIOUSLY THE SAME SIZE-- THIS WORLD MUST SIMPLY BE TOO BIG!
SHHOOP
WHAT IN THE...?
THERE WE GO...A NICE CARROT SOUP FOR MY POOR, SICK ANGEL.
SAY, "AHH."
AAAAAAHHH!

You're Gonna Flip

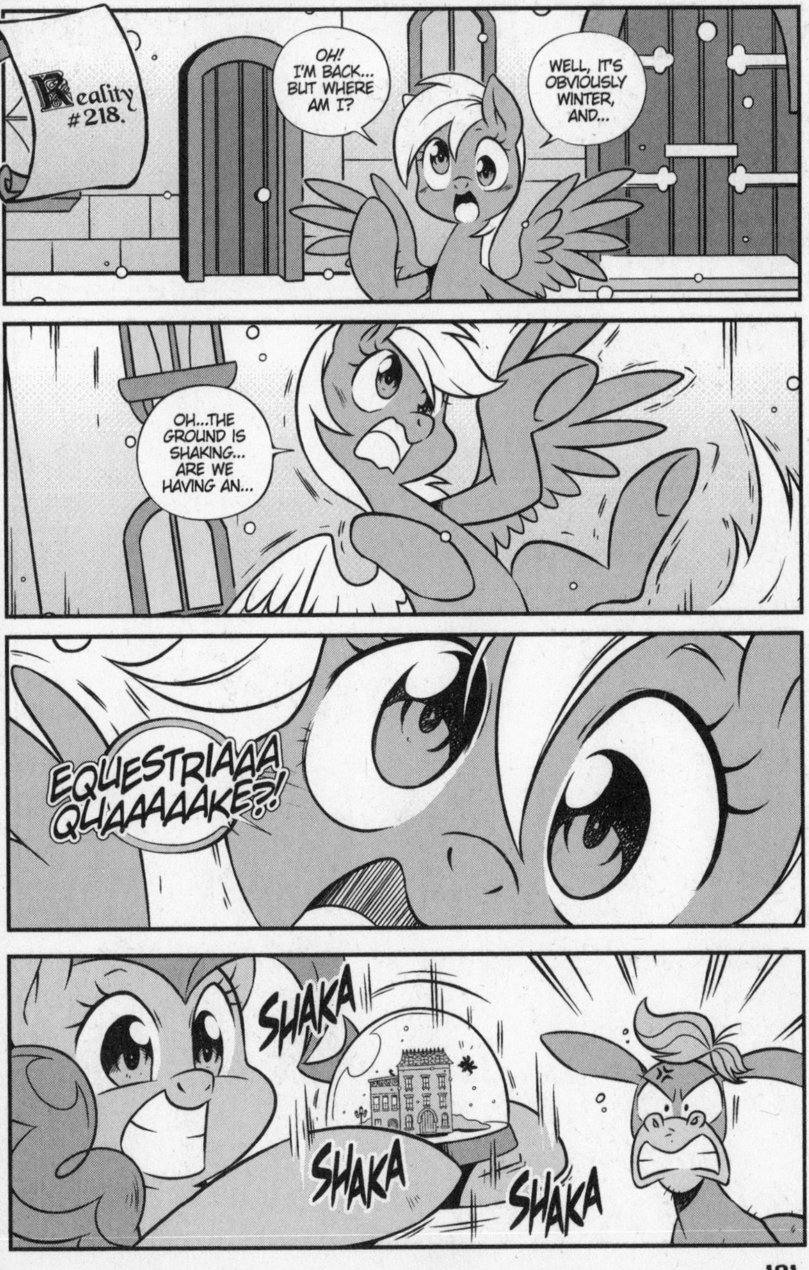
Reality #218.
OH! I'M BACK... BUT WHERE AM I?
WELL, IT'S OBVIOUSLY WINTER, AND...
OH...THE GROUND IS SHAKING... ARE WE HAVING AN...
EQUESTRIAAA QUAAAAAKE?!
SHAKA
SHAKA
SHAKA

Hardly a Reason to Lose Your Head

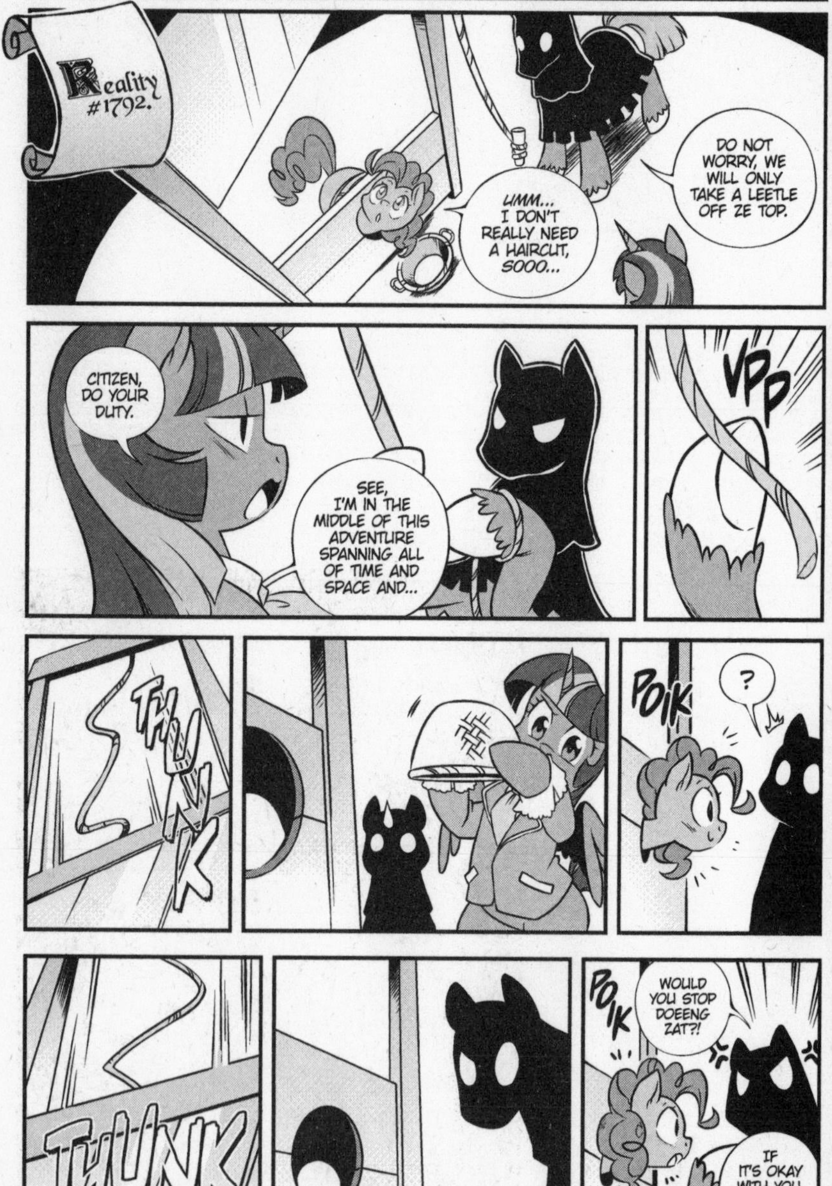
Reality #1792.
UMM... I DON'T REALLY NEED A HAIRCUT, SOOO...
DO NOT WORRY, WE WILL ONLY TAKE A LEETLE OFF ZE TOP.
CITIZEN, DO YOUR DUTY.
SEE, I'M IN THE MIDDLE OF THIS ADVENTURE SPANNING ALL OF TIME AND SPACE AND...
VPP
THUNK
POIK
?
THUNK
POIK
WOULD YOU STOP DOEENG ZAT?!
IF IT'S OKAY WITH YOU, I'D REALLY RATHER NOT!

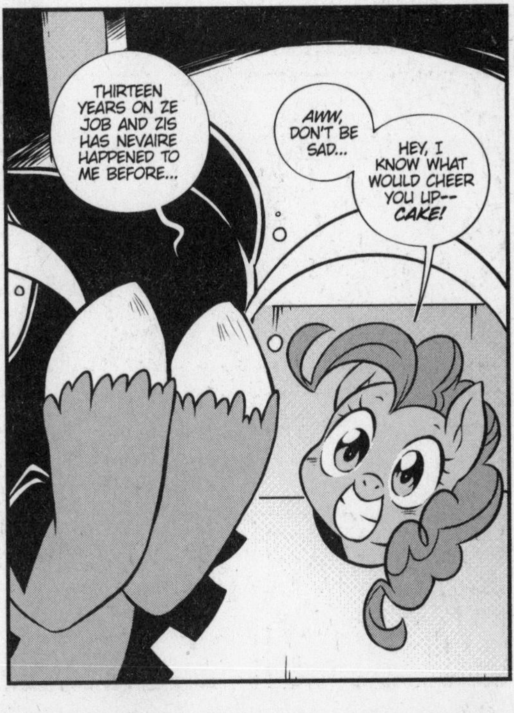
THIRTEEN YEARS ON ZE JOB AND ZIS HAS NEVAIRE HAPPENED TO ME BEFORE...
AWW, DON'T BE SAD...
HEY, I KNOW WHAT WOULD CHEER YOU UP-- CAKE!

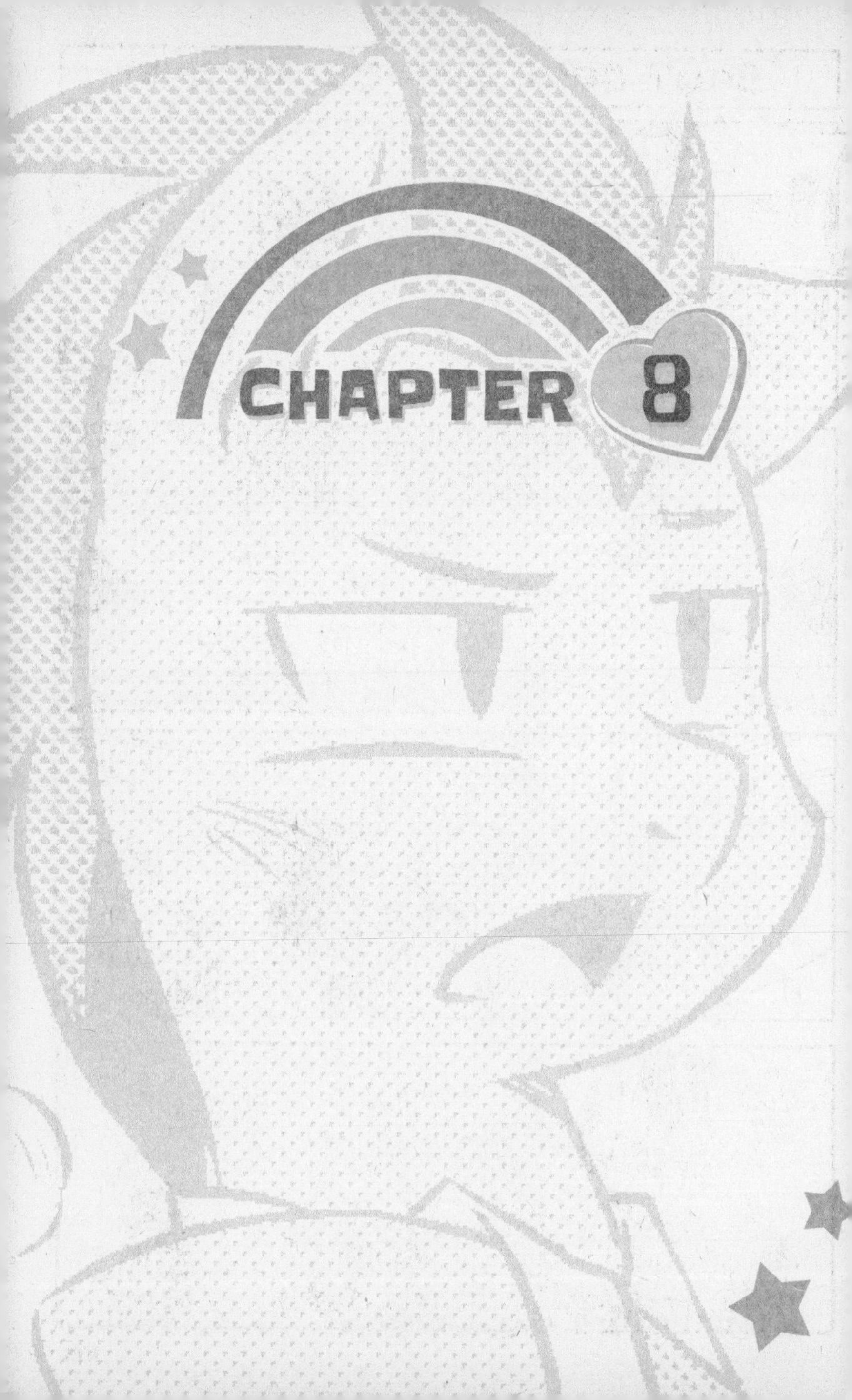
CHAPTER 8

You'll Get a Kick Out of This!

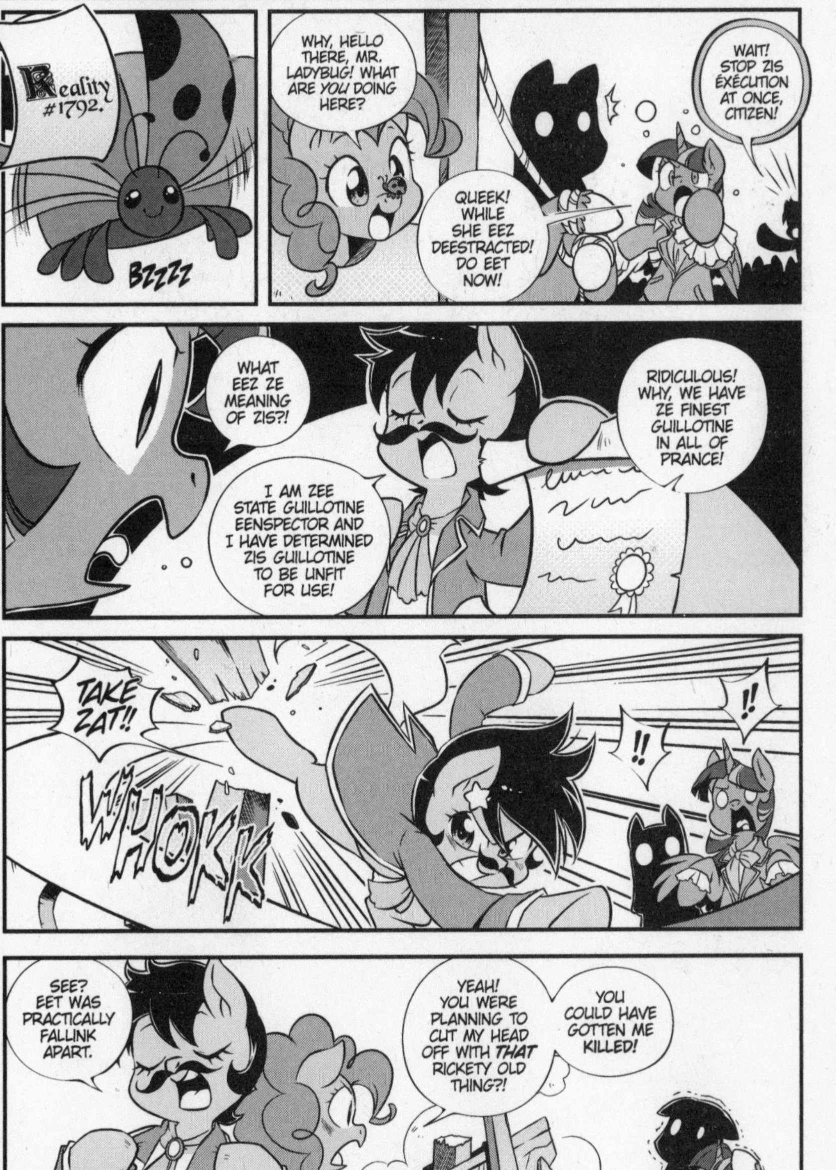

Reality #1792.
BZZZZ
WHY, HELLO THERE, MR. LADYBUG! WHAT ARE *YOU* DOING HERE?
WAIT! STOP ZIS ÉXECUTION AT ONCE, CITIZEN!
QUEEK! WHILE SHE EEZ DEESTRACTED! DO EET NOW!
WHAT EEZ ZE MEANING OF ZIS?!
I AM ZEE STATE GUILLOTINE EENSPECTOR AND I HAVE DETERMINED ZIS GUILLOTINE TO BE UNFIT FOR USE!
RIDICULOUS! WHY, WE HAVE ZE FINEST GUILLOTINE IN ALL OF PRANCE!
TAKE ZAT!!
WHOKK
!!
!!
SEE? EET WAS PRACTICALLY FALLINK APART.
YEAH! YOU WERE PLANNING TO CUT MY HEAD OFF WITH *THAT* RICKETY OLD THING?!
YOU COULD HAVE GOTTEN ME KILLED!

Truth and Pies

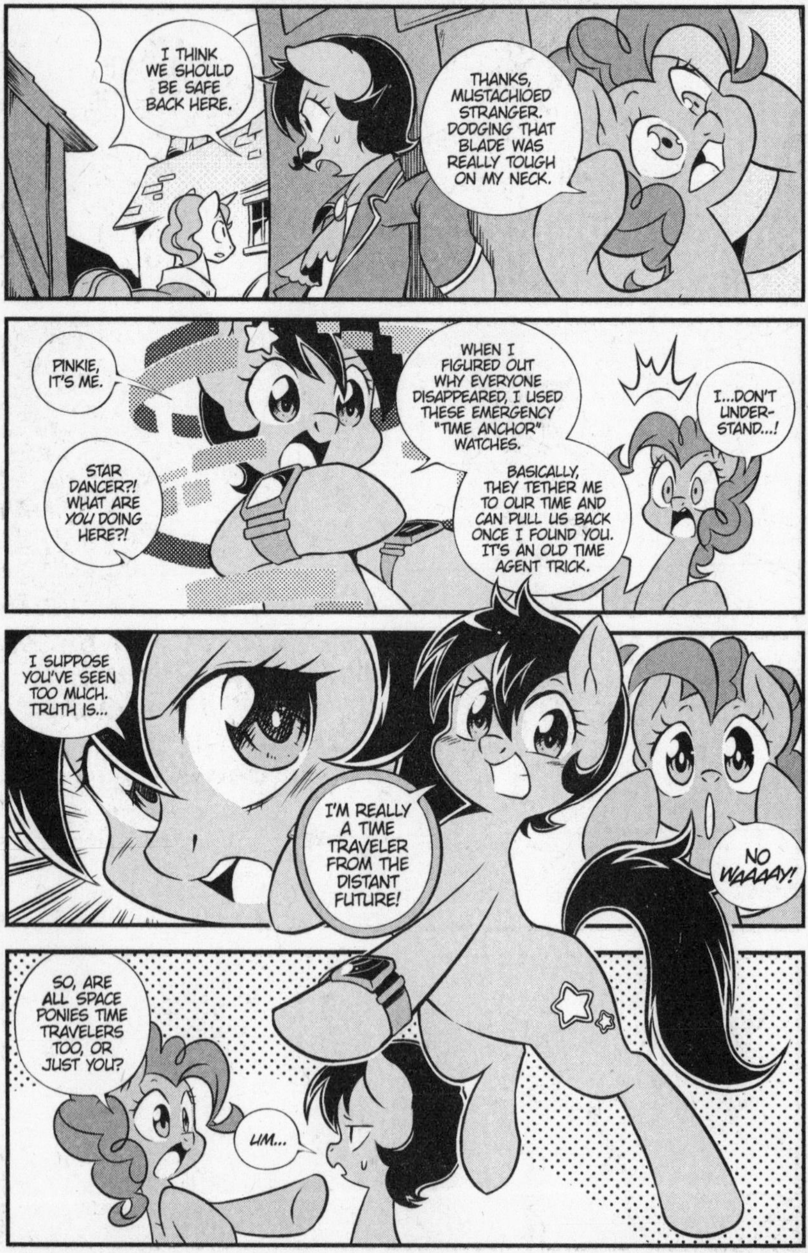

I THINK WE SHOULD BE SAFE BACK HERE.
THANKS, MUSTACHIOED STRANGER. DODGING THAT BLADE WAS REALLY TOUGH ON MY NECK.
PINKIE, IT'S ME.
STAR DANCER?! WHAT ARE *YOU* DOING HERE?!
WHEN I FIGURED OUT WHY EVERYONE DISAPPEARED, I USED THESE EMERGENCY "TIME ANCHOR" WATCHES.
BASICALLY, THEY TETHER ME TO OUR TIME AND CAN PULL US BACK ONCE I FOUND YOU. IT'S AN OLD TIME AGENT TRICK.
I...DON'T UNDER-STAND...!
I SUPPOSE YOU'VE SEEN TOO MUCH. TRUTH IS...
I'M REALLY A TIME TRAVELER FROM THE DISTANT FUTURE!
NO *WAAAAY!*
SO, ARE ALL SPACE PONIES TIME TRAVELERS TOO, OR JUST YOU?
UM...

Watch Out!

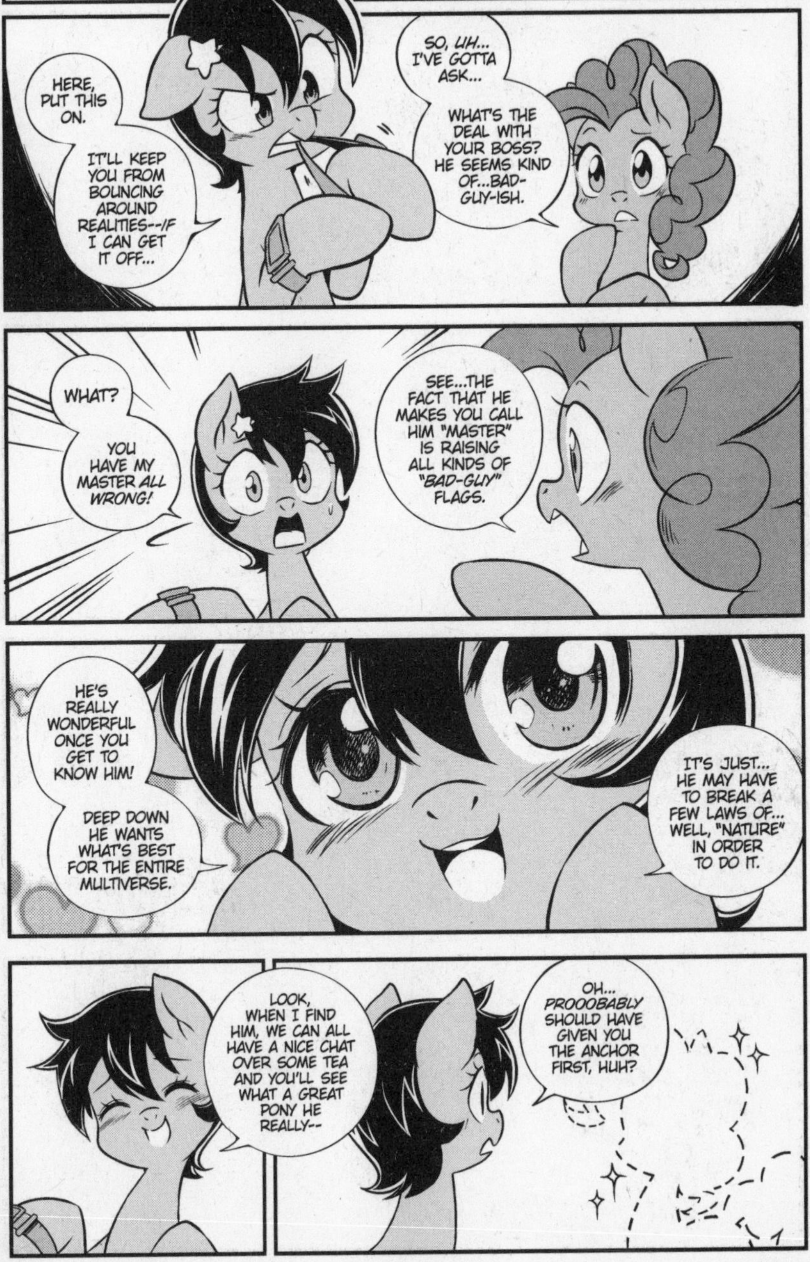
HERE, PUT THIS ON.
IT'LL KEEP YOU FROM BOUNCING AROUND REALITIES--IF I CAN GET IT OFF...
SO, UH... I'VE GOTTA ASK...
WHAT'S THE DEAL WITH YOUR BOSS? HE SEEMS KIND OF...BAD-GUY-ISH.
WHAT?
YOU HAVE MY MASTER *ALL WRONG!*
SEE...THE FACT THAT HE MAKES YOU CALL HIM "MASTER" IS RAISING ALL KINDS OF *"BAD-GUY"* FLAGS.
HE'S REALLY WONDERFUL ONCE YOU GET TO KNOW HIM!
DEEP DOWN HE WANTS WHAT'S BEST FOR THE ENTIRE MULTIVERSE.
IT'S JUST... HE MAY HAVE TO BREAK A FEW LAWS OF... WELL, "NATURE" IN ORDER TO DO IT.
LOOK, WHEN I FIND HIM, WE CAN ALL HAVE A NICE CHAT OVER SOME TEA AND YOU'LL SEE WHAT A GREAT PONY HE REALLY--
OH... *PROOOBABLY* SHOULD HAVE GIVEN YOU THE ANCHOR FIRST, HUH?

Balancing Act

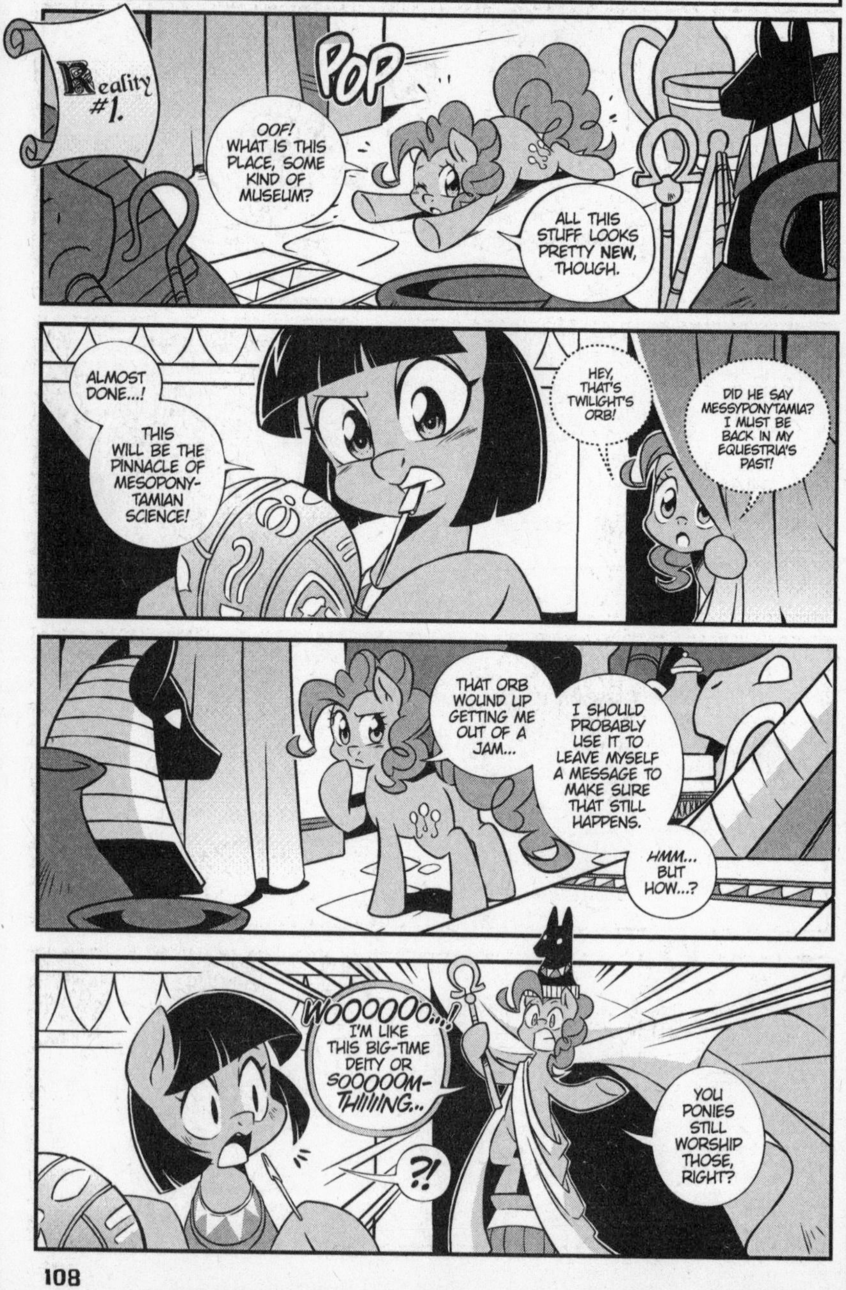
Reality #1.
POP
OOF! WHAT IS THIS PLACE, SOME KIND OF MUSEUM?
ALL THIS STUFF LOOKS PRETTY NEW, THOUGH.
ALMOST DONE...!
THIS WILL BE THE PINNACLE OF MESOPONY-TAMIAN SCIENCE!
HEY, THAT'S TWILIGHT'S ORB!
DID HE SAY MESSYPONYTAMIA? I MUST BE BACK IN MY EQUESTRIA'S PAST!
THAT ORB WOUND UP GETTING ME OUT OF A JAM...
I SHOULD PROBABLY USE IT TO LEAVE MYSELF A MESSAGE TO MAKE SURE THAT STILL HAPPENS.
HMM... BUT HOW...?
WOOOOOO...! I'M LIKE THIS BIG-TIME DEITY OR SOOOOOM-THIIIING...
?!
YOU PONIES STILL WORSHIP THOSE, RIGHT?

Prophesy Pie

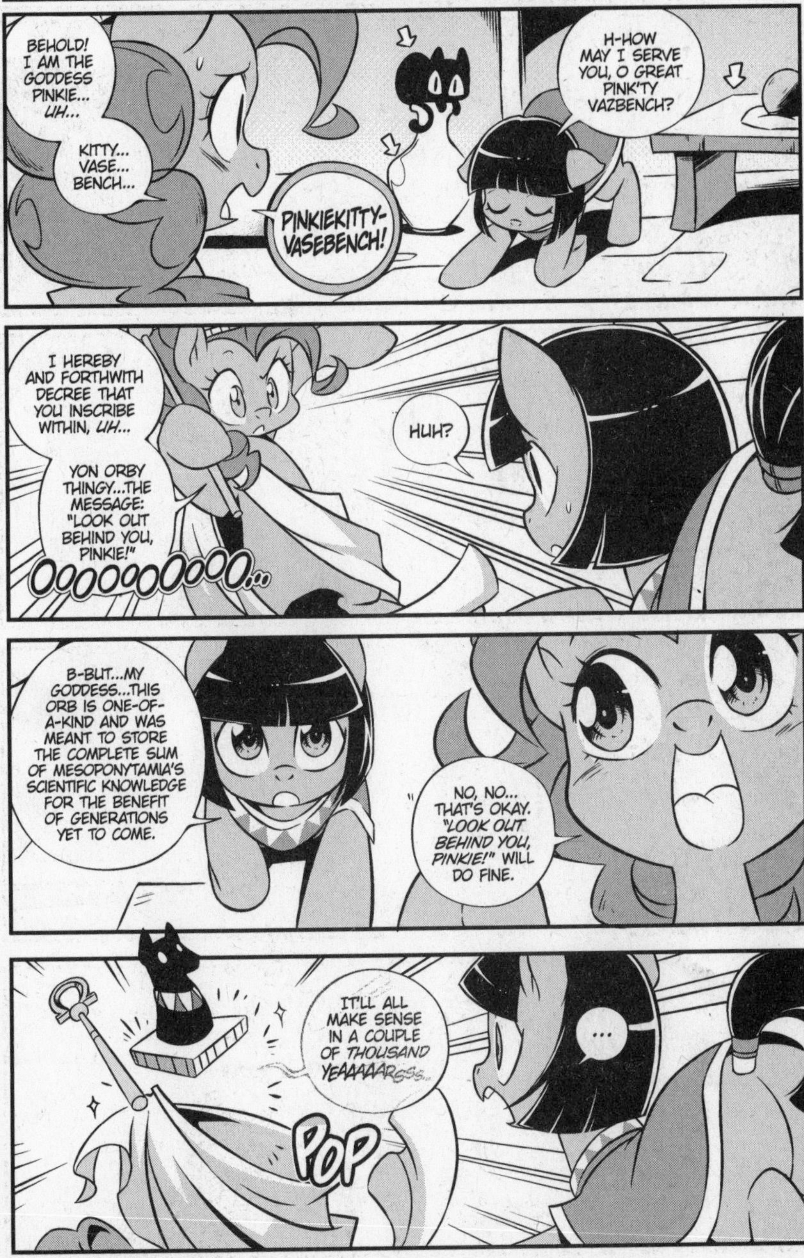

BEHOLD! I AM THE GODDESS PINKIE... UH...
KITTY... VASE... BENCH...
PINKIEKITTY-VASEBENCH!
H-HOW MAY I SERVE YOU, O GREAT PINK'TY VAZBENCH?
I HEREBY AND FORTHWITH DECREE THAT YOU INSCRIBE WITHIN, UH...
YON ORBY THINGY...THE MESSAGE: "LOOK OUT BEHIND YOU, PINKIE!"
OOOOOOOOOOO...
HUH?
B-BUT...MY GODDESS...THIS ORB IS ONE-OF-A-KIND AND WAS MEANT TO STORE THE COMPLETE SUM OF MESOPONYTAMIA'S SCIENTIFIC KNOWLEDGE FOR THE BENEFIT OF GENERATIONS YET TO COME.
NO, NO... THAT'S OKAY. "LOOK OUT BEHIND YOU, PINKIE!" WILL DO FINE.
IT'LL ALL MAKE SENSE IN A COUPLE OF THOUSAND YEAAAAARSSS...
...
POP

The Towering Time-ferno

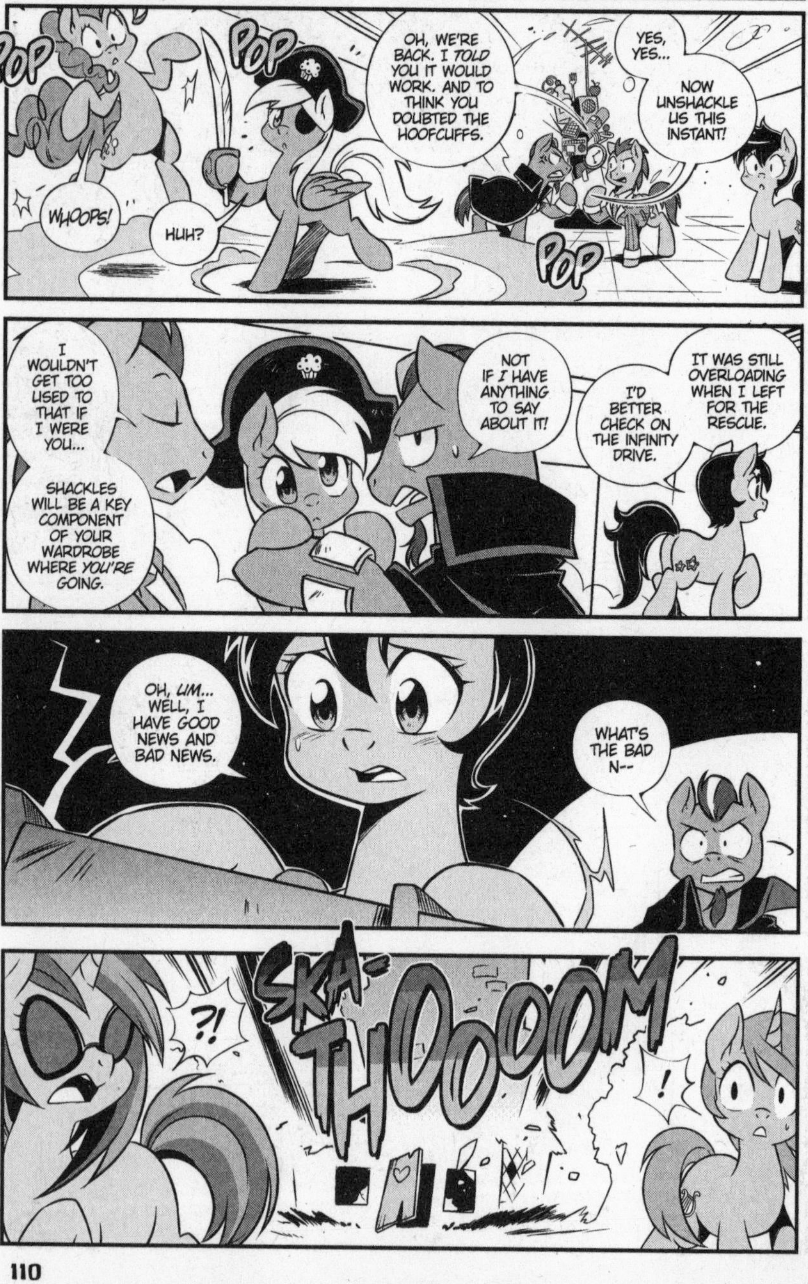
POP
POP
OH, WE'RE BACK. I *TOLD* YOU IT WOULD WORK. AND TO THINK YOU DOUBTED THE HOOFCUFFS.
YES, YES...
NOW UNSHACKLE US THIS INSTANT!
WHOOPS!
HUH?
POP
I WOULDN'T GET TOO USED TO THAT IF I WERE YOU...
SHACKLES WILL BE A KEY COMPONENT OF YOUR WARDROBE WHERE *YOU'RE* GOING.
NOT IF *I* HAVE ANYTHING TO SAY ABOUT IT!
I'D BETTER CHECK ON THE INFINITY DRIVE.
IT WAS STILL OVERLOADING WHEN I LEFT FOR THE RESCUE.
OH, UM... WELL, I HAVE GOOD NEWS AND BAD NEWS.
WHAT'S THE BAD N--
SKA-THOOOOOM
?!
!

Pie-d and Seek

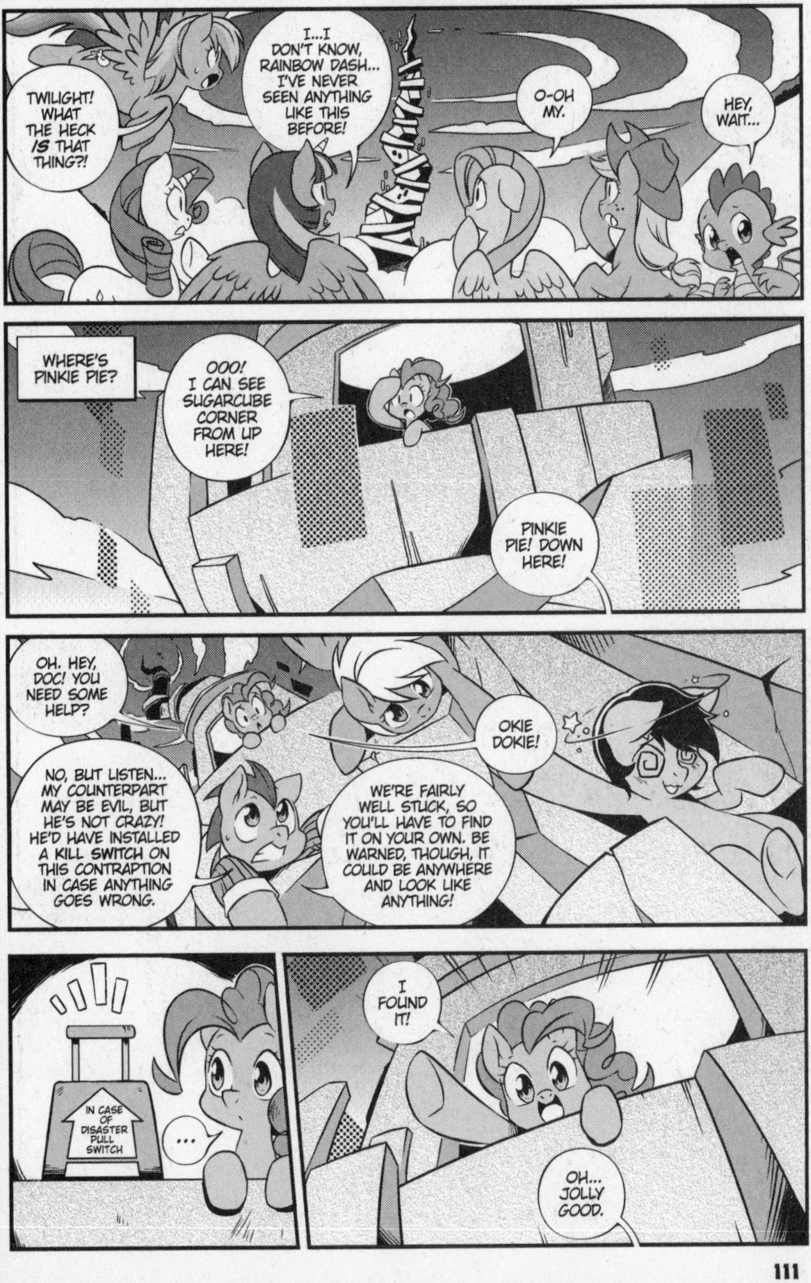
TWILIGHT! WHAT THE HECK *IS* THAT THING?!
I...I DON'T KNOW, RAINBOW DASH... I'VE NEVER SEEN ANYTHING LIKE THIS BEFORE!
O-OH MY.
HEY, WAIT...
WHERE'S PINKIE PIE?
OOO! I CAN SEE SUGARCUBE CORNER FROM UP HERE!
PINKIE PIE! DOWN HERE!
OH. HEY, DOC! YOU NEED SOME HELP?
NO, BUT LISTEN... MY COUNTERPART MAY BE EVIL, BUT HE'S NOT CRAZY! HE'D HAVE INSTALLED A KILL SWITCH ON THIS CONTRAPTION IN CASE ANYTHING GOES WRONG.
WE'RE FAIRLY WELL STUCK, SO YOU'LL HAVE TO FIND IT ON YOUR OWN. BE WARNED, THOUGH, IT COULD BE ANYWHERE AND LOOK LIKE ANYTHING!
OKIE DOKIE!
IN CASE OF DISASTER PULL SWITCH
...
I FOUND IT!
OH... JOLLY GOOD.

What an Offer

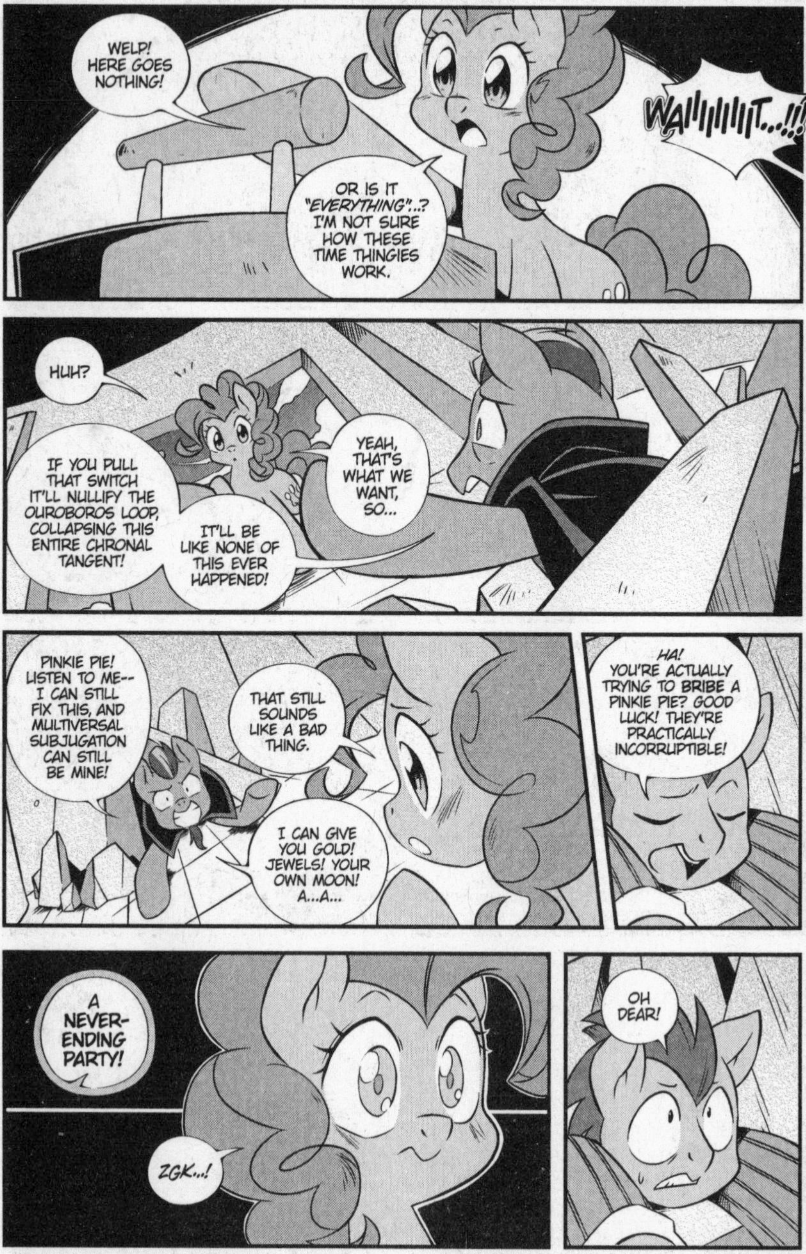
WELP! HERE GOES NOTHING!
OR IS IT "EVERYTHING"..? I'M NOT SURE HOW THESE TIME THINGIES WORK.
WAIIIIIIT..!!!
HUH?
IF YOU PULL THAT SWITCH IT'LL NULLIFY THE OUROBOROS LOOP, COLLAPSING THIS ENTIRE CHRONAL TANGENT!
YEAH, THAT'S WHAT WE WANT, SO...
IT'LL BE LIKE NONE OF THIS EVER HAPPENED!
PINKIE PIE! LISTEN TO ME-- I CAN STILL FIX THIS, AND MULTIVERSAL SUBJUGATION CAN STILL BE MINE!
THAT STILL SOUNDS LIKE A BAD THING.
I CAN GIVE YOU GOLD! JEWELS! YOUR OWN MOON! A...A...
HA! YOU'RE ACTUALLY TRYING TO BRIBE A PINKIE PIE? GOOD LUCK! THEY'RE PRACTICALLY INCORRUPTIBLE!
A NEVER-ENDING PARTY!
ZGK..!
OH DEAR!

The Last Temptatio

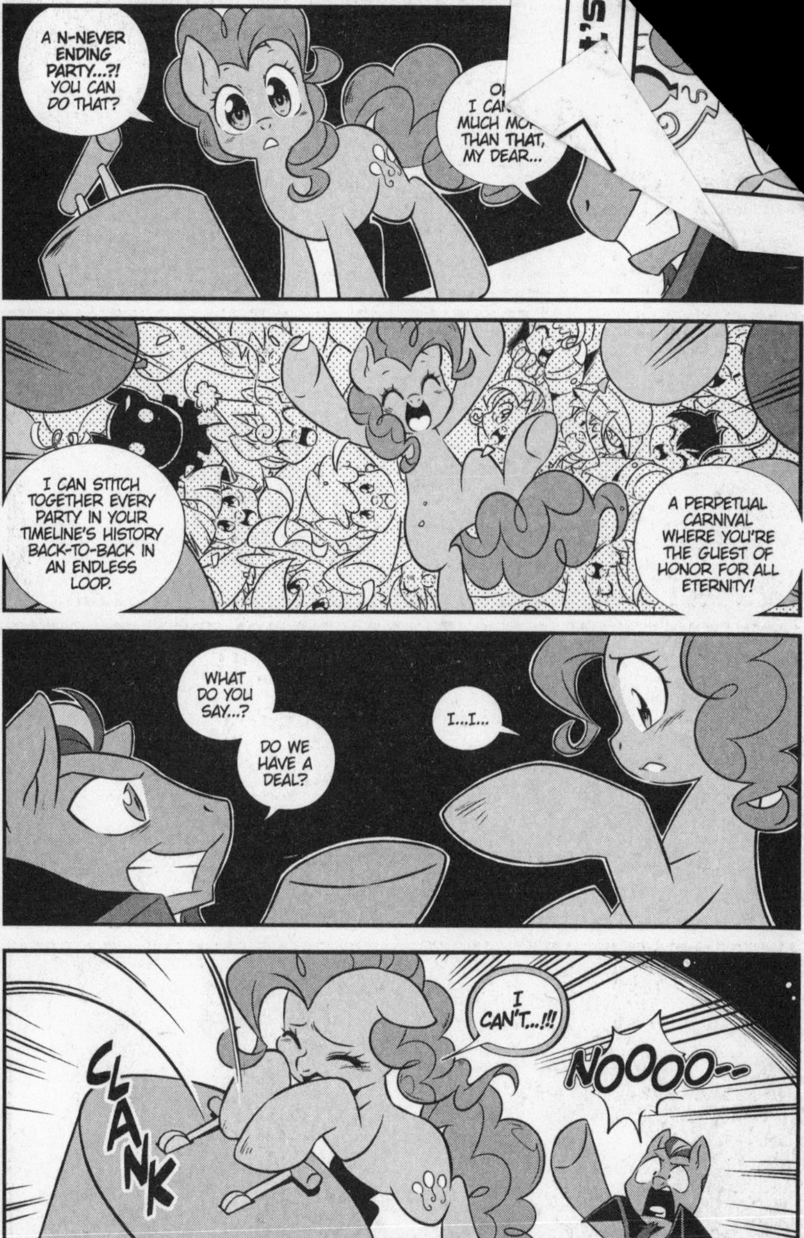

A N-NEVER ENDING PARTY...?! YOU CAN DO THAT?
O I CAN MUCH MO THAN THAT, MY DEAR...
I CAN STITCH TOGETHER EVERY PARTY IN YOUR TIMELINE'S HISTORY BACK-TO-BACK IN AN ENDLESS LOOP.
A PERPETUAL CARNIVAL WHERE YOU'RE THE GUEST OF HONOR FOR ALL ETERNITY!
WHAT DO YOU SAY...?
DO WE HAVE A DEAL?
I...I...
I CAN'T...!!!
CLANK
NOOOO--

[redacted] Hard to Say Good-Pie

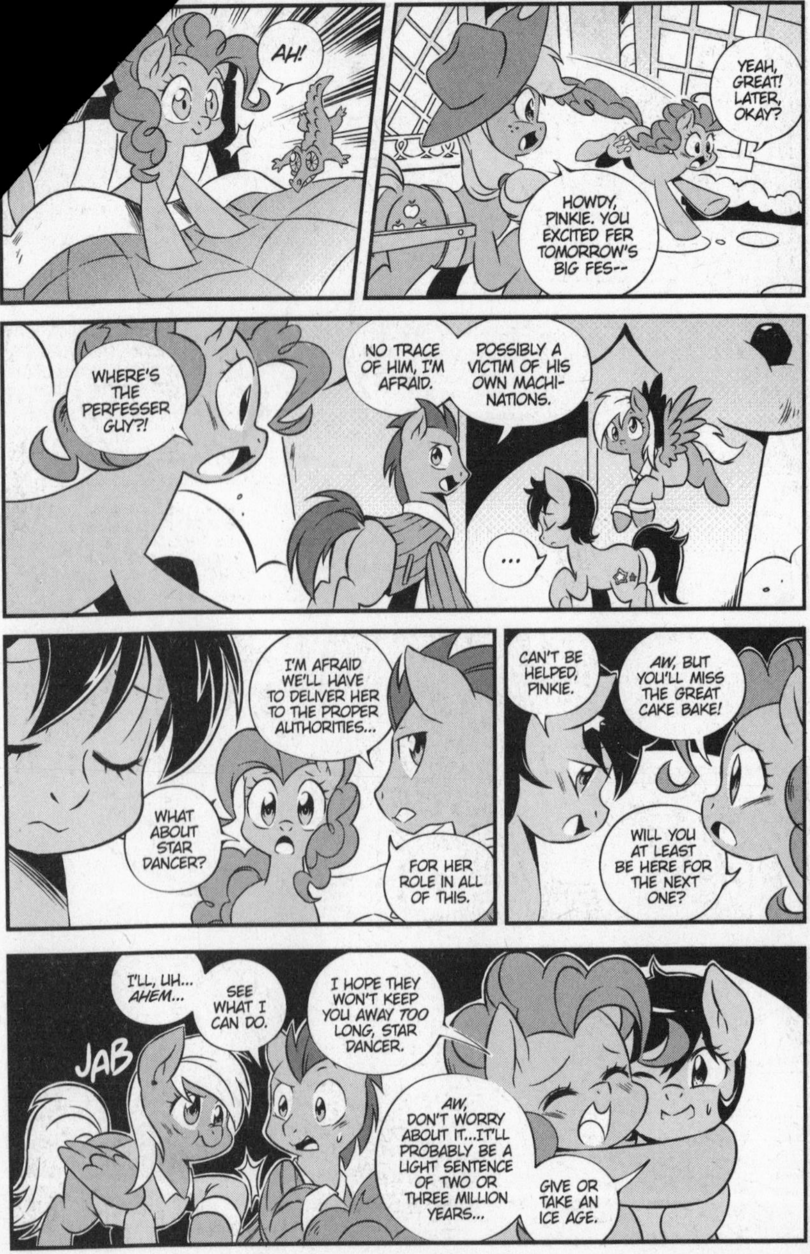
AH!
HOWDY, PINKIE. YOU EXCITED FER TOMORROW'S BIG FES--
YEAH, GREAT! LATER, OKAY?
WHERE'S THE PERFESSER GUY?!
NO TRACE OF HIM, I'M AFRAID.
POSSIBLY A VICTIM OF HIS OWN MACHI-NATIONS.
...
WHAT ABOUT STAR DANCER?
I'M AFRAID WE'LL HAVE TO DELIVER HER TO THE PROPER AUTHORITIES...
FOR HER ROLE IN ALL OF THIS.
CAN'T BE HELPED, PINKIE.
AW, BUT YOU'LL MISS THE GREAT CAKE BAKE!
WILL YOU AT LEAST BE HERE FOR THE NEXT ONE?
I'LL, UH... AHEM...
SEE WHAT I CAN DO.
JAB
I HOPE THEY WON'T KEEP YOU AWAY TOO LONG, STAR DANCER.
AW, DON'T WORRY ABOUT IT...IT'LL PROBABLY BE A LIGHT SENTENCE OF TWO OR THREE MILLION YEARS...
GIVE OR TAKE AN ICE AGE.

Jailfake

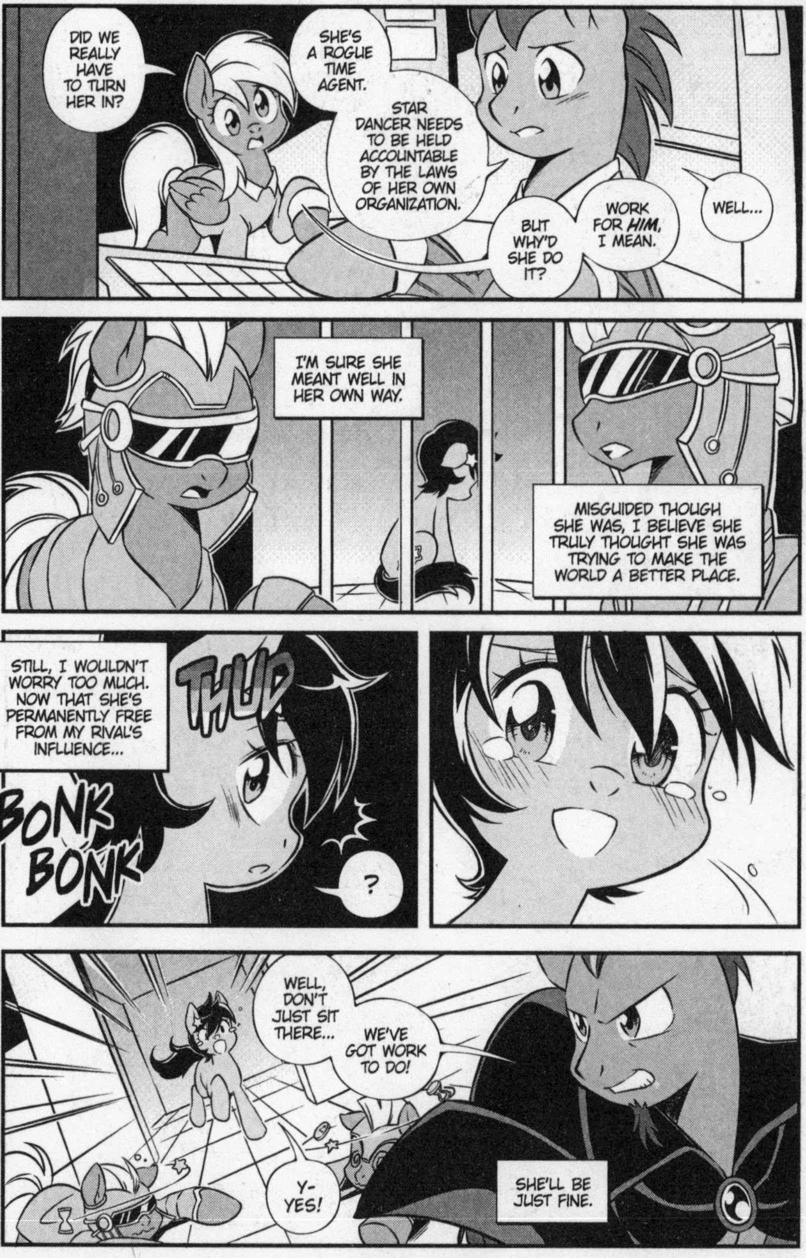
DID WE REALLY HAVE TO TURN HER IN?
SHE'S A ROGUE TIME AGENT.
STAR DANCER NEEDS TO BE HELD ACCOUNTABLE BY THE LAWS OF HER OWN ORGANIZATION.
BUT WHY'D SHE DO IT?
WORK FOR *HIM*, I MEAN.
WELL...
I'M SURE SHE MEANT WELL IN HER OWN WAY.
MISGUIDED THOUGH SHE WAS, I BELIEVE SHE TRULY THOUGHT SHE WAS TRYING TO MAKE THE WORLD A BETTER PLACE.
STILL, I WOULDN'T WORRY TOO MUCH. NOW THAT SHE'S PERMANENTLY FREE FROM MY RIVAL'S INFLUENCE...
THUD
BONK
BONK
?
WELL, DON'T JUST SIT THERE...
WE'VE GOT WORK TO DO!
Y-YES!
SHE'LL BE JUST FINE.

Sleeping Like an Epi-Log

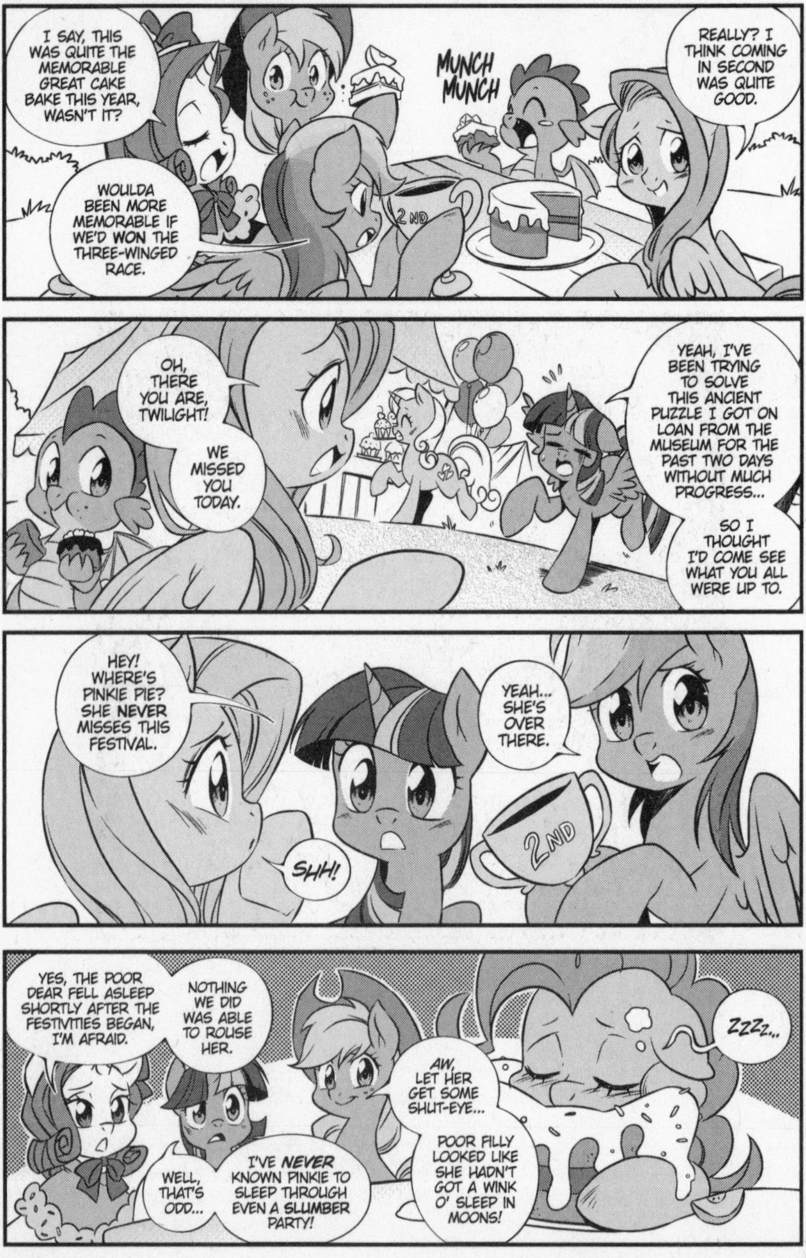
I SAY, THIS WAS QUITE THE MEMORABLE GREAT CAKE BAKE THIS YEAR, WASN'T IT?
WOULDA BEEN MORE MEMORABLE IF WE'D **WON** THE THREE-WINGED RACE.
2ND
MUNCH MUNCH
REALLY? I THINK COMING IN SECOND WAS QUITE GOOD.
OH, THERE YOU ARE, TWILIGHT!
WE MISSED YOU TODAY.
YEAH, I'VE BEEN TRYING TO SOLVE THIS ANCIENT PUZZLE I GOT ON LOAN FROM THE MUSEUM FOR THE PAST TWO DAYS WITHOUT MUCH PROGRESS...
SO I THOUGHT I'D COME SEE WHAT YOU ALL WERE UP TO.
HEY! WHERE'S PINKIE PIE? SHE **NEVER** MISSES THIS FESTIVAL.
YEAH... SHE'S OVER THERE.
2ND
SHH!
YES, THE POOR DEAR FELL ASLEEP SHORTLY AFTER THE FESTIVITIES BEGAN, I'M AFRAID.
NOTHING WE DID WAS ABLE TO ROUSE HER.
ZZZz...
AW, LET HER GET SOME SHUT-EYE...
WELL, THAT'S ODD...
I'VE ***NEVER*** KNOWN PINKIE TO SLEEP THROUGH EVEN A **SLUMBER** PARTY!
POOR FILLY LOOKED LIKE SHE HADN'T GOT A WINK O' SLEEP IN MOONS!

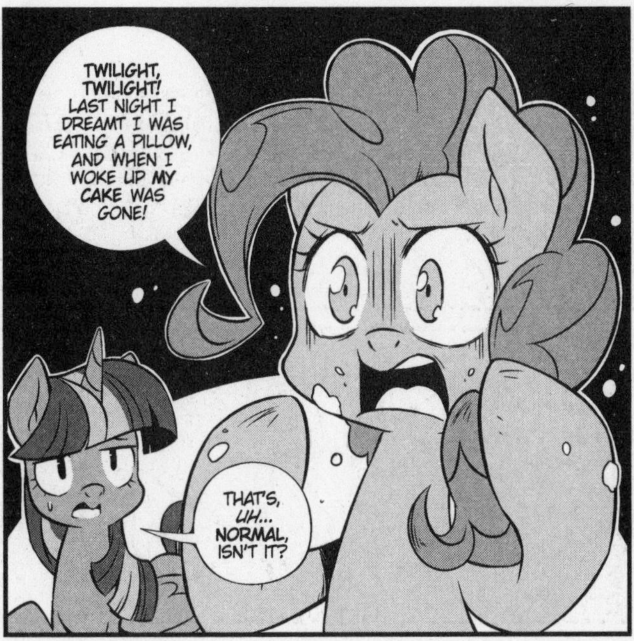
TWILIGHT, TWILIGHT! LAST NIGHT I DREAMT I WAS EATING A PILLOW, AND WHEN I WOKE UP MY CAKE WAS GONE!
THAT'S, UH... NORMAL, ISN'T IT?

SKETCH GALLERY

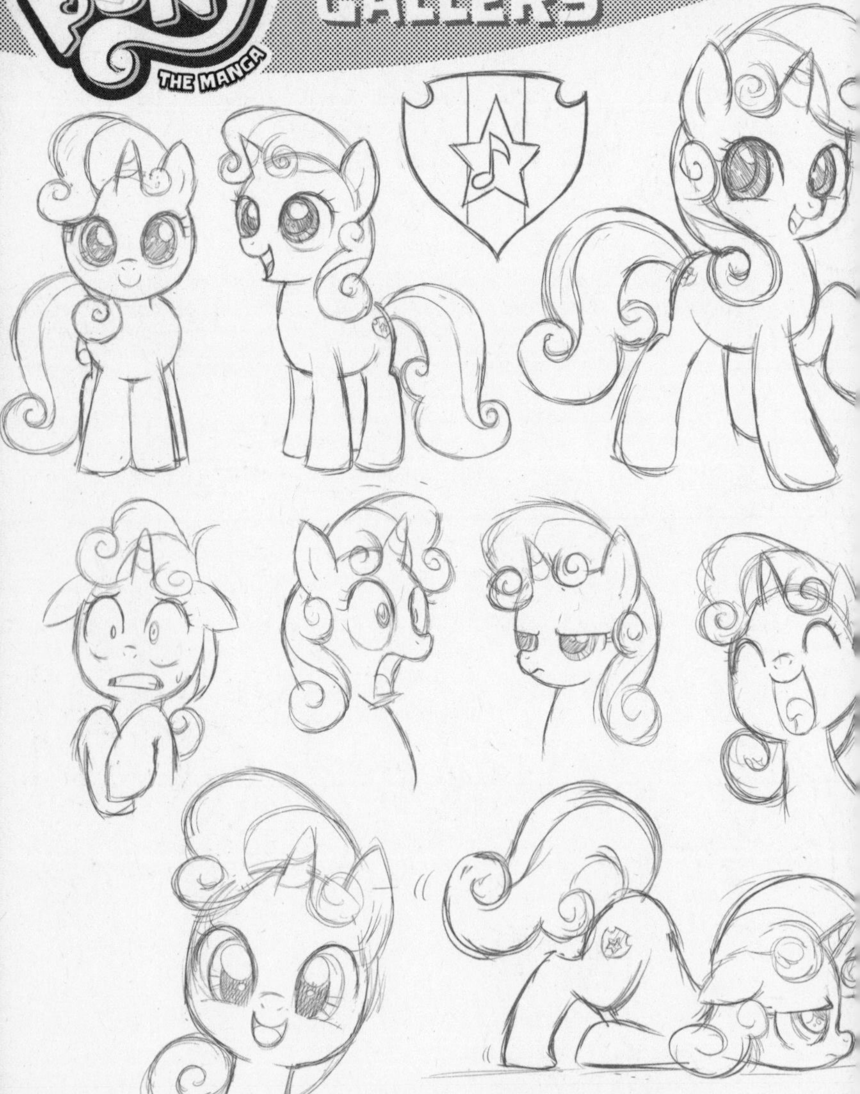

Sweetie Belle

Scootaloo

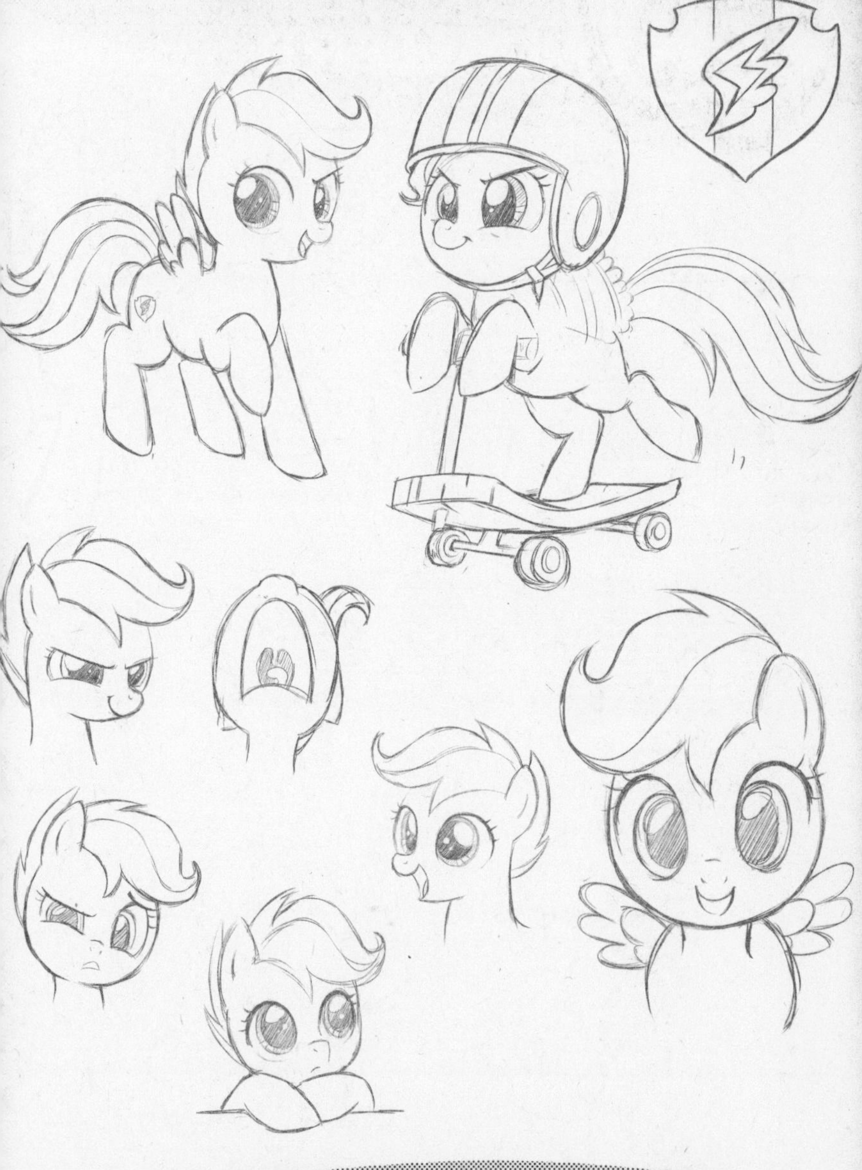

SKETCH GALLERY

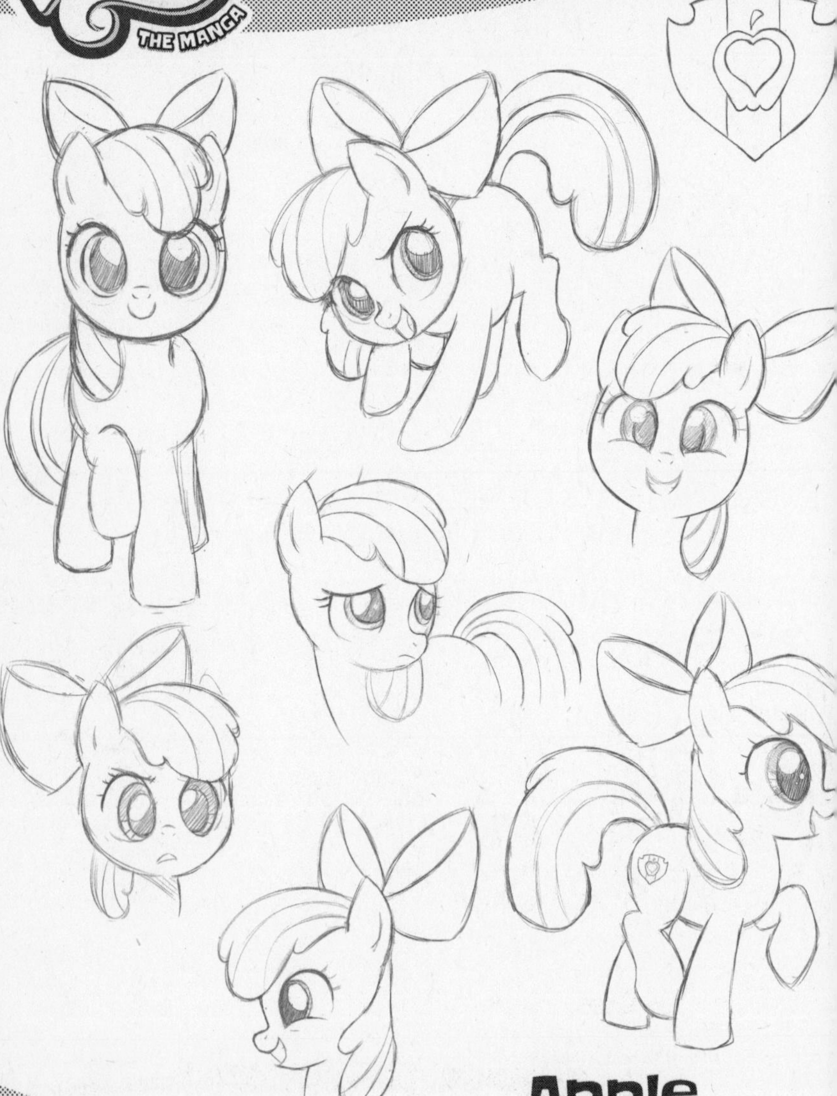

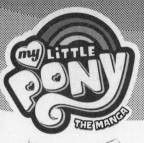

Apple Bloom

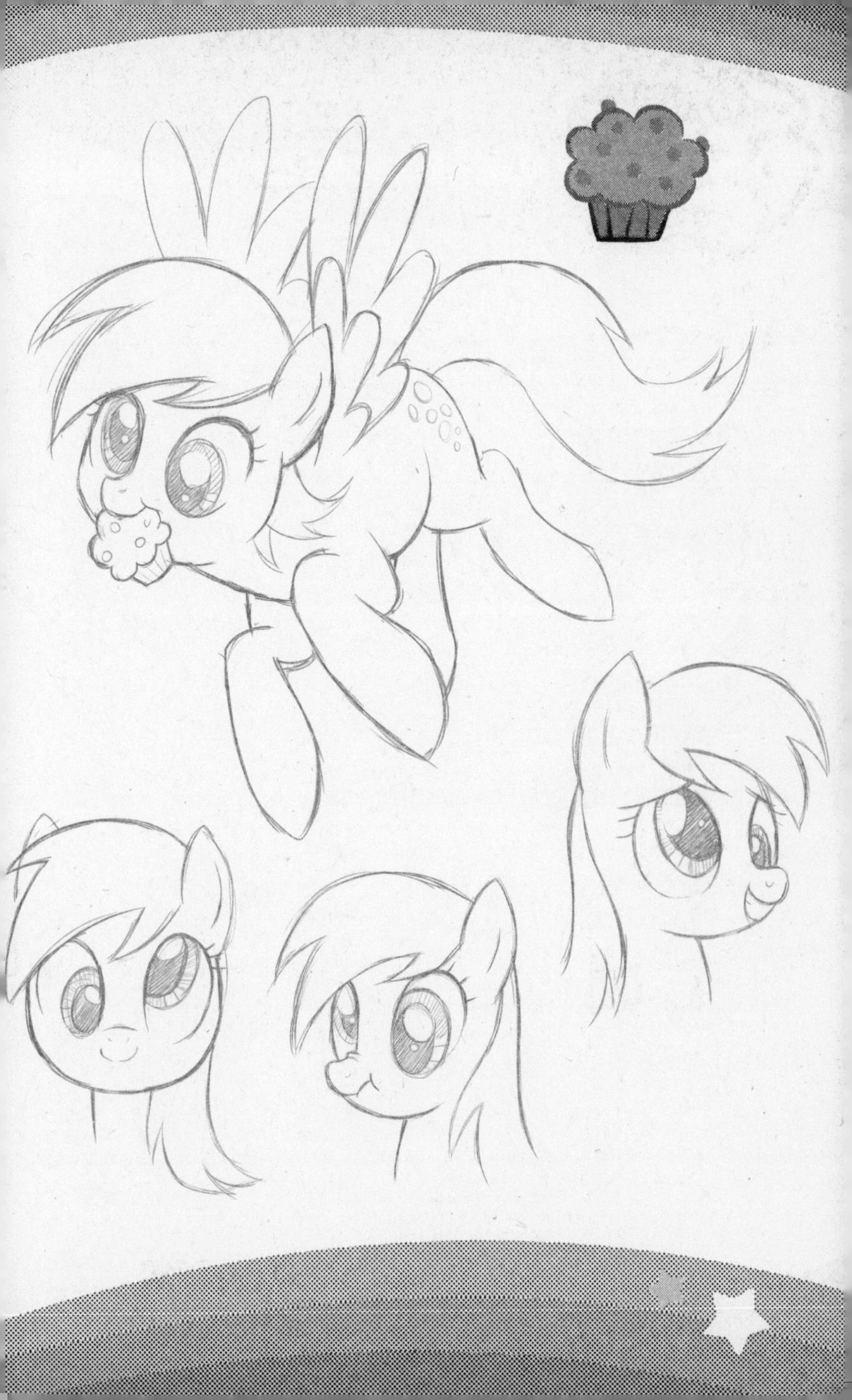

SKETCH GALLERY

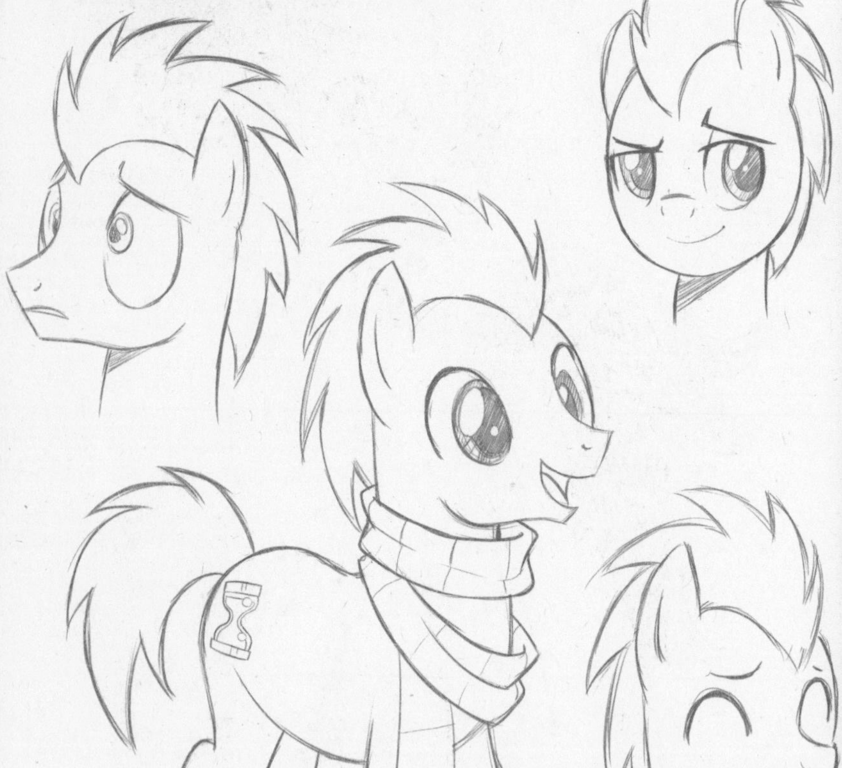

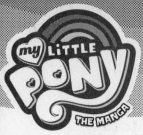

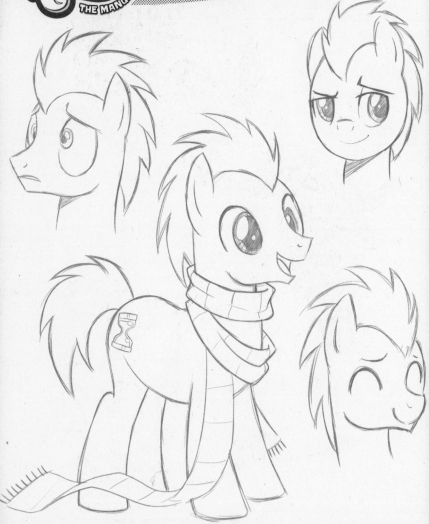

Dr. Hooves